THE COUNTERFEITER'S DAUGHTER

VICTORIA MARSWELL

THE COUNTERFEITER'S DAUGHTER

VICTORIA MARSWELL

Scriptures are taken from the World English Bible (WEB): Public Domain.
All Creatures of Our God and King, St. Francis of Assisi, 1225. Translated by William H. Draper, published, 1919. Public Domain.
ISBN-13-978-1-7350135-1-0 (paperback)
ISBN-13-978-1-7350135-0-3 (eBook)
Production Credits
Editing: T. Morgan Editing Services
Formatting: Formatted Books
Cover Design: 100Covers
Concept Art and Logo Design: Dillon Adams
Published by: Penhallow Books | Portsmouth, New Hampshire, USA

DEDICATION

To Dillon and Rhiannon. Thank you for encouraging me and
believing in my dreams.
I love you, forever and always.

ACKNOWLEDGEMENTS

Thank you:

To my editor, T. Morgan, for her meticulous work and help;
To my mother for her advice;
To family and friends for their constant support;
To Anna Mocikat for her patience with all my questions;
A huge thank you goes out to the incredibly
supportive writing community, for helping me navigate
through the editing and publishing process.

I'm grateful for all of you.

CHAPTER ONE

The ten o'clock train departed, transporting Gretchen and the boys from Berlin to Munich. Sam sighed. Now they'd be safe from the deadly consequences of his poor choices. No more suffering family members as a result of his unscrupulous lifestyle. Sam shivered while he packed a small red suitcase with a few days' worth of clothing. Perspiration exuded from the pores on his forehead as he scuttled between the nightstand and the open bag on the bed.

A cool morning draft whistled through a cracked window in the corner apartment on the twelfth floor. "Are you planning a trip somewhere, Mr. Healy?"

Sam jumped and twisted his body toward the voice. "But how—"

"I'm sure you don't mind a visit from your employer," the man said, "since we have unfinished business."

Sam licked his lips and swallowed hard. "Sorry, you caught me—"

"At a bad time?" His dark eyes narrowed. "I suggest you be careful with your trade dealings and whom you betray."

He wiped his sweaty brow. "I don't understand."

"Think carefully before you speak." He took a few steps closer and reached into his coat pocket. "They may be your last words."

"Y…y-yeah, I will."

"Good. Now, where is it?"

"I already—"

Sam flinched at the sound of the hammer of a gun, ready to fire. Beads of sweat dripped from his temple and down his face.

"Once again, where's the original?"

"It…" He gulped. "It's not here, but I can get it and bring it to you." He loosened the collar of his shirt. "Later. I'll meet you tonight."

Even the silence in the apartment buzzed in Sam's ears with the pounding of his heart. His assailant glared at him then dug in his coat pocket and pulled out a cigarette, lifting it to his lips.

"I'll give you one more chance." He struck a match, cupping his hands together to light the end, then threw the burning stick onto the floor.

Sam's eyes darted to the tiny flame on the edge of the rug. A breath hitched in his chest.

"Next time your wife and kids may not make it to the train so easily." He wore a hard smile on his face, turned his back and headed toward the door. "Be at the beer garden tonight, seven sharp." He patted the pocket that concealed the gun and left.

Sam seized a glass from the coffee table, tossed water onto the small fire and stomped on the remaining flames. A billow of smoke rose, setting off the alarm. Grabbing a magazine, he stepped up onto a chair and fanned the soot from the ceiling. He rushed to the front door, slammed it shut then chained and double-bolted the locks.

A tightness gripped his heart. He smacked a flat palm against his chest and sucked in a sharp intake of air. He bustled toward the writing desk in the room's corner, pulled out a sheet of paper and scribbled a note. Time denied him a moment to dwell on thoughts of Gretchen and the boys.

He only had one chance to react and perhaps, just this once, get it right.

After he penned the letter, he folded it, sealed the back and wrote the name of the one person essential to notify in his despair. Putting on his wool pea coat he shoved the envelope inside his pocket and peered out the balcony.

A silver sedan sat parked across the street. Sam noticed the vehicle when he returned after driving Gretchen and the kids to the Berlin Central train station.

Sam's hands trembled and he closed the windows overlooking the Brandenburg Gate. The room darkened as he pulled the shades, blocking the little sunlight peeking from the thick gray clouds.

He shuddered. An eerie sensation swirled in the pit of his stomach, spreading to his nerves, that he'd never again see the light of day.

* * *

"What he did was unforgivable." The woman's chin quaked, and a tear streamed down her cheek.

Madelyn pulled a tissue from the box on the corner of her desk and handed it to Lainey, her tenth emergency case assigned today. Her clients went through at least three boxes of tissues a week. She knew the struggle well, from her own experience.

"It'll take time. You'll feel a range of emotions. That's why I personally connect you with a licensed professional counselor, to help you through the difficult process." Madelyn stood and stepped from behind her desk. She straightened the side seams of her dark-blue pencil skirt and buttoned her matching blazer. "I authorized a referral to our emergency shelter for thirty days."

"Thank you, Ms. Brighton." Lainey sniffed hard, then blew her nose.

She passed her a business card. "Please call me Madelyn, and if you need an extension, beyond the allotted time, you can notify me."

A small smile flickered. Lainey stood and her legs wobbled as if she were taking independent steps for the first time. Madelyn held out her hand, in case she needed assistance.

She spun, her eyes wet and swollen. "What if he tries to find me?" Her voice trembled.

Madelyn placed an open palm on her shoulder. "We maintain the highest level of confidentiality. You'll be safe." She strolled at a slow pace down the corridor, escorting her into the last office. "Our client, Lainey, needs a ride to the shelter."

"Hello, I'm Cynthia, your case-carrier." She swept back her sun-kissed golden locks and extended her hand. "Please, have a seat and we'll have a quick chat before I drive you." Her smile lit up the drab little room.

Madelyn valued her coworkers; they were the closest she came to having a family. "I leave you in accomplished hands. Let me know if I can further help you."

"Thanks." Lainey turned, her face dry, but flushed.

Madelyn forced an encouraging grin and strode back to her workspace. Out of the corner of her eye, she glanced at the empty lobby and checked her bracelet watch, noting the time: 5:30 p.m. Like any government agency, in Southern California, the Women in Crisis Center remained at maximum capacity daily and most days the staff worked after business hours.

Madelyn slid against the smooth leather of her chair and ran her finger along the metal frame of her desk. She blew a free strand of hair from her face and kicked off her beige, kitten-heel shoes. Flipping through her inspirational calendar, she checked for an available date to schedule a haircut and groaned as she passed today's quote: "You're stronger than you realize."

She tapped the tip of her pen against the stack of files piled on her filing cabinet. Booked solid for the rest of the month.

She'd have to deal with her hair growing past her shoulders. She rested her head against her palm, allowing her gaze to settle on a framed photo. The anniversary date of Mom's death was always a difficult workday, although Madelyn preferred the distraction of staying busy with her job.

Her stare shifted as a soft knock came from the ajar door. "Come in."

"Are you ready for tonight?" Sheryl walked over and set a stack of letters on the edge of her desk.

"What's going on?"

"Ah, come on, it's girl's night out."

"Oh, right. Um…" Madelyn diverted her eyes back to the stack of papers. "I've got a lot to do."

"Seriously? All you do is work. Plus, we're celebrating your birthday!" She shook invisible pompoms. "Woohoo, the big 3-0."

Madelyn rolled her eyes. "It was last Tuesday."

Sheryl folded her arms across her chest and raised an eyebrow. "You know this is the only night Martin can stay home with the kids."

"I appreciate the offer, but—"

"You're not getting off that easy, you do this every year."

Sheryl had no problem speaking the truth. "Exactly. So, you know why today is rough for me."

"I do, but I don't think it's a good idea for you to sit alone at home."

Madelyn shrugged a shoulder and shuffled some documents. "I'll be fine." She glanced at her daily quote on the calendar. "Besides, I'm stronger than I realize."

"I hope those positive affirmations help." Sheryl turned, then swiveled back. "I almost forgot, I picked up your mail."

Madelyn stood from her chair and moved a stack of manila folders, parting the forest of files mounding on her desk. "Thanks, but please don't trouble yourself. I'm sure your workload is big enough."

"No problem. I was picking up my mail, anyway." Sheryl pointed to a large envelope. "I also signed for an express letter from Germany."

"Germany?"

"Yeah, and I'm glad you're as curious as I am about it." Sheryl's hazel eyes glimmered with the excitement of a teenage girl passing on a secret note between classes.

"No need to get excited. I haven't met any men in Germany."

"I can always hope for you."

"My odds are better at playing the lottery." Madelyn pulled the tab on the back of the envelope. "And I witness every day how relationships end."

"Now, wait a minute." Sheryl placed a hand on her hip. "I agree, it's disheartening to hear reports of abuse regularly, but for as many broken relationships, there are successful ones too."

"Should I get the statistics?" Madelyn tilted her head to the side. "I know you mean well and your heart is in the right place, but you and Martin have a rare and special partnership."

"Not really, it's just a lot of compromise and communication." She winked. "I'll keep praying for someone special to come into your life."

"Okay, I'll leave the praying to you." Madelyn swept her bangs across her forehead and opened the letter. She unfolded the piece of paper and read the first line. A coldness swept through her body and she fell backward into her chair.

"Are you all right?" Sheryl squeaked in a high-pitched tone and rushed over.

"I need a moment alone."

The creases deepened around Sheryl's eyes. "Sure, let me know if you need anything." Sheryl closed the door as she left. Madelyn appreciated their friendship; there was no need to give a long explanation, and a simple look between them explained enough.

Madelyn pressed her thumbs against the paper, verifying the authenticity of what she read. She blinked hard and took a deep breath, preparing herself for the rest of the letter.

Dear Madelyn Brighton,

My name is Gretchen Eichel-Healy, the wife of Samuel Healy, who passed away on the 4th of May. Sam and I have two boys, 10-year-old Alarick and 7-year-old Rainor, and our wish is for you to join us in Munich, at All Saints Church. I scheduled the funeral service for Thursday the 10th of May at 1:00 p.m. A gathering for the family will take place before the memorial service on Wednesday. I'll send details when you arrive. If you attend, I've booked you room 511 at the Hotel Füssen. We look forward to meeting you for the first time and regret it is under such sad circumstances. Please contact me with questions.

Geh107@germail.com

Cordially,

Gretchen

Her heartbeat resounded in her ears and heat prickled her nape. The words blurred into random letters as Madelyn stared at the page. Even if she wanted to go, she had clients depending on her services. She curled her trembling fingers, the paper crunching under her grasp. Pretend she never received the request and forget the whole thing?

Madelyn tossed the crumpled paper in the trash and dropped her head into her hands, massaging her temples. The day had gone from bad to worse. Somehow Sam knew where to find her and yet still never called or reached out. She took a swig of her coffee and choked on the bitter taste mixed with the lukewarm temperature.

Sam was dead… The poor boys, losing their dad so soon, even if Sam wasn't much of a father to her, she knew the negative effects of an absent parent. Madelyn blew a heavy breath from her mouth, pulled the note from the trash and did a search online for the first available flight to Munich, Germany. She booked an airline ticket and emailed her supervisor with a notification of time off for two weeks' bereavement period—accounting for travel time, jet lag and unforeseen entanglements with Sam's family. She sent a quick response to Gretchen.

How weird to think of Sam having a family. For years she attempted to disconnect her heart from any thoughts of Sam. She pressed her fingers against her chest and massaged the burning knot growing inside.

Madelyn slipped on her shoes, grabbed the letter, packed up her laptop and case files to pass on to another crisis counselor. Traveling to a foreign country required extensive planning. She paused, then shook her head. Good thing she kept her passport current. The extent of her international travels was a one-time trip to Canada, despite studying architecture for her dream job as a conservationist of historic buildings, before changing her major to psychology at Cal Poly.

Her heart banged with a heavy thud as she closed her office door. If she dwelled too long on the request, she'd change her mind and stay home. She had to follow her gut reaction and go.

Madelyn suppressed a surge of sickness in her stomach and squared her shoulders while she headed to Sheryl's office.

"Can you do me a favor?" Madelyn leaned against the doorframe.

"You got it, what do you need?"

"Please follow up on my clients, while I'm out of the office." She hobbled to the desk, her arms filled with folders and her oversized handbag slipping off her shoulder. "Thanks, I really appreciate it. And I'll be at your place at eight tonight. I need a ride to LAX."

"Wait, hold up." Sheryl removed her square-framed eyeglasses. "Does this have to do with that letter?"

"Yes, it was a memorial announcement."

"I thought you didn't know anyone in Germany."

"I don't."

Sheryl scrunched up her face. "Girl, you make little sense."

"I'll tell you about it on the drive to the airport. I've got to go pack. See you in a few hours." Madelyn turned and hustled down the hall.

She blew out a gusty breath. Madelyn never left the office for an extended length of time and always stayed an hour or two past closing. In her absence, Sheryl would be responsible for taking on extra work. Likewise, it would take a miracle to prepare for a last-minute trip to Munich. What choice did she have other than honor the request of Sam's widow and children?

Madelyn checked her watch and hurried outside. Golden rays of sunlight filtered through the smog layer hovering above the city of Orange. Madelyn squinted and dug out her sunglasses from her bag. Her body temperature increased in the sultry eighty degrees and she cranked up the A/C as she started her white Prius to head home in rush hour traffic on the 22 freeway toward Huntington Beach.

On the regular hour or more drive, she increased the volume on her favorite classical station, calming her nerves. The sun set over the beach when she turned onto Pacific Coast Highway. She never tired of the serene sight of rose-gold hues illuminating the sky. Fiery orange set the Pacific Ocean ablaze while the sinking sun submerged, casting shimmering yellow light on the surface of the water.

Circling the neighborhood four times, she parked against a curb, a block away from her one-bedroom condo. Yet another cost of living two streets over from the beach, but at least it came with a view. She gazed at silhouettes of surfers riding the waves and sailboats floating in the distance.

Once inside her cozy bungalow, her movements were sluggish and mechanical as she searched for her carry-on suitcase. When Grandma died seven years ago, she moved in and felt that leaving most of the décor paid homage to her memory. Grandma's gardenia scent lingered in the back corner of the walk-in closet and she pulled out the small suitcase.

A breeze from the beach swept through her open patio door and Madelyn inhaled the familiar aroma of briny sea air, like her childhood neighborhood of Avila Beach. No matter where she tried to escape, the past followed. Madelyn gazed off at nothing. Sam was dead and had a family in Germany. News of Sam's passing on the anniversary of Mom's death emphasized the difficulty of tackling every trial in life alone. The quick decision to attend the funeral was impulsive and settled in while she packed her clothes. The invitation forced her to face the past or risk being haunted, even in death, by the memory of Sam.

At 8:45 p.m., heading north on the 405 to LAX in bumper-to-bumper traffic, Sheryl kept her eyes on the crawling cars. "Who is Sam Healy?"

A numbness engulfed her heart. Madelyn made a point of avoiding the subject, since she'd have to dredge up suppressed memories. "My mom's ex-husband."

"Your mom's—" Sheryl pressed harder on the brakes. "You mean your dad?"

Madelyn cringed, grasped the interior handle above the window and gulped. "For lack of a better word, yes." Sheryl's response was the reason she never discussed Sam.

"I'm sorry. Do you want to talk about it?"

The hairs on her nape raised. "Not much to talk about, I hadn't seen him in fifteen years."

Sheryl paused with her mouth gaped. "Maybe this is an opportunity for you to find a way to forgive and forget."

Madelyn tightened her jaw and forced half a smile. She'd rather just forget. "I'm going for the purpose of supporting Gretchen and her boys at the funeral service."

"I totally get it." Sheryl glanced behind to change lanes and exit the freeway. "You're going to approach the situation like it's another day at work."

"That's not fair. And you should talk." Madelyn nudged Sheryl. She was never in the company of just a friend since she was also a therapist.

"Hey, I call it like I see it."

"True, and I value your honesty. I don't want to focus on myself or the past and I'm going because I feel an obligation toward Sam's family."

"Want to know what I think?" Sheryl pulled into the drop-off zone for Lufthansa Airlines. "You're brave and doing the right thing."

Madelyn's words swelled in her throat. "Thanks." She grabbed her suitcase from the trunk and shut the door then peeked through the rolled-down window. "I appreciate the ride."

Sheryl's smile shortened and the wrinkle in her brow deepened. "Let me know how you're doing sometime this week, after you get settled."

"I will."

"Hey, don't forget, you're stronger than you realize." Sheryl waved and flipped on her blinker.

"Okay." Madelyn stepped back and laughed under her breath. "I'll call you."

Madelyn stared as Sheryl drove away in her Honda CRV. The sinking sensation in her belly intensified. Why did she feel compelled to support Sam's second family? Madelyn knew all too well the chaos Sam could create. She entered terminal seven and followed the signage for Lufthansa. The nerves tightened in her shoulders and she shuddered. Madelyn risked prolonging the pain from her past and never breaking free of Sam's constant betrayals. She'd seize any opportunity to put the past behind her for good, even if it meant flying halfway around the world for the first time.

CHAPTER TWO

Lufthansa flight LH453 departed on time for a nonstop trip from Los Angeles to Munich. Five hours into the journey the cabin lights dimmed for the many passengers asleep. Madelyn finished her second cup of coffee and tapped her nails on the tray in front of her, until she caught an unpleasant glare from the woman across the aisle. She folded up the tray and rubbed her lower back, wishing she spent extra money on business class. Tightening muscles aggravated the swirling sensation in her head along with the stench of fish and chicken that sickened her stomach. She dug in her handbag for bottled water and Dramamine. The back of her hand brushed against the letter and she reread the note a few times.

Her actions were rash, and she hadn't given a lot of thought to anything. Never mind the emotional consequences of a spontaneous decision, she had planned no details for traveling in a foreign country. She figured she'd use a credit card for most transactions and stop at a cash machine for a little currency. Madelyn closed her eyes, accepting she set in motion a journey into a forbidden territory of the past and there was no turning back.

* * *

The plane landed around 7:00 p.m., after an eleven-and-a-half-hour flight. A stabbing pain in her abdomen set her internal clock spinning in two directions. Pulling her carry-on down from the overhead compartment Madelyn swayed with the weight of her suitcase. Regaining her balance, she squeezed into the tight line departing the plane. Strong spearmint and lingering floral perfume assaulted her nostrils. She twitched her nose and blinked to clear the watery blur from her vision, straining to focus. With a sluggish shuffle into terminal two, the group of passengers from the airplane broke free and dispersed through the crowds. Madelyn stepped aside and extended the handle of her suitcase.

Franz Josef Strauss Airport bustled with fast-paced travelers. The reality of her hasty decision settled in after spending an hour in the customs queue where she overheard two airline attendants chat in German. She grazed her teeth along her lower lip and tried to recall common phrases she learned in high school but doubted her ability to carry on an everyday conversation.

Even worse, she missed her chance to brush up on language skills during the flight. She pulled her burgundy sweater around her hips and straightened the hem. All she wanted was a heavy dose of caffeine, so her body functions normalized.

Madelyn created a mental list to gain control of her circumstances. First, she'd get a strong cup of coffee and something to eat. Second, stop by a shop in the airport for a map and an essential travel guide including a section on useful German phrases. Then, take care of currency and locate her hotel. The subtle aroma of cocoa and toasted nuts stimulated her senses as she fought to push through the fog of jet lag. With poised posture she strolled to the next terminal and tackled her number one priority.

Madelyn waited in line for coffee. Eating dinner would help her body adjust to the proper time zone, but her mouth salivated for breakfast food. She patted down her pockets then dug in her bag, looking for her phone. Idiot. She tossed her hand up in the air and smacked it against her thigh. She forgot her phone on the nightstand at home when she charged it after work. So far, her careless mistakes created major consequences and she'd leave no room for additional errors.

Madelyn stepped up to the counter. The barista greeted her, along with an 'out of order' note taped over the credit card machine.

"Spr-ich-st Du Englisch?" Madelyn scrunched her nose at how awful her supposed German sounded.

"Ja." The girl smiled.

"Cash only?"

The cashier nodded and pressed her lips tight. Madelyn grumbled under her breath and slouched as she walked away. A stale taste filled her mouth, and she ate a mint that rolled around in the bottom of her purse.

Madelyn maneuvered through a sea of people like a fish swimming upstream. Bags bumped her shoulders, rocking her balance, yet she held a strong stance and ran into a convenient shop to purchase a guidebook, including a map. Thumbing through the pages of her *Guide to Germany* book, she unfolded the transit rail system and memorized the stops. The last thing she needed was to end up on the wrong train. It didn't appear too complicated—the U-Bahn and S-Bahn trains ran throughout the city. She traced the S-8 yellow-and-black line with her finger, to Marienplatz, the stop closest to Hotel Füssen.

Under a bright green sign, a row of touchscreen kiosks attracted clusters of people. Madelyn inserted her credit card in the machine and purchased a single fare. With a ticket in hand, she followed the signage for the S-Bahn and rode down an escalator to the train platform. She waited with the large huddled group, behind the white line.

A whoosh from the air brakes screeched through the enclosed station as the rapid transit arrived. The automatic doors for the red-with-white-trim train opened and passengers hustled to any available seats or latched onto the vertical poles extending from the floor to ceiling. Madelyn charged for an empty seat, securing a victory comparable to a touchdown in a football game. She slid into a coupled lounger with luggage racks overhead. A man squeezed beside her. She tucked her carry-on behind her legs and leaned away from the smell of greasy hair.

The S-Bahn bolted with a dynamic force, the rails sleek and smooth as the train bulleted on the track, lurching passengers forward. With a whistling sigh Madelyn tucked herself into the blue vinyl chair and studied the guidebook. Remember, basic phrases and greetings.

"Sprechen Sie Englisch?" she whispered and repeated.

After a forty-minute ride, Madelyn exited the electric train. Her leg muscles stiffened while she climbed the stairs leading out of the station. As she stepped out from the underground, into the historic heart of Munich, her heart pounded, and her adrenaline spiked, increasing her disorientation. She never dreamed she'd arrive at a destination she read about and studied in books. When Sam left, she missed her chance to study abroad and assumed traveling wasn't in her future.

Munich housed many of her favorite neo-gothic architectural buildings. She skimmed through the history in the Germany guidebook on the train. Ample light in the plaza showcased the brick and shell limestone structure of Neues Rathaus—New City Hall. The ornate façade towered almost three hundred feet above the flagstone square.

Surrounded by a crowd, heads tilted, and phones pointed skyward, at the Glockenspiel clock, the forty-three-bell carillon chimed like an old-fashioned music box. Madelyn peered up as illuminates flashed onto mechanized life-sized figures, perched in the niches of the tower. A night watchman blew his trumpet on one side and an angel on the other as they jerked into action and moved behind the curved columns, bidding a goodnight to the city.

The jaunty tune at the end of the performance drew *oohs* and *ahs*. Caught in an intersection of people scampering in several directions, she checked the map and walked a few blocks toward Hotel Füssen. Her suitcase stuck in the cobblestone street, she halted and yanked until a wheel broke. She threw her hands up and a hard breath escaped her lips as she hoisted the case along her side.

The sound of oompah music lured her toward a large, lit-up building named the Hofbräuhaus. She peeked through the double-wide doors at the father of all beer halls, in which trumpet, drum, and accordion blended with the singing and shouting of drinkers, producing a boisterous noise. The comradery between the folks sitting on wooden benches at tables long enough for seating at least fifty people, brought a small smile to her face. She twisted her neck over her shoulder and faced Hotel Füssen across the street.

Madelyn whirled through the silver revolving doors and rolled the three-wheeler suitcase across the black-and-white marble floor. The long hours of travel vanquished her energy and she utilized her carry-on as a crutch at the reception desk. At 10:15 at night, the lobby of the hotel brimmed with men in designer suits and women wearing cocktail dresses. Other guests, arriving late, swung store bags in their hands, from Karstadt and Galeria Kaufhof.

Madelyn propped her elbows on the cool, granite counter and blew a loose strand of hair from her face. Behind the counter, sitting at a desk, a silver-haired man lifted his head from his leather notepad and with a severe look, motioned for the employees to help. Making his silent orders with gestures, he had the workers marching to the snap of his fingers.

A wide-eyed desk clerk rushed to the counter. "Guten Abend."

"Hello." She smiled with confidence. "Sprechen Sie Deutch?"

He nodded and choked back a laugh. "Ja, I speak German."

Her cheeks grew hot and she fumbled with the earmarked page in her book. "I meant, Sprechen Sie Englisch?"

"I speak English too," he said, and grinned. "How may I help you?"

"My name is Madelyn Brighton and I have a reservation."

The young man typed with two pointed fingers as he stared at the computer screen. "I'm sorry, we have no reservation under that name."

Madelyn slumped forward. "Is this the only Hotel Füssen in Munich?"

"Ja."

"Can you please check again?" She rested her cheek against her palm.

"Do you have the credit card you used to make the reservation?"

Madelyn expected complications and delays during her visit, yet she persisted with her fatigue and raw nerves. "No, I'm sorry. Someone else made the reservation. The last name is Healy."

The conversation caught the attention of the older man behind the desk. He stood and spun on his patent-leather loafers and nudged the clerk aside. "I'm Herr Renault, the hotel director, how may I be of service?"

"Gretchen Healy made a reservation for me."

"Gretchen Healy, sehr gut." Herr Renault emphasized the name in a loud voice as his fingers danced across the keyboard.

Madelyn glanced around the lobby. Blinded by a bright crystal chandelier, she blinked a few times and turned her body in the opposite direction. At the far end of the counter a slender man, in a slate-colored suit leaned and tilted his head toward Herr Renault. His ash-blond locks draped at one length just below his contoured jawline and hid his line of vision. Her eyes followed the frantic movements of everyone and revealed him as a possible person of importance.

"We have a single room reserved for five days." Herr Renault swiped a plastic card. "Here is your key for room 511."

"Thank you." Madelyn forced a smile.

"I'll attend to anything you need during your stay at Hotel Füssen."

Herr Renault glared at the young desk clerk and he rushed to pick up her suitcase.

"Oh no, you don't need to—"

"I insist, Ms. Brighton." Herr Renault softened his tone.

Too tired to question the peculiar behavior of the staff, she nodded in agreement. Either it had something to do with her or the mysterious man at the end of the counter. She glanced up, but the man had left. She shook her head; no reason to overthink anything.

Ever since she received the letter from Gretchen, a coldness surged through her body that she couldn't shake. An exaggerated huff escaped her lips. The news of Sam's death along with learning she had two stepbrothers swayed her steps and hindered her regular body functions.

Madelyn followed the clerk to the elevators and stopped. She verified the name badge pinned on his black blazer. "Thank you, Kolt, but I'd prefer to go up to my room alone." She took her suitcase from him.

"If you wish." Kolt held the automatic doors open.

"I appreciate your assistance." She entered the vacant elevator.

As the metal doors slid together, a black wingtip shoe stepped forward and triggered the retracting doors. Madelyn's body jolted with the thump of the elevator.

"Wie bitte." The man that stood at the edge of the counter gave her a single nod.

Kolt stepped aside and turned toward Madelyn. "He begged your pardon."

"Of course." Madelyn licked her dry lips and swallowed.

"You are Amerikanerin," the man stated in fluent English, consonants crooning with his German accent.

Madelyn squirmed inside her sweater. The man towered beside her average height. "Yes, I'm an American." Her words were taut and quiet. She kept her eyes fixed on the sliding doors as they squealed shut.

The number seven illuminated on the operation panel as he pressed the button. "What floor?"

"Five, please." She pulled her handbag close. Two was a crowd in the confined space. She inhaled the mixed scent of cedar with a subtle hint of bergamot in his cologne.

"First visit to Deutschland?"

"Yes, I'm here for a funeral." She snapped her mouth shut. Why did she divulge that information?

"My condolences."

Madelyn stared upward. "Thank you." The floor numbers sequentially lit up: three, four, five… She sighed at the sound of the ding. The pulley shuddered to a stop, and the brushed steel squeaked open.

"Bis später."

Madelyn stiffened her neck and stepped out of the elevator towing her suitcase. The doors glided inward, and she glanced at the man. His chin tilted downward, his gray eyes peering under his narrowed brows.

"See you soon." He disappeared behind the closing elevator.

Madelyn shivered. What a bizarre encounter. She hurried and found her room halfway down the gold-veined, white-marble hall. Fumbling with her key card, she slipped the smooth plastic into the slot then yanked it out at least three times before the green lights flashed for entry.

The door slammed after entering and she jumped. She didn't want to acknowledge the fact the man in the elevator set her on edge. Taking a deep breath, she exhaled with controlled breathing and repeated the anxiety-reducing technique she often taught clients. Her nasal cavities filled with the scents of bleach and a lavender deodorizer. She opened the bi-fold closet, removed her coat and hung it on one of the non-removable hangers.

Wrenching off her ankle boots, her swollen feet ached with the pressure of walking to the end of the bed. She tossed her suitcase onto the bench and laid out her pajamas along with a second pair of shoes.

Madelyn crossed the room to shut the drapes. Down below on the streets people filtered in and out of the Hofbräuhaus. She did travel to Germany on a moment's notice. She rubbed the back of her neck. Sam crept into her mind. What led him thousands of miles away from her and Mom? So many things she wanted to say, confront him about his choices, and now… She tugged the curtains hard, shutting out the city.

Massaging the constricting pain in her chest, she slowed her breathing, inhaling and exhaling—she refused to get emotional. She slipped under the heavy duvet on the bed then thrusted her head onto the pillow. Fifteen years should've been enough time for her to prepare for a rehash of the past. Her abdomen cramped, and she curled into a fetal position. Sheryl's promise of prayers gave her solace. Madelyn wished she could believe in the power of prayer right now—she needed all possible help in the universe. Madelyn forfeited God when Sam left, and when Mom died. Her doubts proved justified and realistic; she expected nothing from prayers. She pulled the covers over her head and closed her eyes.

Madelyn sprang upright in bed. She rubbed the sleep from her eyes as her foggy brain zeroed in on a buzzing noise. Glancing at the clock the time flashed a red 7:30 a.m. She hit the top of the alarm, but the racket continued. She blinked a couple times before identifying the strange ring from the phone.

She juggled the receiver in her hands, almost dropping the telephone. "Hello." Her voice was strained.

"Hallo, Madelyn?" a woman asked in clear English with nuances of a German accent.

"Yes."

"I'm Gretchen. Nice to finally speak with you. I hope I didn't call too early."

"No, it's fine. How are you—"

"I needed to speak with you right away." Her tone was urgent and serious. "Samuel left me specific instructions upon your arrival."

Madelyn rubbed her forehead. "How did Sam know I'd be in contact with you?"

"I can't answer all your questions now, but I can tell you, Samuel trusted you above anyone else." Her voice wavered.

A swirling sensation ripped through Madelyn's body, twisting her emotions with a force beyond the wreckage of a damaging EF5 tornado. She sucked in a heavy breath. "I think Sam trusted that whatever he left behind, I'd take care of again."

"I don't mean to upset you," Gretchen said in a soothing voice.

Madelyn swallowed, dulling the ache in her throat. "I'm sorry, it's a lot for me to process in a short amount of time. I'm sure it's been very difficult for you and the boys."

"It's hard on all of us."

Inhaling a deep, cleansing breath, she exhaled a deliberate breath from her mouth. After all, she flew thousands of miles to comfort Gretchen and the boys. "What was Sam's request?"

"You need to find an item he left for you. Samuel was a regular guest at Hotel Füssen and stayed in room 511."

Her hands trembled. "There's something here in the room? Where is it?"

"The instructions are to reference the Bible and look up Luke chapter 8 verses 16-17."

Madelyn turned and flicked on the small lamp on the nightstand. She grabbed the hotel pen and a pad of paper and scribbled down the information. "What's next?"

"Samuel wrote that the verses would give you further guidance on where to look."

"The way you're talking…" Madelyn rubbed her belly, quelling the sick feeling building inside. "Sam knew he'd die?"

Gretchen cleared her throat. "I think it's best if we discuss this later. Please come to the wake at six. I'll give you the letter and we'll talk."

"All right." Her muscles twitched. "I'll meet you at the church this evening."

"See you tonight. Goodbye," Gretchen said in a quiet voice.

"Okay, bye."

Madelyn lowered the receiver onto her lap and blinked several times before reaching out for a few mis attempts to hang up the phone. Her eyes darted around the room. What had Sam left and entrusted her with after fifteen years of no communications?

CHAPTER THREE

adelyn rolled her neck, sighed and stared at the notepad. She pulled the knob on the nightstand and found the drawer empty. Her trip started with one odd exchange after another. She shifted her shoulders underneath her sweater, adjusting to the rising heat in her body temperature. She hated falling asleep in her clothes.

Before hunting for the Bible and searching for excerpts from scripture, she needed a strong cup of coffee. Madelyn slid out of bed, hunched over, and stumbled across the room.

She stubbed her big toe on the desk. "Ouch."

The hotel squeezed in a queen bed, desk, entertainment cabinet and bench in a standard-sized room. She dragged her fingers along the wall, found a switch and flipped it on. The floor lamp next to the desk flickered with a surge of electricity until the bulb lit. She gulped a mouthful of air at first sight of her reflection in the mirror. She leaned back to see if the image got any better. No such luck. She moved closer, hoping her tired eyes were out of focus. It would be a minimum-of-two-cups-of-coffee kind of morning.

Madelyn poured the last of her drink from the airport into the coffeemaker's reservoir. She opened two packs of grounds and

dumped them into the filter. Pressing the button, the brewer filled the room with an earthy aroma, layered with notes of spices. She gulped down an entire complimentary water bottle, alleviating her raw throat and dry mouth. A throb spread across her forehead and she moved her fingers in a circular motion on her temples. To add to her pain, a noise hummed throughout the room.

While the coffee brewed, she laid her suitcase on the luggage rack. With the airport security stipulations and leaving on short notice, she left most of her toiletries at home. She peeked in the bathroom and sighed. The hotel staff stocked shelves above the sink with a full-sized shampoo, conditioner, body wash and a toothbrush plus paste.

She showered and dressed, putting on a pair of jeans and a sweater. A rumble in her stomach stirred acids and increased saliva in her mouth. She already drank two cups of coffee and her hands jittered with caffeine as she zipped up her boots. Her body needed fuel, and she hadn't eaten a full meal in twenty-four hours. Every movement and thought required great effort.

Madelyn exited the room, and the door slammed shut. She smacked her arms to her sides. Darn it, she left the key card on the desk. She entered the empty elevator and swiped at the strands of hair against her cheek. At least she didn't have to face another encounter with the strange man from yesterday. The doors opened at the ground floor and she walked to the front desk.

"Guten morgen," Kolt said.

"Good morning. I'm sorry, but I locked myself out of my room." She rubbed her forehead. "Oh, and there's a buzzing sound, maybe a loose wire or something."

"No problem. I'll make you another card key and notify our maintenance staff about the noise."

"Thank you." Madelyn leaned against the cool counter and scanned the lobby. Her limbs stiffened. The man she met in the elevator reclined in a wingback chair reading a newspaper.

Madelyn turned and faced Kolt, avoiding eye contact with the man.

"Here you are." He handed her two plastic cards.

"Danke."

"Anything else I can help you with?"

She'd be risking sounding paranoid if she inquired about the stranger. Although, Kolt could provide information and clarify his presence. What had the man done? Greeted and welcomed her to Germany and read a paper in plain sight. If the hotel had any suspicions, they would've escorted him off the property. Best if she kept the questions to herself.

"Does the restaurant serve brunch?"

"Altes Dorfhaus offers Zweites Frühstück." Kolt pointed to the dining room past the foyer.

Madelyn tapped her fingers against her lips. "Second breakfast?"

"Ja." He laughed. Kolt seemed at ease when Herr Renault wasn't lurking over the staff. "Help yourself und I'll add the meal to your room bill."

"Haben Sie…einen…schönen Tag."

"Good day, Ms. Brighton."

Madelyn smiled and waved, heading toward the hotel restaurant. The breakfast rush ended, and a few guests lingered in the dining area. For a restaurant named Old Village House, it had a contemporary décor, everything from the dome-pendant lights to the parquet floor. The antique cabinets below the counter looked like authentic German furniture.

Madelyn picked up a tray and cutlery rolled up in a cloth napkin at one end of the buffet table. The countertop exhibited several food options to entice the largest of appetites. Madelyn scooped fruit from a bowl, grabbed a few slices of ham and with a pair of tongs, selected a croissant from a breadbasket.

"You should try the Bavarian Weisswurst." A man stood too close.

"I—" Madelyn turned toward the voice and faced the same stranger again. "I'm going to pass, thank you."

"It's a delicious boiled sausage served with sweet mustard, a pretzel and beer."

Madelyn scrunched her nose. "I'm good with my choices." She inched down the table and stared at the food.

"Are you going to be eating in the dining room?"

"No." She turned a shoulder toward him.

"Pity."

"Please, excuse me." Madelyn moved around the counter. She refrained from lifting her gaze as she sensed him watching. She poured a cup of coffee, balancing a tray of food and left in haste. She quivered with an unnerving feeling the man's eyes followed her every step until she was out of his sight.

Back in the sanctuary of her hotel room, she set her breakfast tray on the desk and turned on the floor lamp. The light flickered, then illuminated half the room. Madelyn broke off a piece of flakey croissant and bit into the rich, buttery taste, melting in her mouth. She sipped her coffee and slid up the sleeves of her sweater. Enough procrastination, time to get busy and find the Bible.

She slid open the desk drawer and discovered a hotel copy of the Holy Bible. Easy enough. Madelyn referred to the notepad on the nightstand for the information she jotted down. She thumbed through the pages until she reached Luke chapter 8. With her index finger she followed the numbered lines and stopped on verse 16.

No one, when he has lit a lamp, covers it with a container, or puts it under a bed; but puts it in a stand, that those who enter in may see the light. For nothing is hidden, that will not be revealed; nor anything secret, that will not be known and come to light.

Madelyn eased into the chair at the desk, leaning her head over the back as she stared at the ceiling. Why would Sam leave a cryptic message using the Bible? He knew nothing about God's word. He stopped going to church when Mom worked on her PhD. Instead, he drove the two of them all the way to the Santa Anita horse track. Of course, a ten-year-old preferred visiting horses over church services. How would she have known he gambled during that time?

She shook her head. The memories flooding her mind were the reason she didn't want to attend the funeral. If it weren't for the desperation in Gretchen's voice, she would forget the whole thing and leave. She sat upright, tapping her fist to her chin and reread the same section of scripture. One word at a time she dissected the sentences. Lamp. She peeked under the lampshade. She shuffled across the room and checked under every shade in the room.

Madelyn progressed to the next words. She got on her hands and knees, then peered under the bed; nothing but a wood platform. Her head swirled as she stood from the floor. Flipping over the mattress she verified he hid nothing around the bed. She flopped her body on top of the sheets and smashed a pillow against her face. Perhaps this was Sam's final jab, torturing her with a wild-goose chase and inflicting additional pain into her lifelong wound.

Madelyn closed her eyes. The caffeine kept her mind active, but she didn't want to think about Sam or the message in the Bible. If she prayed, would God listen? He remained silent all the times she cried herself to sleep after Sam left. She wanted to call Sheryl and ask her opinion, since she believed prayers worked.

She vocalized her supplications with a slight cough. "Um, God." Perhaps she wasn't ready to speak aloud or say anything. Swallowing the lump in her throat, her heart banged. "I know I haven't spoken to you in years, but I want to help Gretchen, Alarick and Rainor. I'm trying to push through the pain of my past and have a lot of mixed feelings about Sam. I'm still angry." She inhaled and exhaled through her mouth as her eyes remained closed. "I don't know what else to say, except please help me find what I'm looking for?" She lolled on the bed. "And thank you. Amen." She blew out a heavy breath. Although she sounded silly, she did feel relaxed.

The hum of the A/C unit echoed in the air. A cool breeze fanned on Madelyn and she shivered from her feet up through her shoulders. The entire weight of her body rested on her right arm and she rolled onto her back. Pins and needles skewered her bicep down to her fingertips. She pressed her lips together as she shook out the feeling in her arm.

Madelyn opened her eyes and blinked a few times, the digital clock on the nightstand displayed a red 4:56 p.m. She widened her eyes and waggled her head, smacking her palm against her forehead. How did she fall asleep after all the coffee she guzzled? In less than an hour, she'd need to dress and figure out Sam's message. She groaned and tumbled off the white duvet. She didn't intend going to the church emptyhanded and confessing to Gretchen she didn't even try finding anything.

Madelyn read the Bible verses again. Once more, she checked under the lamp and looked beneath the bed. Still nothing. She walked over to the desk and stared at the words. *No one covers a lamp, or puts it under a bed, but puts it on a stand.* She missed the point about putting it on a stand. Whatever she was searching for must be on a stand. She squinted and scanned the room.

The solid-oak headboard, attached to the bed, didn't qualify as a stand and the wood cabinet with a television inside contained a small refrigerator. No other furniture remained. Madelyn stood, placed her palms to the desk and leaned her face closer to the open book.

"Come on, God, just give me a clue." Examining the passages, she paid careful attention to the frequency of the word light. *Puts it on a stand.* Resting her chin on her hand, Madelyn focused on the floor lamp as the buzzing grew louder. "I wonder…"

She turned off the light and unplugged the cord from the outlet. She tilted the entire fixture onto the bed and eased the bell-shaped shade onto the pillow to investigate the structure of the lamp. Madelyn inspected the entire length of the thick, antique bronze stand, attached to a square metal base. Her fingers trailed the path of where the base and stand connected. Turning it counterclockwise she detached the two pieces. The weight of the metal base slipped through her clammy hands and fell on the floor. At the same time the end of the stand hung off the edge of the bed exposing a shiny item inside.

Madelyn reached two fingers into the stand and extracted a silver tube. The object measured about the length of a sheet of paper and the approximate width of a broom handle.

"I found it." A gradual smile spread across her face although she was unclear of what she found.

A coldness ran down her spine. She rotated the object in her hands. No markings appeared on the outside, and the tube had two pieces fit together. Her pulse increased. If she tugged at each end it would separate the pieces. Better wait to open it until she spoke with Gretchen.

Madelyn set the aluminum tube on the desk and glanced at the clock on the nightstand, ten minutes until six. She lost track of time, ensuring her tardiness. Rummaging through her clothing, she selected her black, fitted trouser pants, a white cotton blouse and a versatile taupe pullover sweater; her regular work attire. She chose clothes that represented confidence and relinquished any risk of wavering under the stress of emotions.

She faced a full-length mirror and straightened her posture, certain her self-assured appearance masked the uncertainties stirring inside. At least no one knew her well enough to see past the façade. She convinced herself that no matter how she felt inside if she dressed the part then she succeeded in disguising her feelings.

She tied up her hair in a French twist and stuck in extra bobby pins for the layered pieces that always slipped out, causing her daily annoyance. Her dark hair contrasted her pasty complexion. Limited to a few cosmetics in her handbag, she dusted her eyelids with a shimmery pink powder. Madelyn shrugged a shoulder, she preferred to present herself as a business professional rather than a high-fashion woman.

Madelyn slipped on her flats and layered her clothes with a tweed coat. She stuffed the inside lining compartment of her coat with the aluminum tube, a passport and an emergency credit card.

In the front pockets she shoved in a pair of cashmere gloves, lip balm and a pack of mints. She glanced in the mirror before she opened the door. Pink splotches covered her neck and crept up beneath her cheeks. Her heart pounded as she straightened the collar of her blouse and left the room.

Madelyn exited the elevators and streamlined for the front doors. She glanced at the concierge desk.

Herr Renault waved his hand. "Pardon, Ms. Brighton."

Her shoulders dropped and she strode to the counter. "I'm running late. Can we speak later?"

"The owner of our hotel properties would like to offer you the service of his personal car with a driver."

"That's very kind. Does he usually offer his car to the guests?"

"Nein," he said, in a curt tone and his face tightened. "He's aware that you're staying with us to attend a funeral and wanted to extend his sympathies."

"I appreciate the gesture, but I don't want to inconvenience—"

Herr Renault swatted his hand in the air. "The driver is here." He extended his arm with a firm nod.

"Guten Abend, I'm Herr Drexwyler. I'll drive you to your destination."

Madelyn flashed a polite grin. "Danke. All Saints Church, bitte."

"The car is parked right out front. It's the charcoal BMW 750 LI."

Madelyn followed the gray-haired man out the front doors of the hotel. Herr Drexwyler opened the back-passenger side and offered his hand to help her inside then shut the door. Madelyn glided into the starlight leather seats. He entered the vehicle and waved his hand in front of a motion-controlled navigation display. With the start of the ignition, the engine purred.

"The church is a short distance from here. Make yourself comfortable with the touchscreen controls in the middle console."

Madelyn glanced at the monitor with icons for air, communications, seat adjustments and moon roof. She leaned backward and rested against the contoured headrest. The level of luxury the car exuded, along with the use of it for a guest seemed irregular for the hotel. Herr Renault's answer confirmed the owner presented her with special treatment. Did they single her out? She couldn't be the first lodger at the hotel attending a funeral. Perhaps the owner knew Sam. Gretchen said he had been a regular guest, although none of it seemed Sam's style. What did she know? She hadn't seen Sam in fifteen years. The man she grew up with always burned his bridges.

CHAPTER FOUR

Madelyn stared out the car window. The gothic cathedral spires pierced the tanzanite skyline. Golden rays painted a vista of amber coral with streaks of violet behind the brick structures. Pinnacles peaked above rows of red-tiled roofs a few blocks from the city center. The car stopped at the corner of the square outside the church. Madelyn didn't wait for Herr Drexwyler to assist her and exited the vehicle.

"Thank you for the ride." She tilted her head and peered through the lowered passenger window.

He turned off the motor. "I can wait for you and drive you back to the hotel."

"I don't know how long I'll be here."

"Here's my number." He reached into the front pocket of his ebony sports jacket and handed her his business card. "Call when you're ready."

"Thanks."

Madelyn stepped away from the car and signaled him with a waving arm, but he drove off before she had a chance to tell him she didn't have a phone. A groan rolled up her throat and she stomped away. She never had an issue with organization and punctuality before arriving in Germany.

At the church entrance her gut cramped, and she clutched her clammy palms around her waist. The excessive coffee consumption and limited food intake made her nauseated. Madelyn approached the decorated, recessed arcs spanning the entry. Above the portal, a huge circular rose window adorned the west façade.

An usher stood inside the open doors. "Guten Abend."

"Good evening." Madelyn walked up a couple steps.

"Are you attending the wake for Samuel Healy?"

"Yes."

"They're gathered in the chapter house, down the hall to the left." The usher passed her a memorial prayer card. She examined a photo of Sam displayed on the front and the Lord's Prayer on the back. Her heart plummeted into her stomach, viewing the first image of him she'd seen in years. She held the picture close.

His brown hair had turned mostly silver, although he still had a full head of hair, and his smile deepened the lines around his dark eyes, defining a visual tale of the joys and sorrows he lived. Sightless eyes stared back at her and a sourness burned her esophagus. Madelyn lost all the strength she spent years building. She shoved the card in her pocket. Time to set aside her feelings and stay strong for the sake of Gretchen and the boys.

Madelyn treaded on soft foot into the chapter house. She dawdled near the ingress and pressed her back against the cool, stone wall. Wood benches lined the perimeter of the chamber along with a few tables with lit candles. She sucked in a breath. A polished mahogany casket, rested on a cloth-covered church truck, beside a center column. Madelyn exhaled hard through her mouth. Thank God, it's closed. She'd find it intolerable with the body on display.

About thirty people gathered in small groups, speaking in lowered voices with a few mournful sniffles. Her legs brushed the smooth bench as she inched away from the separate cliques. A tugging in her heart tempted her to turn around and leave, but she would never be free unless she faced the past.

A small-framed woman stood near the casket, talking with an elderly clergyman. She glanced up, and they locked eyes. The woman strolled toward Madelyn. She pulled her black crocheted wrap tighter over her bare arms.

"Hallo. You must be Madelyn." The woman's voice cracked.

"Yes, it's nice to meet you." She extended her arm and offered a handshake.

Her icy fingers clasped Madelyn's hand. "I'm Gretchen. I'm glad you came to the memorial." Gretchen's green eyes were bloodshot and puffy. She brought a shaky arm to her forehead, sweeping her flaxen hair from her lashes. "I'm sure deciding to come here was a difficult choice, but we're thankful you joined us."

A sickness churned in Madelyn's stomach. Her hands balled into tight fists and her nails dug into her palms. Sam showed complete disregard for a family. He abandoned his first wife and child for a younger, healthier woman.

Madelyn coughed to clear the thickness in her throat. "I know how hard it is to lose a parent."

"There are the boys with my parents." Gretchen pointed across the room. "They're excited to meet you."

Madelyn glanced at Alarick and Rainor. Gretchen waved as their eyes met hers. They both had brown hair and the look of Sam in his younger years. "I'm looking forward to meeting them too."

They turned their mouths down at the corners while sitting on a bench, swinging their feet back and forth under a stained-glass lancet window. The sorrowful look on their faces struck her core. Madelyn wasn't much older when Sam disappeared, and Mom died.

"I'll introduce you to the boys." She gestured with her hand for the boys to come across the room. Alarick and Rainor lagged their steps and stood beside their mother.

"Boys, meet Madelyn Brighton." Gretchen glanced at Alarick and nudged his shoulder.

"Hallo." He pulled up his extra-long sleeve, stepped forward and offered a handshake.

Madelyn took his hand. "I'm glad to make your acquaintance." Alarick inherited Gretchen's fair hair and light eyes.

He nodded his head and stepped backward, wriggling with an obvious discomfort of wearing a suit. A gentle finger tapped her forearm and she turned toward Rainor as he gazed upward with the same dark brown eyes as her. He lowered his head and slouched.

Madelyn crouched to his level. "Hello, Rainor, I'm Madelyn."

He stared at her and reflected a younger version of herself. Madelyn recognized the pain and confusion behind his vacant expression. An unfocused look, pale skin and persistent sorrow, the kind he'd carry within his soul for a lifetime. The current weight of her anguish almost knocked her off her feet.

Rainor flung his arms around her body as far as he could reach, and she held him in an embrace. "Dad says whenever someone is hurting you should give them a hug," he whispered close to her ear.

How did Sam teach them about showing empathy? She wasn't aware he possessed any. Madelyn felt a sinking feeling in her stomach and gulped the lump in her throat. "You have a precious gift with your special hug. Thanks."

Rainor leaned away and she searched his face. God, please don't let the death of Sam crush the sweetness and innocence from the children.

"We'll visit more with Madelyn after the service." Gretchen pulled Rainor against her hip and patted his shoulder. "Now, go to your seats, bitte."

"Ja, mutter," Alarick said.

"Bye." Madelyn curved her lips upward to one side.

Rainor waved and grabbed onto his brother's arm. She kept them in her line of vision as they walked across the room and returned to the bench. Madelyn placed an open palm over her chest. If she could do anything to ease their suffering, she'd do it in a heartbeat.

"My sympathy is with you and the boys. Please let me know if you need anything."

"Thank you." Gretchen's emerald eyes flickered. "We're just happy to have you here, as part of our family."

A wave of heat rushed over Madelyn, pushing her back against the bench, and she staggered then regained her balance. She wrapped her arms around her belly. The aluminum tube in her pocket pressed against her body and she straightened her posture.

"I almost forgot; I found the item Sam left in the hotel room."

Gretchen placed her hands on her arms and directed her onto the bench. She leaned close and whispered, "Here, take this."

Gretchen removed a sealed envelope from the pocket of her fitted skirt and stuck it inside Madelyn's front coat pocket. "I don't know the details of your father's involvement, but he had good intentions."

Madelyn flinched at Gretchen's words. She never called Sam her father, yet all at once he was her father again, and they considered her part of their family. The room spun and seemed smaller.

"Ladies and gentlemen." The minister straightened his collar and stepped up to the podium. "Let's honor and celebrate the life of Samuel Healy."

"Please excuse me." Gretchen stood and placed a hand on her shoulder.

"Yes, of course."

Gretchen's heels click-clacked on the floor as she joined the minister. The room grew silent and everyone turned their attention to Gretchen. Madelyn stood, her legs trembled, and she leaned against the wall for support.

"Thank you, friends and family, for your support during this tough time." Gretchen gripped the edges of the podium. "I want to share my joy of having our family member, Madelyn Brighton from California, here with us."

A room of eyes inspected her like a specimen under a microscope. Madelyn shifted her shoulders and stiffened. She appreciated Gretchen's kindness, but the emphasis of being a part of their family tore into a wound that never healed and to embrace them as a family wasn't an idea Madelyn prepared herself to accept. At least not during the current conditions. Brokenness and loneliness lurked in her heart for so long she familiarized the feeling, and the sentiment remained a constant companion. Did anyone or anything exist with power to lift the weight of her sorrow and relieve her pain?

"Gretchen will deliver a brief eulogy." The minister stepped away and sat in the chair near the stand.

"We all know Samuel; a man who loved God, a member of the church, a wonderful husband and father." Gretchen choked on her tears.

Her words were a sharp slap on the face and Madelyn's ears rang with the stinging note of Sam being a loving father and husband. Gretchen continued to praise him about his love, generosity, and sacrifices. Heat seared through Madelyn, causing the whole of her body to shudder. Her mouth dried, and her legs were jelly as she stood with a strong stance. Madelyn squeezed her lips together as Gretchen continued reciting her admirations. How could she reconcile the Sam Gretchen described with the one she experienced?

Madelyn stretched the bottom of her sweater and sucked in a hard breath. She spent her adult life equipping herself with a tough exterior, to defend against any rivals from the past, but never considered having to protect herself against an emotional widow and her children. The genuine hurt and loss Gretchen expressed, echoed through the large, vaulted room with sighs of grief and mournful snivels of loss. The Sam they wept for seemed a different man than the deserter that broke his commitments in his earlier years.

She sympathized with Gretchen and the boys yet hearing how selfless Sam had been during the last ten years forced her to confront suppressed feelings. Had Sam become a reformed man? Madelyn's vision blurred as tears brimmed in her eyes and her chin quivered. She pressed her lips tight. For the sake of Sam's family, she intended on representing a composed woman like she posed as every day. Now wasn't the time to reflect on the past and the complicated present.

Between her thoughts and repressed feelings, she succumbed to the squeezing pressure in her neck and shoulders. She lost the war with her emotional battle. What a fool believing she had the strength to attend Sam's funeral with unresolved feelings. Sheryl was right, she tried to handle the details like a case file from work and evade the personal connection. Far too many years she neglected the pain Sam caused her and now like a dormant volcano her emotions erupted.

The minutes Gretchen spoke about Sam seemed hours long. Madelyn gulped for air as her lungs constricted, and the room spun. No longer able to hold up the pretenses of a poised woman, she dashed out of the chapter house.

Taking long strides, Madelyn hurried outside until she reached the wrought-iron fence that bordered the cathedral. The cold night air struck her face and as she blinked the tears spilled. She swiped the back of her hand across her cheeks. Her body crumpled onto a limestone bench as she tried to catch her breath. How far could she keep running? After Sam left and Mom died, she thought moving south of San Luis Obispo County was far enough to escape. Madelyn discovered she had a deep-seated bitterness in need of uprooting if she would ever achieve freedom from her ensnaring past. Starting with addressing her anger toward Sam. Madelyn pulled the letter from her pocket. In-ground pathway lights provided enough incandescence for her to read the note. Unfolding the handwritten pages, she read the scribbled penmanship.

Dear Maddie,

I write this knowing I will never see you again. This is my last opportunity to beg for your forgiveness. I have no right to ask since I don't deserve it, but I'm ashamed of leaving your mother, in her moment of need, and you to deal with it on your own.

It wasn't fair to expect a kid to take on such a responsibility. I wish to go back and change things. I thought of you every day and there are no excuses for my behavior, but by the saving grace of God I was set free from my gambling addictions and fraudulent activities.

By the time I recognized the errors of my ways, it was too late. I was in too deep with smuggling stolen art pieces, which led to trade in forgeries of documents and replicating relics. The last piece I confiscated over a year ago would be my final job since I wanted out of the business. I need to protect my family and, for once, do the right thing.

I'm relying on you to take on too much, but I know you're a strong, smart woman, just like your mother. Hopefully, you already have the item I left for you. The rightful owner wanted the artifact donated to a museum. I desire to follow through on his wishes. Be careful. Several independent smugglers are in a heavy pursuit of trafficking looted antiquities. I don't want you to get hurt. If you consider my request too dangerous, I suggest contacting the U.S. Consulate to involve Interpol.

Time is crucial and your silence in this matter is imperative.
Above all, protect yourself and trust no one.
I love you,
Dad

Madelyn crushed the paper between her fingers and shoved it in her pocket. Her mind raced with the information in the letter. Did Sam designate her to take care of his family again? What would happen to Gretchen and the boys if she didn't follow through with his request? Having lived with Sam's poor choices, she had an acute awareness of the repercussions of his mistakes.

Madelyn squared her shoulders as she scanned the courtyard. A shadowy figure stood near the entrance of the cathedral. The man leaned against the building, lit a cigarette and tossed the match. He observed the people exiting the church and his line of vision followed a person until settling his gaze on her. Madelyn shivered and glanced in another direction.

Wiping tears from her face, she cursed under her breath. Rash decisions led her here on this unnerving excursion. Madelyn cupped her hands over her face, inhaling and exhaling, hoping to carry on the guise of being in control. She hunched forward until her elbows rested on her knees.

"Geht es dir gut?" Another man stood at the foot of the bench.

Madelyn gasped and flung her head upward from her lap. "What?" She stared at him.

"Sorry, I didn't mean to startle you. I asked if you're all right. Do you need any help?" He spoke with an American accent.

"No. I'm fine." She dabbed the wetness from underneath her eyes.

"Are you sure? Because"—he gestured with his hand—"the tears and all."

Nerves stiffened in her neck and she hopped up, stretching on her tiptoes beyond her five-foot-five height yet fell short of his six-foot stature. She straightened her clothes and smoothed the wrinkles with her palms.

"Look, I've just attended a memorial service." She lifted her arms out to display the structure behind them. "You realize we're standing outside of a church, right?"

He laughed. "Okay, got it, I'll go. Sorry I bothered you." He pulled his hand from the pocket of his distressed, brown bomber jacket and gave a single wave goodbye, turning away. "Have a good evening."

"Wait." She twiddled her fingers. "I appreciate your kindness."

A smile spread across his face and a warm sensation spilled along her spine. His blue eyes shifted focus and his face brightened. Madelyn peered over her shoulder and glimpsed at the older man that caught his attention.

"How are you?" The older British gentleman called out while taking quick strides.

Extending arms, the two men greeted each other with pats on the backs. "Good to see you."

The younger man's smile faded. "Any sign of him yet?"

Madelyn scratched her head; she would add the incident to her list of odd encounters. She had her own puzzle to piece together and needed time alone at the hotel. She turned, hailing a taxi, when headlights with low beams cast a glow on the cobblestone road. Madelyn squinted and peered at a red sports car. She blinked a couple times and shook her head. The vehicle from the hotel drove alongside and she raised her hand, alerting the driver, Herr Drexwyler.

The American guy yanked her arm down. "You need to go."

His eyes narrowed. "Douglas, get her out of here."

She stumbled backward from his grip. "Hey, that's the ride to my hotel."

"You're staying at Hotel Füssen?"

"How did you know—"

He veered and stepped in front of her. The car slowed and stopped with the tinted windows of the BMW lowered. A voice spoke from the backseat. "Jake, I am surprised you chose such a conspicuous location to meet your comrade."

He leaned closer toward the open window. "I thought meeting at a church would keep evil at a distance."

Madelyn eavesdropped, but the British man slipped his hand around her elbow and tugged her in the opposite direction. "Come with me, dear."

"What, who are you?"

"My name is Douglas Wyatt. I work for Cardiff University in restoration and conservation of antiquities. I can assure you, I'm trustworthy."

Trustworthy? He restores antiquities. The letter warned to trust no one. But did she trust Sam?

"I don't understand, I want to return to my hotel. So, if you please…" Madelyn jerked free from his handclasp.

"My associate, Mr. Nolan, will take care of everything, don't worry." He quickened his steps.

A thundering sound of a gunshot echoed throughout the sky.

Madelyn's body jolted as if someone struck her with a bullet. She picked up her pace from a brisk walk to a sprint along the south side of All Saints Church.

"Are we safe?" She gasped and slowed to a stop. Her limbs trembled and she spun around. Douglas disappeared. He'd have to manage on his own. Besides, she hadn't caused whatever went on between those men and refused to die for no reason.

She looked in both directions on the street. Dense fog haloed around the streetlamps lining the charcoal stone streets. With the shops closed, an unnatural silence lingered on the residential lane. A sheen of perspiration formed on her temples as she approached a dead end. Her pulse raced while she rushed to the back entrance of the cathedral and jerked the locked iron gates. Trapped. She kicked her foot against the gates, stubbing her toe, and pressed her lips together to silence her scream inside. Worst of all, she bumped the same toe on the desk earlier.

Screeching tires resounded at the far end of the street. Her body stiffened as the rev of an engine drew nearer. A single headlight targeted Madelyn and the sound of a motorcycle ripped through the road. The motorcycle aimed for her, skidded and stopped with the tail end inches from her feet. She stood motionless with locked knees as if stuck in wet cement.

The hooded figure on the bike flipped up the visor of a black helmet, exposing his blue eyes, revealing the stranger she encountered moments ago.

"Get on," he yelled over the roar of the engine.

"I thought someone shot you."

He removed his helmet. "No, not yet. Here"—he tossed her the helmet—"put this on."

She held it in her hands; her gaze bounced between him and the bike. Cold air seeped through her open mouth. "Why would I go with you? I don't even know you."

"Hurry, we need to get out of here." He motioned with his hand for her to speed up.

"What do you mean, we? I'm not involved with—"

"You're one stubborn lady." He shook his head. "We don't have time to argue, I'm trying to help you."

Did she need help? She surveyed the street and concluded she had no other choice. Her hands shuffled the oversized helmet before she placed it on her head. She raised her foot up and down off the ground, three times, testing her aim until she swung one leg over the seat of the bike while trying to keep her balance. Placing his hand on her hip, he nudged her onto the motorcycle. Heat rose to the surface of her cheeks and she shifted her weight, keeping a distance.

He angled his head over his shoulder. "Hold on tight."

Madelyn scrambled to grab hold of anything but him and secured her grip on the cold chrome rack behind her, where he fastened his belongings. Her abdomen twirled with the swooshing of butterflies in her belly. Sensory receptors under her skin emitted the vibration of the engine throughout her entire body.

He revved the motor a few extra times before bulleting through the street. Madelyn lurched forward against his torso and wrapped her arms around his waist. Her hands grasped for something to pull away from the uncomfortable position, but the high speed of the bike forced her against his back. Darkness surrounded her with the shield of the helmet covering her eyes. Where would he take her? An icy chill paraded down her vertebral column. How did he know the name of the hotel? Madelyn gasped. The front end of the motorbike lifted off the ground as if they had taken flight and would shoot for the stars.

She no longer had an immediate concern for Sam's letter and the item in her pocket. Her mind focused on one question: who was the man she clung to and entrusted with her life?

CHAPTER FIVE

The city lights faded, and the roads widened when they left Munich's city center. The speed of the motorcycle accelerated, and they traveled along the A8 Autobahn. Every muscle in Madelyn's body tensed and she scrunched her knees, keeping her feet from the pavement. Her neck stiffened, distributing her weight while the harsh winds stripped away any feelings of protection. She used him as a shield and found comfort from the warmth protruding from his body. He remained unaffected, navigating with her pressed against him.

He maneuvered the bike following the curves of the road, emulating a cowboy riding his steed in open lands. Madelyn lost conscience awareness of her motions and leaned into every move he made. Her adrenaline raced with the rapidity of the motorcycle, hairs on her nape stood on end and raised small bumps on her flesh. She didn't care anymore about the physical torture of the rip-roaring ride. If she removed the helmet, she'd let her hair flow freely in the wind. With strict limitations on herself, she never acted carefree, but the peculiar events of the evening led her to react on impulse instead of reason.

The motorcycle veered sharp to the left, and she clasped her hands tighter around his waist. She tried checking her surroundings, but the helmet constrained her movement. The force of the brakes slammed her against him and with a sudden increase of speed threw her backward again. As the bike swerved, she pitched back and forth like a ragdoll. Madelyn trembled with a cold sweat.

Headlights of a vehicle behind them illuminated the road and created a spotlight. The car tailed close and the heat of the engine panted on her, growling with the hunger of a lion hunting its prey. The front bumper scraped the rear fender of the motorbike and it took everything inside her not to leap forward. Racing at maximum speed, he shifted hard to the right, gunned the motorcycle, and they zoomed off a crest.

Madelyn squeezed her eyes and opened her mouth, sucking in a sharp intake of air. Seconds passed as they soared into darkness, without a moment to pray, if she had enough faith to believe prayers saved lives. They hit the ground and shook vigorously while he attempted to gain control, steering steady and straight.

Overpowered in the fight against man and machine, the heavy metal mass buckled and forced them to accept defeat. The impact vibrated the bike and moisture on the topsoil caused the wheels to skate on sleet until the front tire slammed into a large boulder. Thrown about fifteen yards in the open terrain, she slid across the grassy knoll.

Battered and bruised, Madelyn laid on the sodden grass for several minutes.

She pulled off the helmet and fluttered her eyelids. Her head swarmed with the buzz of bees in her ears. Muscles twitched, propping herself into a sitting position, then she flopped onto her side.

An immediate piercing sensation of burning pokers shot through her neck and spread across her shoulders. Lying on the grass, her skin tingled with excess dampness and she shivered.

Madelyn glared through her blurred, double vision at the shadowy figure slumped near the bike. Were his intentions to sustain or extinguish their lives? Her blood bubbled, and she gritted her teeth.

Such flagrant carelessness. She balled her hand into a fist. If he didn't already sustain injuries, he would soon.

* * *

Jake rolled onto his hands and knees after he tumbled a few feet from his bike. His arms wobbled with the weight of his body and a tight pinch in his tendons constrained muscles in his neck. He blew a heavy gust. Thank God he didn't snap his spinal cord or have a concussion. With his fingers still curved into the gripped position of the handlebars, he squeezed his limbs, checking if he had broken bones.

An aching groan ascended from the ground mist, resembling an ancient apparition. Jake blinked a couple times before making out the dark outline of her body slouched onto her side.

"Are you all right?" he called out in a hoarse tone and struggled to his feet. He pressed his lips tight as he placed pressure on his knee. An increasing throb pulsated, surrounding the joints.

Limping toward the spot where she laid, he crouched down, slipped his arm around her and raised her torso to an upright pose. She stared past him with wide, glazed, brown eyes. She remained silent, and he waved his hand with the motion of a metronome inches from her face.

"Are you hurt? Can you move at all?" He braced his arm behind her for support.

"Yes"—she twisted her upper body in the opposite direction—"but no thanks to you."

Jake pushed his hair back with his hands. "Yeah, that didn't go as planned—"

"You call that a plan?" Her gaze flicked upward. "And now we have no transportation."

She pointed behind him and Jake followed her finger. "My R50!" He jumped to his feet and winced. Red pieces of plastic, from the taillight, lay shattered on the ground. His shoulders drooped and he collected a smashed side mirror. They survived and dodged major injuries, but a crushing weight on his chest increased, and he hobbled to the final resting site of his R50.

His head pounded, and he massaged his forehead. *Dang it.* He banged a fist against his leg. He damaged his bike, stranding them out in a field at night. Restoring the vintage BMW 1966 R50 500 remained one of his fondest memories he had working with Dad. Jake spent too many years wrestling with his own ideas about his future versus Dad's wishes for him to be his business partner. Building the R50 together welcomed a needed distraction from tensions and was the sole time they bonded as father and son.

Cruising on his motorcycle helped him escape and get away from the pressures of everyday hassles. The highway expanded his mind, gave his thoughts clarity while he deciphered the plans God had for his life. He spent the past year grappling with the direction he should take since Dad passed away. Jake entrusted God with his needs, but lately God's silence loomed, a dark raincloud lingering overhead and in addition to his own trials, he had the responsibility of protecting this lady, whom he met an hour ago. His actions apart from God ended with negative consequences.

"Excuse me, Mr.—"

"Nolan." He peered out the corner of his eye, watching her move with the stealth of a cat. "You can call me Jake."

"All right, Jake." She used his name like a curse word. "I can see you're having a moment with your bike, but what's next on your agenda?"

She stood behind him and heat spread up his neck as if hot daggers stabbed him. Jake turned and faced her fiery glare.

"I'm sorry. I had no choice." He raked his fingers through his hair.

She shifted from one foot to the other and placed her hands on her hips. "No choice, but to drive off the road and crash?"

"You think I wanted this to happen?" He threw his arms upward. "I was avoiding the other vehicle—"

"And that's another thing. Why did you involve me in this mess?"

"I told you. I'm trying to help you."

"You keep saying that, but I recall rejecting your offer." A crease deepened between her eyes and her nostrils flared.

"Yeah, well, you accepted my offer when you left with me." He turned from her and flipped up the light function on his phone, examining the wreckage.

She grunted aloud. Jake pressed his lips tight, holding in his laughter. He managed to push her buttons. Although, he couldn't blame her for being upset. Things hadn't gone the way he hoped for the entire evening.

His gaze bounced from one broken piece of his bike to the next. He hunched forward; the damage looked significant in the dark and he didn't want to imagine it in the daylight. A sour taste crept up his throat.

"Are we going to stand out here all night?" Her teeth clinked.

Jake altered his stance, relieving pressure off his knee. She hugged herself hard and shuddered, her glassy stare on the verge of shattering at any moment. He glanced at the trees and bushes surrounding them.

He swiped his hand across his face. "Okay, I'll make a call." He held up his phone and tapped on Douglas' number from his contacts. "Don't worry. Phone towers are everywhere, roadside service should arrive within the hour." After a few seconds and three short beeps, the call dropped.

"How about your phone, maybe you'll have better reception?"

"I don't have one with me." She raised a hand skyward. "Oh great, we're stuck here."

"Now hold on, Miss…"—Jake offered a handshake—"I didn't catch your name."

She stared at his open palm, her gaze rising until their eyes met. "Madelyn Brighton."

Her smooth, delicate hand slipped into his. Jake smiled. She yanked her arm backward and shoved both hands into the front pockets of her coat.

"Are you always so pessimistic, Madelyn Brighton?"

She slanted her head to the right. "Are you always this reckless?"

Jake swallowed the thickness in his throat. "Everything will be fine. You'll see." He patted her on the arm. "I'll try sending a text message."

He forced the crook of his mouth to curve upward, finding it difficult to encourage her when he had his own doubts.

A heavy breath escaped from her lips. "Sure, I'll wait and see."

True, he showed a level of risk and trashed his motorcycle, but they survived. Every time he tried doing the right thing, something or someone got in his way and botched his plans. He inspected pieces of his R50, positioned his motorcycle upright, and propped it up with the kickstand. He rubbed the back of his neck. At least they escaped unscathed.

Jake drew in a deep breath and exhaled through his mouth. He relished having a minute of silence after Madelyn Brighton challenged every word and action. He presumed she'd evaluate his decisions and demand an account of all his deeds. He found her unobtrusive demeanor refreshing, compared to her constant ridicule. However, the sooner he returned her to safety, the better. He chewed on the inside of his cheek and waited for a response from Douglas.

Jake appreciated her lack of questioning, but the stillness unnerved him. Straining his eyes, he peered in the dark. "Madelyn." He scanned the area with the light on his phone, searching in every direction. In the distance, she hiked the hill toward the Autobahn.

"Madelyn," he hollered across the field.

Jake tossed on his backpack and jogged toward her. He pursed his lips as the ligaments in his knee tightened like strings on a violin, ready to snap any instant. There she stood, out on display, after the trouble of getting away. He guessed by her comments she'd try to take control of the situation.

He respected she didn't play the damsel-in-distress role, yet her hasty decision could cost them their lives.

Jake swallowed hard, standing at the bottom of the incline. Madelyn waited under a light alongside the road. He climbed on all fours while his boots slipped on the wet pasture. Reaching the top, he wiped his hands on his jeans. "Why did you leave?"

"Wait and see." She swished her hair and strutted along the edge of the express highway.

She gestured to a car coming into view. The vehicle slowed, and she crossed her arms above her head. The BMW 750 LI braked to a full stop.

"You have no idea what you've done."

"But how?" Madelyn stumbled backward and into his arms.

"Let me take care of this," he muttered from the side of his mouth. Her extremities stiffened and she scampered out of his grip. She stepped aside, straightening the collar of her coat.

"What are you going to do?" She gathered her hair to one side, petting the length of her locks.

"Get behind me." He tightened his hands into fists. He'd avoid a fight but had to protect Madelyn.

She eyeballed him. "If you hadn't crashed your motorcycle—"

"You're right, I shouldn't have jumped my bike." Jake slouched and relaxed his hands.

Madelyn raised an eyebrow with a sharp nod.

"Then again, you flagged down the same car chasing us."

"You're keeping score?"

Jake shrugged with a slight smile. "We're even."

The passenger door of the vehicle opened. Madelyn leaned close and whispered. "That man is from my hotel; I think he's following me."

Jake parted his lips, then sealed them tight.

"Hallo, Jake."

"Leon," he said in a blunt tone.

A sneer wavered across Leon's face. "I'm so contented we're still on a first name basis. Please, get in, we'll give you a ride."

"That isn't necessary."

Leon opened the door, motioning with his hand to get into the backseat. "I'd lose sleep tonight, if I left you stranded on the Autobahn."

"I bet." Jake rolled his eyes.

"I'm certain the Audi in high pursuit of you will return."

Madelyn glanced around, searching for another escape route. The burden pushed into his abdomen. She'd ditch him at her first chance. She used concise words expressing her disdain for him and the ambitious off-road jump.

Mr. Drexwyler exited the car and marched to the passenger side. He accompanied Leon everywhere and his actual job description remained ambiguous, but Leon used him as brute force between the duo. Drexwyler advanced and flashed a handgun in a shoulder holster under his sportscoat.

"At least I'll offer a proposition and protection." Leon held the door open for them. "I'm certain your pursuers will not be as generous."

No point in avoiding the inevitable. Leon would continue his quest until he got what he wanted. Jake proceeded forward and Madelyn grabbed the hem of his jacket. He turned and ogled at her dark, distressed eyes.

"Stay close. You'll be fine." Jake wrapped his hand over hers and trudged toward the car.

He offered her the backseat, and she slid across the leather interior. She leaned against him as he shut the door. Leon and Drexwyler loaded into the front seats.

"Why do you make everything difficult?" Leon said.

"It's debatable who creates the difficulties." Jake rolled his shoulders and stretched his neck.

Drexwyler turned on the ignition and shifted the gear from park to drive. "Ms. Brighton, I'm unable to provide you with a return trip to the hotel tonight."

Jake peeked at Madelyn. She bit her lower lip while she twirled her hair with her finger and fixed her stare on the window. Jake angled his head forward, her pallid complexion showed she didn't trust him.

"I prefer your new companion to that bumbling British fool who tags along with you." Leon turned; his leering gray eyes trailed down the length of Madelyn's body.

Heat rose beneath Jake's collar. "I don't care about your preferences."

"I forgot how sensitive you are since the great Dr. Henry Nolan passed away."

Jake inhaled and exhaled hard through his nose. Leon's voice grated on his nerves. He heard tons of condescending remarks from him before and refused to let his words get under his skin. But now he had gone too far, taking them hostage. Jake needed more than his own strength to get them out of their predicament.

He bounced his knee up and down. A Bible verse came to mind about loving your enemies and praying for those who persecute you. Maybe he had taken it out of context, the phrase couldn't apply to Leon.

"I'm glad you recognize my father was great. And Douglas has always been dear to my family. He's stayed loyal, unlike others who've worked with my dad in the past."

A snigger hissed through Leon's teeth. "You're referring to those who worked for your father and expected more than a pat on the back, while Dr. Nolan received the glory and recognition? Then, I'll agree with you on the matter of Douglas' so-called loyalty. He'll continue working for nothing as a servant to the Nolan family, whereas the memory of Henry Nolan lives on forever."

"You fail to recognize my dad worked for a greater purpose. He honored God and kept serving the Lord, knowing he'd obtain eternal rewards. I'm sure he's enjoying the benefits now, just as I will someday."

"Now that's a delightful thought of you joining your father." Leon faced forward and eased into his seat. "Perhaps sooner rather than later."

Jake scraped his palm over his face. "You're wasting your time. I don't have what you want."

With animatronic movement, Leon pivoted in his seat and peered at him. "We'll determine what I want when we arrive at our destination." He selected the classical music icon on the car's touchscreen and played Mozart's Sonata No. 11, increasing the volume during the Turkish March.

Jake massaged his forehead. Most of the time he ignored Leon's arrogance and pomp, but the mention of Dad hit a sensitive mark, a gnawing inside that his recent actions would disappoint him. Nausea rumbled in the pit of his stomach. Would his overzealous behavior lead them into danger? The circumstances got out of control and godly ambitions developed into willful desires, extending the roots of deep-seated pride. He closed his eyes with a heavy sigh.

Jake spent years dealing with Leon and speculated where he'd take them. The location made it almost impossible to flee. He concentrated on planning how they'd get away. If they had an opportunity to break free, it would be risky.

His gaze settled upon Madelyn. She sat poised with straight posture, and her hands folded on her lap. Yet, a pained stare exposed a loneliness she couldn't disguise, even with the greatest efforts of composure. What was her story and why did Leon follow her? The draw to know Madelyn Brighton since the second he set eyes on her increased beyond what he intended to discover.

CHAPTER SIX

Madelyn peered out the window of the speeding vehicle. Her line of vision followed the painted dividers on the highway. Farther away from the city, later into the night hours and deeper into trouble. A pinched nerve in her neck tensed every muscle. The conversation exposed a link between Jake and Leon. She chomped on the inside of her lower lip and picked at the clear polish on her thumbnail while she pieced the information together. Abduction by a stranger worried her enough but being pursued for the sake of vengeance would be worse.

Leon showed up in every location she'd been, then Jake appeared at the church about the same time as Leon. For all she knew the three men were in cahoots. They probably singled out tourists that appeared to be vulnerable, led them out into the middle of nowhere, and battered them up a bit with crazy motorcycle stunts before they closed in for the kill. She glanced at each of them in the car, her gaze lingering on Jake. What was the connection and how did she fit into the scenario?

She acted foolish, accepting Jake's offer of help. Madelyn massaged the tightness in her chest. With her lack of senses, she destroyed all credibility of being a streetwise woman; she didn't even have a cell phone. A sickness churned in her stomach and she tucked her knees closer to her chest. Her body quivered, and she pulled her coat around her torso. The odd cylinder item Sam left with his instructions pressed against her ribcage. Her throat constricted and her resolution faded fast.

After a forty-five-minute intense car ride the vehicle exited the Autobahn. She dozed off for a few seconds, and with a twitch her instincts shook her awake. Gazing out into darkness, she searched for visual markers, creating a mental note of her surroundings, in case she survived the ordeal and could recount where they drove. Full foliage covered the landscape and she squinted at the faint mountain peaks in the distance as they passed a village.

Another half an hour later, the car drove off the paved road with the nearest town miles away. The tire tread crunched on gravel until the BMW rolled to a stop and parked. Holding her breath, she arched her neck, leaning against the headrest, and lowered her eyelids, exhaling aloud. If she made a run for it, she'd possibly end up with a bullet in her back. Either way, she'd undoubtedly die in the countryside of Germany. At least if she cooperated, they might spare her life.

"Make the call," Leon ordered Drexwyler and they both got out of the automobile.

With a gentle clasp on her hand, Madelyn flashed her eyes open and her gaze spiraled into two blue whirlpools. Jake whispered inches from her face, "Stay calm."

She kept quiet while she sank into the depths of his eyes.

Drexwyler opened the door and the cool late-night air rushed into the backseat. She tumbled out of the vehicle and Leon gripped her arm. He escorted her toward a boat tethered to a dock. She glanced over her shoulder; Jake followed behind with Drexwyler.

Unlike the consoling caress of Jake, Leon tugged her along and held her close to his side. Determined to stay strong and optimistic, despite Jake calling her a pessimist, she twisted under Leon's grip.

"Do not fret, Madelyn Brighton. You'll find I can be quite hospitable when entertaining my guests." Leon bent close. "If you cooperate with me."

"Perhaps if you explained what you want from me—"

"I'll inform you of my intentions when we arrive at Schloss Von Füssen."

In the stillness of night, water lapped against the wooden stilts. At the end of the pier a young man stood under a single light, wearing a black turtleneck and dark jeans. Resembling a thief in the night, he wore a beanie over his short blond curls, peeking out from beneath the cap. He chatted on his phone, until Leon approached, and the man shoved the device in his pocket.

Leon snapped his fingers. "Alles nach Plan?"

"Ja, Herr Von Füssen." The young man verified everything went according to plan and hurried to his post at the helm of the watercraft.

"Please, step aboard." Leon positioned his arm around Madelyn as they boarded the passenger ferry boat. A beige awning draped above them for minimal coverage from the damp air. Two vinyl-covered benches lined each side of the boat with enough space to seat about eight people.

"This is a waste of time and now you can add abduction to your list of offenses." Jake halted before stepping onto the boat.

Leon crossed his arms. "I'm simply providing comfortable accommodations due to the extenuating circumstances."

Drexwyler prodded Jake on the shoulder, forcing him onboard the boat. The young man from the docks untied the vessel and started the motor. He steered away from the pier and navigated the ferry toward the northeast side of the lake.

Leon sat close on the plush seats. "Pardon the mode of transportation while we cruise to the island. They docked the yacht at the port in Stock. It's a short ride to my castle."

Madelyn scratched her head. She hadn't just traveled to a foreign country, she felt transported to an alternate time. It seemed difficult to wrap her mind around what transpired within the past twenty-four hours. The discussion alone boggled her along with her new acquaintances. The name Von Füssen hadn't escaped her attention.

Leon's presence at the hotel made sense, yet it still didn't account for her relevance in the matter between Jake and Leon. She gasped as if shards of ice lanced her skin. Maybe the article Sam left factored into the chaos. His letter warned of danger and she suspected they involved Sam in something terrible. The constant rocking of the boat stirred the sickness in her stomach and the chance to break free slipped away as they journeyed farther from land.

Thick fog layered the lake. Madelyn rubbed her hands up and down her arms. They traveled with a simple spotlight guiding them to the castle. A string of lanterns hung from the edges of the canopy and Madelyn stared at Jake, sitting across from her. His eyes shined with a bold light she couldn't define—a spirit glowing inside him—and she found comfort in the calmness. For a moment she allowed herself to gaze deeper into his cobalt eyes.

Leon inched closer. "I'll tell you a brief history of the Von Füssen family, so we'll get better acquainted." He interrupted the eye language between her and Jake. "The house of Von Füssen is of royal descent, dating as far back as 1180, through my great grandfather's rule of Bavaria in the 1800s. Our enthusiasm for the arts influenced my family's reign. We created an artistic legacy procuring the commission and financing from prodigious art collections for the major cities. My second cousin, twice removed, financially supported the construction of many elaborate structures in Bavaria, including Herrenchiemsee, one of the three islands on Lake Chiemsee."

"Until their eccentric lifestyle forced them into bankruptcy." Jake dropped his shoulders with a hard eye roll.

Leon ignored him and recounted his story. "It's true my ancestors lost a substantial amount of the Von Füssen wealth at the end of the Bavarian kingdom in the early 1900s. Later in the 1960s the Von Füssens staked their claim on several of the properties built with our personal funds. Unfortunately, we did not acquire Herrenchiemsee, but of course we reap financial benefits from the attraction. Now I gain most of my fortune from the chain of Füssen Hotels."

"I'm curious, does the tale of your family actually impress anyone?" Jake bent forward, resting his elbows on his knees. "Are you impressed, Madelyn?" A wide, cheeky grin spread across his face.

"Well…it's a lot to take in." She tucked a corner of her lower lip under her teeth and glanced at Jake. A warmness spread up her neck, she turned toward Leon and swallowed hard.

"Your depiction of the Von Füssen family history is intriguing, but I can't imagine an important person like you having any business with someone as insignificant as me."

Leon leaned closer, making direct, probing eye contact. "You possess something of immense value."

Madelyn pressed her rigid body hard into the cushion of the seat. The echo of her heartbeat pounded in her ears. "I…I'm certain you're mistaken—"

"Leave her alone." Jake stood and the oblong fenders on the ferry bumped against the dock. He lost his balance and grabbed a support pole above his head.

An arrogant laugh rumbled in Leon's throat. "I'd forgotten how your mere presence entertains me."

"Wish I could say the same of you, but you're a joke that isn't funny anymore."

Drexwyler situated himself between Jake and Leon. Madelyn shook her head. The verbal assaults reeked of battle of the male egos more than any real physical threats. She intended to stay on guard and didn't trust any of them. She even found it difficult to rely on her own judgment.

"Sie können jetzt gehen." Leon dismissed the young man as they disembarked the ferry and stepped ashore.

Madelyn twitched her nose with the peaty smell of algae circulating in the breeze. Reeds sprouted up from the shore and they strode off the jetty onto the island. Ground mist swirled around her feet and she halted with a sharp poke from a pebble on the bottom of her foot. Leon halted and held her arm while she shook the stone from her shoe. Her boots were the ideal footwear for the unexpected outdoor undertakings rather than her flats. She sighed with relief when the path led to a boardwalk trail.

Blackness encroached, ambling under a row of towering trees and without Leon's supportive hand Madelyn stumbled. She wouldn't have known Jake walked behind her if it wasn't for the couple times he tripped on her heels.

"In a moment you'll see Schloss Von Füssen." Leon guided them to the end of the passageway.

At night, the monumental structure remained visible. Shadowy limestone turrets pierced billowing clouds with lights twinkling from the windows like stars in the sky. Madelyn trembled. The massive edifice revealed the material power Leon Von Füssen possessed.

Leon directed the group through a courtyard with a topiary garden of geometric-shaped shrubberies, bordering the slate stone footpath. Fire-lighted lampposts lined the walkway leading them to a marble fountain in the hub. Cherubim encircled the fountainhead with water flowing from their lips.

Beyond the center, they arrived at the entrance of the castle. Leon paused in front of the large oak doors and pointed at the crest. "This is the Von Füssen coat of arms. The heraldic shield encompasses charges of a golden rampant lion in the first quarter for bravery. The second is a purple acanthus leaf signifying an admiration for the arts. The third presents three black chess rooks representing strategic thinking"—he raised a deliberate eyebrow—"und the azure dragon, in the fourth quarter, is a valiant defender of treasure. At the middle of the escutcheon, the white-and-blue diamond shapes symbolize Bavaria as an entity." He scrutinized her while waiting for a response.

Madelyn glanced around and smoothed her palms over her coat. "You must be proud of your legacy—"

"A little too proud." Jake shoved his hands in the front pockets of his jacket. "Are we going inside?"

Leon pulled open the doors. "Welcome to my home."

Her breath caught in her chest. For a second she had forgotten under what pretenses Leon took them to the castle. Entering the foyer, a five-tier glass chandelier crowned the vaulted ceiling with four ribbed pillars beside the wrap-around staircase. To the right of the entry, a gold-laced, hand-carved mirror hung above a cabriole-leg console.

"Your reaction reveals your exquisite taste." Leon loosened his grasp on her arm.

Heat flushed her cheeks, and she pushed her shoulders back, lifting her chin as she straightened the lapels of her coat.

"When can we leave?" Jake said in a level tone.

"Let us get comfortable in the assembly room." Leon escorted them through the next corridor. "We'll have light refreshments und I'll clarify the terms of our business."

Strolling the great hall, Leon shared his oil paintings of the Von Füssen lineage decorating the walls. He hesitated in front of a picture. "A family painting, twenty-five years ago, a few months before my eighteenth birthday. It's the last depiction of my parents, Otho and Elisabeth. They both died nine months later," he said, expressionless, with an unfocused stare. "My older sister, Annelise, married Baron Henriksen, und now lives in Viborg, Denmark."

On instinct Madelyn clasped her palm over Leon's hand. He rotated and faced her with calculated movement, his eyes dim with a grim twist to his mouth. Madelyn withdrew her hand and curved her chest inward.

"Shall we continue to the next room?" Drexwyler rushed ahead into the next location.

Half a minute passed before Leon tore his gaze from Madelyn. "Come into my treasure chamber and have a seat."

Inside the assembly room, burgundy-colored rugs, with blue-and-beige trim, covered the hardwood floors. Aromas of wood oil and musk permeated the air. Floor-to-ceiling windows, draped in indigo and gold colors, bordered the far end of the room. Madelyn sat with a stiff posture in a Baroque, gold-leaf chair and Leon settled beside her in a giltwood Louis XVI chair, upholstered in scarlet velvet. Jake slumped into a cerise striped settee beside Drexwyler.

"Please, help yourselves. Helga, my pastry chef, makes a delicious Prinzregententorte."

Leon offered a tray of coffee and sponge cake, served on a brass-and-onyx table. Madelyn poured herself coffee from the white, scroll-handled ceramic pot into a matching cup and waited until Leon drank before taking her first sip.

"How do you like my collection, Madelyn Brighton?" Leon lifted an outstretched arm.

Paintings of master composers, in retrospective order, framed the walls. Mozart, Beethoven, Chopin, Brahms, Handel, Bach and other classical artists—presented to proclaim their prominence in the musical world.

"Looks like a museum in here. It's clear you're a music enthusiast."

He scoffed under his breath. "It's my field of study and expertise. As a conservator, I have an extensive private collection, and many contributions at public galleries. Come with me." Leon stood and held out his hand. "I'll show you a few of my great achievements."

Madelyn glanced across the table. Jake clanked his cup onto a saucer and folded his arms over his chest. He averted his gaze, checking his phone. His mannerisms expressed he still didn't have cell service and hadn't received a response from Douglas.

Sauntering the perimeter of the room, Leon introduced his historic findings. "Handel's clavichord." He raised his hand, presenting the small piano staged in a corner.

Below each composer identified, elevated panels with glass casings exhibited an historical object of the musician. "I acquired Beethoven's fountain pen during an excavation of his belongings in Vienna."

Madelyn nodded. She bowed forward for a closer observation and clasped her hands behind her back.

Leon continued his tour. "In Paris I authenticated Chopin's intimate, handwritten letter to George Sands, dated around the time of his death. In Baden, I located and verified Brahms' Orgel composition." Leon tucked his starlight hair behind his ear. "A favorite of mine is Bach's goblet. If you look closely at the mysterious etchings in the crystal, you'll see the name 'Bach' with musical notes in the form of an acrostic puzzle. I uncovered the goblet in Leipzig, und a matching one is on display in Eisenach."

After Leon presented all his items, fulfilling an article for almost every artist, he stared at a vacant case beneath Mozart's portrait.

"Isn't it disappointing to see an empty display for Mozart?" His eyes narrowed to slits.

"I suppose, but your other pieces are magnificent."

"Ja, my treasures are superb, but incomplete. However, circumstances have changed und soon everything will be where it should be." He raised his voice loud enough for his words to be heard throughout the room.

"As much as I admire your décor and art presentation, I still don't get why you brought me here." Her sight skimmed the room, and she locked eyes with Jake.

"Perhaps you need time to reflect on your position before deciding," Leon said.

"Haven't you figured out she has nothing to do with your delusional conquest?" Jake stood and walked across the room. "She was in the wrong place at the wrong time."

"I grow wearisome with your failed tactics to deflect the truth. Now we'll retire und continue our conversation in the morning. My servant, Edmond, will show you to your rooms."

"Wait, what? We're staying here tonight?" Her voice squeaked.

"Leon, this has gone far enough," Jake said.

"I agree. So, when the ferry returns in the morning, I'll expect you to return my rightful property."

"I told you, I don't have it."

Leon stroked his jawline. "A fascinating fact about archeology, you'll find many artifacts have passed onto unsuspecting hands and turn up in the most unpredictable places."

"If you follow me, I'll accompany you to your quarters." The middle-aged servant stood in the doorway, dressed in the traditional butler's three-piece suit, complete with a bowtie and white gloves. "You will find the highest level of luxury at Schloss Von Füssen."

"Guad Nachd und pleasant dreams." Leon jutted his chin and waved a dismissive hand, excusing everyone from his presence.

Edmond directed the way to the bedchambers. They climbed five flights of burgundy carpet stairs and halted at a door in the middle of the hall. Edmond opened the double doors, holding his arms out, inviting Madelyn into the room.

"I think you'll find all the amenities you need." He lit two pink, princess-feather oil lamps. "Herrn Von Füssen requires your attendance in the dining hall for breakfast at 7:00 a.m. sharp. Will there be anything else before I take Herr Nolan to his room?"

"Ah…" She arched her body to look at Jake while he waited in the hall. "I guess I'm fine at the moment."

"Sehr gut."

Madelyn glimpsed at Jake, as Edmond left and shut the door. She found it difficult to distinguish the sound between the thud of the door and her heart. She petted her neck to ease the lump in her throat, faced with the dilemma of sleeping in a castle with strange men, one with a gun and another who held her captive. With no other options, she'd have to stay and hope she'd make it to see the light of day.

* * *

"Herr Nolan, I'm sure the room is suitable." Edmond opened the door to a suite at the end of the hallway.

"You're not throwing me into the dungeon?" Jake followed him into the room.

"Not yet, although if it were up to me—"

"I knew there'd be one." Jake laughed. "Leon doesn't consider me a serious rival?"

"At least not worth the effort of escorting you to the tower. On the other hand, it would serve you well to remember breakfast in the morning." Edmond swung the doors shut.

Jake shrugged a shoulder. Leon and his staff shared similar traits with their lack of personable skills. Jake curved forward, placing his hand on the crystal knob. With a tight grip and a wary turn of the handle, the door creaked open. None of Leon's lackeys stood outside. Weird, Leon didn't post a guard at an unlocked door and left him unattended. He rubbed the back of his neck.

Jake closed the door. He mulled over schemes and scenarios Leon might formulate. The caffeine from the black coffee kicked in and he paced the dark-stained plank floor. Leon's courtesies were a crude attempt to coddle the two of them before acting upon his sick will. There was no point of forcing them to stay the night if Leon knew he didn't have the item. Maybe Leon assumed Douglas had it and planned to hold them for ransom. Leon seemed convinced Madelyn had something to do with their connections and that she wasn't just an innocent bystander.

Pulling back the full-length drapes, he peeked out the glass. Jake cracked his knuckles. The pressure and responsibility of protecting Madelyn intensified his headache. He experienced her strong-willed temperament, but also witnessed a vulnerability in her when she sat in tears outside the church. He had to consider her disposition before devising an escape plan.

Jake sat on the edge of the bed, away from the unlocked door, removing the temptation of making any rash decisions. Their getaway would involve more than strolling out the front door. He took off his jacket and sweater, getting comfortable in his heather-gray t-shirt. With heavy thoughts and throbbing pain in his knee, he lowered his head onto a pillow and relaxed on the down-filled comforter.

If they stayed until morning, he needed to devise clever persuasions and convince Leon to let them go. Yeah right, he wouldn't listen to reason and nothing Jake said made a difference. Leon deceived so many people and they followed him or his money blindly.

Jake stared up at the candle chandelier above the bed. He closed his eyes and inhaled through his nostrils then exhaled hard out his mouth. Charred wood lingered in the air from the marble fireplace.

Leon expected him to give up the job and walk away like he did before Dad died. If he possessed what Leon wanted, then he'd consider surrendering the victory without a fight. But Jake would be an idiot to allow Leon to win. This assignment became too important, and personal. Leon's ambitions cost Dad his life. He would do whatever was needed to ensure Leon would pay the price and lose this time around. With or without Madelyn Brighton, no one would deter him from completing his mission and finishing what Dad started.

CHAPTER SEVEN

Leon stood in front of the opulent white stone fireplace. He drummed his fingers against the sculpted frieze-and-acanthus-scrolled jambs, forming an intricate design and creating an ornate mantel. A sense of calm filled him. He demonstrated his authority to Madelyn Brighton, pressing upon her the importance of giving him what he wanted. He earned the right to demand the return of his property. Jake lost and Ms. Brighton would soon discover she'd be no match for him. Leon glanced at the French Baroque clock, the hands pointing to the roman numerals indicating twenty minutes past midnight.

"Do you think it wise to leave our two guests unattended?" Drexwyler entered the room, uninvited, and closed the doors, stationing himself with the posture of a night watchman.

"Where will they go? We're on an island." Leon poked a log with a fire iron, watching the embers float up the chimney and the wood smoldered. "I never lack wisdom. I have them perfectly positioned, with a sense of security, yet imbued with the uncertainty of any escape."

"Are you certain the woman has what you want?"

"Ja, she holds all I desire." His eyes narrowed, staring at the flickering flames, thinking of Madelyn sliding her hand over his when he mentioned his family. Did she think him inept, and he'd fall for her temptress ways? Nothing would distract him from his goal of obtaining his rightful possession. He wasn't blind to her beauty, yet quite aware she used flattery and charm to manipulate her plight.

Leon glared at Drexwyler, sitting and finishing a cup of tea. "Mason." He called him by his first name in a stern voice to get his attention. "In case Ms. Brighton needs further persuasion, find out everything about her."

"A prudent decision. I'll run the regular reports along with a personal investigation."

"The usual essentials—where she resides, place of employment, her hobbies and interests, down to the inconsequential, such as romantic entanglements."

"Wie bitte?" Mason popped his head back.

"You heard me." Leon squinted his eyes and glowered.

"Ja," he said with a sharp, single nod. "I heard you loud and clear."

"The information might prove useful; people act irrationally when they're in love." Leon stabbed the log a few times until the wood collapsed and the fire died.

"Indeed." Mason avoided eye contact and set his cup on the table. "I'll get to work straight away."

* * *

Madelyn blew out a heavy groan. The scent of kerosene and beeswax filled the air. What a horrible day it turned out to be. Pure fatigue and the ache of her muscles forced her to sit on the canopy bed, with floral fabric draped along the four posters. Her palms slid against the champagne, satin sheets and the small of her back leaned against the mattress. She didn't dare lay down, in case she fell asleep.

She hadn't relaxed or had a moment to herself since she left Hotel Füssen. With a weighty head in a fog of confusion, she bowed forward. If going to Sam's funeral and meeting his family wasn't enough, she ended up with strange men, stranded on an island. She massaged the tight pain in her chest. The mysterious item inside her coat tapped and nudged, begging for exposure. Heat spread throughout her body.

Madelyn removed her coat, reached into the inner pocket and wrapped her fingers around the cool, aluminum tube. She held it vertically, close to her face, inspecting the item. A blurred, contorted reflection mirrored her image in the silver metal canister. She gawked at the defined, connecting line in the center and pulled at both ends. The moisture on her hands hindered her from separating the two pieces. A gusty huff blew from her lips. She tossed her hands onto the bed, threw her head back, and her shoulders dropped.

Madelyn licked her dry lips. She dug in her front pockets and withdrew her cashmere gloves, lined with finger and thumb grips, covering her hands with a snug fit. She tugged at the opposite ends of the tube with all her strength in a final effort until one end of the canister loosened. Her fingers trembled and she removed the top portion, exposing a cream-colored parchment rolled up inside. Gulping in a mouthful of air, she flattened her lips tight together while she extracted the paper.

Setting the aluminum container aside, she used both hands, unrolling the documents. Her heart throbbed as she extended the four oblong sheets. Handwritten musical notes were scrawled over pre-printed staved lines. Madelyn never learned to read music, but she squinted, reading the legible autographed signature in ink. Her eyes widened and her mouth went dry as she focused on the name.

Wolfgang Amadeus Mozart

Her hands quivered and her blood ran cold.

After viewing Leon's gallery collection and listening to his odd statements, she knew the valuable documents made her his main target. Did Leon know Sam left her Mozart's music, and if so, how much did he know about Sam and his instructions? Gretchen stated Sam stayed as a frequent guest at Hotel Füssen.

She scrunched her nose and forehead, rolling up the papers and sealing the documents in the protective case. Sam once again had forsaken his responsibilities and left it for her to manage. Madelyn missed a chance to decide if she wanted to help while whisked into a spiraling tornado of actions that swept her away. She retrieved Sam's crumpled letter from her pocket and reread the note with her eyes settling on his closing words to trust no one.

Madelyn tapped her fingers on her lips. Jake and Leon were far from friends and weren't working together. If anything, they were on opposing sides. How did Leon, Sam and Jake all intersect? She had so many questions and no answers. She held the letter tight in her fists and tore the paper in half. After she ripped the note several times, she tossed the scraps in the cold fireplace.

The less anyone knew about Sam's directions the better. Did Mozart's music arm her with the leverage needed for breaking away from her current position? Refusing to succumb to fear she'd take the initiative and get herself out of her dilemma. Madelyn prided herself on being sensible; there were no knights in shining armor ready to rescue her in her moment of distress. She smiled at the thought of her gallant cavalry—he didn't ride off with her into the sunset, he rode his steed straight off the Autobahn.

Madelyn flattened the hem of her sweater and straightened the collar of her white blouse. She inhaled and exhaled hard through her nose. Jake Nolan expressed his intentions of helping her and so far, proved to be unreliable. She rested her chin on the back of her hand. The hasty decision she made on the Autobahn resulted in them being confined to Leon's castle. Although, she wouldn't wait for Jake to do anything heroic, or anyone else; she would take matters into her own hands. Her chest caved inward with the weight of her heavy heart. Whenever she depended on people in the past, the relationships ended in disappointment. She sighed.

The struggle with relationships amplified a little over two years ago when she thought Brennan Moore would propose after they dated for three years. They finished their degrees and he'd been a major support during Mom's death. He promised to take care of her and stay by her side, but his drive and ambition for a career in politics lured him away. Or at least she liked to believe that was the reason he left, and he'd been urged not to propose marriage, rather than accept he didn't love her enough.

Either way, Brennan moved on with another. The image of him saying goodbye remained vivid with his maple-brown hair, dipping into his jade-green eyes, capable of inducing a slight natural buzz while he spoke words of hope, trust and love, tenderly crushing her dreams. Through the sobs, she proved, in her own strength, she would manage independently. Madelyn was convinced her idea of the "right man" was as flawed as the nuclear family. She had two failed romantic relationships, no family, and daily encounters with battered women, pushing her beyond a cynic. However, she learned one important lesson: never fall for a guy with dreamy eyes, especially if he rides a motorcycle.

Madelyn gripped the cold brass handles of the solid oak armoire, pulling the double doors open and glimpsed at her reflection in the full-length mirror. Taking a second to fix her hair, she combed her fingers through the tangled strands, coiling the back tight into a twist and replaced the bobby pins. Removing her glove, she ran her index finger back and forth on her teeth to substitute for a toothbrush. Her skin, a paler shade of light ivory, emphasized the dark circles forming under her eyes.

She rummaged through her pockets in the same manner a soldier checks supplies before going into battle. The hidden penned parchment provided the only sense of security and she didn't know if possession of Mozart's music created an advantage or disadvantage. Drawing in a deep breath, she squared her shoulders and headed for the exit.

Madelyn cracked the bedroom door open and peered through the crevice. The hallway appeared empty. The light from a dim-lit ceiling chandelier cast a soft glow in the center of the hall. Her heartrate increased as she slipped out into the corridor. On tiptoe she peeped over the handrailing into a dark labyrinth of stairs and passages. One of the oil lamps from the bedroom would help guide her downstairs. Pivoting around, her body slammed into a muscular structure and her nose pressed hard against a firm chest. Her palms roved over his defined pectorals.

"What are you doing?" Jake whispered.

Madelyn jolted and smacked her head on his jawbone.

"Ow," they said in unison.

She massaged the top of her scalp. "I'm trying to get out of here."

He rubbed his chin. "Come with me, I figured a way out." Jake slid his hand around her wrist, leading her down the hallway.

She grunted under her breath. In the few hours she spent with Jake Nolan, he gave her directives at least three times. At the end of the hall, they entered Jake's assigned suite.

"You should've waited for me, it's too risky standing in the hall."

Heat rose from her neck to her cheeks. "You were taking too long."

He lowered his gaze. "I was working on a plan."

She placed a fist on her hip. "You fell asleep?"

"Well, more like a quick nap." He flashed a wide smile of gleaming, straight teeth. "But I know how we can get out."

"Another one of your clever escape routes?" She bit her lower lip. "I'm afraid to ask." Should she give him a second chance to talk her into following a new reckless scheme?

"Quick, let's pack up our coats and shoes." He sat on the bed and laid his backpack next to him as he unlaced his boots and shoved them into the gear.

Madelyn crossed one arm over her chest and propped up her elbow, resting her chin on her fist. He folded his black sweater and a brown leather jacket, stuffing them inside the pack.

"There's room for your coat and shoes too." He ran his hand through his rich brown hair. Every strand fell perfectly out of place—although he wore a helmet, tumbled from a crash, and slept, it still didn't affect the style.

Madelyn rolled her eyes to the side. "Don't you think we'll at least need our shoes?"

"Trust me, you'll thank me later."

Everyone involved expected her trust, and yet they had done nothing trustworthy. Did Jake have an interest in Mozart's music too? Right now, he was the only one with an escape plan. She had no other options. Madelyn pulled off her coat, rolled it tight and squished them on top of his jacket, sweater and boots at the bottom of the large, waterproof bag. Would the aluminum case and their clothing protect the documents? She couldn't wait to get to a phone, contact the US Embassy and get out this mess.

"Put your shoes and gloves in the front pocket."

She crammed her gloves and ballerina flats inside. "Now what?"

"Okay, let's go." Jake adjusted his backpack on his shoulders.

He rushed around the bed and paused in front of the floor-to-ceiling ivory, damask-style drapes. With a swift sweeping motion, he flung the curtains back and opened the thick glass-paned doors leading out to a small balcony.

Jake stepped outside on the limestone terrace and observed the surroundings, stretching over the edge as if taking mental measurements. The pace of her heart hastened, vibrating in her veins. Based on his recent track record she had a good idea what Jake planned. She knew next to nothing about him and yet in the time they'd spent together he exposed her to multiple life-threatening situations. Knots tightened in her stomach when he waved her over to join him outside.

"See over there?" He pointed his finger to the right of the castle. "We'll use the small boat, docked at the servant's entrance."

Madelyn shuffled her feet a little closer and extended her upper body while keeping her back planted against the stone edifice. She peered out the corner of her eye above the ledge.

"We're jumping?" Madelyn swallowed hard.

He nodded his head. "It's approximately seventy feet, give or take."

She did a double take. "There's no other way out of the castle? Back staircase, a secret passageway?" Her voice trembled. "Anything?"

"Not unless you want to wander around, waking Leon and his staff."

Madelyn blinked long and hard. Maybe she'd awaken from her nightmare. "I honestly regret meeting you."

"Everything will be fine." He spoke in a soothing tone and laid a palm on her shoulder.

"Didn't you say that earlier, before we ended up here?"

He cocked his head to the side with a slight frown. "What do you suggest? We give in to Leon's demands and stay for breakfast."

Too tired for an argument, she shrugged her shoulders. She had no other choice but to trust Jake again. "I'm going against my better judgment."

He launched himself onto the stone balustrade. She inhaled hard as he stood at his full height on the foot-wide ledge. Jake squatted then outstretched his arm. Madelyn secured her grip on his forearm and gained a foothold on the limestone support. She sprung off her bare foot, and he pulled her up to his side. Her body swayed backward and forward until she latched onto his bicep and stabilized her balance. She glanced beneath her; the darkness bled into the depths of the lake.

"You may feel disoriented when you hit the water." He clasped their hands together. "Hold on tight."

She gulped, lacing her fingers into his and prepared for the perilous plunge.

"Are you ready?"

Words piled on her tongue, but nothing came out of her gaping mouth. She sucked in her breath and ballooned her cheeks with air. Her heartbeat pounded in her eardrums.

"On the count of three," he said. "One, two…"

By the end of two, she felt invisible hands thrust her off the ledge. She screamed, but only the sound of air whistled in her ears. The sensation of her stomach wedging between her ribs then plummeting to her knees stirred a biliousness. Within seconds, the feeling of thousands of prickly needles piercing her flesh fired through her body as they crashed into the water.

Shooting toward the bottom, Madelyn tried to remain conscious of holding Jake's hand while she struggled through the dark liquid space. Whether her eyes were open or closed seemed irrelevant beneath the pitch-black water.

Gravitational force ripped free her tethered grip on his hand. In a panic she kicked her feet wildly and rose to the surface. Lake water lapped her nose, her hair like seaweed covering her eyes. Blackness engulfed, and she gurgled. "Ja—"

Her arms and legs weighed her down as if filled with lead. With her head emerging, ripples of water slapped her in the face, and she went limp. A gust of air expanded her lungs, and she coughed up fluid. He buoyed her up from behind and gave support under her arms.

"How are you doing?" Jake uttered in a wet, breathless tone. "Okay?" He panted against her ear.

Her neck locked when she tried to nod.

Jake navigated toward the shining torches lining the docks, propelling against the current, and keeping them afloat by fluttering his legs hard.

Madelyn regained her bearings, flexed her ankles and pointed her toes to create less drag. The great escape plan would be a failure if they drowned in the middle of Lake Chiemsee. Jake stopped paddling, removed his backpack, and moved ahead of Madelyn. She latched on, using it as a flotation device while he towed her with one arm and managed an impressive sidestroke. She helped relieve the weight on his upper body, flapping her feet and legs faster than she knew possible.

They arrived at the wooden dock and Jake made one last exhausted lunge for the dinghy tied with a rope to the post. Madelyn clung to the edge of the craft as it rocked. Once again water filled her mouth, and she gasped for air. She mustered the little strength she had left and raised her chin up out of the water. Jake tossed his backpack onboard and helped prop her upper body atop the bow. She lifted her leg and hauled herself inside for safety. The shock of the cold water settled in her bones and intensified her rigid movement.

With a worn-out heave, Jake rolled into the boat with a sluggish thud. He laid on his side, his wet t-shirt clung to his ribcage, his torso rapidly rising and falling. Madelyn clutched her chest, trying to control her erratic breathing. She wavered with depleted energy, but they weren't in the clear yet, with the plausible chance of being caught.

Her arm quivered with fatigue, her fingers fumbling as she untied the rope from the dock post. Jake rotated his body to an upright posture and pressed his hands against the dock, pushing the boat farther on the lake. With a heavy intake of oxygen his shoulders drooped while he exhaled hard. Droplets streamed down the bridge of his nose. He cupped his hand over his mouth and swiped the water from his face then pushed his soaking hair back from his forehead.

Madelyn shivered. Her clothes stuck to her flesh and her tresses now hung at full length. Water dripped from the saturated strands. Her chin trembled and her teeth chattered. She sat with her knees tucked to her chest and her arms wrapped around her body to produce extra heat.

"Here." Jake handed her his backpack. "There're supplies in the small pocket."

Madelyn unzipped the bag and retrieved a hand towel. She dabbed it against her face, dried the ends of her hair and passed it to Jake. He patted his skin dry, smoothed the cloth over his head and tossed it in with his stuff. Resting his hand on the throttle of the outboard engine, he watched the gentle roll of the waves drifting about a hundred yards from the castle. He shifted the lever in neutral and tugged the starter rope. He yanked the cord two additional times, and the motorboat started.

Jake positioned the control, aligning the arrow lines up with the shift mark. He angled his body toward the motor with his head slanted over his shoulder and guided the boat across Lake Chiemsee. The soft light of the moon, set in the dark-blue hue of nautical twilight, cast a glow on the surface of the water and illuminated a path to shore.

In a silent, shivering shock, Madelyn's skin burned like raw meat packed on ice. A chill surged through her veins and her temperature dropped. With wind-whipped flesh, crimson lashes lined Jake's exposed arms.

After a thirty-minute boat ride they reached the shallow water of the east end of the lake. Jake switched off the motor and hopped out into the knee-deep water, pulling the boat up onto the rocky shore. Anchored down with her soggy clothes, Madelyn strained to climb out of the dinghy. Numb and freezing, she stood in the crisp, biting breeze, nipping at her nose and cheeks as she shrunk to her feet.

Damp hair draped across her face as she bowed her head toward her legs. She exhausted her physical capabilities, heart palpitations increased, and her mind spun with the force of a tilt-a-whirl carnival ride. They evaded fatalities in both the motorcycle crash and a seventy-foot jump into a lake, yet she felt death hover. Hypothermia spread through her respiratory system. Ready to surrender, she collapsed to the ground.

CHAPTER EIGHT

adelyn's wet clothes clung and constricted her movement in the dank air. She sat upright and gritted her teeth. At any moment she would awaken from the nightmare and it would all be over.

"Madelyn." Jake crouched and gripped her arms. "Are you okay?"

She slumped forward against him.

"Hey, Maddie!" His voice strained. He raised her chin with his finger, and she fluttered her eyelids. No one called her Maddie since she was a kid. She forced her eyes open. His lips pouted, and a defined line creased at the bridge of his nose. Jake bent on one knee and dragged his backpack beside him.

"Sit tight," he said.

He pulled her coat from the bag and wrapped it tight around her chest. Madelyn flinched at his touch and tucked her arms in close to her sides. She hated him making a fuss. With every ounce of energy left she pushed herself off the ground.

Jake held his arms out in front of her as she swayed. "I think I'll be fine."

"You're sure?"

She wriggled her shoulders, struggling to slip her soaked arm through her sleeve. At least Jake attempted comforting gestures. His tactics had been risky, yet relative to the situation. Her reasoning became fuzzy from the adrenaline rush and extreme fatigue. She lacked the stamina to sort out in her mind Jake Nolan's character and his true intentions.

Madelyn watched his movements. He peeled off his drenched shirt, replacing it with a dry sweater, then put on his jacket and zipped it before she blinked again. Jake glanced up while tying his boots. Her cheeks burned, warming her neck and chest.

Rummaging through his belongings, he paused, patting himself down and pulled his waterlogged phone from the pocket of his jeans. Jake shook the device and frowned. He organized his backpack according to his immediate needs, as if everything that had happened was a daily routine. He didn't seem shaken by the events, although his strong jaw implied repressed tension rather than only an attractive facial feature.

Jake moved closer and set the bag at her feet. "At least your shoes are dry." He winked. "Use anything you find helpful—except the phone, it's dead."

Tiny pebbles stuck between her toes. She brushed off her soles before putting on her flats. His gaze dipped with his arms folded across his chest. Pity crossed his face as he assessed her appearance. She stood there with the desperation of a sunk cat. Perhaps he pitied himself for taking her along. Heat spread up her nape and flooded behind her ears. He probably considered her foolish, and incapable of managing things on her own—a helpless girl. So far, his impression must've been an emotional, headstrong… Why did she care what he thought?

Whatever his perception, he would be in for a big surprise from here on out. Sure, Jake provided certain resources, had knowledge of operating machinery along with strong swimming skills, and his cunning strategy got them out of trouble…then again, he had been at the center of all the turmoil.

"I guess I should thank you for being lucky enough to pull off an act of heroism?"

He shrugged a nonchalant shoulder. "I thank God we survived not only one, but two death-defying acts."

Madelyn tilted her head, paused and searched his face for any signs of falter. He looked serious. She hadn't given the conversation with Leon in the car much thought, but Jake had no problem professing his belief. Trusting in an invisible God was no worse than her depending on a stranger.

"Your actions were a literal leap of faith?"

"You could say that."

"And to think my choices were to stay with an egocentric man in his luxury castle or follow you, the guy who believes 'when God closes a door, he opens a window' and literally jumps out."

"You may have a chance to reconsider if we don't get moving." He slid his backpack over his shoulders. "Sun will be up soon."

Jake directed his steps toward a thicket of white birch trees. Madelyn sucked in a breath of cold air and strolled two strides behind.

He peered over his shoulder. "By the way, that quote isn't from the Bible, it's from the Sound of Music."

"Well…" Madelyn grazed her top teeth over her bottom lip. "I love that movie."

A hazy shade of orange burst across the horizon. Trees towered with pearly dewdrops sparkling in the opaque light. The sun peeked through the snow-topped mountains, encircling Lake Chiemsee. Jake navigated through a grove of trees. Did he know where they were going? The closest town and train station would be ideal. As soon as they arrived, she'd check into a bed and breakfast inn, take a long hot bath, eat and get rid of the burden bestowed by Sam. The entire fiasco created further hassle than she intended handling.

She rejected the idea of extending her time away from work, neglecting clients, schedules, and responsibilities. Sure, she didn't lead a life of adventure like Jake Nolan, but she also didn't end up in life-or-death situations.

"Do you know any local towns or where I can take transportation back to Munich?"

"Yeah, we're going to Ruhpolding."

"How much farther do we have to walk to get there?" Madelyn paused with the throbbing pain of her heels rubbed raw.

"About five hours." Jake glanced at her shoes and attire. "Actually, that timeframe is for experienced hikers."

"Are you kidding? Can't we catch a train or a bus? Isn't there anywhere closer?"

"Yes, but I'm staying in Ruhpolding. Leon will check the local stations and the expressway. We need to stay out of sight."

"I don't care what you think is best. All your ideas lead us into danger." She waved her hand, brushing off his suggestion. "No thanks, drop me off at the closest village."

"I'm not leaving you in a random city."

"Who delegated you to be my protector? You're not responsible for me." She straightened her damp blouse under her sweater. "I can take care of myself."

"I'm sure you can." His eyes narrowed to slits. "What about Leon following you? For some reason he's convinced you have something he wants." He lowered his head with a deliberate gaze. "Do you have any idea why he singled you out?"

"I…I don't know. I'm visiting Germany to attend a funeral."

"Yes. Sorry for your loss."

"Thanks." Her voice cracked, and she swallowed the lump in her throat. "It was someone I knew a long time ago. I came to comfort the family."

"You mentioned Leon followed you."

"He seemed to be everywhere, but now learning he owns Hotel Füssen my assumptions need a reevaluation."

"Uh-huh." He stroked the short stubble on his chin. "Did Leon say anything at the castle that clued you in on why he'd taken an interest in you?" He studied her expression. "Other than the obvious."

"Excuse me?" Heat singed her cheeks.

"This is beyond an attempted courtship, even for Leon."

"I don't know why he's interested in me. I told you all the facts." She rubbed her wet clothes and fidgeted.

Her eyes darted toward the tree roots crisscrossing under her shoes.

"Okay, if that's all you know." He shrugged a half-hearted shoulder and strolled along the rocky path with a slight drag of his right leg.

Madelyn followed in his footsteps. Her sticky sweater caught in her sleeve as she slipped her hand in the inner pocket of her coat and ensured the aluminum tube remained safe. Did the protective encasing for the documents and Jake's waterproof bag spare the papers from water damage? Leon desired the prized possession of Mozart's handwritten music, but she didn't know what Jake wanted. He acted like a Good Samaritan, but she had a feeling personal interests motivated his actions.

Madelyn shivered despite the increase in her body temperature. She needed to learn specifics about Jake before entrusting him with her information. She'd prefer to blame Jake for getting her mixed up in this mess, but his persistence to help appeared genuine, and she had the item Leon coveted. Jake didn't give the impression of being aware Sam left the music in her care.

Leon had a straightforward, aggressive approach, but possibly Jake utilized a calculated, and manipulative method. She encountered plenty of men like that at the Women in Crisis Center. She shook her head. So far, he showed honesty and true concern for her wellbeing.

Jake confessed he knew Leon well and professed he attributed God for circumventing injuries during their exploits. Did he plan on making all faith-based decisions? The possible answer wasn't as alarming as her fascination with a man accrediting God for their safety and directing their path. Getting to know him better, for the sake of profiling, would be challenging, and enlightening during the process.

He kept a steady pace and stared straight ahead. She staggered a couple steps behind. An earthy scent with hints of clary sage and grapefruit stirred in the light breeze. A giddiness swarmed in her head with the fluttering wings of a bird on its first flight. Sleep deprivation overpowered her sense, and she pressed a hand against her belly. A sinking swirled in her stomach like an unplugged drain. She would fail at gaining answers if she lost control.

Madelyn pushed up her damp sleeves and hurried alongside him. "So, what's the story between you and Leon?" He peered out the corner of his eye.

"We can't exactly sit and discuss it over a cup of coffee right now."

Sweet coffee. The hearty, bold blend of a balanced medium and dark roast on her tongue. A sharp pain seared through her brain and she massaged her temples. Served her right for being a caffeine addict.

"Believe it or not I'm the kind of woman who can walk and chew gum at the same time." She swung her arms back and forth, keeping his pace.

He spun around. "Oh, I don't doubt that." His eyes blazed like torches. "You've proven yourself perceptive and resilient in moments of crises."

Stricken with a heaviness in her body, she froze in her tracks. The inflection of his words speared her, splintering fragments of the preconceived notion that nobody had the capability of breaking through her protective barriers. Did he recognize qualities that people she'd known her entire life never uncovered? The confidence in his statement unnerved her and filled her with an inexplicable desire to keep as much emotional distance from Jake as possible.

She straightened her posture. "I have a right to know why you're determined to protect me from Leon."

"Let's just focus on getting to our destination, then we'll talk." His jawbone tightened and twitched.

"Are you worried about Douglas?"

He paused and scratched his neck. "Nah, this is sort of a regular thing for us."

"Right"—she curled strands of her hair behind her ear—"which leads me back to my original question. What's the deal with Leon?"

Jake hiked the trail. "What do you want to know? He already shared his entire family history and personal achievements. What else can I tell you?"

"What business do you have with him?" She numbered the questions off on her fingers. "If Leon thinks I have something he wants; will he continue to pursue me? I mean, Drexwyler carries a gun for protection, but is he dangerous?" Her pitch raised an octave.

Jake rotated on his heels; the gravel crunched under his boots. Madelyn slowed her steps to a stop and clasped her hands behind her back.

"We're on a need-to-know basis and I'll let you decide about Leon. He worked for my dad and deceived him. The betrayal resulted in my father's untimely death." His voice trailed off and he drew in his brows close together.

"I…" Madelyn raised her hand toward Jake, but then lowered it to her side. "I understand."

Mom lost her battle with cancer after Sam left. The stress during chemotherapy caused painful treatments during remission and ultimately the disease ravaged her cells.

Jake gave a slight nod and inhaled hard. "Regarding your security, it's my moral obligation to ensure your safety and keep Leon's deranged behavior away from you. I'm partially responsible for him assuming you have"—he glanced at his shoes—"what he wants. And I'm at a loss trying to figure out his intentions and actions. I think that covers it for now. Anything else?"

Her mouth went dry. "I want to know if I can trust you."

"Well, you've followed me this far, along with our fair share of accidents. And, hey, on the brighter side, no more jumping off balconies." He held his hands out to his sides and stumbled a step backward. "You can trust me. I'm a man of my word and have my feet firmly on the ground—"

His foot slipped and his arms flailed as he staggered, falling onto his back.

Madelyn clasped her palm over her mouth. Pressing her lips together, spurts of laughter escaped like air from a balloon as she rushed toward Jake. His arms and legs sprawled out, his nose crinkled, and his body rumbled with hilarity.

She stared with a hand on her hip. "What were you saying about the fair share of accidents?"

The weight of his backpack anchored him to the ground. She wrapped her hands around his outstretched forearm and pulled.

Jake hopped to his feet. "Yeah, I couldn't have timed that any better." He brushed the dust from his pants. "At least we're starting the day off with a good laugh. I find laughter creates the right balance between life's hardships and enjoyments."

She folded her arms over her chest. "That makes me feel so much safer."

An hour later, the thick woodlands of oak and pine trees opened into broad valleys of meadows, with splashes of rich greens, reds, pinks and purples. Wildflowers decorated the rolling hills. Madelyn dragged her feet along the grassy trail. She destroyed a pair of her favorite shoes as she smashed the heel down to relieve her blisters.

Sunrays on her face warmed her clammy skin as the sparkling sunshine invigorated every pore, awakening her senses. Clean air, free of pollutants, cleared her lungs. With each breath, she inhaled the intoxicating aroma of sweet woodruff floating in the tepid atmosphere. The hustle and bustle of home became distant as if months had passed. The floral scenery reminded her of Mom.

She heard her mother's voice in her head, naming the species of plant life.

Her nerves unknotted in the relaxing surroundings and she strolled, half-dazed, half-gingerly while the lush landscapes preoccupied her daunting circumstances. A contentment filled her even though she wandered the countryside of Germany with a stranger. She admired his confidence and constant optimism despite all their calamities.

A few steps ahead, Jake tossed his backpack into the tall grass with yellow flowers that appeared fuzzy with white hairs on the petals. He stretched his arms up over his head and behind his back and sat.

"We're taking a break?" she squealed.

His eyes narrowed and his lips curled up at the corners. "Is that okay or should we keep walking?"

"Please, let's stop." Her body crumpled under her weight and she dropped to her knees. Madelyn's stomach growled. He dug in his bag, retrieved a protein bar, a small Ziploc of assorted nuts and a twenty-ounce bottle of water.

"Want something to eat and drink?" He offered both options.

"Do you have a thermos filled with coffee and a buttery blueberry scone?"

"What you see is what you get." Jake titled his head to one side. "But I think there's a piece of Kartoffelpuffer here in my backpack."

"Oh, no. I'm fine. I don't think I want any Kart-o-whatever."

A throaty laugh rasped out of his mouth. "Kartoffelpuffer, they're potato pancakes." Jake handed her half the protein bar.

Madelyn reached for his hand, and a slight smile tugged at the corners with a twinkle shining in his eyes. She ogled. No, the sunlight caused a reflection in the iris of his eye. She rubbed the knot in her chest and settled into the cool grass. "How much longer till we arrive in Ruhpolding?"

He scanned the terrain. "About four hours, more or less."

She expected him to pull out a compass and give her the direct coordinates. "Feels like we've already walked for hours." She hung her head low, feeling the little strength she had vanished. "Then there're options for public transportation to Munich?"

"Yeah, you can catch a train from Ruhpolding, and you can go your own way." His voice dropped, losing clout. He gazed with eyes as deep as the Bavarian Sea sweeping her into the undertow.

Madelyn diverted her stare. Did he hope she'd stay, or had she mistaken his tone? After all, the physical exertion he produced would make anyone tired. She pressed her hand against her belly. Her stomach fluttered, and she nibbled the crunchy peanut butter bar. Beyond hunger and the threat of danger, the appeal of Jake and his ability to remain calm while trusting in the unseen distracted her mind. Regardless of his kind offers and gestures, she'd work out her problems on her own. Even if holding onto Mozart's music lured her into a false pretense of empowerment, she'd prove she wasn't a mere weepy woman in need of a hero.

* * *

Leon sat alone at the head of the vacant dining table. The Hermle wall clock chimed seven o'clock. He propped his elbows on the polished wood and rested his chin against the tips of his steepled fingers. A fire crackled in the hearth and he glared out the window. He squinted at the beams of sunlight strewed through the sheer white curtains.

He thought he made the importance of following his orders clear, and yet they disregarded his request.

Leon banged his fist on the table and his porcelain cup clanged against the dish. He reached for the teacup and the cold Frisian tea splashed on his hand. He glowered at the dissolving little cloud of cream artfully billowing in the dark liquid.

Tea drinking was a sacred moment and more than a beverage choice—it had been since the time of his childhood. Mutter introduced her ceremony of East Frisian tea traditions from the north and taught the family a ritual three times a day. As a boy, he studied the custom with fascination. The minute the eyelet-lace-trimmed linen covering the walnut trolley rolled into the sitting room, he stood with eager six-year-old hands, holding a pair of tongs, waiting for Mutter to set the cups on saucers. She'd wink and brush her delicate fingers along his cheek. Her smile radiated the warmth of a summer day. Proud of his task in preparations, he'd drop the rock sugar into all the cups. Mutter poured the kettle while Annelise finished by adding a dollop of cream on the rims.

After tea, Mutter allowed them to pick one sweet from Grandfather's assortment of Schogetten chocolates that he stashed in his old cigarette box. They gathered around the Fortepiano as Mutter settled onto the bench and played her favorite Mozart piece, Sonata No. 5 in G, K283 II Andante. The gentle touch she had on the keys emulated the original sound Mozart intended for the musical notes written.

Leon closed his eyes. The music was active in the air, floated around the room, filling him with a sense of peace and purpose. With all his childlike wonder he believed he had arrived in the presence of eminence and his own greatness possible to achieve if the genius minds of composers were represented in the Von Füssen home.

His throat constricted and he lost his taste for the tea. It wasn't only a childhood dream. Mozart's music on display in his personal gallery would keep Mutter's spirit alive in the same room she introduced him to the brilliance a mere man could create.

The fire flickered as a gusty swoosh of air swept through the room while the door pushed open.

"They've fled." Mason soared across the mahogany hardwood floor. "Sometime in the early morning."

Leon pursed his lips and drummed his fingers in triple time. "I'm aware of your blunders." Jake always constructed nonexistent problems and the element of surprise dispelled. The solution would've been forcefully taking his belongings and leaving them stranded on the Autobahn. Instead, as a gracious host he offered luxury amenities, and they repaid his kindness by running off in the middle of the night. Due to their ingratitude, he'd no longer extend any generosity.

"What is your next move der Herr?"

His eyes fixed on the flames and he reveled in the idea of a hunt. "Have the men patrol the shores of Stock und Lambach." He drew his forefinger across his cheekbone. All along he intended for Jake and Madelyn to flee. "You and I will go to the east shore. Jake knows where to find me, and I always know where to locate him."

CHAPTER NINE

Jake leaned back on his elbows in the long, green grass, the blades glistening with a slight sheen of moisture and his denim jeans nowhere near dry. Grateful for the nourishment, he savored the mealy texture of a handful of almonds. Splitting a protein bar and bag of nuts with Maddie hardly made a meal. He sat up and passed her half a bottle of water. One side of her lips curved upward, and she wiped the lid with the inside of her blouse. After several gulps, she handed him the bottle.

"Please, finish the rest."

Maddie shook her head with a mouthful of water and swallowed. "I've had enough, thanks."

Never had he encountered a woman so adamant about taking care of herself, to the extreme that even in desperate circumstances, she rejected provisions. He scratched the back of his head. Her commitment to absolute self-reliance left him bewildered with slight amusement. Mom showed remarkable strength, deciding to open an inn when Dad preoccupied himself with expeditions. He admired strong and independent women. Although, his ex, Angelina, took her self-sufficiency to the next level, breaking off their wedding engagement. Maintaining independence was one thing, but Madelyn Brighton reigned in a league of her own.

He rested his head on his hand. Did she have a process to her meticulous behavior? Maddie swiped a finger under each eye and applied lip balm. She dug in her pant pockets, retrieved pins, pulling tresses back, and clipped her cocoa-colored hair back. Jake sighed. He liked her wavy, tousled locks framing her face. His head slid along his arm and he rolled onto his side.

What would it take to unravel this tightly wound woman? He caught glimpses of her carefree spirit. Few people would leave on a motorcycle with a stranger, and even fewer would jump off a balcony into a lake. He imagined, behind her tough exterior, she repressed a playfulness. He envisioned her frolicking barefoot through the fields, her hair flowing free, laughing. Jake tore away from his watchful stare, blinked hard and stood while bundling his backpack.

Reaching for her hand, she rejected the offer, shifted her shoulders and used the tree trunk beside her for support. She lost her balance and latched onto him. Her smooth palm pressed against his and he swiveled in the opposite direction with an increase in body temperature.

"Thank you." She leaped to her feet, lowering her chin while dipping her gaze and hiding behind long dark lashes.

He stretched out the collar of his sweater and removed his jacket, unable to deny her complex aura.

"You can put your coat in my bag if you—"

"No. I…I'm comfortable." She wrapped it tighter at the waist.

"I'm guessing you spend a lot of time indoors." He trudged through the grassy meadow.

"I work long hours with overtime." Maddie shifted her shoulders straight and lifted her chin. "Although I live across the street from the beach."

Now he seemed to get somewhere. She spent most of her days inside working. She had the beach outside her front door yet had creamy ivory skin that revealed evidence of a half-life, living out only a portion of a human existence. He formed the opinion from his own experience, prior to leaving Boston. His job had been his world and identity until Angelina found solace in the arms of another man. The devastation awakened him to the harsh reality he'd made his career a priority over anything or anyone else in his life.

The day Angelina told him about her affair a piece of him died and by the time they achieved reconciliation and continued with their marriage plans, tensions grew, straining the already damaged relationship. Months passed, and he discovered they wanted different things. He recommitted his life to God, following his original plan to work with Dad and return to Germany.

Angelina confessed her reluctance to marry him—she wasn't in love with him, only with the idea of the two of them together, and she needed time to flourish as an individual.

No, he wouldn't allow himself to get caught up in details about Madelyn Brighton. He needed to accomplish getting her to safety and far away from Leon. She hid something greater than her private matters.

Jake cracked the surface and it was only a matter of time until he unearthed what she buried inside. With enough small talk, nothing serious, for the next few hours, he would urge her to share details about her life and get answers.

He glanced over his shoulder. "You've a room with a view at your beach house?"

"Yes, a bay window overlooks the Pacific Ocean."

"Do you ever lie on the sand or put your feet in the water?"

She stared with a blank look on her face. "Ah…"

"Let me guess, you watch people from a distance and assess their lives?"

"That's presumptuous of you." She folded her arms across her chest and raised her brow. "You couldn't possibly make that assumption based on the mere hours we've spent together."

"Enlighten me. I want to hear about A Day in the Life of Madelyn Brighton."

"I thought you said we're on a need-to-know basis?"

"I meant that regarding Leon, for security reasons and your protection. But I should know some pertinent information about you. You know, in case of an emergency."

Maddie stopped, angling her body away as she stared him down for a moment before walking again. "Oh, sure. That makes sense."

He didn't fool her. She'd remain guarded while pushing to find out about Leon and his pursuit. Jake would give her minimal information about Leon, but he wanted her to know as little as possible, if they encountered Leon or his henchmen again. Diverting the conversation to a personal subject wasn't ideal, but it was a risk he'd be willing to take.

"What's your demanding job that keeps you indoors for so many hours?" Jake said.

"I'm the director of client services at the Women in Crisis Center in Orange, California. I counsel abused women, aiding them and their children to find refuge."

"Now I understand."

"What?"

"Evaluating people's lives and being a skeptic. The everyday exposure to the hurting and suffering of people must be difficult." He placed his hand on her shoulder. "Takes a dedicated, and good-hearted person to subject yourself to that level of pain."

Her shoulder arched into his hand, embracing his touch as she leaned closer. As hasty as she responded to his caress; she sidestepped and moved away. She wriggled her arms and straightened her posture.

"My mother, Dana, hoped to start a center for women. She passed on before achieving the dream. In my heart I needed to continue the work my mom started." Her chin quivered.

His gaze settled on her mouth for a minute longer than he intended and he cleared his throat. "That's exactly what I've decided, to finish my father's job."

"You actually have a profession? I thought you had a goal for breaking the world's record for 'Most Attempts to Risk your Life in a Day.'"

Her smile lit up, a glow of lightheartedness he wished to draw outward. Did he dare delve any deeper and unveil the curtain that covered her heart? She defined an intuitive, strong-willed woman, beyond voicing an opinion or instigating an argument, and appeared rooted in her protective ways. However, a sadness eclipsed her demeanor like she experienced enough hardship for one lifetime.

"Where do you work?"

"I teach musicology and do research in the field of paleography at Boston University." The job didn't sound exciting. "I specialize in paper types, watermarks and how music staves are drawn."

"Doesn't seem too dangerous."

"No…" He lowered his head and rubbed the back of his neck. "Should I stick with trying to break the world's record for risky ventures?"

"You said Leon worked with your dad?" She spoke in a professional manner.

Jake lost any opportunity of intriguing her with the details of making a living and she looked unimpressed. She pushed hard for facts like any minute she'd pull out a notebook with a pen and take notes. Perhaps gaining information helped her feel secure in her circumstances. Although, when she arrived home, nothing kept her from creating a story to her advantage and naming him as an accomplice in her abduction, but he believed in her authenticity.

"My dad, Henry Nolan, worked as a professor of liturgy at Boston University, School of Theology."

Maddie did a double take and scrunched her brows inward. "Leon doesn't appear the religious type."

"He isn't. My father retired from the University and pursued his passion for historical context and analysis of musical pieces. After a few years of collaborating with museums and conservators around the world, he traveled abroad on archeology expeditions."

"Now that makes sense." She tapped her finger against her lips.

A heaviness swayed his steps with the weight of his backpack and the ache in his knee. The discussion progressed to a full circle. He massaged his forehead. She dodged his inquiries and all her questions led to additional answers about Leon.

"Yeah, and for whatever reason he followed you to the church too. Whose funeral service did you say—"

"I didn't."

"Fair enough, you're not an open book. You can keep all your deep dark secrets hidden."

"You think I have secrets?" She bit the corner of her lower lip and her eyes darted toward the ground. "Never mind."

Jake grinned, filled with a feast of gained knowledge. His words shook her, and he had an eagerness to discover his effect on Maddie. She posed as a tower of strength while insisting on doing everything for herself. At times, she'd soften her look and speak with sincerity, revealing moments of vulnerability. So much mystery surrounded her. Would it be worth the trouble of figuring her out? He assumed that whenever anyone met Maddie, they never forgot her. One thing seemed clear, she seldom lost composure and whatever caused her to break down into tears outside the church would be the key to unlocking what she shielded in her heart.

Half an hour later, strolling in silence through hypnotic waves of rolling green hillsides, sunlight danced through the valley in rays of rippled light. Golden eagles soared through the sky as orange-spotted butterflies fluttered across the fields. The Savi's Warbler bird chirped a wild song that echoed over the tall grass. Jake never tired of hiking Bavaria's diverse terrains and with his motorcycle in pieces off the side of the Autobahn, he'd be spending extra time walking.

A heavy sigh escaped his lips, and he clenched his fist. Leon caused frequent trouble, more than he considered worth the effort of being on the run. After he finished Dad's job, he would escape the circus of his life with Leon playing the ringmaster. There's only so much of him a person could endure, and Jake exceeded the threshold. Thank God they avoided having to withstand time at breakfast listening to his pretentious stories.

Jake glanced at Maddie. She shuffled her shoes through the meadow a few feet behind. "I didn't mean to scare you into silence. Your secrets are safe."

She stopped with a fixed glare. "Don't give yourself any credit. I'm exhausted."

"Hang in there, it's only a few hours."

"Why did you have to remind me?" She groaned in a raspy voice and flung her arms over her head.

A buzzing sound reverberated in the distance. He scanned the dale they'd crossed. He didn't count on Leon catching up with them so soon. "Come on." Jake ran back and grabbed her hand.

"What's—"

"Hurry."

The roar of motorcycle engines grew louder. They rushed toward a grove for tree covering, and she squeezed his hand. The sound of sprinting, heavy breathing, and revving engines amplified in the open meadows. Perspiration beaded on his forehead as they raced for a sloping hillside leading into a covert of shrubs. Their stalkers closed in on them. Motorcycles thundered and shook the land like a Spanish running of the bulls.

At an entry of the woodland, Maddie slipped on wet leaves that blanketed the grimy ground. He lost his grip, and she tumbled down a hummock. "Maddie," he yelled over the chaotic noises of the motorcycles and the rustling of shrubberies.

She rolled to a stop, entangled under a large bush. Jake dashed for cover in the underbrush, diving toward her with one leg extended as if he were sliding into home plate in a baseball game.

In mass confusion of undergrowth, branches and vegetations, she clawed to break free of the bushes. He pressed his weight down, holding her in a still position.

"Let me go." She squirmed under his chest.

"Stop moving, this is our only hiding place."

He wrapped his arms around her body, and she twitched with an animalistic instinct to flee instead of sitting as prey. She squeezed her eyelids shut, and he held her in a close embrace. Their rhythmic breathing orchestrated a harmony with his pounding heart and the motorcycles racing along the hilltop. Jake tucked his bag tighter against his back, making certain it stayed hidden behind the shrubs. The branches were talons reaching out, snagging and scratching his hands with the slightest movement.

He mouthed a silent prayer for protection as a motorcycle stopped and rumbled above on the hill. Maddie flashed her eyes wide open.

"Keep quiet and still," he whispered.

She muffled her whimpers and pressed her lips tight together.

The front of the motorcycle directed aim toward the shrubbery. Jake held his neck stiff, as sweat dripped down the sides of his head, while the bike idled in place. Would Leon order a kill-on-sight or were these men making their own decisions? The rider throttled the engine a few times before he sped off to join the other cyclists circling the area. Minutes that seemed like hours passed before the echo of speeding motorcycles faded into the distance.

Maddie expelled her breath with a burst. She blinked and tears streamed from the corners of her dark eyes. Jake moved his hands over her head, untangling her hair from the clutch of twigs. He writhed his body from the underbrush and rolled onto his side.

"Take it easy." He lifted the branches higher, and she shifted her hips, inching her way free.

Lying on her back, she coughed, and her eyelids fluttered with dust stuck on her lashes. Jake gazed at her pale skin with a slight rose blush that highlighted her features.

Small scrapes streaked her forehead and her beauty overwhelmed him. Swiping his thumb across her cheekbone he cleaned the dirt-trailed tears from her face. She parted her lips with a hard intake of air and her body tensed. He looked downward with a sinking feeling in his stomach. He had the strictest objective: helping her to safety, figuring out why Leon followed her and if she knew anything about Mozart's missing musical piece. Yet, a personal sentiment infiltrated his mind that he inducted his own agenda, instead of following the will of God.

Maddie struggled onto her feet, tottering and she grasped his bicep for support. He swooped his arm around her back, drawing her forward. "How am I doing with the world's record? I've still got time, the day's not over."

* * *

Leon peered out the cracked window from the back seat of his parked BMW 750 LI, off the side of the A-8 Autobahn. He scanned the area and tightened his jaw. At any minute he'd finally have Mozart's music, where it belonged, in his hands. He massaged his temples. Careless people had handled his treasure over the past several months. Mason failed at executing a deeper investigative background check on the discovery team in Vienna.

All the arduous work and knowledge he invested into the project, wasted, and he ended up chasing after his own possession. His expertise led the group to the final location of the lost music.

Tapping his fingers on the leather armrest, he blinked hard and pursed his lips. The buzz of Motorrader zoomed across the grassy knoll, stopped beside the vehicle and two men turned off their engines. Mason exited the driver's seat and opened the passenger door.

Leon stepped out of the car, straightening his Armani suit, lifting his chest with a jutted chin to accentuate a military stance and demonstrate his authority. The riders removed their helmets, dismounted and stood at attention.

Leon glared at them, dressed in black leather from head to toe. "What is your report?"

Both men shifted their gaze and waited for the other to respond.

"Am I to understand Jake and his accomplice managed to get away on foot?" he said in a sharp tone.

Staring forward, they avoided eye contact. The man standing on the left spoke. "Entschuldigung, we—"

"Your apology means nothing to me. You're dismissed. Go to Munich und await my instructions." Leon swatted at the air.

The bikers scurried onto their motorcycles and zipped off on the Autobahn. He gritted his teeth with forced restraint. "How long must I endure the incompetence of the men you hire? You need to do better vetting the employees or I'll find someone to take your position."

"Ja, mein Herr." Mason closed the back door and climbed into the front seat. "Should I contact the local Polizei?"

"Nein. Drive to the hotel."

"Wie Sie wünschen."

"I count on Jake to slip up. His new companion will distract him and weaken him at any moment." He stroked his chin. "In the process of collecting my music, I may be inclined to accumulate another valuable from Jake."

CHAPTER TEN

The sun disappeared behind the gray clouds that rolled in as rapidly as the motorcyclist appeared out of nowhere. A soft drizzle strafed Madelyn, and she blinked a few times, clearing her blurred vision.

Lines deepened in Jake's forehead. "Maddie?"

He wrapped one arm around her waist, and she hung on the other for balance. "I've got you, take it easy."

An instant cold-to-hot tingle swept across her nape and chest. An overwhelming sensation surged through her body. She summoned all her willpower to refrain from turning toward him and succumbing to his embrace. With no recent memories of a genuine hug from a man, she longed for him to hold her and reassure her everything would be all right. Refusing to submit in her brokenness she pushed against him and he released her from his grasp.

Madelyn swallowed the dryness in her throat. "I got dizzy when I stood up too fast."

She invested years on the construction of the fortress she built to shut people out. The time spent with Jake illuminated an emptiness in her soul, revealing the potential of allowing someone to get close and a yearning for relationships. It wasn't even a romantic notion; she avoided all rapports. She had only shared details about her life with Sheryl, and everyone else remained distant acquaintances. Since her breakup with Brennan, she steered clear of the dating scene. She wouldn't get carried away with an adventure-seeking man she met in the middle of a pursuit in a foreign country.

"You've been through a lot." He raked his fingers through his hair.

She brushed the dirt from her clothes, readjusted her hairpins and dug in her pocket for a lint-covered mint.

Jake swiped his palm across his face and threw his backpack over his shoulder. "We'll stay on a path along the trees and keep out of the open terrain." He spun and trekked onward through the evergreens.

Madelyn slumped her shoulders and sighed. "I didn't mean to sound unappreciative." She hurried and followed a few steps behind Jake.

His reaction validated the reason she shunned relationships with constant misinterpretations, skewed perceptions and wounded pride, yet while they'd been together, he pushed beyond her comfort zone. Not that she lacked an explanation of how his show of concern touched her heart—she refused.

She didn't need to set herself up for disappointment. If he had any interest, she'd wager it would be temporary. She developed a fondness for Jake, and the longer they spent together would increase the difficulty of her departure. At this point, she'd rather have him believe she despised him than have him learn the truth.

Scattered trees grew thicker along the edge of a brook. Verdant land invited her to stop and slip off her shoes. Being barefoot in the long blades of grass relieved her blisters and the soft soil pressed into the soles of her feet. The relief urged her toward the creek, and she rushed past Jake.

Sticky, damp clothes chafed her skin while the misty rain added weight to her coat. She removed the outer garment, peeled off her sweater and rolled up her blouse sleeves.

"We can drink the water."

Madelyn stooped, cupping the fluent stream. "Really?"

Jake withdrew the empty bottle from his backpack and a small package. "Here's the trick." He filled it and opened the packets. "Iodine tablets." He dropped two inside, and his eyes gleamed.

The day felt like a reality TV survival series, starring relic hunters. "You're full of resourcefulness."

"There's a worse thing to be full of."

She pressed her lips together and coughed. "At least it stopped drizzling."

A shock pulsated her nerves with the sting of cold water as she dipped a toe into the brook. Madelyn stared into the clear liquid coursing over half-buried pebbles and gravel at the bottom. She swayed, and laid on the moist ground, the scent of wet earth and algae lingered in the air.

"We have to wait a little over thirty minutes before drinking the water." Jake sat close on the grassy bank. "For now, we'll rest." He pulled a twig from her hair.

A warmth flooded her body. His soul-searching stare put her on edge, and she found it difficult to look him in the eyes. Madelyn wanted to trust him and tell him her secret, but she wasn't ready for complete surrender and planned on keeping the music close, for her own protection.

"You think those motorcyclists will track us out here?"

"I'm confident they don't know the area like I do."

Jake acted a little too assured. On the rocky ground, she shifted and straightened her body, staring at the sky. Why did she feel comfortable beside him? The structure of her everyday life had shattered. She'd experienced threatening scenarios and followed a near-stranger based on his assurance. Either she started to trust him, or pure fatigue engulfed her senses.

"How do you know this area?"

"I used to hike these trails with my dad before I left for Boston." Jake rolled onto his side, with a bent elbow, propping his head on his fist. "What about your father?"

"What about him?" Her voice cracked.

"You mentioned your mom passed, and it's clear you don't like to talk about yourself—"

"Let's enjoy the silence."

"Okay, sure." He turned onto his back, shifting his shoulders with rigid movements and slipped his hands behind his head.

Water trickled over rocks, creating a natural lullaby. Her nerves relaxed and with every blink she forcefully lifted her lids. Sleep would win the current round of the fighting against staying awake.

Madelyn struggled opening her eyes and awoke with birds chirping in the tall trees. She cringed at the sharp pain in her neck and shoulder as she rolled into an upright position. Stretching her arms overhead, several muscles in her body double knotted, twinging from head to toe. She rubbed her face and cleared her vision. Jake and his backpack disappeared.

Madelyn scanned the immediate surroundings as her heart raced. Did Jake abandon her in the middle of nowhere with no phone, no provisions and people chasing her down? She tripped over the coat covering her lower extremities and fumbled onto her feet. The garment dropped to the ground, and she tied her sweater around her waist. She grabbed her clothing, slipped on her shoes and spun in every direction.

Did he continue upstream? She hadn't figured out what he wanted. At first, she thought Jake wished her harm, then he stepped into the role of protector. Why ditch her now? She might wander for hours before finding anyone to help. Sickness churned in her stomach and she swallowed the nausea creeping up her throat, taunting a gag reflex. Madelyn inhaled and exhaled hard, repressing rippling waves rolling out from her heart, spreading throughout her body.

Following the creek, she rounded a bend and came to a halt after exiting a cluster of trees. Madelyn gasped. Jake sat on a rock a short distance away. Her spirit burned with the flicker of a kindled flame. With a cautious step closer, his icy blue stare chilled her to the bone, the spark snuffed out and the fire died. His gaze lowered to a silver object clutched in his fist. Her fingers grappled the lining of the inner pocket of her coat. She gulped the lump in her throat and wrestled with the smooth polyester fabric.

"Looking for this?" Jake held the cylinder up in his hand.

Madelyn froze and her heart skipped a beat. Her mouth dropped open with no sound.

"You're as surprised as I was to discover it hidden in your coat."

A heatwave surged through her body. "You had no right to go through my pockets." She stomped toward him.

"That's not what happened."

"Oh, really?" She grabbed for the tube, but he jerked it away.

"Yeah, when you dozed off, I covered you with your coat and the case flew out."

Madelyn expelled a hard breath and stared at a random rock. "All I can say is, everything happened so fast and I'm not sure if I can trust you."

"That's understandable, but I've been honest—"

"After I pressed for information. I'm certain you didn't intend on volunteering anything." She dared to look him in the eyes.

Jake glanced at the aluminum container in his hand. "You're right. I kept it confidential to protect you."

"How convenient." Madelyn cocked her head. "Whenever you keep things secret it's for my protection, and if I don't tell you everything, I'm deceitful?"

"No, that's not true." Jake sighed, pushing a palm through his hair. "How did you get this?" He clutched the canister close to his chest. "Do you know the contents inside?"

Madelyn offered a simple nod. Her mouth went dry, and she squirmed under his interrogating stare. Sam set up another disaster and left her with the repercussions. How could Madelyn describe the mess Sam made of lives? Perhaps telling Jake about the immediate concern for Gretchen and her boys would help. Forget explaining Sam's shady deals and the past.

"Someone left the item for me with specific instructions."

"That person had no right to give it to you." Jake frowned and swiped a hand over his mouth. "Didn't they realize the danger… and when Leon—"

"I realize that now…" Her tone wavered.

"You shouldn't get further involved." Jake stepped back, rubbing the stubble along his jawline. "At least now I'm aware and it's clear why Leon is so persistent. Don't worry, we'll sort everything out and you can go home."

A piercing like tiny daggers pricked her heart. Jake had no desire to build an alliance. He created an agenda and didn't care about anyone else's involvement and the reasoning behind those choices. No way she'd submit to a man's will and retreat. He wasn't a godsend.

Madelyn squared her shoulders, pulled down the hem of her blouse and stepped alongside. "I'm sorry, but that doesn't work for me." She snatched the canister from his hand. "Autonomy is a strength, and I'll complete the task without the need of a savior." Madelyn strutted past and didn't glance back.

She quickened her pace, swinging her arms for momentum. For the first time since the chaos commenced, she gained control of the situation. The decision still required his help navigating to their destination, but without tagging along. She made a definite choice regardless if he liked it.

"Maddie, wait." Jake rustled through the grass. "Why are you rushing away?" The tips of his fingers brushed her shoulder. "You don't even know where you're going."

Madelyn spun and faced him. "You're mistaken if you think I will leave without following through on a commitment. And stop using that nickname."

"Okay, fine." Jake passed the water bottle and gazed beyond the pasture across the creek. "It's important because my father spent over three years searching for, locating, then authenticating that piece of Mozart's music and the job cost his life." He pivoted, flashing lightning eyes. "So, excuse me if I disregard the final request of a thief."

She shoved the drink into his hands. "I take nothing that wasn't given to me."

"It was stolen from my father and anyone working for those involved, I consider a thief." Jake tossed the bottle in his bag and walked beside the current.

She fumed with an increase of body temperature and her pounding heart. Madelyn tightened her grip around the cool aluminum cylinder. She journeyed too far to lose a last chance of forgetting her past. She calmed her irregular heartbeat, using yoga breathing techniques. Emotions gushed with the water downstream as she hurried to catch up with him.

Madelyn reached out and yanked his arm with no restraint over her actions. He jolted his head with a dazed look on his face.

"We're not finished talking." Her words caught in the ache at the back of her throat and her vision blurred with watery eyes. "I wanted to tell you, earlier during the first break—"

"I know, you don't trust me. Even after helping you escape from Leon and a crazed cyclist on a rampage." He slipped his hand around her arm and lowered into a sitting position in the grass. "Now will you explain what happened?"

She still wasn't sure if she trusted Jake. Speaking always proved her strong characteristic of communication, yet articulating words presented an immediate challenge. He expressed a temperate demeanor waiting for an explanation and his eyes brightened in the light-blue sky. A searing pain recurred on the side of her brain, begging for relief only a triple espresso provided. She massaged her head and sniffed with the added congestion from allergies.

"When we met outside the church, I…" Madelyn twisted a button on her shirt so hard it unthreaded and fell into the grass. Blowing her cheeks out with a gusty breath, she slumped forward.

"You'd been crying."

Her gaze flicked upward as if someone tugged the ends of her hair. His direct observation cornered her, and she wished to flee into the thicket of trees. Madelyn wanted to confess how she got Mozart's music, but if possible, to avoid the details about Sam.

"Yeah." She cleared her throat. "I finished reading a letter Sam Healy had written for me before he died."

His eyes narrowed. "Sam Healy is the man who left you Mozart's sheet music?"

Madelyn swiped a loose strand of hair tickling her neck. "The note never mentioned the contents, so at the time I was unaware."

"Leon knew." Jake knocked a fist against his knee. "That's the business he hoped to discuss with us and why he's continuing in a heavy pursuit." Jake vocalized thoughts aloud rather than adding to the conversation. Madelyn nodded her head in agreement.

He leaned close, tilting his ear forward. "What else did the letter say?"

"Sam regretted his choices and wanted to make things right, for the sake of his family."

His eyebrows scrunched together. "Why did he leave it for you?"

"He asked me to clear his name by restoring the documents to the rightful owners. Sam stated the artifact belongs in a museum but didn't give any names." She grazed her palm along the blades of grass. "Perhaps he didn't know, but I've decided he meant you and your father."

"You've decided?"

"Yes."

Was it only fifteen hours ago they met? Too much had occurred, forcing Madelyn to bargain with a stranger. For the sake of principles, and unloading the burden of Sam, she'd compromise. She searched his eyes for answers. "Are we going to work together?"

Jake arched a brow with a glassy stare. "I guess we are."

Jake rose and offered a hand. She smiled and reached, but he pointed to the aluminum tube. "I should hold on to that—"

"I've got it for now." Madelyn tucked the item inside her coat, pushed herself off the ground and stood.

"In a tiny pocket while we're on the run from people willing to kill for it?"

"Aren't you protecting me?" She pursed her lips together in a satisfied smirk and patted his bicep.

"Right." The corners of his mouth curled into an indolent smile. "We should get going if we're to arrive in Ruhpolding before sundown."

The journey would test and reveal his true character. Would his concern be for her safety or the music? Jake protected her earlier, unaware she carried the sought-after handwritten Mozart music. Madelyn hoped Jake would follow through on their agreement and while she kept the item in her possession, she maintained leverage. Although, she'd remain cautious of Jake and make certain he didn't dig deeper into her personal life.

She flattened the lapels of her coat, finally on track with her plans to correct Sam's wrongdoings, help his family and move on from the past. Unattached and free to leave for the comforts of her lifestyle in Southern California. Once home, Jake and Leon's quest for treasures would be a distant memory, a faded dream. Madelyn accepted her deluded sentiments about Jake emerged from shock, fatigue and hunger.

Madelyn peered at him walking ahead. Jake agreed to the terms and wasn't as angry as she thought he'd be about her secret. His initial intentions seemed genuine, keeping her from harm, and when he held her in his arms, the deep look in his eyes displayed an honest care. A rise in temperature swept over her body as if a spotlight followed her steps. She fanned her face with her hand. Madelyn agreed with Jake on one thing: the sooner she returned home, the better.

CHAPTER ELEVEN

Jake sighed and snapped a twig, tossing it aside. What a day it turned out to be. He peeked over his shoulder about every twenty minutes. Each time, Maddie straightened her collar and forced a smile shrouded in mystery. He shook his head, refusing to get caught up in the wonderment of her intricate personality.

Something puzzled him—a piece of the story seemed to be missing. A rational person would rid themselves of the trouble of a missing artifact and a half-crazed lunatic in pursuit. If she believed in Dad's efforts to secure the music at a museum, why did she insist on continuing the journey? What other secrets were hidden behind her dark-brown eyes? Jake believed Maddie got the music with no knowledge of its origins and deduced she didn't have any prior encounters with Leon. The muscles in his neck tensed. What relationship did she have with Sam Healy and why the importance of clearing his name?

The day progressed from bad to worse. An hour ago, she appeared angelic in a peaceful slumber, until an enchantress awakened and clutched in her claws the power to make or break his future. Jake glanced out of the corner of his eye again, watchful that she didn't fall behind and cast any spells. He pushed his palms through his hair, relieving the pressure in his head.

He'd focus on God's mission and finishing Dad's work without further distractions. If he remained obedient to his faith, he'd extend grace to Maddie and her headstrong determination. Jake sighed heavily. The personal struggle of falling short all the time. Compassionate, patient, slow to anger, keep no record of wrongs, were all attributes Dad demonstrated and Jake aspired to attain.

"You've been quiet for at least half an hour." She hurried alongside.

"I thought you enjoy the silence and you've already told me everything there is to know about your involvement with Sam Healy." Jake spun to catch her reaction.

Maddie tightened her lips with a flinty stare. "You have enough information and you'll be able to complete your dad's work."

The remark provided the evidence and confirmation that she withheld details. Should he press to discover the truth about her connection to Sam? Something about her avoiding the topic of family and Sam left him unsettled.

"At least Sam did the right thing before it was too late, instead of leaving you to deal with the authorities."

Maddie scoffed. "Sam always..." She bit her tongue and cringed. "No, he wouldn't. Why are you making assumptions?"

"I don't know, maybe because he led you into the middle of a dangerous circuit of theft and forgeries." The sour words stung his lips like lemon juice poured on an open wound. Jake pushed too far. Her cheeks glowed fiery red, and she slowed her pace to a stop. "I meant, it's unfortunate you're mixed up in everything." Jake didn't want to upset her; he wanted the truth.

"Unfortunate for whom?"

"Wait a minute, I've been watching out for you since the moment I set eyes on you and that was before I discovered your secret."

Maddie twisted and treaded closer toward the creek. The breeze swirled through her hair, stirring sun-warmed honeysuckle filling his nostrils as he stood beside her. Sunbeams shined light twinkling diamonds on the water's surface and highlighted her figure, illuminating a rare gem. She rolled her head over her shoulder, with lips curved up on one side, emitting her own sunshine, a jewel from the sun.

"I know, that wasn't fair. Can we call a truce?" She faced him and held out her hand, silky skin slipped against his palm. Her eyes brightened to a caramel brown, sprinkled with flecks of golden honey, and his gaze stuck in her entrancing wonder.

The revving of an engine ripped through the sky and she threw herself into his arms. Jake held her and stroked her loose strands of silken hair as her body trembled against his chest. He scanned the field on the other side of the river, cows herded for miles across the land.

"It's not a motorcycle. It's a tractor."

Maddie pushed free from his arms, pivoted in the opposite direction, then lowered her gaze toward the ground and started walking. "I'm not usually jumpy."

Jake studied her mannerisms and failed at figuring her out. One moment she'd enjoy the comfort of his arms, then turn away. Another moment her lashes curled upward, unveiling inviting eyes with sincerity, and soon after flash a look of sheer disdain.

"Do you usually have people chasing you?"

"No, but should I really fear Leon?"

Without alarming her, he needed to explain and be honest. Jake rubbed the facial hair growth on his chin. Perhaps a slight warning. He'd assure they were safe, but also make it clear they should proceed with caution and keep away from Leon.

"I trust that Leon will not be a serious threat to us, but better if he's avoided."

"Are you speaking cryptically or in code?" A crease between her eyes deepened as she crinkled up her nose.

"I believe we'll persevere, no matter what happens."

Maddie stopped mid-stride. "That's a strange response. Are you talking about trusting in God?"

"Yes."

"I can appreciate faith works for you. Personally, I've experienced nothing spiritual that made any difference in my life." She shifted her eyes to her feet and strolled through the grass.

"Let me explain. Leon's ambitions fulfill his own purposes. He's only interested in satisfying a personal conquest—"

"Aren't we all?"

"I don't think so." He reached out, brushing the side of her arm. "You said you wanted to help a widow and her children. Sounds selfless to me."

"You know nothing about me. Remember all my hidden secrets?"

Maddie hurried her steps—a woman on the run, in a foreign country, mixed up with men willing to kill for material possessions and she wasn't only surviving, she almost conquered.

Jake strolled beside her. "I'd like to know more about you."

A deep shade of pink crept across her neck and face. "What were you saying about Leon?" she said with a somewhat convincing poker face, holding personal details close to her chest. But he would call her bluff. Jake figured she practiced her technique daily. Maddie needed to hear the dangers involved for the person carrying Mozart's long-lost sheets of music.

"Leon is driven by selfish greed and demands retribution when he's been double-crossed. Ever heard of Clyde Zimmerman?"

"No. Who is he?"

"Clyde worked as a field technician in Vienna and was hired before I arrived. From what I gathered from the excavation team, once my dad passed away, Clyde engaged the services of a professional counterfeiter to create a copy of Mozart's sheet music. Maybe Sam Healy?" Jake angled his head and studied Maddie's expression. A lack of making eye contact confirmed the theory. "Anyway, Leon hoped to take advantage of the opportunity to steal the authentic piece and pass a forgery on to me." He shrugged a nonchalant shoulder. "As if a fake 'd fool me."

"Then what happened?"

"Clyde betrayed Leon. I imagine Clyde promised Sam or whomever a hefty cut for keeping the original and handing a counterfeit to Leon. Too bad Sam made the right choice when it was too late."

"Where's Clyde now?"

"He was lucky. Picked up by the authorities."

"Lucky?"

"The forger endured a worse fate."

"Are you telling me—"

"The situation is serious, and you asked about the dangers involved. Now you know."

Maddie nodded with a slack expression. Jake stopped, pivoted and held her arms. Her body stiffened, and she leaned backward with wide owl eyes. "Why are you willing to get involved? What is the purpose?"

Wool fibers scraped his fingers as she yanked free from his grasp. "I told you. Sam Healy requested my help for the sake of his family."

"Knowing the risk, you'll still continue?"

"Yes. I have to finish the journey." Her glassy, puffy eyes stared through him. "And I know you're anxious to get rid of me, but—"

"I don't want to see you get hurt." The weight of an anchor pressed on his chest. "Help me understand a reason for continuing to place you at risk."

She squeezed her eyes shut, blowing a hard breath from her cheeks, and walked faster. He stopped and gawked. Her shoes dragged through the thick grass as she swung her hips side to side.

"Maddie." Jake outstretched his leg, taking a wide step forward. His boot slipped on the moist ground, sliding his foot into a hole and his limb bowed to the side, tearing his injured ligaments. A burning sensation of hot coals poured over his knee. He gritted his teeth, grunting as he bent on his opposite leg for relief.

Maddie turned and dashed toward him. "For someone claiming to know the area so well, you sure stumble a lot."

"When I'm hiking, I stay focused on the trail." She stood inches away, her trim legs in front view. His gaze traced from the ground up toward her face. "You're a little distracting."

She looked in another direction, unable to meet his eyes, and tucked her arms close to her sides as a soft glow highlighted her facial features.

Jake placed his heel down with added pressure and clenched his jaw. He tossed his backpack aside and removed his damp t-shirt. Pulling at the seams, he ripped the shirt in half, then tore another strip.

"Can I help?"

"Yeah, stop running away." He extended his leg, rolled up the denim and wrapped the torn material around his knee.

"All right. I'll stop running." Her voice wavered.

Maddie picked up his bag and glided it over her shoulders. "Sam Healy was my father." In one breath she had confessed, spitting the words out like ingested poison.

Jake jerked his head and glanced up at her. Maddie curved her neck, concealing flushed cheeks and an unfocused gaze toward the brook. He unrolled the denim, covering the tourniquet, and applied a little weight on his leg.

His body swayed as he stood. "I understand why you kept that private."

"I hadn't considered Sam my dad in over fifteen years." With tightened lips, her chin quivered.

"Sorry, I should've realized when you changed the subject about your father." Jake wished to pull her close into his arms and cloak her in comfort. If he touched her, she'd probably push him away.

"Sam's wife contacted me, requesting my presence at the funeral. Everything I told you earlier about how I received Mozart's music and the letter is true. I wasn't sure—"

"If you trust me."

Maddie nodded and placed her trembling fingers on her lips. "I still don't know."

"Trusting someone is developed over time. That's why I always place my faith in God before people."

She gazed into his eyes with a searching stare as if she tried to view deep into his soul. "I want to trust you."

A knot swelled in his throat and he gulped. Jake paused, glancing at the sign posted on the dirt trail. "Good news, we reached the crossroad. Ten kilometers to Ruhpolding." He pointed his finger toward the path.

Maddie curved her body, following his hand gesture, and whirled back around. He stepped backward to avoid another head-to-chin collision. A breath escaped her parted lips.

"Everything will be fine. We should arrive in fewer than two hours." He imagined how difficult it must've been for her to tell him about Sam. She revealed more of herself in that intense gaze than she had at any other time. Behind her swollen eyelids she possessed raw beauty, real sincerity highlighting a sparkle of hope suppressed inside. It would be destroyed if she found out he switched the original Mozart music with the counterfeit copy. Jake flicked his eyes heavenward and silently prayed for forgiveness.

* * *

Leon entered the private entrance to the top-floor apartment suite at Hotel Luxur in Ruhpolding. Flipping on the light switch by the door, he winced at the dreary décor. A single watercolor painting of the Bavarian Alps hung on the eggshell-white wall. He suspected the bedroom displayed an awful floral design. Considering Mason booked the best accommodations in Ruhpolding, he'd contact his developers right away to construct a Hotel Füssen in town. He ran his hand along a light-oak side bar in need of varnish and rubbed his fingers together. At least the furnishings were clean, and a pleasant aroma of lavender circulated from a reed diffuser.

The room would suffice—he wouldn't stay long. In the meantime, he would indulge in a refreshing drink while he waited for Mason to return with his report on Madelyn Brighton. The bar stocked plenty of choices and he grabbed a glass from the cabinet above the sink. He selected a cold lime seltzer without ice. He'd send Mason with the bucket to fill later.

Drained after pursuing his ungrateful guests, Leon removed his tonal-stripe suit jacket, loosened his silk tie and unbuttoned his top collar button. He skimmed the room for amenities and glanced above at the dark-wood beams stretched across the slanted ceiling. A bit rustic for his taste. The suite needed elegance to enhance the ambiance.

Leon selected Pachelbel on his music player and connected the device to the surround sound system. Canon in D fit the mood. He placed his glass on a small chairside table and slid into a sage-color armchair. Every note absorbed through his body, sinking into the depth of his soul. He closed his eyes, relaxing his nerves in a conscious meditation.

To achieve an internal peace required reigning in thoughts about Mozart's music in Madelyn's hands while she remained in the company of Jake. The muscles in his face twanged. Things appeared to be benefiting them, for the moment.

Leon inhaled deeply through his nostrils. Citrus and jasmine bloomed in his lungs and he blew a slow breath out his mouth. His shoulders dropped; his mind clear of distractions. The enticing smell of honeysuckle permeated his senses. The familiar fragrance of his fallen angel, Leyna.

Leon pictured his first encounter with Leyna like it happened yesterday, although it had been more than twenty years ago at the annual banquet of Schloss Sommersdorf. The minute they were introduced, and he kissed the back of her hand with her pale-pink lips smiling, he knew she was his little angel. She wore a Bavarian-blue dress; the silk clung to the curves of her body.

Creamy-colored locks flowed over her bare shoulders as she sat beside him in the dining hall. They barely consumed their food, satisfied with the nonstop conversation through the three-course meal. From that evening on, they were inseparable.

Three months of traveling, dining, music, dancing, and living life to the fullest. Then the villa in the French Riviera, where he confessed his feelings and proposed marriage…yet Leyna refused. The abysmal excuse, claiming as the daughter of an aristocrat, her family expected an agreement for an arranged nuptial. Although Leon acquired his own wealth along with an inheritance, the Von Füssen name remained tarnished during those years from the near bankruptcies in the sixties.

Leyna tore his heart out, creating a hollowness in his chest. At the tender age of twenty, he was never the same. If she saw him now. Everything he possessed, his assets, status and more wealth than her greedy father desired. He hoped she lived with regrets all the days of her life. Na, if he had the opportunity to show her the powerful man he was today, he'd never let her go. A knock on the hotel door interrupted his thoughts.

Leon opened his eyes. "Komm herein!" He paused the mp3 player.

The plastic key card swiped, unlocking the door. "Hallo." Mason's loafers squeaked across the hardwood floors.

"Incessant noise." Leon glared at Mason.

Mason sat and removed his shoes. "You don't look well—"

"What do you expect? One disaster after another." He sighed, rubbing his forehead. "Fetch me a paracetamol."

Why did Mason treat him as a child? Leon's parents gave specific instructions to protect and serve, but for the love of Beethoven, he neared middle age.

"I'm certain, you'll find interest in these reports." Mason handed him a file folder before rummaging through the pharmaceuticals.

Leon thumbed through three pages. "Not much information."

Mason set two pills on the table beside his drink. "Madelyn Brighton lives a somewhat solitary life. No family, few friends."

Leon skimmed the documents. "Madelyn Nicolette Brighton." Her name rolled off his tongue. "She is independent, well educated, fulfills a directorial role at work." He leaned closer to the page. "Fascinating."

"What is that?"

"She writes quixotic poetry und is free of any romantic entanglements." A slow smile built. "Good," he said under his breath and glanced up, avoiding direct eye contact. "She'll cause plenty of trouble for Jake."

"I verified there were no prior communications with Jake Nolan. The only phone calls in the hotel room I traced to Frau Healy."

Leon sipped his lime seltzer. "Seems Jake had been following us. If he was unaware Samuel left Mozart's music for his daughter und by pure chance met Madelyn, he'll soon discover his luck is ending."

"How will you proceed?" Mason sat on the edge of the sofa with a quirked eyebrow. He placed the papers on the antique mahogany coffee table. A colored photo of Madelyn stared at him from the cover page. She displayed a shy closed-lip smile as if the camera had the capability of stealing her essence.

"I'll allow some time to pass for her to become a millstone around Jake's neck. Not too much, I don't want her to sympathize with Jake. Ensure we're notified upon their arrival in Ruhpolding."

"I'll contact the men on patrol." Mason pulled his phone from his sports jacket. He poked his index finger on the screen and sent a message.

"Tell the Munich crew to increase their efforts to locate the rest of those involved in betraying me und causing my treasure to end up in the wrong hands."

Leon finished his drink, stood from the table and set his empty glass on the picture of Madelyn's face, the image a magnified blur. "Shall I tell you what makes a man fall?"

"Ja."

"A woman."

CHAPTER TWELVE

Madelyn massaged her wrist, missing her watch and other necessities. A toothbrush and comb, for starters. If Jake estimated their arrival time for Ruhpolding accurately, they must be close. A light breeze stirred the aroma of ripe berries infused by intermittent rain. Her palms pressed against her abdomen; stomach acids raged a violent storm and her parched throat inflamed as the glands in her mouth increased saliva. Trudging forward, her leg muscles protested in agony, but she continued pushing the limits of her body.

Even with an injury, Jake kept a steady pace a few feet ahead with physical stamina that defied human capabilities. The hours spent sitting at her desk during a regular work week didn't help build endurance.

Her weighty head felt fuzzy, and she rubbed her temples. Jake stayed quiet after the confession of her relation to Sam. Was all the secrecy evidence of linked corrupt genetics? After all, she was the counterfeiter's daughter. Madelyn balled her hand into a fist and banged her thigh. Maybe he entertained the thought of her working with Leon to finish what Sam started. She shouldn't care about Jake's opinion, yet she did.

Madelyn massaged the tightness in her chest. At least she revealed the truth and he would have to accept her decisions, however flawed and illogical her choices seemed. What if Jake despised her? A breath hitched, and she struggled for air in her lungs. She wouldn't blame him if he never trusted her again. Darn it, she had to clarify her position on the situation.

The heels of her shoes smacked the bottom of her feet as she rushed toward his side. He did a doubletake and scratched the peppered hair growth on his chin.

"I don't support or condone any of Sam's past offenses."

"I wasn't thinking that…" Jake rubbed the back of his neck.

"Go ahead, ask questions about Sam."

"Did Sam's wife set you up? She must've known about Sam's involvement with Leon."

Her step skipped as the front of her shoe caught on the root of a tree. Gretchen and Leon? "No…well, I guess it's possible." The pores on her arms pimpled. "But I think she's been honest about the little information she received and"—she shook her head—"funny thing is she believes Sam reformed his ways."

"You don't believe he changed?"

"You didn't know Sam."

"I can see he hurt you."

Madelyn wished he hadn't seen. She shrank behind and paused before her next step. "I'm moving on from the past."

"If you need to talk—"

"Want to hear how Sam verbally abused my mom and abandoned us when the doctors diagnosed her with cancer?" She progressed emotionally beyond tears after all the years that passed. "I was fifteen when delegated with taking care of my sick mother by myself."

Jake rested a hand on her shoulder. "I'm sorry. Sounds like a difficult and painful time," he said in a gentle tone. "You can find real peace and healing through forgiveness." With a pat on her back, he completed the pep talk as if they were teammates getting ready to face the opposing side.

A hotness, near boiling, surged from the top of her head spreading throughout her entire body. "Oh sure, that's easy, just forgive and forget."

"No, forgiving is difficult, and I guarantee you'll never forget."

"Then, what's your point?"

"You'll be free."

A lump swelled in her throat. Madelyn desired freedom from the weighted past and horrible memories that crept into her thoughts. However, for years, she listened to clients describe a similar disparaging home life that she endured. With each new case she expected deliverance through the process of aiding and helping women achieve liberation.

It didn't work. And although comforted by protecting the mothers and children from further abuse, she still stared into their hopeless faces, and *was* them—with all the hurt, anger and captivity they encountered.

"How do you find forgiveness?" She paused and tilted her head, studying him. "Oh, I get it, you're going to say it's faith or a God thing, aren't you?"

A wide, closed-lip smile crinkled the lines around the outside of his mouth. Madelyn searched and scrutinized his facial features for an indication he'd burst into laughter. She stared into the indescribable glow in his eyes, like she had seen on the ferry ride across Lake Chiemsee, and the radiance beneath flesh and bone burned inside him.

A quiver, close to seeing an old friend after a falling out and never expecting to see them again, rocked her nerves. The presence of something engulfed her and embodied a life all alone, whether residing in the essence of someone's belief or omnipresent. She closed her eyes and shook her head. Fatigue must've overtaken her senses.

Madelyn drew in a heavy breath and exhaled hard. "So, faith will help me forgive Sam?"

"For me, knowing God forgives my offenses helps me to forgive others." Jake focused on the path straight ahead.

Madelyn panted as she kept his pace. Her legs wobbled, taking two steps for every one of his strides. She hurried to face him, stare into his bright-blue eyes and validate the honesty of his words.

"Have you forgiven me?" Madelyn snapped her teeth down, biting the tip of her tongue. She squeezed her eyelids shut with a lightheadedness. Did she say that aloud? She angled her head toward Jake, allowing loose strands of hair to sweep over the side of her face.

Now he'd know she regarded his view and surmise her concerns. Would Jake use the knowledge for his advantage and attempt to confiscate Mozart's composition? If only she had been well rested and nourished, then her judgment would be clear, and she would've kept tight lipped.

"You're asking for my forgiveness?" He stopped and pivoted, leaning his head closer with the smallest curl of his lips to one side. "Why?"

A hotness swarmed across her chest with a tickle of marching ants over her skin. Madelyn raised an arm to swipe the prickly sensation from her limbs. Jake stepped forward into her open arms, capturing her in an embrace. He slid the backpack from her shoulders, and it fell onto the ground. The warmth of his torso against the damp material of her shirt skipped a chill down her spine. His scratchy stubble scraped the top of her ear as he drew closer. The pounding of her heart resounded throughout her entire body.

With an awkward jerk of motion, she flung her arms around him, pressing her cheek into his shoulder. She encountered a peace in the comfort of his grip. Jake held her in a tight, consoling hug while displaying compassion with no words, and only actions.

"I guess forgiveness is easy for you." She spoke in a muffled tone with her face squished against his bicep. His grasp slackened, and he shifted his boots, taking a step backward. As quick as she found herself in the coziness of a cuddle, with one swift move she stood in the stark reality that she enjoyed his company.

"Hardly." He shrugged with a forced smile and picked up his bag. "Besides, there's nothing to forgive. I understand why you did what you did. You were protecting yourself and Sam's family."

"Yeah." Madelyn rubbed her forearm.

Jake reached his arm behind, and with a gentle push forward, he encouraged her to continue walking. When did she become a lost individual, incapable of sorting out her thoughts and feelings? Not that she procured sentiments for him, only emotions about the situation. Madelyn glimpsed out the corner of her eye and her pulse increased as if he possessed the power to read minds.

Jake focused on the path, his jaw twitched, and he remained quiet. Did his silence reveal humility or his own internal struggles? Madelyn wished to hear all about his life, beyond the circumstances of Mozart's musical piece and Leon. Jake talked about his career, traveling and Henry. What about his mother or siblings? Did he have a girlfriend?

Madelyn stumbled over her feet. An urge to run the rest of the way to Ruhpolding coursed inside and jogged the silly sentiments out of her head. She'd check into a separate hotel, gaining a nice distance from Jake and communicate by phone until it became necessary to meet then deliver the sheets of music to the museum. Yes, and acting herself again, she'd follow through with her original plan. She wouldn't bother with a guy she recently met. Her stomach dove with the sensation of air turbulence on a plane. No point in developing an acquaintance with a man she'd never see again.

The sun dipped behind the snow-capped mountains in the distance, submerging into colored layers of lilac, coral, and deep saffron. A wind rustled the leaves on arched tree branches that interweaved to create a tunnel of foliage. The atmosphere inspired Madelyn, and she would've sat and penned a poem, if circumstances were different.

Pollen allergies added to the fatigue and she traipsed with a heavy head a couple steps behind Jake. Each muscle in her body begged her to stop. She left the hotel in Munich over twenty-four hours ago and never imagined traveling on foot through southern Germany, yet she pushed herself to move forward, beyond physical strength, to finish the journey.

Madelyn hoped they were close to Ruhpolding, since she reached her breaking point, and any moment she'd collapse. Jake seemed to think so too, because he peeked over his shoulder a couple times, checking she hadn't already crashed onto the ground.

"Here we are." Jake stopped, flashing a white, toothy grin.

"Where?"

"Less than a kilometer to the Glaubige Haus. Also known as The Nolan Family Inn."

The gravel dirt trail led out to green meadows adorned with bluish-purple bell-shaped flowers, dangling from narrow oblong plants. An ivy-covered fence bordered over several acres of land.

"Your family owns an inn?"

"Yeah, my mom needed to keep busy while Henry traveled."

Jake sighed and stared off into the distance. She visited that place of memories many times when thinking about Mom. Her hand rested on his arm to bring him back from the stroll down memory lane.

"Do you stay here often and help at the inn?"

"Sometimes."

"That's kind of vague."

"Depends on my work." He raised open palms heavenward for a second then dropped them to his sides. "Whether I'm teaching at the University or freelancing for a museum. I try to visit often and stay as long as my unpredictable life allows."

Yep. She had him pegged as a guy that wandered around, trying to discover himself while finding the adventure in dangerous circumstances to test his own mortality.

"Is it difficult for you to settle down in one location?"

"Not particularly." He lowered his brow, squinting as he peered. "I don't have a problem with commitment if that's what you're asking."

Thunder clapped. Her body jolted with the boom and echoed through her nerves. Metal-colored clouds hovered, and Madelyn flicked her gaze skyward. "Only curious since I see the destruction of the family unit regularly because of lack of dedication—"

"You're talking about relationships? I thought we were discussing wanderlust."

Raindrops pelted her head, drumming the rhythm of a marching band. "Well, yes. Consistent travel weakens unity in the bond."

"To a certain extent you're right." He raked his fingers through his hair. "But depending on the couple, traveling may strengthen a relationship." Jake turned, shining two warm and inviting eyes that caressed her face as he clasped her hand. "At any minute we'll be drenched."

What did Jake insinuate? Madelyn shook her head at the ridiculous contemplations about his degree of interest. He coveted Mozart's music and nothing further. She hobbled behind, and he extended his arm while he strode at a quicker pace. The random taps of raindrops increased to a steady rainfall.

It rained more in one day than an entire year in Southern California. After complete submergence in Lake Chiemsee, she still had wet clothes. Flashes of lightning bolted and illuminated the sky a silvery purple. Thunder boomed, opening a torrential shower on them and they hurried toward the picket fence.

Rushing down an incline, Jake trekked faster and her soaked fingers slipped from his grip. "Jake," Madelyn yelled as water streamed down the tip of her nose and into her mouth.

He stopped at the railing and spun around. Near the bottom of the hill she slid on the irrigated clay. She leaned forward to catch her balance, but her speed increased on the slope, propelling her onto her hands and knees into a puddle of mud. The force of the fall threw her chest down onto the soil. With a sharp reflex she held her head up, sparing a total faceplant into the sludge.

"Maddie!"

As she opened her eyes, his boots were inches away from her face. Glued to the ground, she laid in shock, waiting for her mind to grasp what happened. Mud cemented to her body as Jake gripped her upper arms and pulled, lifting her off the field. He placed a firm hand around her back and wrapped his other arm under her legs.

Fluttering swirled in her belly with a swinging motion as he raised her up and over the waist-high fence. The support of his arm behind her thighs released, and she dropped onto her feet. Madelyn wobbled for a minute, while gaining her stability. Jake pressed his palms onto the wood railing, hoisted himself and flung his legs over like a gymnast on the high balance beam with an impressive landing.

He stood close; his eyebrows drawn together with a searching gaze. "Are you injured?"

Madelyn glanced down, clothes caked in mud and arms lead pipes, dangling beside her hips. Stunned by her appearance, she bobbled her head and gawked at Jake. Physically she wasn't hurt, yet emotionally she was wrecked.

"Let's go. Don't wanna be out here in a lightning storm."

Madelyn despised his energy, and he already gained several steps ahead. She inhaled wet earth and minerals as the downpour washed the dirt from her coat. Struggling fingers attempted to comb through a tangled mass of hair bunched at the collar of her blouse. With staggering steps, she held her arms outward, allowing the water to rinse the mud off as murky rainwater stained her skin, teeming over her hands and feet. It ruined her clothes, standing covered neck to toes in filth as if she wrangled a pig. If Jake planned on using a back door, they had an opportunity to delay introductions with his mother, but she didn't have anything else to wear.

Jake disappeared over the hill. Did he forget she carried the item he desired? She reached into her pocket, the cool, dry aluminum casing still protected Mozart's sheet music. A scream built inside; she'd erupt if she stood in the rain one minute longer.

Climbing the last grassy incline, mud oozed between her toes as her foot pressed into her shoe. On top of the rise, Jake gathered the reins on a chestnut-and-cream horse, tethered to a post. The horse pranced in a circle around Jake and whinnied.

"I need to bring Brunhilda into the stable before we head into the house," he yelled over the hammering rains.

A milk-white barn sat next to the three-story inn. Madelyn plodded past Jake toward the double apple-red doors and tugged the iron, wagon-wheel-shaped handle for him.

"Thanks." Rainwater spluttered from his lips.

Madelyn gave a quick nod and followed him inside the barn. Jake led Brunhilda into a stall, removing the horse's tack, then gathered dry hay.

"She's a beautiful mare. What breed?"

"A Westphalian." He closed the gate with water flinging from his sleeve. "You're familiar with horses?"

"If time at the racetrack counts." Madelyn moved back, tucking her saturated arms in front of her coat and sneaked a peek at his expression.

Jake narrowed his eyes and pulled out a towel from a shelf of shed supplies.

She grazed her teeth against her lower lip. "Sam took me every other Sunday for about three years. He'd let me choose the horse, a beautiful black-and-white Appaloosa. Good ol' Lucky Jackson. Never lost a race."

Heat spread up her nape and behind her ears as her eyes darted to the door. What would he think about her being a child gambler? The truth of her past wouldn't help her case to win his trust.

A fluffy cotton towel swept across her face and Jake tilted her chin up with his finger, drying her skin. Droplets formed on the tips of his hair, hanging over his brow. As he leaned forward, water dripped on her forehead, and the warmth of his breath on her scalp curled her toes.

"We should go inside the house," he said.

"Like this?" She opened her arms wide, displaying muddy clothes.

"I've come home in worse conditions."

"Yeah, your mother expects that from you, but—" Dust formed a lump in the back of her throat, scratching like straw with a hard swallow.

"Come on, it'll be fine." He linked his arm around her elbow, exiting the barn, and following a cobblestone walkway.

The rain drizzled and golden patches from the skyline contrasted the charcoal clouds, creating a silhouette of the inn.

On the porch, Jake dropped his backpack, threw himself onto a bench swing and removed his Doc Martens. Under the entry light, Madelyn smoothed the hem of her shirt. Nothing helped— smears embellished her entire outfit. Her moist feet wriggled free from her shoes and she set the pair beside Jake's muddy boots.

Jake stood and reached for the knob. She grabbed his wrist before he gripped the handle.

"Wait…"

"Don't worry. I'll take you straight to a guest room."

The door swung open and Madelyn stepped back from the light, hiding in the shadows. What kind of first impression would she make covered in grime? Jake said his mother had seen him arrive home in a worse state. Did he bring women to the inn regularly?

"Jake, my boy." The woman gathered him into her arms. "I started to get worried."

"I'm all right, Mom." He choked as she squeezed harder.

His mother eased her clasp, moving her hands onto his shoulders, and on her tiptoes stared him square in the face. "I've just about had it with your dangerous escapades." She wrinkled her brow. Her lips stretched upward at the corners and she kissed him on the cheek.

Jake's mother appeared above average height and taller than Madelyn. Her dark-blonde hair hid her grays well and made it difficult to guess her age, but her face had a few deep lines around her eyes and mouth. Madelyn knew she experienced loss, and no doubt suppressed her sorrow for Henry.

Madelyn relaxed her tightened muscles as the warmth of Jake's fingers slid across her skin, maneuvering her to his side. "Madelyn Brighton, I'd like you to meet my mother, Katherine Nolan."

Katherine's blue eyes gleamed while flitting between the two of them before her gaze settled on their handclasp.

Madelyn yanked her hand from Jake and stepped forward with an extended handshake. "It's nice to meet you."

Katherine prolonged the greeting, tugging her into a side-hug. "Come inside, let me take your coat."

"Thank you, Mrs. Nolan." Madelyn removed the mire-encrusted outerwear, retrieved the items from her pockets and passed Katherine her coat.

Katherine widened her almond-shaped eyes. "You poor dear. What happened?"

Where should she begin and how much did Katherine know? A conversation with Jake would be best before answering the question. She didn't want to make unnecessary trouble for Jake. She caught a glimpse of his eyes roving toward Katherine and he pressed his lips into a straight line.

Madelyn cleared her throat. "I slipped as we were walking in off the trail."

"Why were you—"

"Excuse me, Mom, do you have any rooms vacant?"

"Yes, sweetie, you must be exhausted. I'll take you upstairs, so you can get cleaned up for dinner."

The walnut hardwood floor creaked as they followed Katherine to the stairs. She turned at the first step. "Jake, you'll stay in your regular room two, I never rent it out and your clothes are hanging in the closet. Madelyn you'll be in room three."

"I appreciate your hospitality, Mrs. Nolan."

"You're welcome. And please, call me Kate."

Kate climbed the navy, textured carpet staircase. Jake stepped aside, his palm open and arm outstretched, directing Madelyn up the staircase. Ascending ten steps then another set of four, she swayed with the weight of her body and shadowed Kate down a split hallway.

"Have you heard from Douglas?" Jake's voice deepened.

Madelyn whirled her head around and gasped at the mention of Douglas' name.

"Yes, he arrived last night." Her eyes gleamed as she stared at Jake standing in front of her, at home.

"Praise God." A huge breath escaped from his mouth.

Madelyn pressed her palm to her heart and glanced at Jake with a sigh.

"Where is Douglas now?" Jake scrubbed his hands over his face and massaged his forehead.

"He's in town, but I'll let him know you're here when he gets back."

"Thanks, Mom." Jake pecked his mother on the cheek. "I'll see you in a bit, Maddie," he said in a listless tone.

"Sure." Madelyn blinked a few times, clearing her hazy vision.

Jake strolled into his room and tears glistened in Kate's eyes. "Here you go, dear." She unlocked the door for room three and handed Madelyn the key. "The room has an en-suite and there's a robe you can put on after you clean up." Kate settled a tender hand on her shoulder. "I'll see if I can dig up a change of clothes for you."

"Thanks." Her voice cracked.

Kate furrowed her brows. "Are you all right?"

Madelyn inhaled hard, awakening her senses. "I'll be fine."

Kate flipped the light switch on by the entrance and cocked her head to one side. "I know my son's expeditions all too well—"

"Oh, no. Jake has been…" Her eyes danced around the space and her head spun. If she were honest, Jake had been too adventurous, yet also protective, generous and patient. Words eluded the extent of her thoughts and feelings for Jake while only knowing him for a day.

Madelyn gawked at Kate. "Sorry, I forgot what you asked."

Kate smiled and the lines around her eyes deepened. "Go have a rest and your thoughts will be clear later."

Madelyn staggered into the room. "You've been very kind."

"Don't give it another thought, it's my pleasure." Kate turned and shut the door.

Madelyn's limbs hung heavy, and she stood for a minute, staring at nothing in particular. The silence in the enclosed area buzzed inside her ears. Her brain became incapable of sorting out the events of the past twenty-four hours. Sweet woodruff flitted around, and she closed her eyes, swaying with the weight of her own body. A wave of nausea rolled through her as the day's occurrences caught up with her and she sank to the floor.

CHAPTER THIRTEEN

adelyn stirred in her sleep and winced at a tight pinch in her shoulder while positioned with one arm tucked under a memory foam pillow. She pried her eyelids open, struggling to blink as a neon green 6:18 P.M. glared from the small black clock on the nightstand. A thirty-minute nap? Madelyn thought she would've slept through the night after forty-five minutes of shampooing, scrubbing, then rinsing until the murky water ran clear in a hot shower and snuggling into a white cotton robe.

Baked ham wafted in the air, taunting her senses. She tossed and turned under the sheets with a rumbling stomach, confirming hunger was the true culprit that lured her awake. A soft knock on the guest room door forced her out of bed. Every muscle protested as she slid her bare feet off the bed and dragged herself across the comfy area rug covering the hardwood floor.

"Yeah." Her voice cracked like a croaking toad.

"Sorry to disturb you, Madelyn," Kate said outside in the hallway.

"No problem." Madelyn tightened the robe's sash. A rush of basil, thyme and garlic seasonings infiltrated the room when she opened the door. Severe hunger tautened her abdomen as she lurched forward and leaned against the wall frame for support.

"Here's a change of clothes while I have yours laundered." Kate gave Madelyn a folded dress and blouse. "I sell authentic Bavarian outfits, hopefully you don't mind wearing a Dirndl dress. If it doesn't fit, there's a few other sizes."

"I'm sure it'll be fine, thanks."

"Supper is being served in the dining room, whenever you're ready, unless you'd rather eat in the comfort of your own room."

"Is Jake downstairs?" She bit the corner of her lip.

"Not yet, but I'm sure he'll be down soon. He never misses a home-cooked meal."

"I…I'll eat in the dining room."

"Great, see you in a few." Kate smiled with a slight wink as she pivoted and closed the door.

Madelyn stared across the room. Did she have the clarity of mind to carry on a tangible conversation with Jake while suffering from sleep deprivation? She already shared too much about Sam and the past. If she dined with Jake, she needed to maintain a serious focus on the mission, to deliver Mozart's music to the museum. No getting caught up in his words about him being her protector, no matter how caring he appeared. Completing Sam's request required her full attentiveness.

Madelyn laid the dress on the bed and raised a corner of her upper lip. She surveyed the classic Dirndl design—a black square-cut bodice including embellished princess seams, with a decorative tawny-and-juniper vines pattern on a dark-green poly-cotton skirt. "Wow, Kate didn't exaggerate the traditional style."

As her only option for clean clothes, she shrugged her shoulders and put the top on first. Buttoning the lace-trimmed blouse, she slid the bodice over and fastened six small brass buttons up the front. Kate made an accurate guess on the size—the garment fit as if tailored made. She stared at her reflection in the full-length floor mirror, holding the skirt out with her fingertips, swooshing her arms to fluff the material. The dress looked nicer on than displayed across the bed.

A deep rose tint spread up her neck and crept across her cheeks. She dropped her chin toward her chest. No one would take her seriously wearing a costume.

Fierce hunger left no other choice but to go downstairs and eat. She combed through the strands of her freshly washed hair, infused with the scent of lavender sage as she used her last two bobby pins to clip the sides back. Red lines on the whites of her eyes mapped out the rugged trail she traveled. Swatting her hand at her image in the mirror, she whirled her head around and walked toward the dresser.

Madelyn sprawled the contents from her coat pockets on top of a crochet doily. She swiped lip balm across her lips then stared at the canister containing Mozart's music. She ran her palms along the material, searching for pockets, and tapped an index finger against the drawers. Tilting her head downward, she frowned at the inability to hide anything in the front of her dress since she lacked a voluminous female figure.

Madelyn scanned the room for a place to store the music. She opened the first drawer of the nightstand, rolled her gloves around the aluminum tube and pushed it far inside. Jake seemed trustworthy and the artifact would be safe in a locked guestroom. She closed the drawer, wiping her palms on her skirt and glanced in the mirror one last time. Shaking her head that, in addition to wearing the getup for public dining, she wore slippers and completed the ridiculous ensemble. She inhaled a deep, slow breath and exhaled hard through her nose, preparing for a spectacle downstairs.

Madelyn stood at the entrance of the dining room. Her mouth watered with the enticing mix of spices, meats and bread. She was famished to the extent she would dispel her personal restrictions on sweets and foods with high carbohydrate contents and consume anything available. Heck, she'd eat Schnitzel or the Weisswurst Leon suggested at Hotel Füssen.

Massaging her clammy hands, she slinked out of the entry and leaned against the wall by the kitchen door. No sight of Jake or Kate. A few guests sat on wood benches at elongated tables, covered with scalloped-edge, white linens. Floral, folk-art-painted plates, displayed in rows, decorated the shelves on the far wall. An elderly couple cuddled in a secluded corner, while at the opposite side of the room, a loud group of five young adults laughed and celebrated. A family gathered at the center table with two girls and a little boy, giggling as he blew a kazoo in one girl's ear. Madelyn curved her neck, spotting a silver-haired gentleman in a gray-tweed suit, sitting at the dinette, close to a cultured stone hearth. The gentleman drank from a porcelain teacup as he read a newspaper. She straightened her posture and waltzed toward him.

Madelyn cleared her throat. "Excuse me, Douglas Wyatt?"

He squinted behind squared-framed lenses and glanced up from the paper. "Yes." Douglas blinked a few times. "Oh indeed, I heard of your arrival." He stood from the chair. "Please, join me, Ms....Brighton?"

"Yeah, Madelyn, and thank you." She settled into the seat across from him. "I was relieved to hear you were safe, after the chaotic events in Munich."

"Truly, and my deepest apologies for the hardships you endured once we were separated."

"You heard about what happened with Leon?"

"I was gobsmacked when Jake disclosed what transpired."

"Jake told you...everything?" She glanced at the glass bottle filled with water on the table, her throat dry as if she swallowed sawdust.

"I learned plenty. Dreadful business."

Did Jake tell Douglas about her relation to Sam and how she acquired Mozart's music? Stomach acids stirred. She needed to drink and eat anything. "Do you mind if I have a glass of water?"

"Please, allow me." He opened the bottle and filled a goblet.

"Thank you." Madelyn gulped the cool liquid when the first drop touched her tongue.

"You really have been through an ordeal. I warned Jake of the dangers involved." He crossed his arms over his chest and leaned back in his chair. "All in the name of preserving Henry's legacy."

"You don't approve of Jake continuing his father's work?"

"Not when the job results in injuries…or worse." His wrinkles deepened on his forehead as he spoke in the tone of a concerned father. How wonderful for Jake, having the love and concern of people around, carrying the burdens for one another. A coldness rippled through her body and now she wished she stayed in her guest room, tucked into blankets and eating a hot meal.

Madelyn refilled her water goblet and sipped rather than downing the entire glass. "I understand why Jake wants to finish his dad's work."

"And thanks to you, he'll complete the job." He smiled with a quick wink. "Rest assured, my dear, Jake will first ensure your safe return to Munich."

Madelyn gathered loose strands of hair, petting the ends. "Jake and I agreed—"

"Well, it looks like the two of you are getting better acquainted." Jake's voice broke into their conversation. "Hope I didn't interrupt." With a gesture of fondness, Jake patted Douglas on the back of his shoulder.

"Not at all, we're discussing that despite all the risk, you're home safe."

Douglas stood and peered over the rims of his eyewear, arching a deliberate brow.

"Are you joining us for dinner?" Jake asked.

Douglas pushed his spectacles higher onto the bridge of his nose, his eyes flitted between Jake and Madelyn. "Thank you, but I ate earlier. The two of you enjoy your meal."

Jake turned. "Hello, Maddie. Did you get settled into your room?"

Madelyn tilted her head toward Jake. He looked handsome with a clean shave and hair combed back, emphasizing the depth of his eyes, a deeper blue than the Pacific Ocean. His dark jeans and graphite-colored sweater hugged his physique. She opened her mouth to speak and he grinned as if her expression said it all.

"I see my mother found you an outfit to wear."

A hotness singed her cheeks, and she averted her gaze, focusing on her water glass. "Ah yeah, I look a little ridiculous."

"You're lovely."

Her eyelids sprung open with the force of a starting gate, and her heart raced, staring at his face. The stampede of emotions galloped at the pace of a stretch runner on its final lap. A slight curl of his lips tugged to one side. He pulled up a chair from behind and sat close. A fluttering swarmed in her belly as her gaze darted between Jake and a pale-yellow napkin.

"What a wonderful sight." Kate approached, beaming with a spring in her step. "My sweet Jake, dearest Douglas and our new friend Madelyn, gathered together, getting ready to break bread." She placed a cloth-covered basket on the table.

"Thanks, Mom." Jake tapped Kate's hand resting on his shoulder.

Madelyn smiled and reached into the basket. "Thank you, Kate." She ripped off a piece of warm bread and chewed, the light fluffy texture melting in her mouth. Food never tasted so good. Closing her eyes, she savored the same bite for at least two minutes before swallowing. As she lifted her eyelids, Jake observed her, and she slinked backward into the chair.

"Fresh-baked Bauernbrot is the best," he said.

"Time used to allow me to bake the loaves, but with the increase of guests, I now send out for the local bakery." Kate's voice dropped.

"If you'd please excuse me." Douglas stepped away from the table. "I'm feeling peckish with all this talk of food."

"Head into the kitchen, I'll fix you up a plate."

"I thought you said you already ate?" Jake wrinkled his brow.

"I did, but lunch was hours ago." Douglas shifted his gaze back and forth with an eye rolling gesture toward Kate.

"Ah, right, Douglas and I have business to discuss, and I'm sure you're both looking forward to a quiet supper."

"Mom—"

"I'll have your meals out in about two minutes, and we'll join you later." Her eyes glinted with the special bond between parent and child as Kate kissed Jake on the cheek. She spun around, bustling in her faded slim-fit jeans, a collared blouse with the sleeves rolled to the elbows and a bright turquoise apron while her low ponytail swished below her shoulders.

Jake propped his elbow onto the table, resting his chin in the palm of his hand. His eyes followed Douglas' steps toward the kitchen door. "I think Douglas and my mother are scheming."

Her fingers coiled around another piece of bread, she only cared about food at the moment. "I can't imagine what you think they'd be plotting."

"Can't you?" Jake leaned forward, staring, speaking in a rich tone laced with serious inquisition.

Madelyn squirmed under his piercing gaze. "I…" She swallowed her bread. "I guess…" She trembled, trapped in a trance. *Remember, don't fall for his words or mesmerizing blue eyes. Focus on the mission.*

"You're blushing." His lips bent into a confident smile and he reached his hand out.

Her cheeks scorched with fury, heat spreading down her body as she budged a few inches away from his grasp. She straightened her torso, taking a deep breath while she blinked long and hard. "Don't bother, I'm sure you have a girlfriend that appreciates your charm."

"No girlfriend, a fiancée."

A sensation of a sharp dagger twisted in her heart and her chest pressed inward. Madelyn pursed her lips, with tensed muscles, and squared her shoulders to hold composure. "You're engaged?"

"I was, we broke up over a year ago."

"Oh, I'm sorry…" Was she? A coolness swam over her skin like jumping into a pool on the first hot day of summer. Curiosity stirred her interest, and she opened her mouth to speak then snapped her jaw closed. Did she want to hear the details about Jake's broken relationship? She needed to learn how to turn off work mode. Personal or professional, the news of his engagement distressed and piqued a significant reaction entrenched inside.

"Yeah, we realized our lives had taken different paths. I guess she didn't appreciate my charm." Jake reclined in his chair, folding his arms across his chest. "Although, it's nice to hear you find me charming." His gaze full of life, a bright spring day in full bloom.

"Ah, no, you misunderstood." Madelyn pressed her lips together to hold back a smile.

* * *

A darkness draped a curtain around the town while Leon strolled the cobblestone streets in the quiet village of Ruhpolding, on the way to Hotel Luxur. The walls of the hotel room, along with Mason, became a millstone around his neck and suppressed clear thinking. Leon convinced himself taking a walk and dining alone at the Rathskeller would be an ideal setting for strategic planning. His shoulders slumped as he swallowed excess saliva.

Both day and evening resulted in a bad mood. Even the restaurant disappointed with the service, a bland meal and distasteful public behavior from tourists. The environment, zu klein, zu laut and if too small and too noisy of quarters weren't enough, the people ate pizza out of their hands then left scraps of food on their plates. Leon paused, pressing a hand against his abdomen as a sudden onset of nausea brewed a storm of sickness. He should've stayed at the hotel and sent Mason out for take away.

Leon followed the streetlamps to the entrance of the hotel; he gazed beyond the town, into the black where only the faint flicker of lights in windows were visible on the hill. It took every ounce of willpower, abstaining from taking a detour and demand the return of his rightful property at The Nolan Family Inn. He had a single opportunity to finish victorious; there'd be no margin for errors. His work taught him persistent patience is a guide, and a necessity to get him through sleepless nights.

A rippling image of the full moon shimmered in a rain puddle. Leon stood leaning on the hard, cold iron of a lamppost. Hairs on his neck raised as a chilling breeze whipped under his unbuttoned collar. The one night he forgot his scarf, the temperature dropped to the mid-forties with a wind chill of thirty. He wrapped his wool coat tighter around his chest. Sliding up his left sleeve to glance at his Blvgari stainless-steel watch, he read the time: seven thirty-seven. Time taunted him and he would suffer a long, restless night. With a visible heavy breath in the air, the warmth of shelter beckoned him out of the bitter weather.

Walking through the double automated doors a rush of hot air greeted him inside the hotel lobby as forced heat blew from the vents. Leon meandered through a grove of guests. He twisted and bent his body, avoiding the people herded together like sheep to use the lifts. Choosing the stairway, he climbed the flights of steps and hoped his opponents incurred mutual misery.

Leon needed to unwind, challenge his mind to detract his thoughts of the unsettling situation. Perhaps a game of chess then extra investigative reading on Madelyn Brighton. He anticipated the information would be useful, playing her as a pawn, and discovering the perfect move to avoid the possibility of reaching a stalemate. With the board and pieces arranged in his mind, the next move became crystal clear.

* * *

Jake finished every morsel from his plate and licked the taste of red wine vinegar from his lips. Devouring their Sauerbraten, they spoke few words. Fulfilled with food and fatigue he lounged back into the wooden chair and wiped the napkin from his lap across his mouth. "Did you enjoy your meal?"

Maddie set her fork on the table after her last bite. "It was delicious. Your mother's a wonderful cook and the inn seems busy with guests."

"Yeah, Mom is amazing."

"It must be difficult for Kate to manage the business, a home and barn too."

"It's challenging since my dad passed away, but she has great support from friends, the church and Douglas. He's been an honorary member of our family for years, and spends most of his retirement here, helping Mom with everything." He sipped his water.

Maddie pushed her dish aside and leaned closer. "How long has the inn been open?"

"My parents started the bed and breakfast a few years ago, but Kate was left to operate the business alone when Henry started work on the Mozart excavation. Dad was a brilliant teacher, an encouraging father, a loving husband and a godly man."

Her eyes fixed on his and she bobbed her head with understanding. She seemed accustomed with being a quiet listener and made it clear her job required hearing heart-wrenching stories from women and their families.

"At times I questioned my dad's priorities when he would go on his expeditions and leave Kate for months at a time. I was angry with him, wondering if he had put his own passions before his family. All relationships have ups and downs, and my parents had their share, but they always trusted each other and kept God at the center." Jake shrugged one shoulder and sighed.

"Are you concerned you may have the same struggle with balancing work and relationships?" The tone of her voice changed to a soothing calm as her facial expression remained neutral with a softness around the eyes.

"Isn't it obvious? It's one of the many reasons that led to my broken wedding engagement."

Maddie lowered her thick lashes, her rosy-tinted lips parted, and she took a breath. Did he confess too much? He admitted his work obligations caused his last relationship to fall apart. Maybe she already pegged him as one of those guys who bolts at any sign of trouble or struggles with commitment issues. She questioned him earlier about having a reluctance to settle down. Great, he appeared to be a sleazy vagabond, looking out for himself. No wonder she didn't trust him.

A thickness built in his throat and he swallowed hard. Did it even matter? He'd never see her again after tomorrow and she'd despise him after he confessed what he did.

"It's remarkable that even as adults we're burdened by the choices our parents made. We fear we'll choose a similar path, or we feel the need to fix their mistakes so we can move on, expecting we'll find a way to put the past behind us and focus on our own lives. You've acknowledged your battle with priorities, that's half the fight." She cocked her head to one side, her eyes glinted with a promised aspiration. "In the short time I've spent with you, my welfare seemed to be of high importance. As a matter of fact, Douglas mentioned something about your first priority is my safety and you'll make sure I return to Munich right away."

Maddie squinted with an endless depth in her sight filled with suppositions. Rich chocolate-brown eyes poured over him. The lump in his throat swelled. He tore his gaze away and swigged his water. As his internal temperature soared, he slipped his fingers under the edge of his crew-neck sweater, pulling it away from his chest, circulating the air.

"Are you charging by the hour?" Her intelligence coupled with empathy shined in her words and gentle expression. Jake imagined she observed everyone she met through professional lenses and anyone close enough she viewed with a magnifying glass.

"I'm sorry if it came across as routine. It's only my opinion based on what you shared. My friend and colleague Sheryl is always…" Her mouth gaped open, and she sucked in a sharp breath.

"What's the matter?"

"Sheryl." Maddie shook her head. "I can't believe I forgot to call her. She must be so worried."

"If you'd like, you can make an international call from the landline in your guestroom."

"You don't mind?" She pushed her chair from the table and stood.

"Not at all, take your time."

For at least a minute she stared, her face bright, shoulders relaxed, and she flipped her chestnut-colored hair back. "I'll meet you here?" she said in a silky tone and turned.

Stopping mid-step, she whirled around. "For dessert, of course."

"Of course."

A full smile flashed pearly white teeth, and she hurried out of the dining room. Hints of the true Madelyn Brighton emerged from beneath the reserved poise, revealing a vibrant woman, willing to open and share her life with the right man. Most of the day he spent trying to scale the fortress she built, but he didn't need to climb or break through, she deconstructed the barrier one stone at a time. Certain to be a lengthy process, although he guaranteed worth the wait.

Jake couldn't deny the level of comfort, familiarity and connection he felt—as if he'd always been aware of her in the world. The desire to explore the many facets of her personality intrigued and unnerved him. He enjoyed spending time with her. However, reality grounded him in truth, and he'd be a fool to contemplate the possibilities of anything beyond. She lived in California, consumed with a life filled with friends, a career, and a conceivable boyfriend. He didn't know much about her, but he already knew he met someone extraordinary.

The dining room cleared and fire from the hearth crackled as flames died down. Jake rubbed the back of his stiff neck. Finding the words to tell her she couldn't continue with him to the Mozart Museum would be difficult; she'd argue and insist on going. The minute she learned he swapped the music with Sam's copy, any possibility of a friendship would be destroyed. Jake swallowed a sour taste in his mouth.

If only Leon didn't pose a threat, he'd tell her the truth and take her on the journey to Salzburg. What was he thinking? Jake swiped a palm over his face. He rejected getting involved emotionally. She needed to leave, and he'd complete Dad's work. Perhaps the call to her friend would give her some practical sense and a longing for home.

Maddie entered the dining area, her lips curved into a sweet smile that Jake wished she intended for him. She sashayed across the floor; the bodice of the Dirndl dress hugged her feminine form. The difficulty with tearing his gaze away increased as she approached the table and his heart raced. She lit up the room and he lost the courage to articulate his thoughts. For now, he'd savor the precious moments together. No rush. He'd tell her the truth in the morning.

"What's that look?" She ran her palms down the front of her dress, tugging at the material.

"You've got it wrong." He stood, slipping his hands into hers. "You have the appearance of walking into a scene on a motion picture set."

A deep pink color crept into her cheeks. "Which movie? The Sound of Music?"

"Well…" He choked on the laughter rising in his throat. "You said you love the film."

Her lavender-scented hair swirled in his nostrils. Jake stepped backward, allowing her hands to slip from his sweaty palms. How was she capable of turning him inside out in one day? He coughed under his breath, reaching for his water, and sipped.

"Did you talk to your friend?"

"No, I left a message. I told her everything's fine and I'm taking a few extra days in the country for a quiet retreat."

"Mm-hmm…"

"Should I have said something different?"

"Ah, no—"

"How did you enjoy your meals?" Mom bustled up toward the table.

"Delicious as always." Jake smiled, thankful for her impeccable timing. He didn't want to spoil his evening with Maddie.

"Everything's wonderful, thank you." Maddie clasped her hands together.

"Our community group is gathering for fellowship. I'm serving tea and cake in the living room. Will you be joining us? Everyone is welcome."

"I don't want to impose on your guests." Maddie swooped her gaze up and down.

Overwhelming fatigue kicked him in the gut and made him physically wiped out yet staying awake longer meant additional time with Maddie.

"You can think about it. Even if you come and visit for a few minutes, that's fine too."

"All right, Mom." Jake reached for the plates. "I'll clean the dishes."

"Nonsense, I'm getting the tea and if you want, we'll meet you in the other room." She turned toward the kitchen; her arms loaded with tableware. "About five minutes."

"I haven't been to a church meeting in years." Maddie bent her shoulders downward.

"It's really a time to socialize, ask for prayer and talk about the past week. You might enjoy the company."

"I'm sure I will."

CHAPTER FOURTEEN

Madelyn entered the living room, the hardwood floor creaking as she ambled across the large mulberry area rug. The warmth of the fire burning in the red brick hearth produced ample heat for the entire area. She stared at a framed portrait of Jake and his parents above the fireplace. Jake emulated the youthful vision of his father Henry. Same facial structure, the square chin, defined cheekbones, even the same dark thick hair. All but the eyes—Jake had his mother's eyes.

She scanned the surroundings as guests filtered into the room; she ran her hand over the floral-print, linen sofa. Bright-colored throw pillows decorated two lounge chairs flanking both ends of the couch. A yellow-green-hued ottoman positioned at the far corner contrasted the color schemes of neutrals, splashed with seasonal greens and blue lilac. The atmosphere created a sense of constant springtime, a welcoming place to gather and grow.

The elderly couple from dinner walked in, along with a few other unfamiliar faces as they chatted while settling on a seating choice. Madelyn stood against the wall, in a low-lit spot next to the piano. Everything she experienced today stretched her beyond her comfort zone. The noise level increased, and the walls echoed with conversation. Her eyes roved the social and charismatic group.

A dizziness swirled in her head. Maybe she still had a chance to sneak upstairs.

Inching along the perimeter of the room, she fixed her eyes forward, her hands a visual guide around any obstacles. She banged her knee on the piano bench and froze, pressing her lips together. Madelyn bent and massaged her joints then jolted her body straight—she didn't want to draw attention.

After fifteen minutes of hiding in a corner while the others chatted and laughed, she glanced at the tall, dark-wood grandfather clock, displaying eight-twenty.

Kate carried in a three-tiered dessert stand with assorted cakes and cookies. "The tea is coming. Please help yourselves."

A couple minutes later, Jake brought in a kettle and cups on a silver tray, setting it on the mahogany coffee table in the center of the room. Through a sea of arms reaching for desserts and pouring tea, she leveled her line of vision, and her sight anchored on Jake. The banging of her heart drummed in her ears as he advanced, holding a cup.

"Have a seat." He gestured with a nod of his head toward a sitting chair beside the piano.

"I brewed coffee for you."

"Mm." Madelyn sat and wrapped her hands around the hot ceramic mug. She inhaled the rich dark roast aroma and swallowed a slow long drink. "I'm beginning to like you."

"All it took was a cup of coffee?"

She covered her smile, placing the rim to her lips. At that moment Jake showed more than an offering of her favorite drink, easing the suffering of the intense squishing pressure in her brain from caffeine withdrawals, he tuned in to her needs like no one ever had in her life. Why had she met him now and in the worst circumstances?

"I've asked my son, Jake, if he'd lead us in a song," Kate said, standing in the middle of the room.

Jake maneuvered around the bench, positioning his body, and facing the upright piano. He turned his head over his shoulder.

"I chose one of my favorite hymns by Saint Francis of Assisi, All Creatures of Our God and King, translated by William H. Draper and melody by Peter Von Brachel, three verses in keys E and B."

Madelyn opened her mouth and Jake handed her the sheet music. "If you want to sing along."

"Um, I can't."

"I'm sure you'll be fine."

Nope, her vocals were intended for the shower or while alone in the car and she only received a passing grade for choir class in high school based on participation. Singing in the presence of people was best when performed as a lip sync.

His fingers danced across the glossy black-and-white piano keys as he played the introductory notes then sang. "All creatures of our God and king, lift up your voice and with us sing. O, praise him, alleluia, alleluia." Jake led the group in a chorus.

His tone was pitch perfect with obvious musical talents as the warm texture of his baritone swept over her like a heatwave. Madelyn stared at the paper and a tightness expanded in the back of her throat. Coffee in one hand, sheet music in the other, and fingers trembling with caffeine-infused anxiety.

"Thou burning sun with golden beam, Thou silver moon with softer gleam, O praise him. O praise him. Alleluia, alleluia, alleluia." Everyone raised their voices in unison, vitality reverberated off the walls and her skin tingled.

She browsed the radiant faces, a few eyes closed, a couple uplifted hands, a few quiet, and others loud with different ranges of tone. They didn't seem concerned with their singing capabilities; they sang from the heart.

"Thou rushing wind that art so strong. Ye clouds that sail in heaven along. O, praise him, alleluia."

Madelyn gazed at the paper and hummed along with a timid voice. "Thou rising moon, in praise rejoice. Ye lights of evening, find a voice. O praise him. O praise him. Alleluia, alleluia, alleluia. Let all things their Creator bless, and worship him in humbleness, O praise him. Alleluia…" In her heart she revered God. "Praise,

praise the Father, praise the Son and praise the Spirit, three in one." She raised her voice a little louder with the closing lyrics. "O praise him. O praise him. Alleluia, alleluia, O alleluia, alleluia."

Jake rolled his fingers over the piano keys, playing the final chords. Madelyn pressed her palm against her heart, kneading the burning sensation rising in her chest. Either a blatant adoration for God stirred inside or the heavy meal topped with coffee triggered indigestion.

"Thank you, Jake," Kate said. "Before we get started, I'd like to introduce and welcome Jake's friend, Madelyn Brighton." Kate extended her arm with an open hand. "I'm so blessed to have them both here with us tonight." Her speech strained with emotion.

All the faces in the room turned, smiling and waving greetings. "Hello."

Madelyn forced a grin and shifted in her seat. Jake swiveled on the bench, angled his body away from the piano, and caressed his palm over her hand, sliding the sheet music through her fingers. Her body stiffened as a slight hitch caught her breath. The guests introduced themselves, clockwise around the room.

The introductions finished, and everyone quieted. Kate sat in a hunter-green chair near the doorway and opened a Bible. She pushed her glasses up further on the bridge of her nose. "Last week we discussed the parable of the lost sheep and read Matthew 18, verses 21-35, the allegory of the unforgiving debtor."

Madelyn surveyed the room as a few people pulled out their Bibles or a smartphone.

"We can share." Jake opened his Bible to the passage.

"Thanks."

Madelyn perused the pages, fluorescent highlighter pen marked several passages, with notes written in the margins and prayers scribbled anywhere the words fit. His Bible resembled a collection of letters bound, the leather soft and worn, with earmarked sections; more than an old book he owned for years, collecting dust on a shelf. The book embodied personality and life, accompanying him on his journeys. She felt the Bible contained something personal, an actual part of Jake.

"Does anyone have anything they want to share?" Kate removed her spectacles, her vibrant blue eyes searched for a volunteer.

"Ja," a woman said with hair the color of honey wheat and eyes like two Granny Smith apples.

"Great, thanks," Kate said.

"Hallo, I'm Svenja. About three years ago, my spouse and I, with our three children, moved from Munich to Ruhpolding. My father was ill, and I needed to help care for him after heart surgery. After the move, my husband became angry and distant. One day he packed and left, we didn't know where he went or what we should do."

Madelyn nodded her head. She heard similar stories every day at work. She marveled at Svenja and her openness; they weren't alone in a private office. The courage to share with a group, with strangers present, impressed on her the power of their community, providing support and comfort.

Svenja folded her hands in her lap, her eyes settling on Madelyn. "A year passed and not a word from my husband. I was distraught, brokenhearted and bitter. It confused my children and they felt abandoned."

Madelyn twisted her torso with the pain of a dull blade in her side that tore into the old wound of Sam leaving without a trace. A sickness swirled with the memory of hurt and anger she suffered as a teenager and still as an adult. The emotional disaster at the funeral proved she was far from healed.

Madelyn lifted her gaze as Svenja continued. "My father died that same year and right after I received divorce papers. All seemed lost, until one day, a little over a year ago, I was in town at the bakery and met Kate. We talked about children, losing loved ones and baking bread. I told her how angry I was with my husband, but feared I was teaching my kids the wrong response, so she invited us to church." She smiled and glanced at Kate. "The children and I continued attending and found healing through prayer as God worked in me a forgiving heart. We prayed for their dad, every day for a year and he finally called Friday. Praise the Lord, he is working in Munich and getting treatment for depression. I arranged a meeting at the end of the week with him and the kids."

Madelyn lowered her head and wrapped her arms tight around her waist. How did Svenja forgive her husband's betrayal? Yes, the man sounded tormented, but he still left his wife and children. Svenja believed her husband changed, like Gretchen trusted in Sam's supernatural transformation. Was it possible for people to have a change of heart and character?

"Thank you, Svenja, for sharing your testimony of compassion." Kate tilted her head to the side, her eyes crinkled at the corners with a closed-lip smile. "We're truly blessed by your faith. We'll be praying for your meeting."

Madelyn double blinked and focused her attention on Svenja as she smiled and mouthed a voiceless thank-you to the group. She picked up her cup of tea, hands steady, shoulders relaxed and reclined on the sofa.

"Your story is inspiring." Jake inhaled hard and deep. "As we've been discussing forgiveness, I'm convicted of my struggle with resentment. I've allowed pride to distort God's direction for my life." He raked his fingers through his hair and exhaled aloud. "Most of you know my dad passed away and I've continued his work, despite many trials and obstacles from opposition."

Madelyn dipped her chin toward her chest and shrank down in the chair. Did Jake consider her an obstacle and opposition? He claimed to understand her choices, yet her presence created a hinderance.

"Please ask for God's clear guidance and strength for tolerating this person. Also, pray for this man's soul, as he persists with instigating trouble." Jake pursed his lips, the corners curved downward.

"We'll continue praying for you and lift Leon up to the Lord," Douglas said with a single nod.

A wet film masked Madelyn's eyes and her heart pounded with a longing for experiencing that kind of faith. Madelyn wanted to encounter the freedom accompanied with true forgiveness. The forgiveness Sheryl, Svenja and Jake spoke of through their faith. The room spun, her stomach swinging in rhythm with the pendulum of the grandfather clock. She gripped the edge of her seat to keep from leaping up and rushing outside.

"I'll close us in prayer, and we'll continue with our fellowship." Kate closed her eyes.

Madelyn observed the guests close their eyes and bow their heads. She bent her neck forward and Jake clasped the top of her hand. Her nerves loosened under his touch. Surrendering to the serenity of human contact, she rotated her arm and uncoiled her fingers, kindling the heat of their palms clutched together.

"God, we're so thankful you've blessed us with our group here tonight and praise you for the work you're doing in each individual. We thank you that because of your mercy, we can forgive others. Please give us an insight into the scriptures, speak to our hearts, so we may glorify you with our lives. In your name, Jesus, we pray. Amen."

"Amen," the group responded in unison.

Jake gave her a slight squeeze before he removed his hand. With heavy lids Madelyn opened her eyes. The need for sleep hit her as she wrestled between physical and emotional fatigue. Challenged by the words Svenja spoke about forgiveness and the lyrics of the hymn, her mind and heart required time to process her feelings.

"Are you beyond exhausted? I know I am." Jake stood and shook himself awake.

"Yes. I'm ready to head upstairs."

Better retreat and think in quiet before doing or saying something rash. Curiosity would lead to questioning Svenja like a client during an intake interview and digging deeper into the real question Madelyn wanted answered. How do you forgive the unforgivable?

"Yeah, a gathering of people revealing their hardships is too reminiscent of a regular workday." Jake rubbed the back of his neck and sighed.

"A little." She stood, staring him in the face. "But you surprise me, and I commend everyone's courage to disclose personal matters in a group setting."

"My mom has created a safe environment and the support from this group is amazing."

"I can see Kate is a model of faith and how grateful you are for her in your life."

An ache amplified in her chest with the growing need for friends and solace. Even Jake surmised she lived as a spectator, keeping relationships at a distance to avoid attachments and the pain of disappointment. Years of sorrow, guilt and anger pent up simmered inside, ready for an explosion. She controlled her reactions with a slow deep breath through her nose.

"How are you both doing?" Kate reached her arms around them, pulling them into a semi-huddle.

"Beat," Jake said.

Kate patted them on the back. "You must be wicked tired, but I'll admit, I'm overjoyed that you joined us tonight."

"Thanks for including me. I found the group inspirational," Madelyn said.

Kate leaned close into a side-hug. "If you need anything, I'm here for you."

A knot looped in her throat and she gulped a mouthful of air. "I appreciate your kindness." Madelyn wavered.

"Go have a good night's sleep," Kate said.

"Goodnight." Jake kissed Kate on the cheek.

Kate smiled and tended to the few people dawdling by the entry hall. Tears brimmed in the corner of Madelyn's eyes. Everything she missed; Mom, friends, a family room with worn furniture and peeling paint on the doorframe embodying real life, it all happened in this house. For the first time in years she longed for companionship, even if it meant exposing her painful past and risking being hurt again. A surge of nausea rocked her off her feet, forcing her onto the piano bench.

"Whoa, are you okay?" Jake sat close, his body inches away.

"I…I guess I'm not as strong as I thought." She swiped her fingers across her cheekbones, rotated her head with her eyes following in the direction of the last guest exiting. The fire popped as the cinders burned out, and she rubbed her hand along her arm.

"Hey, I'm shocked neither one of us passed out earlier."

Madelyn fixated on the empty mug in her grip. A slight perspiration broke with the weight of his stare. "I meant…I don't have strength like Svenja to break free of my bitterness."

She stood, crossed the room, placing her mug on the coffee table, then collected small plates and teacups, cleaning as a distraction from confessing her conflicting thoughts.

"Maddie, it wasn't strength that helped Svenja work through her hurt, it's grace and mercy that led her to finding peace."

The candor of his words shook her limbs. The porcelain cups clinked as she set them on the tray. If real healing occurred with forgiveness, no matter the offense, then she remained confronted with absolving Sam, the man who turned his back on his family, abandoning his dying wife and child.

She'd have to extend mercy regardless if she cleared his name or believed he changed. Did she possess enough grace to forgive Sam?

Madelyn tapped a finger to her lips, her shoulders sagged, and she spoke under her breath. "There's a lot to process."

"Hey, I don't pretend to have all the answers," he said through a heavy exhale and approached from behind, his arm brushed her shoulder. "It's not something that happens overnight, give it time."

She shot a glance. "It's been fifteen years."

Fifteen long years of suppressed resentment festering inside, anticipating an opportunity to discard past events and allow her to live life.

"I know, but Sam's gone. Your best chance for moving on is to accept forgiveness doesn't change the person forgiven, it changes you."

Completing Sam's request accomplished two goals: casting a positive light on the dark shadow of his nature and deliverance from their unresolved relationship. As much as she contemplated forgiving Sam, mistakes and all, she believed the process would help her heal. Didn't Jake recognize they both wanted to achieve the same thing?

"Why haven't you asked me for the music?" She pivoted her body and faced him, sweeping her arm against him, a pang quaked in her chest, sending aftershocks to her heart.

Jake shrugged a nonchalant shoulder. "I wasn't thinking about it."

Lost in the details of his face, she memorized every fine line and bone structure, a magnificent piece of art. The hairs on her nape raised with an acute awareness of the proximity of their bodies.

"We're in this together, right?" Seconds gazing into his eyes seemed like forever, entranced by the tropical blue, her mind reached a permanent vacation destination. She blinked and the heaviness of her head thrust her onward.

Jake leaned forward; the smooth caress of his lips sealed a confectionery kiss on her mouth. Weakening in the knees, she slid her hands over his biceps, resting them on his shoulders. His muscles tensed under her touch. Suspended weightless, she felt a sensation of floating into space, as their lips worked into a synchronized motion.

Jake shifted his body and drew away. Gasping with a loss of oxygen her eyelids flashed open as she plummeted toward earth. His eyes were blue ice as he stepped back, banging his leg on the coffee table.

"It's been a…" He ran his fingers through his hair. "Difficult and revealing day," he said, in an uncertain tone. "Among other things."

His gaze darted toward the floor then the entry, jerking his limbs forward, he picked up the tea tray. "Well…" Jake lowered his lids with a fleeting glance. "Night."

"Goodnight."

His lips slanted upward to one side, and he strode out of the room. She stared off at the empty doorway, dizzy as she kneaded the back of her head. Did she act too eager? Madelyn ballooned out her cheeks, releasing her breath. Did she let her guard down again? Rubbing her lips, the feeling of their mouths pressed together moments ago rippled through every nerve ending and stirred a fluttering in her belly. Why did she respond like a schoolgirl with a crush? She smacked a palm against her forehead and plodded upstairs to the guestroom.

Madelyn climbed into bed and replayed the events of the evening in her mind multiple times, and concluded she lacked any expertise in the field of successful relationships. She considered turning in a letter of resignation upon returning to work. All her experience involved case studies of broken and dysfunctional families. Days and hours exposed her to the cruel aspects of the human condition, distorting her interpretations. Wasn't she supposed to come to Germany to severe relational ties? Instead, her travels inundated her with added emotional turmoil.

She tossed the pillow over, fluffing the down filling with her fists. She would carry on with her initial plans and take Mozart's music to Salzburg. Following her strategies, without fickle feelings provided the comfort of completing a commitment which always proved reliable.

Madelyn flattened her back and wriggled her shoulders below the pillow. Jake's help ensured the beginning of a temporary agreement and if a friendship developed then so be it and if not… She hoped for too much.

Rotating onto her side, the sheets cocooned around her waist while she wrestled to break free. Out of breath, she sprawled her arms and legs, extending her limbs the length of the bed. Lingering in the pit of her soul like a song repeating in her head, hope whispered to not let go, urging her to believe in more than what she had known and experienced. She threw her arms upward and yanked the duvet, covering her entire body. At least for tonight she would dream.

CHAPTER FIFTEEN

Jake strolled from the barn back to the house, removed his boots and swung the side door open. The scent of maple wafted through the kitchen. He rolled his sleeves and washed up in the sink, rinsing chicken and horse feed from his hands. Funny how he missed being home in the country and tending animals, after spending months traveling or working in metropolitan cities. He settled onto a stool at the center island, popping a fresh piece of sliced coffee loaf into his mouth. Cinnamon melted on his tongue as he chewed the savory cake. Mom made the best Blitz Kuchen. Jake reached in the back pocket of his dark-blue jeans and sighed. He forgot his phone suffered water damage from Lake Chiemsee—the reason he put his wristwatch on this morning, the one Angelina gave him the Christmas before she split.

At 9:30 a.m., if Maddie had awakened, she'd come down for breakfast at any moment. After swallowing a second bite of cake, he massaged the tightness in his chest. Today he'd tell her to leave, even after they kissed last night. The risk to her safety appeared greater than sacrificing the pleasure of her company. If they'd met under different circumstances, he wouldn't waste another minute and ask her out on a date. No chance of that happening now.

Jake slouched and propped his elbows on the counter. Who was he kidding? Maddie lived in California and he failed at making a relationship work on the east coast, let alone the west coast.

The urgency for caffeine pounded in his brain. Jake pressed his fingers into his temples as he got up and brewed a pot of coffee. If Maddie wasn't already on her way, the smell of a steaming cup of java would lure her downstairs. Sickness swished in his gut; he didn't have time to prepare for a fueled discussion. He credited hunger as the culprit for his queasiness, even though he spent half the night tossing and turning, thinking about Maddie.

A full meal would hit the spot and he'd make breakfast for her too. At least he'd seem less of a jerk with a nice gesture. He fired up the stove and cracked six eggs into a cast iron pan. As he cooked sausage in boiling water, he scrambled the yolks and whites on low heat. Staring into the beaten blur, he mixed them with a spatula, and deduced there were no other options but to send Maddie home. He placed the Weisswurst in a bowl of hot water and scooped the eggs onto a serving plate. Setting dishes out on the kitchen island, he stayed positive since he finally gained Mozart's music and met a fascinating woman, even if it ended as the last day of their acquaintance.

Jake pushed through the swinging door into the dining area. Maddie rounded the corner and entered the room. Her hair hung loose with slight waves framing her face, sweeping just below her shoulders. He blinked hard and his pulse increased.

"Good morning." She tucked her hair behind one ear.

"Sleep well?"

"Yeah." With three quick steps, she stopped and surveyed the empty chairs. "It's a slow start to the day."

"Breakfast rush is over by nine and Douglas drove Kate into town." Jake extended his arm. "Come with me."

A slow smile built as she reached for his hand. He escorted her into the kitchen and pulled out a stool at the center island. "I hope you don't mind eating in here with the mess I made."

"You prepared breakfast?"

"Sausage and eggs." Jake turned on his heels and grabbed the glass carafe off the coffee brewer. "And your preferred beverage."

"Sounds delicious, thank you."

"Don't thank me yet…"

Jake stood across at the counter, her dark lashes curled up, and he found it difficult to tear his gaze away. Her eyes, the color of golden topaz with flecks of amethyst, shining like precious gemstones. Her stare burrowed into him.

"I'm glad we're alone, so we can talk," Maddie said in an inviting tone.

He took a large gulp of coffee. Jumping off a balcony into Lake Chiemsee seemed like nothing compared to plunging into a serious conversation with Maddie.

"Yeah, sure." Jake scooped the eggs with a serving spoon and plopped half the portion onto her plate. He pierced a sausage with a fork, placed it beside her food and poured two cups of coffee. "The cream and sugar are here." He pointed toward the center of the counter and served himself the other portions. He sat on the opposite side of the island.

"Everything looks great," she said.

"You know, looks are deceiving?"

Maddie flaunted a small smile before taking a bite. His eyes fixed on her mouth and the lips he kissed only hours ago. Jake inhaled deep and lost the nerve to initiate the conversation. He shoved in a mouthful of grub.

"This is good." She held up a piece of sausage skewered on her fork.

"You should try the coffee cake."

"I'll be honest." Her pause signaled him to give her full attention. He wanted to finish eating and allow his stomach to settle prior to any difficult discussions. When he tilted his head upward, their eyes locked.

"I thought you were one of those thrill seekers, you know, trying to defy your own mortality." A sheepish grin curled her lips.

"Now what do you think?" Why did he ask her that question? Her honest reply wasn't as unsettling as what he hoped she'd say. If she answered with positive remarks, he'd continue his internal battle with confessing and sending her home.

"I believe you live an adventuresome life and found a balance with your responsibilities through faith."

Jake liked that she interpreted his experiences as adventurous. If she only knew the reality of his life; nine months out of the year spent in classrooms teaching and the remaining three helping Mom in the small village of Ruhpolding. "Yep, tons of adventure. Things were super exciting in the barn this morning."

"I'm serious, I was wrong about you. I've appreciated your help and everything you've done."

The sincerity of her words surged heat through his body. He'd be a true disappointment to her now. "It's just sausage and eggs." Jake shrugged a careless shoulder.

Maddie slanted her head to one side. "Anyway, thank you." Her eyes peered over the rim of the mug as she sipped her coffee.

What was it about her? She called him out on everything. He expected a certain level of astuteness in analyzing relationships, yet there was something more. One thing for sure, he would contemplate the many ways Madelyn Brighton mystified him for a long time.

"What's our next move?" Her face shined with excitement. "When do we deliver Mozart's music to the museum?"

"Ah…"

"Grüß Gott," a voice called out from the dining area.

"What the—" Jake dropped his fork on his plate. He jetted his hand forward, knocking half his drink on the table.

Maddie jumped from her stool. "Who is it?"

Jake grabbed a wad of paper towels and cleaned the spilled coffee. Maddie glanced around as if searching for answers. He tossed the saturated cloth into the trash and headed for the dining room. Maddie followed close behind.

Jake pushed through the kitchen door. "Leon," he uttered under his breath.

"Ah, there you are," Leon said in a flat tone.

"What are you doing here?"

"Is that any way to greet and welcome a guest into your family's inn? I'm sure your mutter would disapprove." Leon stepped closer, his eyes shifting to Maddie.

"Well, you're not a guest." Jake clenched his jaw.

"I thought your Christian upbringing taught you better manners—"

"What can we help you with today, Leon?" Maddie stepped forward. The fabric from her dress slipped through his fingers as he tried to pull her backward.

Leon reached out and lifted the back of her hand to his lips. "Nice to see you again."

She tugged her hand from his grip.

"Like she said, why are you here?" Jake said.

Leon flashed an icy glare capable of freezing the tundra, then returned his attention toward Maddie. "I admire how you're embracing the traditional dress of my country."

She pressed her palms against her waist and lowered her chin. "Yes, well, I didn't have any other options available. My clothes were wet, covered in mud and torn. Jake's mother was gracious enough to provide the outfit."

"Ja, I took the liberty und ordered your belongings from my hotel, they should arrive sometime later today."

A nausea rumbled in the pit of his stomach. Jake sensed earlier Leon knew Maddie received Mozart's music and his actions confirmed it. He should've expected a rash reaction after they escaped from Schloss Von Füssen. Leon made bolder moves, taking them to his residence and now strolling straight into the inn without so much as ringing the bell. Jake hoped to avoid a reckless and unpredictable Leon—he seemed insistently arrogant, beyond usual.

"How considerate, after you held us hostage." Maddie lifted her shoulders and chin with a defensive stance.

Jake encountered her bearing the same position on a few occasions, but he didn't like her challenging Leon, and his unpredictable reactions. Jake stood close enough to feel the brush of her arm.

"Meine Liebling, hostage? I simply invited you into my home, und offered you the luxuries of royalty. If you'd stayed with me, I would've provided you with an entire new wardrobe." Leon hesitated with a slight smirk, as his eyes feasted on and devoured Maddie. "Nevertheless, you fled unexpectedly, leaving me very displeased."

"How do you expect me to respond?" She crossed her arms over her chest.

"An apology would've sufficed, but you failed to keep our rendezvous. I suggest you meet me this evening und we'll discuss things, alone."

"As I mentioned earlier at your home, I'm sure you'd find my conversation dull and I lack the sophistication of your artistic taste."

"Come, don't be modest. I'm certain others have shown interest in you." Leon rolled his eyes toward him with a hard stare.

"That's enough of your games," Jake said.

"I'm under the impression that our real competition has now begun." Leon raised a deliberate eyebrow. His gaze focused on Maddie. "Now, if you would be so kind as to indulge me with the pleasure of your company. In addition to our business matters, I'd enjoy learning about the prose you write."

Maddie dropped her arms with a slack posture. "How did you—"

"Please, don't be embarrassed. You possess a natural talent."

"I haven't written since my college years." Her tone softened and a rose tint deepened the color of her cheeks. What on earth were they talking about? Heat billowed under Jake's collar. Maddie wouldn't give into Leon's attempts at smooth talking or coercion. She was too smart, determined and level-headed to fall for cheap flattery.

"Perhaps you need the right inspiration. Shall we plan on six o'clock, at Hotel Luxur? I'm in the private suite, on the top floor."

She opened her mouth, but Jake positioned himself in front of her and said, "You must be joking."

"On the contrary, I've exemplified patience." He glowered and faced Maddie. "I'll anticipate your arrival at six." Leon turned to leave. "Pity I missed your mutter, Jake. Please give her my regards," he said over his shoulder and exited the room.

Leon's orders and behavior were the reason Maddie needed to depart Ruhpolding as soon as possible. He despised watching Leon toy with her. "Can you believe that guy?" Jake threw his hands upward in the air. "I mean, the nerve of him coming into my family's house."

"Don't let him get to you." Maddie placed her hand on his arm and an electrical jolt surged inside.

"I know, but he's ordering us around and demanding you to meet him alone at his hotel…"

Jake slumped into a chair, resting his elbows on his knees. What did Leon hope to gain? Leon's intimidations wouldn't sway her decision, he had to realize that when she ran from his estate. Her silence unnerved him, and he jerked his head up. She rested her chin on a fist and stared off to the other side of the room.

"Don't tell me you're thinking of going?"

"No…" She sat in the closest chair, took a deep breath and exhaled with a small cough.

"But, isn't there a compromise—"

"You heard him, he believes the music is his rightful property, and he'll display it in his private collection."

"Maybe if somebody listened, making an effort to understand him and try reaching an agreement."

"That someone means you?" He puffed out his cheeks and shook his head. "Forget it, you're not getting further involved, besides Leon requires more than family counseling."

Maddie pinched her lips together. "Whether or not you like it, I'm connected—"

"It's not safe, and you can't trust Leon." Jake crept into treacherous territory delivering his opinion as fact. He needed to tread carefully; he'd already witnessed her disdain for being advised on how to proceed in any situation.

"I don't think he's dangerous."

His body tensed, her words a powerful blow to the gut. "What led you to that conclusion? Was it before or after Leon took us against our will?"

"It was something I noticed when he spoke, a glimmer in his eyes, and a softening demeanor."

Nausea rolled inside his stomach and he swallowed the lump in his throat. Did lack of sleep muddle her senses to believe Leon had an ounce of decency?

"You were looking into his eyes?"

"I wasn't staring at him like that." She glided her palm over his forearm. "Besides, you were the one praying for him last night."

Jake hopped from his seat, moving out of reach. "So, you think you can trust him because he discovered poems you'd written in the past? That's another thing, don't you find it strange Leon went out of his way to gather that information?"

"I didn't say he's trustworthy and I'm sure he researched me online."

"His investigations go beyond a basic search on the internet."

She sighed with exaggeration. "I'm trying to help."

Why would she want to assist Leon after everything that happened? Didn't she consider he might've had something to do with Sam's death? His stomach twisted in knots, a feeling all too familiar after what transpired between Dad and Leon.

Jake turned and stared straight ahead. "Who are you trying to help?" He glimpsed out the corner of his eye, aiming to avoid any response. "I'll let you know when we're ready to leave, I'm taking you back to Munich." He strode toward the hall.

The moment he dreaded since they met, pushing her away, for the sake of her safety. At least he'd try and convince himself he accomplished it with no harm being done.

"In case you forgot, I still have Mozart's music," she called out across the room.

Jake ignored her as he left the dining area and headed upstairs. He didn't want to see the displeasure in her eyes. He wanted to remember the look on her face when he held her in his arms. The way her lips still puckered, yearning for his kiss, after he stepped back. He'd never get that chance again.

Jake sat on the edge of his bed in prayer. He sought to let go of the anger he harbored for Dad's death. The pain over the circumstance that Henry seemed to depart earth too soon, lingered in his heart and mind. Dad didn't suffer from a long term, bedridden illness and it left Jake unprepared for his passing. Since Dad's spirit and ambitions were that of a youthful man at the time of his death, it filled Jake with a weighted disturbance.

Deep down, Jake recognized Leon wasn't the direct cause of Dad's death. Although Henry's persistence to finish the excavation and the hope to reconcile with Leon pushed his physical boundaries. Henry opted to take on the work of several men in Domgasse, Vienna. He directed a team of eight men, documented progress in a daily journal, managed field members, plus dealt with the public relations for Grobt Holding Company and Mozart's Museum. Jake blamed himself for not taking on more work and delegating the extra jobs to others in the group. Too many personal agendas impeded business and Leon's determinations left no one to trust. If Jake arrived earlier in Domgasse, before things spiraled out of control with the employees, perhaps Dad…

Henry began working at five in the morning the day he died. In the cold January air, relentless with his work until the instantaneous massive heart attack brought his work to a finale around seven in the evening. In the passing of seconds, he perished. Jake wasn't even in the room, and Dad dropped to the ground with no chance of survival. Jake worked in another location on the job site all afternoon and hadn't seen Dad for hours. Hopelessness ensued as the paramedics arrived—the medics were unsuccessful in reviving him and calling Mom with the terrible news resulted in the worst day of his life. He wanted to go home and comfort Mom in her grief, yet Jake struggled with the decision to either continue the work or to curse the entire assignment and walk away.

The conviction to complete Dad's efforts outweighed his sorrow. When he finished authenticating Mozart's sheet music, he gained a little peace that the team earned a chance to accomplish the job. Jake would never allow Leon to steal Dad's final project and render his death meaningless, even if it meant personal sacrifice. Jake prayed.

"Father, you know my pain, guilt and anger that burdens me. Please heal me of my inflictions…"

CHAPTER SIXTEEN

Peering out the window of her guest room, Madelyn rested her head, heavy with thoughts of Jake, against the windowsill. She acted foolish from the second she arrived in Munich. The story of her life, wishing to go back and say or do something different. She messed up Sam's last wishes and if any hope existed for letting go of the past, she needed to fix things with Jake.

He must loathe her, judging by his evasive eyes and how quickly he offered to drive her to Munich. A sigh escaped her lips. Thankfully, she didn't mention the kiss they shared.

The memories of Jake Nolan would remain a short prose in her mind, once upon a time in Ruhpolding… She wouldn't dare risk her heart. Last night she believed if she handed him the composition, he'd still accompany her to Salzburg and aid her mission of finding peace and forgetting Sam. She sighed with the possibility of relinquishing the piece and demanding to stay.

Once Jake got Mozart's music, he would have what he wanted and send her away. Even if he concealed a mutual feeling, she doubted he would allow his emotions to change his course. A strong inkling that none of her words mattered forced her to cling to the music as if it were life or death.

Should she confront Jake and demand he take her with him to the Mozart Museum? He didn't have enough trust in her to deem she wouldn't betray him like Sam. A sickness stagnated in her stomach as she clutched at her waist. She needed to correct her mistake and make her intentions clear.

Madelyn opened the drawer of the nightstand and removed the aluminum canister containing the musical artifact. How did scribbles on paper by a composer cause so much chaos? Was there something extraordinary about the piece of music? Compelled to discover a hidden truth and shed light on any secret meanings in the coveted item, she slipped on her gloves and removed the delicate parchments. Without the ability to read music she searched for keywords and assistance in finding an answer. Her eyes roved over the title *Great Mass in Minor C* scrawled in the top corner of the first page and she traced her finger along the staff paper.

On the second page a handwritten Credo labeled the music sheet and on the third sheet Agnus Dei identified the rest of the composition. The bottom of the fourth page marked the date of 1783, next to Mozart's signature. An online hunt would give her information and a clue for why the stakes were so high for that artifact.

A quiver swept through her chest as she rolled the pages with careful precision and secured the papers in the slender tube. She hid the item at the back of the drawer. An adrenaline rush moved her body faster than her mind settled as she hurried downstairs. Last night she noticed a computer on a desk in the living room.

Madelyn tripped on the rug, entering through the double-wide sliding doors, and caught herself before she hit the floor. She glanced at the spot where she stood with Jake. A tingle rippled throughout her body as a vision of him flashed in her mind and she froze in the place he held her in his arms. She hoped the reminder wouldn't prompt a physical reaction and vowed to disregard any emotional effect, blaming it on fatigue. She inhaled and exhaled hard with a fast-paced stride toward the writing table.

Madelyn sat at the chestnut computer desk, facing the wall, on the opposite side from the piano. She slid the mouse around and the desktop screen illuminated. A search engine appeared, and she typed in the title with Mozart's name. She scrolled the responses on the topic, reviews, opinions, and papers written about lost and unfinished portions of Mozart's Great Mass. She rested her elbow on the desk with her hand cupped over her mouth. The results confirmed the music in her possession contained lost segments of the Credo and the undiscovered Agnus Dei.

Beyond the initial awe of the missing musical segments being recovered, another fascinating article captured her attention: *The Story Behind Mozart's Credo*, authored by Jake Nolan. She read details about the broken relationship between Mozart and his father Leopold.

Leopold beckoned Mozart to visit Salzburg. Mozart expected the half-written score would please him and, in a letter, he wrote a declaration: *"I made a promise in my heart of hearts and hope to be able to keep it. The score of half a mass, which is still lying here waiting to be finished, is the best proof that I really made the promise."*

Her eyes filled with tears when she read that Leopold and Mozart never reconciled. Mozart never returned to Salzburg, and the world assumed Mozart did not finish the Credo with Agnus Dei. An ache burned in her chest. Madelyn stared at the screen through a wet blur covering her vision. She allowed anger and bitterness toward Sam to hinder her chance to forgive.

Madelyn understood Jake's need for restoring the music to the proper place in Salzburg. Mozart promised his father the Credo in Salzburg, and Jake made a vow to his father that the composition would end up at Mozart's Museum.

Restoration of the musical arrangement in Salzburg would bring a sense of peace to Jake and a closure for Mozart and Leopold. Jake deserved the music even if it meant her returning to Munich today. In her heart, the music held nothing personal between her and Sam, only a mere symbol of reinstating Gretchen's faith in her husband and Madelyn's effort to close the painful chapters of her past. No agreement to fulfill a dying man's wishes or honorable act on Sam's behalf would heal her wounds. No external remedy existed for easing her sufferings and after hearing Svenja's story, the real healing needed to take place within her soul.

The truth about her own personal journey presented a clear decision, one she figured would benefit everyone, except Leon. Was it possible to convince Leon the artifact belonged in Salzburg? It didn't matter, she wouldn't meet Leon at his hotel and soon Jake would have the music. If only…

"I was looking for you." Jake stood in the doorway and rocked back onto his heels.

Madelyn jolted in her seat, swiped the tears from under her eyes and clicked her index finger on the mouse, closing the internet pages.

She twisted her body. "I, um—" She swallowed the dryness in her throat. "Good timing, we need to talk."

Jake shoved his hands into his front pockets. "What's going on?"

"I can't leave right now." Not the best choice of words. Madelyn opened her mouth, but nothing came out. *Go on, tell him about the research and the decision to give him Mozart's finished Credo.*

"Yeah, the plans are delayed. Kate loaned the car to Svenja until tomorrow and the trains are on strike." Stepping closer, he rubbed a finger against his chin. "How did you know about the transportation issue?"

Madelyn trembled with a hyperawareness of the closing gap between them. "I didn't, I…" All the things she intended to say swelled and stuck in her mouth.

"Then why did you say you can't leave?" His face brightened in the light and his tone evoked a longing as if he hoped to hear she desired to stay with him.

Positive she misinterpreted his question she bit the inside of her lower lip. "I wanted to explain—" Swept into his stormy blue eyes she lost her nerve while staring into the center of the hurricane. Once she surrendered the music to Jake, she'd never see him again. Her breath hitched, and she ripped her gaze away. "Ah, my clothes are at the cleaners."

"Right." He scratched his head. "We can pick them up in town. But let's not forget Leon's selfless act of having your belongings delivered later today." He pivoted his body.

"Jake."

He halted, stiffened his torso and squared his shoulders. "Huh?"

"I'd never offer Leon the music."

Jake spun. His lips slanted up on one side. "I'm confident you'd never be able to."

*　*　*

A cool wind rustled the umbrella covers for the tables outside the cafés in downtown Ruhpolding. "Kerr Café makes the best creampuffs." Leon consumed a mouthful as they exited the café. "Wouldn't you agree?"

"If you say so, Herr." Mason stared ahead.

"I'm feeling exuberant today." Leon sat at a table under a navy-and-white striped umbrella. "You want to know why?"

Mason settled into the adjacent seat. "Ja." His expression remained stoic to uphold his image of obedience and manly brute. Leon appreciated the harsh demeanor on most occasions unless his mood demanded an enthusiastic response.

"Madelyn Brighton."

"You're excited over a woman?" Mason glanced out the corner of his eye.

"Not in the way you're suggesting. Don't be crude."

"Herr, I only implied—"

"She's softening toward me und with proper persuasions she may succumb to my request sooner than I thought." His lungs expanded to their fullest with a deep, satisfied breath.

"What about Jake Nolan's influence on her?"

Leon eased backward into a wrought-iron chair, folding his hands. "Ja, it is imperative she meet with me alone at the suite tonight."

Mason held a fist to his mouth to suppress a cough. "I agree—"

"You think Madelyn will listen to Jake?"

"She left Schloss Von Füssen with him in the middle of the night. How will you ensure she'll accept your invitation?"

"I'll make her an offer she can't refuse." He leaned in close and spoke in a lowered voice. "My knowledge of her written prose impressed her. I told you the information would give me the upper hand."

"Ja, Herr, I see." Mason continued to avoid eye contact and maintained the same manner.

He observed him grow from a child to a man and Leon surmised Mason understood all too well.

Leon stood from the table. "Here"—he shoved his half-eaten creampuff into Mason's hands—"have a Windbeutel."

Mason cracked a small smile. He amused Leon, but he remained poised. Was his fascination with Madelyn obvious? Leon treaded on new ground and the unfamiliar territory made him uneasy. After Leyna, he proclaimed any viable women in his life remain dispensable. Being a man with money, honorable reputation and an inexhaustible taste for the finer things in living, he secured access to Frauen whenever he desired.

His intrigue with Madelyn both bemused and disturbed his nerves. Leon attempted to justify his curiosity as strictly being motivated by gaining Mozart's music. Why would he place himself in the same quandary as Jake? He'd prefer to use Madelyn as the needed distraction to cause Jake to lose. He only hoped Madelyn would be the source of Jake's downfall instead of his own undoing.

* * *

Sunbeams sifted through patchy gray clouds rolling over the bright-blue sky. White daisies sprung from flowerboxes lining the windows, filling the area with a floral fragrance. The scent of berries, citrus and a hint of mint from freshly baked pastries drifted in the air. Madelyn pulled a beige trench coat Kate loaned her tighter over the Dirndl dress.

"Are you cold?" Jake asked.

"No, I wanted to wear my own clothes before visiting the town." She huffed and blew a few strands of hair from her face.

"Too bad it's not Oktoberfest, I would've worn my Bundhosen."

Madelyn pressed her lips together with the image of Jake wearing traditional Bavarian garb. "How unfortunate October is months away and after today we'll never see each other again." Her eyes darted toward a shop window. What a dummy, making that comment aloud. The remark displayed a blatant yearning for continual communications, after he clarified wanting her gone and out of his life.

Jake wrapped his fingers around her hand. A heat bubbled below the surface of her skin. "Allow me to buy you a coffee." He guided her to a set of outdoor tables on the corner of the pedestrian path. "Kerr Café has the best pastries too."

"Please order for me and I'll grab us a table."

"All right." Jake strolled inside the café.

She sat at an umbrella-covered patio dinette and closed her eyes for a moment. In a few minutes she'd surrender Mozart's music to Jake and their brief partnership would cease. Madelyn fooled herself into a fantasy, ignoring the advice she offered women at the center and warnings of acting on initial feelings rather than depending on rational thinking.

"I did not expect the pleasure of seeing you so soon."

Madelyn's eyelids flashed open and her body jerked at the sound of the man's voice. She glanced up, and raised a hand above her brow, shielding the sun. Leon stood with perfect posture, and his hands clasped in front of his pressed Kiton suit.

"Pardon the intrusion," Leon said.

"Um, you're not intruding. Jake is inside Kerr Café ordering coffee."

"To be frank, I have no interest in conversing with Jake. I've found good fortune in finding you alone."

Leon's steely gray eyes fixed on hers. A prickle sensation raised the hairs on the back of her neck, and she swallowed hard. "Then I hope I don't disappoint you."

His lips slightly curved up at the corners. "I'm so glad you're willing to oblige me. Madelyn—" He pulled a chair out and gestured with a nod for permission to sit. "May I address you by your first name?"

His ashen complexion now reflected a soft candlelight glow. The structure of his face almost seemed to change, with a faint smile lifting his chiseled cheekbones, and illuminating his ageless skin. Leon defied aging, no laugh lines and no wrinkles encircling his eyes. She assumed years of being expressionless gave him the look of a youthful man. Did the loss of his parents create a joyless existence? His face lacked a detailed map of the discovered treasures on his journey through life. All the money and successes he obtained wouldn't fill the void of an absent family. Each encounter she had with Leon deepened her empathy for his griefs.

"Have a seat, and as you said, I've been a *guest* in your home." She emphasized the word guest. "I'm sure we're on a first name basis now."

"Indeed, we are." He tossed his blond locks back. "I'll be quick. I presume you've taken time to consider my earlier invitation?"

Madelyn held her breath for a moment. Leon presented an opportunity for her to decline his offer. "Yes, and I regret that I can't meet you at your hotel tonight."

She stiffened, his eyes a silvery scrutiny that poured over her like liquid steel. She tucked her hands under the table, hiding her trembling fingers. He tilted his neck back and flicked his gaze upward. "I confess, you've put me in an unfortunate position of having to disclose my unsettling news."

Madelyn suspected Leon would try and manipulate the situation to his advantage. It didn't matter; she planned on giving Jake Mozart's music and it would finish her usefulness. Leon wouldn't bother with his pursuit of her once she surrendered possession of Mozart's Credo to Jake.

"What is this difficult information that troubles you?"

"My sources have revealed the man behind my betrayal, the same people responsible for Samuel Healy's death, are under the impression his wife, Gretchen, acquired my artifact."

A sudden coldness hit her core with the real dangers Jake cautioned her about. "So, it's true? They killed Sam?" She pressed her palm to her throat to control the shakiness in her voice.

"Ja, you see my dilemma? I'd like to help—"

"Leon, there are children to think of and this person already committed one murder. I…"

Madelyn searched in a panic. Where was Jake when she needed him? He promised to keep her safe. She had doubts about Leon's information and his integrity, but she couldn't risk the safety of Alarick and Rainor, not when she was in a position to protect Sam's family.

In a frantic state of mind, she turned toward Leon. "Please, if there's anything you can do to save them—"

"Now, now, Schatzi." He rested his hand on her arm. Her body tensed under his touch and he gently squeezed then patted her forearm. "I will settle the matter. After all, he only wants money und I have plenty."

Her heart thumped in her chest, the sound thundering in her ears. If she enlisted Leon to protect Gretchen and the boys, he would ask for something in return for his aid. He'd want to bargain for Mozart's Great Mass, and she'd have to give in to Leon's demands.

"Don't worry, I'll take care of everything und we'll discuss the details when you visit me tonight." He leaned close, his cool caress brushing strands of hair from her face as his fingers trailed along her jawline. "Best if we keep this between the two of us. Very high stakes involved—we don't want to tip off those working with this deplorable criminal."

Madelyn gulped air to keep her breathing calm and nodded in agreement. "I'll be there."

"Splendid, I look forward to seeing you." He stood from the table. "Pfüad Di." One side of his mouth tugged up at the corner.

She stared through a wet film as Leon strolled around the block. Talk about things taking a turn for the worse. Following Leon's directions required her lying to Jake. She ingested the sickness rising in the back of her throat. Everything she planned collapsed in an instant and was now left in the hands of Leon, to do as he pleased.

"Here we are." Jake set two glass goblets on the table and sat in the seat beside her.

"German coffee with cream on top and you gotta try the strudel."

Madelyn forced a half smile while fixing her eyes on the ground. "Thanks."

He angled his head toward her face. "What's wrong?"

"Nothing." Her tone dithered. Madelyn latched onto the goblet and sipped her coffee. She sensed Jake's vision following her movements. Every cell in her body wanted to climb into his arms and tell him what transpired with Leon. The dream of creating a meaningful relationship with Jake would never happen, now or ever, and shattered in a blink of an eye. He would despise her for betraying him.

"Sorry about before." He took a bite. "You're right, I shouldn't let Leon get to me. I care about you and I'm trying to watch out for your wellbeing." Jake licked a piece of sticky strudel from his thumb. "At least while you're here and my responsibility."

She tugged at her earlobe. He said he cared and yet in that instance of declaration, he rendered it void by clarifying the temporary obligation. A tightness swelled in her throat. Madelyn had no right to expect anything from Jake. He made no affirmations of feelings for her other than compassion for a fellow human being.

"I know, things happened so fast." Her voice cracked. If she intended on deceiving Jake it required better acting skills to succeed. She wanted to throw up and now had no way out. She was trapped.

"Will you do me a favor"—he slid his arm around her back—"and have supper with me this evening?"

Her belly gurgled as she drank her coffee and debated whether to tell Jake about Leon's quick visit to the table along with her new predicament. If she rejected Jake, he'd be suspicious.

"I'd enjoy dinner with you." She glanced at him and the genuine smile on his face caused her to crumble inside.

"We'll pick up your clothes at the cleaners then go back to the inn. Should we say around six?"

"Sounds good."

"At least you're not considering the alternative and meeting with Leon."

Madelyn sucked in a breath and her heart resounded, echoing in her ears with the sound of racing hooves. Did Jake see them conversing?

She exhaled and sat at the edge of her seat. "You made a valid point this morning."

"I hope so, because he only wishes to create trouble, and if needed, inflict harm to get what he wants."

There'd be no opportunity for turning back and she'd pay the price of making a deal with Leon. "I understand."

Jake raised his goblet. "Prost," he said, with a slight wink. "To new friends."

She lifted her glass. "Prost."

CHAPTER SEVENTEEN

The sun dipped into the horizon, striking shadows across the walls, her heart sinking with the weight of hiding the truth from Jake. Madelyn glanced at the small digital clock on the nightstand. The glowing numbers taunted her as six o'clock ticked closer. Out of time and choices. Leon expected her at his hotel the same hour she agreed to dine with Jake. What options did she have, but agree to help Gretchen and the boys? She fanned her sticky palms in the air as she dressed and contemplated meeting Jake downstairs for dinner.

At least her suitcase arrived as Leon promised and now, she'd be comfortable in her regular clothes again. She counted on Leon keeping his word to protect the Healy family, especially at the cost of a friendship with Jake. Slipping the container with Mozart's Great Mass inside her coat pocket, she prepared for her first decision, meeting Leon at Hotel Luxur. The current plan involved leaving before her date with Jake and standing him up.

Exiting the guestroom, she sucked in several breaths with an inability of filling her lungs. She twisted her gloves in her hands and peered down at the top of the stairs. Jake stared up at her from the entry, his thumbs hooked in the front belt loops of his jeans. She winced as her conscience creaked with each step down the wooden staircase. She'd resort to her second plan and excuse herself from dinner because of a sudden onset of illness, although at this point it wouldn't be a lie. Her internal temperature spiked, and she felt the break of a cool perspiration on her nape.

Madelyn swallowed several times to loosen the knot in her throat and ran her palm along the polished railing to gain stability as her knees wobbled.

"Ready to go?" he asked.

"Yes, now that I'm back in my own clothes."

"You're beautiful no matter what you wear." His face brightened, standing under the candescent ceiling lights.

An inward tug in her heart revealed that at any minute she would cave and all she hid inside would collapse, suffocating her under the pressure of deceit.

"Everything okay?"

Madelyn lowered her gaze, picking lint from her coat and nodded. Things would be a lot easier if he didn't stare in a way that invaded the alcoves in her mind, crushing her under the tides of his ocean-blue eyes.

"Let's forget the madness of the last two days and enjoy a nice dinner together, all right?"

"Sure." She kept her sights focused forward as Jake opened the door.

After their short walk into Ruhpolding village, they arrived on time for their six o'clock reservation at the restaurant, Stassenburgs. Jake excused himself with a twist and turn of his shoulders, parting a path to follow through the crowd of people waiting under a stucco overhang outside the double glass doors.

"This is a popular place."

"Yeah, and the owner is a friend." Jake tapped a round, brawny man on the shoulder. "Hello, Felix."

The proprietor spun around. "Jake! Where have you been?" Felix opened his bulbous arms and squeezed Jake until he murmured with a slight gasp for air. "Sorry, I forget my strength."

He released Jake and flexed his bicep muscles. "Not only filled with flab."

"Yes, it's been a while and business looks good as usual."

"Ja und I see you're doing very well." Felix directed his extended handshake toward Madelyn and bumped Jake aside. "Who is your guest?"

"My friend, Madelyn Brighton."

"Nice to meet you."

"The pleasure is all mine." Felix shook her hand. "Jake hasn't brought in a lady friend in over a year."

Jake coughed and knocked his elbow into Felix's ribs. His eyes skimmed the full maximum-capacity dining room.

Inhaling the intoxicating aroma of robust wines, heat warmed her cheeks and a fluttering swirled in her belly. Her body reacted to the news of hearing Jake hadn't been on a date in a while. Madelyn glanced at him and hoped the physical response had gone unseen.

"Yeah, well, work is demanding." Jake combed his fingers through his hair. "So, do you have a dinette available?"

"Ja, your usual table." Felix guided them through a maze of rectangular, lacquered wood tables toward the back corner of the dining area. "I'll pull up an extra chair."

"What can I say, Felix? Your level of accommodating me above and beyond dining solo is incomprehensible. Stellar service, seating two people as opposed to one."

Felix rumbled with a hearty laugh from his belly. "I missed you, Jake."

"Good to see you too." Jake placed a hand on his upper arm.

Felix pulled out a cushioned, upholstered chair for Madelyn and offered to take her coat. Her muscles tensed and she clutched the coat in her hands. The Mozart artifact, hidden in her pocket, represented more than a lost piece of music, more than a paralleled story to restore a parent and child relationship, it was a payment to save lives. Her eyes flitted between Jake and Felix; both their faces crinkled with confusion by her response.

"No thank you, I feel a slight chill." She released her grip, draping the coat on the back of her chair. She smoothed the wrinkled rayon fabric of her blouse and settled into her seat.

Felix handed them a list of options. "Enjoy your meal."

"Thanks," Jake said.

Madelyn nodded and smiled. "He's a fun guy." Her eyes fixated on the propped-up menu on the edge of the table.

"Felix's a kind and honest man."

"He seems to think highly of you too."

"Yeah, but right now I'm interested in your opinion of me." Jake peered over the top of the drink selections.

She shrank into the seat, hiding behind the 'specials' and wishing he wouldn't bait her. Even without words, she was in jeopardy of risking her heart and falling for him. The torture of longing to express her admiration for him and withholding information filled her with a queasy sensation.

Madelyn shifted in the chair as Jake kept his eyes locked on her. A waitress came to the rescue, setting a glass bottle of sparkling water on the table, and asked for their order. "Was darfs sein?"

The woman repeated the question twice before Jake responded. He asked Madelyn, "What would you like?"

Madelyn glanced at everything written in German and looked at Jake. "Any suggestions?"

He flipped through the choices and ordered. "Zwei mal Schwäbische Käsespatzle bitte."

"Is that an authentic German cuisine?"

Jake cocked his head and flicked a hand upward. "It's like mac and cheese."

"Sounds perfect."

"Danke." The waitress collected their menus and left. Madelyn now had to face Jake without the safety of hiding behind items. She slid the fan-shaped, cloth napkin off the table and laid it across her lap, twisting the edge around her finger.

"You seem a little preoccupied."

"I do?" Perspiration broke on her hairline and she wriggled in her chair under the heavy weight of his gaze. She twitched as dishes clanged in the kitchen nearby, taunting every anxious feeling that encumbered her mood.

"Yeah. Is something bothering you?"

"No. I'm fine." She twirled her napkin tighter. "Maybe a bit distracted with my thoughts…"

"What are you thinking about?" He slanted his head, arching an eyebrow, and outstretched his arms around the back of his chair. "Or should I ask whom are you thinking about?"

Her heart sank and lodged into the pit of her stomach. Madelyn wrestled with the possibility Jake knew Leon spoke with her earlier at the café. Did she have a defense for why she kept everything a secret?

"Why question if someone's on my mind?" She hated herself for asking a loaded question. Jake presented her with an easy resolve to abandon her secrecy, and she still held things close to her chest. She couldn't allow herself to risk the safety of Sam's family, not even for Jake Nolan.

"I don't know." His voice dropped as he lowered his sight to the candle in the center of the table. The look on his face, yearned for her to confess she thought of him. Or perhaps he worried she'd name him and create a big melodrama. She wanted to admit she dwelled on him but refrained while in the middle of double crossing him.

Jake already forgave her for keeping one secret—she doubted he'd pardon her for a second offense. How long would he accept her quietness before pressing for an answer? The server brought their plates and spared Madelyn from giving false excuses for a moment.

She stared at her plate, picking out caramelized onions with her fork, hidden in layers of egg noodles. Better focus on anything to avoid eye contact and work on a plausible reason for leaving. The seconds passing felt like minutes evolving into an eternity of silence.

"Is it something Leon said to you?" Jake's eyes searched her mannerisms.

"Huh?" She shoveled noodles into her mouth. Her eyes darted from the candle, to the framed watercolor painting of the Alps hanging on the wall and back toward her dinner plate.

Jake reached forward across the table, his fingertips grazing her knuckles. "You can tell me anything."

Madelyn attempted to ingest the gobs of cheese stuck in her throat; she choked and grabbed her glass, chugging water down. She gasped for air, triggering a hacking fit.

Jake jumped from his chair. "Are you okay?"

Her sporadic coughing allowed her a second to reply. "Yes. Please, excuse me." Madelyn hopped up, yanking her coat from the chair and hurried down a flight of stairs toward the lavatories. She pushed open the door labeled *Madln*. As she rounded the tight corner, she almost crashed into a young woman engaged with her phone.

Madelyn used her basic language skills and asked for the time. "Wie viel Uhr ist es?"

The girl glanced up from her device. "A quarter to seven." She stepped forward and Madelyn blocked her path.

"May I please use your phone? It's an emergency." She hoped her act of desperation crossed cultural barriers.

"Ja, sure." She gave it to Madelyn.

"Vielen Dank." Madelyn leaned back against the cold tile wall. Her fingers trembled as she swiped the touchscreen and searched for Leon's hotel. She tapped the contact information and waited for an answer.

"Guten Abend, Hotel Luxur."

"Sprechen Sie Englisch?" Madelyn said to the concierge on the other line.

"How may I assist you?"

"Please ring Herrn Von Füssen's room."

"One moment, bitte."

Madelyn prayed, while the phone rang, that Leon wasn't angry. Her breathing became erratic whenever she encountered Leon and her throat constricted while she expected his reaction.

"Von Füssen—"

"Leon?"

"You're late, where are you?"

Madelyn swallowed hard. "I'm sorry, but I can't get away."

"You disappoint me again," he said, in a curt tone.

"I tried, honestly—"

"Na freilich!"

Her body quaked, and a chill rushed through her veins despite the hotness spreading from her ears to her face.

"May I ask what took precedence over our rendezvous?"

"I'm in town having dinner and wanted to keep our meeting discreet." Madelyn stared with pleading eyes at the woman waiting and mouthed, "Sorry."

Leon seethed with heavy breathing. "Discretion is of the utmost importance und I will tell you what to do now." Her nerves tightened with every accentuation of his words. Leon continued with his instructions. "You'll meet me tomorrow at five o'clock sharp with no delays, and no excuses. I expect your arrival with my item in hand, wearing a pretty smile filled with gratitude for what I've done for you und Samuel Healy's family. Do you understand how imperative it is for you to follow my directions?"

"Yes."

"You will be here tomorrow," Leon demanded.

"Tomo—"

Leon hung up before she responded. Madelyn handed the phone back to the woman.

"Thank you, I appreciate it." Madelyn's shoulders drooped with relief.

She smiled and said good luck. "Viel glück."

At the top of the stairs, Madelyn straightened the hem of her shirt, and gathered composure before returning to meet Jake. He already expressed his concerns and suspicions about her behavior.

She inhaled a deep calming breath. Leon gave her extra time and for now Sam's family would be safe.

"Sorry about that." She sat in her seat.

Jake visually searched her face with a wrinkled brow. "Are you sure you're all right?"

She waved a dismissive hand. "I'm fine." Why did he have to look so distraught? She wasn't a good liar, and deception seemed difficult with Jake. If only there were another way… She faltered and suppressed her sob by guzzling the rest of the water in her glass.

"I paid the bill, figuring you'd want to go back to the inn." The defeat in his tone tore into her heart, shattering the dream of them ever being more than passing acquaintances.

"Thanks for dinner. I know I wasn't the greatest company tonight."

Jake leaned, pressing his chest against the table, his irises flickering in the candlelight. "If there is anything you need, count on me." He reached out, coiling his fingers around her hand. "I'm here for you." His eyes smoldered with a low blue flame.

A gush of warmth flooded her body. She needed to remain tough and not weaken with his heartfelt expressions, but she collapsed under the weight of his words. Which was worse, obeying Leon's commands or denying the demands of her heart? She pressed her hand against her chest.

"Jake, I wanted to tell you before—"

"How was your meal?" Felix sneaked up as quiet as a thief, stealing an irreplaceable moment.

Jake moved, his fingers trailing along her skin as he eased back into his chair. "Wonderful, as always."

"Can I get you a dessert or Kaffee?"

Madelyn slid her coat over her shoulders. "No, thank you."

"Thanks, Felix. We're all set." Jake stood and shook Felix's hand.

Madelyn got up and joined him around the table as he made his way toward the exit.

"Next time you come, save room for my famous Prinzregententorte." Felix escorted them out of the restaurant.

Madelyn shadowed him. "Thank you, goodnight."

"Guten Abend." Felix rested his arms on his large belly and smiled.

Jake said a friendly goodbye, "Servus."

The brisk night air left a tingle on the tip of her nose. Standing outside, the full moon cast a vibrant glow over Ruhpolding village. Madelyn stared at the sky, the stars sparkling diamonds, and she wished for a different ending to their story. Jake wrapped his arm around her back, and with the sensation of freefalling from dizzying heights, her stomach dropped. She longed for him to grab her into an embrace and press a firm kiss against her lips.

"I'll go call for a taxi."

With a sudden jerk she grabbed his arm. "Can we walk around the village?"

"I thought you'd want to get back to the inn."

Madelyn inhaled a deep cleansing breath and would try to make the night last if possible. "Something about tonight's air, I don't know, it enlivens me."

"You have livened up a bit."

"Sorry I ruined dinner."

"You didn't, I'm just concerned." Jake caressed her cheek with the back of his hand. She closed her eyes and savored the experience. He leaned closer and whispered near her neck, "You had me worried."

Madelyn held her breath and her eyes popped open, certain he noticed her peculiar actions. "Why?"

"I thought you never refuse coffee."

Madelyn exhaled aloud. It didn't matter if his words were playful, he could say anything while speaking in her ear. She turned, with their faces close, creating an intensity foraging her soul. She stepped backward, conscious of the fact she desired Jake to know every part of her being. The conflict of her secluded life and the rare occasion of opening up to someone hindered her now. Madelyn forgot how to be herself, always trying to fit into the mold she created of a self-reliant woman. Whenever she felt misunderstood, she became defensive, but she had a pang in the core of her existence that Jake understood. Her deficiency in intimacy seemed irrelevant, since he saw past her façade and accepted what was beyond. The realization comforted her, and yet frightened her. She linked her arm around his and he escorted her through the cobblestone streets.

The dimmed interior lights of the closed shops and the streetlamps guided their stroll round the quiet town. The only noises were from occasional soft chatter of passers and clacking shoes on the pedestrian walkway. Madelyn beamed, appreciating the time alone with Jake, and hung onto his arm, while resting her head against his bicep. Yes, she missed the feeling of holding someone close.

Blinding bright headlights flashed on at the end of the street, spotlighting the exact place they walked, casting them center stage. She froze, tightening her grip on Jake. He halted and lifted his hand above his brow, squinting while viewing the idling car.

"Do you think we have a problem?"

"Maybe. Keep walking." Jake redirected their steps and crossed the walkway to the next block over. They quickened their pace, turning down an alley. She crooked her neck, peeking over her shoulder to see if they were being pursued.

Blackness surrounded them as if night itself tracked them down. Madelyn pivoted toward the light. "We're probably overreacting," she said, in a breathless tone.

"We've taken enough chances."

The soft purr of a slow-moving vehicle nuzzled up behind Jake and Madelyn. She twirled, and a dark car, with no visible lights, stalked them like a panther. The engine growled, and she shuddered amid the vibrations. Jake grabbed her waist, pulling her closer, with his back alongside a wall and her breath left with a force as her body crashed into him.

He held her pressed against his chest. Tires screeched as the wheels of the car spun hard on the road and the vehicle zoomed away.

Jake stroked the length of her hair, settling the shakiness in her limbs. "You okay?"

"Yeah." Once again, she discovered refuge in his protective arms. He cuddled her a little tighter and she rested her head in the nook of his arm and chest, falling into a trance with the rhythm of his heartbeat.

"We should leave now," he muttered into her hair.

Madelyn nodded in agreement, yet her body refused to let go. Every time she ended up in his arms she wanted to stay. She despised the constraint of being tough all her life. The minutes in his embrace offered her hope in having a partner, someone caring for her needs, and not always staying the strong one.

"Is it safe?"

Jake released her from his grip and the once-inviting evening air in her face turned biting and harsh. If only he'd continue holding her close—not just in times of impending danger or emotional breakdowns. Night flaunted sincere cruelty, tempting romantic notions with an alluring moon while harboring fears in the black blanket of nocturnal hours and waiting to pounce on the unsuspecting.

Jake stared off toward the end of the street. "The car drove off," he said with his breath visible in the cold air. "Let's move. We'll get a ride home."

Madelyn hurried her steps to keep up with him. At the end of the alleyway they reached a major road. Jake paused and looked in both directions.

"Is there somewhere to make a call?" She shivered and rubbed her arms up and down her sleeves. The temperature wasn't too cold, but she couldn't shake the disconcerting events of the evening.

"I know where we can go."

CHAPTER EIGHTEEN

Rushing up the steep incline, Madelyn glanced over her shoulder again, ensuring the car abandoned pursuit. Her legs wobbled with the twitching of her muscles and an uneasy feeling they remained in jeopardy because of her deal with Leon. She shivered with the fluctuation of internal heat increasing with all the rapid movement and stress.

Approaching the top of the hill, the shadow of an onion shaped dome peaked above the trees. Of all the places to take her, he brought her to church. Her shoulders slumped with defeat, certain with all her secrets and lies, she'd burst into flames upon entry.

"Someone will be here at night?"

"Yes, Pastor Fredrick lives on site."

Entering the iron gates, a light shined in the front window of the cottage-style parsonage. They followed a slate stone path to the front door. Jake rang a large, rustic hanging bell and knocked on the door. He glanced and gave a quick reassuring nod. Her anxieties were as twisted as a Bavarian pretzel.

The brass peep-hatch opened. "Hello," the man answered with a British accent, only his eyes and forehead observable.

"Pastor Fredrick, it's Jake Nolan."

"Jake?" The door flung open, revealing a man of medium height and build, dressed in khaki slacks and a short-sleeved button-down shirt. Madelyn guessed his age as mid-fifties, and assumed he'd be wearing a clergy robe with an oversized gold cross dangling around his neck.

"Sorry to bother you—"

"Is everything all right?"

"At the moment, can we please come inside and use the phone?" Jake asked.

"Yes, you're always welcome." The pastor stepped aside. "Make yourselves comfortable."

"Pastor Fredrick, this is my friend Madelyn Brighton."

"Lovely to meet you." He closed the door behind them.

Spiced cinnamon and licorice scent filled the dimly lit room. Candles burned on top of a bookshelf in the corner of the living space—about the size of a standard small apartment.

"Thanks for welcoming us into your home."

"Please, have a seat." Pastor Fredrick offered the choice of a threadbare green sofa or a brown leather armchair. "I'll put on a kettle of tea."

"That would be nice, thank you." A quivering feeling consumed her, and a hot drink would soothe her tensions. Pastor Fredrick strolled into the kitchen.

Madelyn's life became a series of chase scenes. She no longer had one person to blame, with so many intersecting lives involved, including Wolfgang and Leopold Mozart lingering in her mind and factoring into the situation. Madelyn chewed the inside of her cheek and dawdled by the front door.

Jake extended an arm around her shoulder and guided her toward the couch. "Don't worry, if that was Leon in the car, you did nothing wrong." He crouched and eased her down onto the cushions. "He'd be an idiot to believe he had the power to demand a meeting tonight."

Madelyn tucked her chin downward and fixed her eyes on her lap. She needed to confess she agreed to meet with Leon, for the sake of protecting Sam's family. Would Jake presume she intended to deceive him from the beginning? Her words required accuracy to convince him she wanted him to achieve his goals and how she read the article he wrote on Mozart's Great Mass. On the verge of an emotional setback, she wished to mend things with Jake.

"I'm sorry, you tried to warn me—"

"None of this is your fault." He rubbed her back; his tender touch and words were more than she deserved.

"I hope you like chamomile." Pastor Fredrick cruised into the room, setting a tray on a two-tier trolley beside the couch.

"I do, thanks." Herbal tea helped her relax.

Jake stood from the sofa, placing his hand on her shoulder. "I'm going to call for a ride."

"Go straight into the kitchen." Pastor Fredrick instructed Jake and poured the drinks.

Madelyn glanced around the room. Bare, pale-yellow walls with a Celtic iron cross on the far wall. An eight-by-ten silver-framed photo of the pastor and a copper-haired woman sat on an end table. He handed her a ceramic mug.

"Any sweetener?"

"Plain is fine." She settled back into the worn cushions and blew on the hot tea. "You know, you're the second British man I've met in Germany over the past few days."

The pastor sat in the leather chair. "You're referring to Douglas?"

"Yes, I suppose he's part of the congregation?"

"Actually, he's my brother-in-law. I was married to his sister, Wynn, for thirty-five years. She passed away; it'll be three years this June…" His eyes locked onto the framed picture.

"Oh, I'm so sorry," Madelyn said.

"Thank you. God has helped me through the difficult time."

Madelyn nodded in agreement, although she never experienced God's comfort through tough times but prayed for the encounter.

"Do you know Jake from the University?" Pastor Fredrick sipped his tea.

"No, we met by chance a couple days ago."

Pastor Fredrick arched his brow. "How intriguing."

"Why do you find that intriguing?"

"What would you call it?"

"I'm not sure, it's complicated," she said, with a nervous laugh. "We happened to be connected through mutual interests, placing us together at the same location."

"Seems forces beyond circumstances brought you together."

"I arrived in Munich for my father's funeral service."

Madelyn figured Pastor Fredrick would say their meeting was by divine appointment. She wasn't in the mood for a theological chat and stared at her tea mug. Her presence in Germany appeared to cause problems for everyone. Gretchen and the boys' safety wouldn't be in jeopardy if she ignored Sam's request and relinquished Mozart's composition to the authorities. If she had delivered the item to Interpol, there was a strong chance the music would have ended up in Salzburg and without all the trouble she created for Jake.

"My condolences."

"Thanks." She drew in a deep breath. "We weren't close. I hoped attending his funeral would help me forget the past." Since when did she make candid remarks to strangers about her personal life?

"Did you forget?"

Heat radiated under her coat and she fidgeted on the sunken couch cushion. The conversation was reminiscent of the earlier discussion with Jake about letting go of her painful childhood. Why did she expect forgiveness when she hadn't extended the same to others? "I think I need to attempt forgiving my father before I can put the past behind me."

Despite finishing a full cup of tea, her mouth had gone dry.

"A prudent choice. If you surrender your resentment and ask God to change your heart, you'll find real peace. In the Bible it says love covers over all offenses," he said, in a gentle tone.

Her gaze darted from Pastor Fredrick toward the cross on the wall and she exhaled, feeling her spirit lightened. The time arrived to relinquish her anger and forgive Sam. Mom managed to absolve Sam's deceitfulness and abandonment.

"Taxi is on the way." Jake entered the room. "Ready to go?"

Madelyn dabbed tears in the corners of her eyes with the tips of her fingers. Jake stepped closer, and stood in front of her, squinting, with his head tilted to one side.

"Trust me, everything will be fine." He reached for her hand.

Madelyn gripped the end of the couch to keep from leaping into his arms. Heaven help her, she trusted him—enough to admit she collaborated with Leon and believe he'd understand. She slid her hand into the warmth of his palm and already felt a little at peace.

She gazed into his eyes. "I trust you."

Jake's lips crooked upward with a steady eye contact as she lost self-awareness in the dark abyss of his pupils. With a soft squeeze, he awakened her from a stupor and removed the mug from her grasp.

Jake turned and faced Pastor Fredrick. "Have a good rest of the evening. I appreciate your hospitality."

"I'm here to serve." Pastor Fredrick escorted them toward the front door.

"I enjoyed our chat over a cup of tea. Perhaps we'll continue our conversation sometime," she said.

"I'm available in the afternoons, if you'd like to stop by before you leave town."

"I'll try."

The taxi dropped them off at the inn around ten-thirty at night. The lights in the windows cast a soft glow, and they strolled into the entry. Madelyn glanced at Jake as he removed his brown bomber jacket and hung it in the coat closet.

"Do you think we can talk for a few minutes?" She crossed and uncrossed her arms, deciding to shove both hands in her pockets.

"Sure." He turned, rolling the sleeves of his gray shirt. "What a night, huh?"

Madelyn licked her dry lips. "Ah, I wanted to tell you earlier…" Her eyes flitted around the space. Why did she find it difficult to tell Jake the truth? He'd been honest and forthcoming with plenty to lose. She lacked the courage he embodied and proved with his morality.

"Let's have a seat in the living room."

She followed him, taking slow, deep breaths. The smell of soot billowed in the air. Jake halted as they stepped into the area. Kate sat in a chair under a floor lamp.

"You're still up?" Jake said.

"What happened? I heard you called and needed a taxi from Pastor Fredrick's place."

"Nothing to worry about, I'll tell you about it in the morning."

Kate removed her squared-framed eyeglasses, pressing her lips into a fine line. "If you say so, dear." She stood from the chair, a blanket in one hand, Bible in the other, and pecked Jake on the cheek on her way out. "Goodnight, you two." She rounded the corner down the hall on the first floor to her bedroom.

"She didn't sound convinced."

"Yeah well, I guess she has reasons to be suspicious." He raked his fingers through his hair. "Another day to be thankful we returned safely." A gusty breath escaped his lips as he plummeted onto the sofa, tossing his head back and closing his eyes.

Madelyn sat in the middle of the couch, leaving a cushion space between them. "Yes, and a good thing Pastor Fredrick was home."

His eyelids lifted with a raised brow and a side glance. "Seems like you had an interesting discussion with Pastor Fredrick." He straightened his posture and faced her.

"We did. He helped clear my thoughts on something that's been troubling me."

"I know what you mean." His gaze shot to the floor, ricocheting back to her. "Ever since we escaped from Leon's house…it's clear you've had concerns about trusting me"—he rubbed his nape— "and tonight when you said that you trust me, it meant a lot—"

"I'm glad because I think we can finally be open and truthful with each other." She hated interrupting, but she'd lose all her assurance about telling him if she didn't hurry and get the truth out.

"I'm thinking the same way. I know we got off to a rocky start with the mix up with the music and concealing our true intentions, but I think we can get everything out into the open."

Inhaling hard through her nostrils, she held her breath for a few seconds before exhaling.

"I agree." Madelyn gulped as his stare intensified. "I need to tell you—"

"Excuse me." Douglas walked into the room. "Jake, do you mind if I have an urgent word with you before you turn in for the night?"

"Sure, have a seat."

Douglas sat in the armchair by the sofa. "It's a bit of a private matter."

"I understand." Jake cleared his throat and his eyes searched her face. "Sorry, perhaps it's best if we finish our conversation tomorrow, after a good night's sleep."

Madelyn nodded. The opportunity to tell Jake about the negotiations with Leon slipped away and sickness swirled, rolling her stomach like a ride on a dilapidated carousel. How much longer did she expect to endure the pressure of Leon's demands while anticipating Jake's reaction to the truth?

Jake stood from the sofa, escorting her to the foot of the staircase. "I can walk you to your room." His eyes, a blazing shade of blue, sparking a flickering flame deep inside.

The offer to walk with her upstairs held the promise of another kiss. Every part of her existence longed for his lips, pressed against her mouth. She shivered with the realization that if she declined, she'd lose the last opportunity of him holding her in his arms, depending on his response to her confession. The more intimacy they shared, the harder the blow of deception would hit.

"It's all right, Douglas is waiting."

With a slack look on his face, he stepped backward. "Then, I'll see you in the morning."

Madelyn stood on the first step; he turned his head over his shoulder with a lingering stare before entering the den. The torment of having to go to bed still carrying her secret to wrestle within her sleep, along with the image of Jake in her mind, would keep her tossing and turning throughout the night.

* * *

Leon paced back and forth across the sitting room in his suite. Mason sat at the writing desk, with his head resting against his hand and heavy blinks.

"Am I keeping you up?" Leon said.

His eyes widened, and he shook his head. "I'm deep in thought about what we were discussing."

"Discussing? I believe I'm the only one talking."

"You're correct, I'm listening."

"I need to ensure Madelyn Brighton does not waver on account of Jake's supposed acts of righteousness. The last thing I'd want is for her to gather with his group of churchgoers, trying to lure her into a false hope of salvation." He fiddled with the sapphire and diamond, white-gold pinky ring—his family heirloom he'd present to the woman he intended to marry. "I need her to believe I'll protect her and Samuel's family above and beyond Jake's claims to guard her."

"Ja, that'll be a real challenge, since they seem to have developed a close relationship."

Leon shot a sharp look at Mason. "Perhaps if you hadn't literally run her into Jake's arms this evening then it wouldn't be a concern." Heat flushed through his body and his muscles quivered. He questioned Mason's loyalty. Mason wittingly made comments to negate his resolutions. Did he intend to support or provoke him?

"With humble respect, I think she already trusted Jake when she dined with him instead of keeping her meeting with you."

"Careful of your words. I don't keep you in my presence so I can subject myself to your off-point opinions."

"Herr, I only implied—"

"I know what you imply." He quite knew of the treachery women were capable of inflicting. After twenty years, Leyna's cut to his heart still gaped wide as the day she wounded him. He settled into the armchair. There'd be no risk of losing himself to Madelyn Brighton. She proved to be headstrong and impetuous, acting in panic. Nevertheless, she was pleasant to look at, revealed blatant compassion for family and, to his delight, resisted any attempts Jake made to send her out of town. The personal details that Leon read, that she remained unattached and distant from people, provided confidence she'd follow his instructions tomorrow.

"Are you getting a report twice a day on Frau Healy and her children?"

"Ja, she is at her family's country Haus outside of Munich," Mason said.

"What news do you have on Clyde Zimmerman?"

"His bail was set, and we'll monitor him closely. I'm certain the man responsible for Samuel Healy's death will go after Clyde next."

"Keep them well protected and relocate the family, if necessary, to one of my hotels. I must convince Madelyn that she can trust me."

"Have you contemplated other methods of persuasion, to ensure success?"

"I warned you about your vulgarity."

"You should consider a subtle approach."

"Don't take the liberty of offering advice to me about the treatment of women. I'm an expert on how to make a woman succumb to my biddings." Leon slammed his hands down, propelling himself out of the chair, and marched across the room toward Mason. "My masterful technique involves manipulation of all emotions. Jake will fail with his attempts to charm her with hopeful suppositions. She'll come willingly to me because I have implanted the idea in her mind, she has no other choice. Fear always dominates over any other emotion."

Leon loomed over Mason sitting at the desk and emphasized his point with his physical stature. He leaned in the chair, sliding his arm away from his chest, exposing his SIG P210 gun resting in his shoulder holster.

Leon smirked and relaxed the tension in his muscles. "We understand each other so well."

"Fear instilled in a person's mind is the greatest tool to deceive a person into acting against their own will."

Leon placed his finger to his chin. "There is more truthfulness in intimidation than in romanticizing the ideals of freedom through love."

"Then we have nothing to fear but fear itself," Mason said.

"How profound," he said, in a flat tone. "I believe you've adopted a beneficial philosophy during your time of service to me."

"Merssi," Mason thanked him.

"Now get some sleep. You're a dreadful sight und we have important work to do in the morning."

"Very good, Guad Nachd."

Leon stepped aside, allowing Mason to retire for the night in the adjacent room. Taking a moment to savor his solitude, he stayed up to have a drink. He poured a glass of Riesling, adding a splash of lemon seltzer water. Turning on the music player, he scrolled through a selection of classical and clicked on Bach.

Leon slid lengthwise onto the sofa, stretching his legs over the edge as he loosened the top collar button of his shirt. He sipped his drink while he waved his other hand around in sync with the notes of Orchestral Suite No. 3. Closing his eyes, he rested his head against a cushion. "Madelyn Brighton, you'll see I'm your destiny."

CHAPTER NINETEEN

O n Saturday morning, after a restless night, Madelyn stirred from her slumber at 7:30 a.m. She squinted at rays from the sun projecting shadows of oscillating leaves on the vertical blinds. Stretching her arms upward, she yawned and shook the fatigue from her head. Slumping out of bed, she dragged her feet to the bathroom. With heavy eyelids she gazed into the mirror and flinched at the sheet marks pressed onto her cheek.

Eager for a cup of strong coffee, she quickly showered and threw on a garnet-colored, fitted pant, a sandstone cotton shirt, and a camel-hued cardigan. She combed through her damp hair and left it to air dry. Her comfort level grew with Kate, Douglas, the community group and Pastor Fredrick, each day she stayed at the inn.

Over the past couple of days, Jake became her real source of solace. She surprised herself at how fast he gained her trust. Today she would discuss everything with Jake. No more secrets and no more lies. She removed the tube containing Mozart's Great Mass from her coat and slipped it into the pocket of her sweater as she exited the guestroom.

Delicious aromas of coffee, sausages, breads and eggs infused the entire downstairs as Madelyn strode into the dining area.

"Good morning, Madelyn. Sleep well?" Kate greeted her and whisked by with a tray of dishes.

"Can I help with anything?"

"Goodness no, please have a seat in the kitchen and I'll serve you breakfast."

Kate bustled around the tables, assisting the two other servers. She remained attentive and energetic to both the guests and the employees.

Madelyn pushed through the swinging kitchen door, grabbed the largest mug off the almond-gold granite countertop and poured a cup of coffee. She grabbed a warm, flaky pastry from a cookie sheet and sat on a stool at the island counter.

Kate swept through the entrance. "Good, you helped yourself to the coffee." She squinted at the croissant. "Don't you want something other than a piece of bread?"

"Actually, it's perfect."

Kate shrugged her shoulders. "Suit yourself, but if you change your mind there is plenty of food already made."

"I only need solid food in my stomach to consume an outrageous amount of caffeine."

"Rough night?"

If she answered honestly, it had been a rough couple of days. She needed to face uncertain reactions from both Jake and Leon. "I have a lot on my mind."

Kate tilted her head with a thoughtful expression. "It's a beautiful, sunny day. Would you prefer to sit outside and talk?"

"I'd really enjoy that, but I don't want to take you away from your guests."

"The breakfast rush is over, and you are my guest."

Madelyn picked up her mug and followed Kate out the back door, stepping onto a dark-stained farmer's porch, wrapping around the entire perimeter of the inn. At the rear of the house,

Kate offered a seat on one of the four sets of woven wicker patio furniture.

Madelyn slid into the cushioned chair, gazing out over the deck. Morning dew on the meadow sparkled on emerald blades of grass. Fog haloed the top of the Alps, a sculptural art piece on display in the distance as the field rolled out toward the base. "I bet you never tire of this view."

"After seventeen years of settling here, I call this home. At times I miss family and friends in New England. But to answer your question, no I never tire of the view." Kate sat down.

"We built the deck after the first year we lived here. I needed familiarity, and we always loved having neighbors over for summer barbeques." She laughed. "I guess that idea eventually evolved into the inn."

"I can imagine that it was a tough transition, moving out of the country, away from family and the comforts of home."

"It was a challenge at first, but we had a lot of support from friends and people here in the community." Kate stared off into the distance.

Madelyn didn't want to dredge up any painful memories of Henry. "The church group seems close and supportive of one another." The nutty and sweet flavor of her coffee poured over her taste buds.

"That is the true blessing of being part of God's family and having the fellowship of other believers together." Kate pulled down a blanket draped over her chair and covered her legs. "They welcomed us, and it helped make our transition easier, although Jake didn't settle for a while."

"I'm surprised, he's so grounded and confident."

Kate giggled under her breath. "Oh, my dear, Jake is a wonderful man and I love him very much, but like everyone else he struggles too. I'm sure he's doing his best at trying to impress you, and you've just met him."

Heat crept up the back of her neck. She allowed herself to get caught up with the idea of Jake being some kind of extraordinary man. "I'm a little embarrassed to admit I've gotten swept up in a whirlwind of excitement and…" She averted her eyes and sipped her coffee again. Madelyn couldn't bring herself to say anymore aloud, especially to his mother, about the feelings stirring inside about Jake.

Kate smiled and placed a motherly hand on her knee. "He should be so lucky to have gained the affections of a strong and beautiful woman."

A lump swelled in her throat. She had become an emotional wreck over the past few days. "You're sweet to say such kind words, but I'm afraid I've made a lot of mistakes since I've arrived. At this point I think Jake has serious regrets of ever meeting me." Madelyn's voice strained, holding back the pain of speaking the truth.

Kate shook her head with disbelief. "Jake is fond of you. I can see he has a deep care and concern for you."

Did she believe the accuracy of Kate's remarks about Jake having feelings for her? A fluttering of butterfly wings in flight swarmed in her belly. The idea filled her with hope and yet dread over the level of disloyalty she committed against Jake. Would she disappoint Kate too? Tears swelled in her eyes and her chin quivered. "I'm sorry." She swiped her finger under her eye, preventing any waterworks.

"You've been through a lot. Don't be so hard on yourself. You're tougher than I ever was when Henry was in the thick of one of his escapades."

"So, this is nothing new for you?"

"No, but I never got used to it and, to be honest, it relieved me when Jake decided he didn't want to work with his dad."

Madelyn set her mug on the beveled glass table and leaned back into her chair. "Did Jake move to Boston during that time?"

"Yes, and it broke my heart when he left at the young age of eighteen, but he needed to discover God's plan for him on his own."

"Sounds like a rough period for everyone."

"As a mother, it was hard letting Jake go and as a wife, witnessing Henry's disappointment when Jake declined a partnership with him"—Kate glanced away—"Jake knew how much it meant to him for them to work together, a father-and-son sort of business. Jake continues to battle a guilty conscience and believes the choices affected his dad's health issues."

"Doesn't he realize Henry wouldn't have viewed the situation like that?"

"Jake doesn't see it so cut and dry. When he left for school, Henry needed to recruit a team of philanthropists, paleographers, field workers and museums willing to support their efforts with funding. The work required more than one man to secure all the positions."

Madelyn picked up her warm coffee mug, heating her cold fingers. "I thought Douglas worked with Henry on the jobs?"

"Yes, but Douglas was still employed with the University of Cardiff. Henry needed someone full-time by his side at the work sites."

"Is that when Leon became involved?"

"Mm-hm. Henry met Leon in connection with one of many museums in Vienna. With Leon's knowledge of historical documents and financial position it seemed like an ideal collaboration."

Kate shifted in her seat, tucking her knees up on the chair. "For the first few years the partnership worked well until Henry discovered Leon's individual ambitions and his goal to keep a portion of the pieces for his own profit."

It all started to make sense, the personal ties binding everyone together, and the bitter rivalry between Jake and Leon. She should have talked to Kate earlier to learn the facts. The truth always seemed to become muddled whenever she sought answers from the men involved.

Was it possible for both Leon and Jake to get what they wanted? Leon vocally expressed his position about keeping the Mozart piece for his own private collection. Perhaps if she persuaded Leon, he'd surrender the artifact over to the museum.

She didn't know if she should risk asking him after being a no-show for their original meeting and the threat to Sam's family. After all, a murderer remained on the loose. She shivered and wrapped her cardigan tighter around her torso as a cool breeze rippled through the air. Was Leon aware that Sam wanted to return the music to Henry's team? The connection between Sam and Leon was unclear. Did Kate hold Leon, and those involved, like Sam, accountable for Henry's death? She trusted Jake kept the information about Sam being her father a secret.

"Sorry if I sound insensitive, but do you think Leon attributed excessive stress and caused Henry additional health issues?" Madelyn bit her lower lip; she may have asked too much.

Kate lowered her gaze and sighed, shaking her head. "No. The truth is Henry liked Leon, despite his vainglory, Henry thought his motives would change. I know Jake blames Leon for his dad's heart attack." Kate paused with a pained expression and down-turned lips. "I think Jake is internalizing his own guilt for choosing to leave. Eight years went by before he returned and when he found out about Leon's intentions, Henry treated them as if they were brawling brothers. I suppose Jake believes if he stayed, he could have prevented everything."

Madelyn pressed a palm against her cheek while listening to the particulars of Leon's association with the Nolans. She had figured Leon contested Henry and the entire family. Maybe there were details that Kate didn't realize about Leon. Did she hear of the illegal dealings involving Sam and how Leon forced them to his estate?

"I didn't think Leon and Henry were close. I can understand Jake's hurt and frustration toward Leon." Her gaze drifted into the distance as she processed the news.

Steam rose off the blades of grass while the sun melted the morning dew. A tingle tickled her nose after learning so much about Jake without him disclosing the information.

"You've been helpful with giving me clarity on the situation." Madelyn took a deep breath and looked at Kate. "Like Henry,

I thought of the possibility of reaching out and reasoning with Leon."

Kate kept her eyes fixed on Madelyn's as she said, "Grace is always available for those who need it and want to receive it."

"Do you think some offenses are too great for forgiveness?" Madelyn asked with the interest of Sam on her mind too.

"Not at all, especially knowing the heart of God. The Bible says, 'where sin increased, grace increased all the more.'"

Madelyn gulped the last of her coffee. Perhaps all the testaments she heard from family and friends at Sam's service were true. It's plausible Sam changed. His final letter seemed genuine and now she'd be the only one to benefit from forgiving him for the past.

"I've really enjoyed talking with you." Madelyn smiled through the ache for her own mother. Many times, she had daydreams about conversations with Mom, similar to the chat with Kate.

"Me too, dear." Kate patted her hand.

* * *

Searching downstairs for Maddie, Jake scrubbed his hands over his face to wake from his stupor after poor sleep and his mind reeling all night. He avoided the necessary talk about switching the original Mozart music with the forgery and the time for delays expired. Transportation didn't pose an issue since Svenja returned the car. The moment of truth approached; options were few and despite the consequences of his choices, he valued the moments he shared with Maddie.

Cutting through the kitchen, he strolled the deck around the inn. Mom and Maddie sat close and engaged in conversation. An empty feeling rolled in the pit of his stomach, and it didn't help that he skipped breakfast.

"I hoped to find one of you, and here you both are together." Jake squinted as the sunlight beamed into his eyes. A slight chill ran through his body. The two of them looked too comfortable chatting.

"Good morning." Mom stood and folded the flannel blanket from her lap and laid it on the back of the chair.

She pulled up her sleeve and glanced at her watch. "Goodness, I better check on the guests."

Jake stepped aside next to the table, and his heart missed a beat when he caught a glimpse of Maddie staring at him. What did they talk about? Part of him liked Mom and Maddie getting along, but a nagging feeling they discussed more than jobs and hobbies gnawed at him.

"You're up early this morning." For a minute he scrutinized her eyes, lost in a dark grotto, all the wonders of her hidden deep inside. Her lips pressed together, hiding a shy smile as she lowered her gaze to the mug in her hands. Every time he worked up the nerve to confess his deceit and send her home, he caught himself staring at her face too long—thinking about sitting by a fireplace and leisurely talking. He wished she'd still trust him once he broke the news to her. With a slow blink he cleared his mind.

"I invited Madelyn to join me out here on this lovely spring day. Now, if you please excuse me." She winked, patted him on the arm and walked toward the backdoor. "I'll see you in a bit."

Jake shoved his hands into his jean pockets and rocked back and forth onto his heels. "So, did my mom bore you with stories about me?"

"Not at all, I enjoy her company very much."

He glanced at her, then stared out into the distance at nothing. Why did he care about what they discussed? In a few minutes, she'd probably tell him off and hop on the first train out of town. It would be for the best if she left before serious problems commenced with Leon.

"Are you bothered by my conversation with your mom? If so, you have nothing to worry about." Maddie stood and set her mug on the table.

"What? I'm not worried," Jake said with a nervous laugh. "It's fine." Heat rose from his chest. He stretched the collar of his white t-shirt, layered under his long-sleeved, button-down shirt. "I guess you heard about my moody, rebellious teenage years." Poking fun at himself would lighten whatever character blows Mom caused.

"Yeah, something along those lines."

"Seriously, that's all you're giving me?" Jake threw his hands upward in the air.

Maddie moved closer, with an intense stare. On her tiptoes she reached up cupping her hand around his chin and leaned forward. "I'm playing with you." She stepped backward and created a space between them.

"I'd say you're definitely teasing me."

Her cheeks bloomed into a rosy pink. He grinned with satisfaction; he enjoyed causing her to blush.

Maddie fumbled with loose strands of hair draping along her jawline and avoided his gaze.

"Kate helped me sort out something I've been struggling to tell you."

"Oh yeah, what's that?" Jake tilted his head to get a better view of her face, still delighted he flustered her and stirred up fervor.

"She told me how the partnership started with Henry and Leon."

The playfulness faded and a dull pain throbbed in his brain. "Why were you talking about my family's personal business?"

Worse than hearing they talked about his awkward teen years, she had hit him with the disturbing news they discussed Leon. Why did she always mention Leon during their intimate moments?

"I thought if I talk to him—"

"Stop, whatever you're thinking or planning."

"You won't even let me finish what I want to say." She flung her hands up and smacked them against her thighs.

"You're right, because there's no point."

Her face reddened. "Now you're telling me what to do and when to speak?" Maddie raised her voice and a small crease deepened between her eyes.

"I know that sounded bad, but you need to listen to me. I've witnessed what Leon's capable of. He's unstable." Jake reached out, and she turned her back toward him. "Please understand, I don't want you to get hurt."

He stood behind, placed his hands on her shoulders and she stiffened under his touch. "You said you trust me." Jake lowered his arms. He didn't deserve her trust.

Maddie twisted around and faced him. Her eyes flickered like breath on the flame of a candle. "I believe you and want to help everyone involved."

"And that's a beautiful and compassionate gift you have but trying to reason with Leon won't work." Jake lifted the back of his hand to her face and brushed her cheek. She trembled and leaned into his caress.

Maddie closed her eyes for a moment. Tempted to kiss her, he bent forward and her eyelids flicked open as if ice water poured over her. "I made plans to meet with Leon yesterday." She spewed the sentence, faster than a wicked snake bite, and the words sank into him like venom.

His lips parted, but no sound came out. Jake stumbled backward and caught himself on the arm of the chair. Gaining his stance, he did a double take. What he suspected turned out to be true. No trust existed between them. The desire and possession of Mozart's Great Mass brought out the worst in everyone. Maddie schemed behind his back while she unknowingly held onto a counterfeit copy of the music.

Jake's mind whirled in confusion and he stared into her tear-filled eyes. "I thought I saw Leon at the café." He slanted his body and created a defined space. "I figured you'd tell me if he talked to you and assumed you wouldn't give him a chance, but like my father—"

"Your mother too."

Jake clenched his jaw as her words struck with the force of a slap against the face. "How can you comment on things you don't know about?"

"I know, you've made the situation personal to you—"

"It is personal, Leon betrayed my father."

"And you feel responsible for Henry's betrayal because of your absence." Maddie gasped and snapped her mouth closed.

His stomach hardened as if she kicked him in the gut. It appeared he carried out the correct decision, keeping the original of Mozart's Credo. Jake didn't know her at all. Perhaps Sam instructed Maddie to gain his confidence then backstab him and support Leon. She never produced Sam's letter.

"Regardless of your chat with Kate, you've no right to make that kind of comment."

Her chin quivered. "That's true and I'm sorry." The color from her cheeks faded from pink to chalky white. "I'm only trying to do what's best for all involved."

The pain in his throat tightened, and he swallowed hard. Jake walked toward the end of the raised porch, leaning against the railing. He stared at the Alps in the distance, avoiding eye contact.

He couldn't risk falling into the deep, dark lure of her eyes. Her footsteps drew near and she stood beside him, resting her arms on the rail. Jake wanted to give her the benefit of the doubt and try to comprehend her rationalization for choosing to meet Leon.

"If that is your true intention, then why not tell me sooner about your plans with Leon?"

"I tried to explain last night—"

"When you were eager to leave dinner, and meet with him?" Jake flashed a sharp glare. "Or when we were almost run down by his car, I suppose that was after you were a no-show for your appointment?"

Maddie remained quiet, standing still with her hands clasped in front as if he denied her an impartial trial, awaiting a public lashing.

"Perhaps you meant to tell me while cuddled in my arms, flirting with me?"

"Hey, that's not fair!"

"No, it isn't. None of it's fair." It wasn't reasonable for him to judge her when he maintained his own secrecy.

"So, you've concluded I'm a horrible person because you don't like my decisions?" Maddie shrugged with her palms facing upward. "You're not the only one who has a personal interest in the matter."

"Yeah, you told me, clearing Sam of his wrongdoings, but I've a feeling you wouldn't reason with Leon, and you'd give him Mozart's composition." Jake glanced out the corner of his eye, hoping she would correct him, and yell at him for suspecting her of such an act of betrayal.

Maddie placed a palm against his back. "I want to explain, but I can't. Please believe I intended on giving you Mozart's sheet music since yesterday afternoon until Leon said…"

He sensed Leon used manipulative tactics against her, and tried pressuring her into giving him the Great Mass.

"What did he say to you?"

"I know you have no reason to trust me after my mistakes and secrets over the past few days. I will be honest with you; I've based all my decisions on those I care about, including you."

In the span of half an hour Maddie said the most hurtful words to him since his breakup with Angelina, and now confessed she cared for him. Jake lacked the cognition for processing everything that transpired. He required time to think and pray. One thing he knew for certain, he needed to be as honest as she had been. He turned; facing her eager response as she bit the corner of her lip.

"You're not a horrible person. I've made plenty of poor choices and I'm certain I'll make several by the end of today." Jake rubbed her arms and stared into her eyes. "Speaking of making mistakes—"

"At least I'm leaving soon, and you'll be rid of me forever." Her voice cracked and she pressed her lips tight. She whirled around and made her way inside the house.

"Maddie, don't go."

She walked away and never turned back, not even a quick glance over her shoulder.

CHAPTER TWENTY

Madelyn rushed through the side door into the kitchen. Her heart raced with the same pace of her feet, exiting the dining room. She'd go anywhere to escape the hurt and guilt that plagued her at the moment.

Dashing out the front entryway, she wished to rewind time to early in the week when she left California. She would have changed her mind about traveling to Germany. No, if she had known in advance everything that would happen, she'd still make the same decisions. Perhaps, without the problems she caused for Jake. The wounded look on his face haunted her, and she slowed her steps at the end of the gravel driveway.

She meandered the dirt trail leading into the village. The late morning sun cast a spotlight on the peaks of snow-tipped Alps. A light spring breeze blew open her cardigan, sending a chill throughout her body. Madelyn strolled the mile stretch, flanked by golden, green grass with ivory flowers scattered like fallen snowflakes across the fields. She inhaled the mineral scents of wet soil and meadow enriched by the early morning rainfall.

Madelyn halted at a wood post marker on the trail, one path for the village and the other toward the church. The chapel bell rang, and her feet pointed in the church's direction and she climbed the incline before she even made up her mind.

At the top of the hill, Madelyn checked the rectory for Pastor Fredrick. After knocking and standing at the door for about two minutes, she perused the front of the pale-yellow chapel. In the daylight, the copper onion dome towered above the church building and outside the iron gates, she stood at the open entrance of large oak doors. Straight ahead in her line of vision, the image of Jesus on the cross, hung on the wall.

With slow, precise steps she entered the empty sanctuary. Other than a few holidays and Sam's service, she avoided churches since Mom died. The small interior with vaulted ceilings created the illusion of a larger room. Three stained-glass windows lined both sides of the building. Colors of green, blue, red and yellow reflected a rainbow across the rows of benches.

Madelyn walked the center aisle, and dragged her fingers along the polished pews, the scent of furniture oil lingered in the air. Her eyes focused on the cross in front of her, behind the simple, chestnut pulpit.

Settling onto the first bench, folding her hands in her lap, she gazed up at Jesus. Dizzying thoughts of everyone and everything involved with Mozart's music swarmed in her mind. How could she figure stuff out when her offenses stared down at her through the image of Jesus? She bowed her head and tears teemed in her eyes.

As a child she developed a personal relationship with God, before Mom's sickness and Dad's abandonment. At fifteen, she felt alone, angry and gave up praying, although Mom demonstrated unwavering faith during her battle with cancer.

A burning sensation inflamed her heart. Heat rose up her neck and she palmed her chest. So much time lost, running away from the pain. Other people moved on from their emotional hardships, but she remained the same. No matter her age, education, career status—she stayed the usual wounded and scarred fifteen-year-old girl inside.

"Lord"—warm streams of tears spilled down her cheeks as she closed her eyes and hunched forward, bowing her head into her lap—"please, help me. I need to know what to do." She swallowed the sharp pain in her throat with a slight choke.

"Madelyn?"

Sucking in her breath, she swiped her fingers across her wet cheeks and jerked her body upright. "Ah, hello." She turned and glanced over her shoulder. Pastor Fredrick stood at the edge of the bench.

"I came to visit with you." Her voice cracked.

He shifted his gaze from her sight to the cross on the wall and smiled. "I think someone else is here to meet with you."

Madelyn laughed through her breath. "Funny thing is I didn't have any intentions of coming here. I planned on heading toward the town."

"I find that is the way of God." He sat beside her on the pew. "We always end up exactly where we need to be."

Pastor Fredrick stated the idea Madelyn spent days pushing from her mind: none of the events were a coincidence and her involvement with everyone had a purpose. "I'm starting to believe that's true." She redirected her attention to the cross. "While I was sitting here, I remembered."

"What did you remember?"

"I committed my life to Jesus in my youth, read the Bible and walked daily with the Lord, but I was shaken when my mom passed." She stared down at her hands folded in her lap.

"I wasn't only angry with my dad and God all these years, but I was mad at myself too."

"I understand."

She flipped her head up in his direction. "You do?"

He nodded. "I struggled with similar feelings when my wife, Wynn, passed away. I questioned the power of my prayers, that they weren't enough or concise and lacked the ability to make her well again."

She stared at his tawny eyes, magnified by his thick, black-framed spectacles. "How did you stop blaming yourself?"

"I opened my heart to God and accepted I couldn't let go of my self-loathing without allowing God's love to fill me up in my brokenness. I shut God out because I didn't feel worthy of his grace and if I ignored the relentless tenderness of Jesus, I would've continued to be angry."

A heaviness in her soul weighed the words of Pastor Fredrick to be true. Too many times she turned away from God, denying herself freedom and forgiveness. She ran so far from God because she didn't feel deserving of his love. "The real obstacle has been feeling like I haven't earned the love of Jesus."

"That's why I stand at the altar of grace with a spirit of gratitude." Fine lines deepened around his mouth as he smiled. "Perhaps now you'll allow God to love and comfort you. That would be your first step on the path toward forgiving your father."

Madelyn longed to surrender the burdens of her heart. Did the answers exist with inviting God back into her life? "How do I begin?"

"If you'd like, we can pray together." Pastor Fredrick placed a tender hand on her shoulder.

Madelyn nodded in agreement, closed her eyes and bowed her head.

Pastor Fredrick opened the prayer, "Father God in heaven, we praise you for your mercy and grace. I thank you for Madelyn and the work you're doing in her heart and bringing her here to Ruhpolding. We praise you for your plans with perfect timing and amid trials, you are calling us to draw near to you. Lord, you know the difficulties and challenges Madelyn is facing. I pray you give her strength and wisdom."

A feeling of peace washed over Madelyn, a flood of joy like an old friend visiting for the first time in ages, filled with a tinge of sadness for losing years spent apart. The evidence of God's presence shined through her answered prayer, leading her into the lives of people already praying for her guidance.

Madelyn prayed after Pastor Fredrick, saying, "God, I've given into my doubts and unbelief. I ask your forgiveness for my anger and bitterness. I thank you for your patience and humbly accept your gift of grace. Please create a new heart in me, so I may forgive as you have forgiven. Amen."

Startled with an unexpected gust rippling through her body, followed by an immediate calm and stillness inside, the knowledge of God's love permeated beyond anything she'd experienced before. The weight of self-loathing dissipated with a deep, cleansing breath and a new hope filled her as she opened her eyes. An excitement buzzed, sparking a certainty toward her journey in life.

"Thank you for praying with me," she said.

"You're welcome. I'll keep you in my prayers. Now"—he stood—"how about a nice cuppa?" Fredrick said with a tilt of his head and a twinkle in his eye.

After a refreshing cucumber sandwich lunch and Darjeeling tea with Pastor Fredrick, Madelyn possessed a new confidence by trusting in a renewed hope in God. She strolled down the streets leading into town with a spring in her step. A heightened awareness of all her senses made her feel spiritually awakened.

Rising dough swirled in the air, the taste of yeast on her tongue—the smell forever associated with her time spent in Bavaria. Passing the shops, she stopped and glanced around. Madelyn turned her head toward the modern, beige-stucco, seven-story building at the end of the street.

A tall flagpole in front waved in the breeze. She gazed upward at the horizontal letters, alongside the entrance for Hotel Luxur. Once again, without intention, she arrived somewhere that required her presence and knew Leon would meet, regardless of the time of day.

Entering the lobby of Hotel Luxur she strolled across the black-and-white checkered flooring. A group of guests crammed into the small elevator. She squeezed in with five other people pressed in on each arm, the confined space a mix of strong cologne and bad breath. Heat radiated through her chest and her pulse increased after each stop. Riding alone after the fifth level the sounds of the working machinery exaggerated until the final ding. Saliva filled her mouth and she gulped as the doors squeaked open.

Madelyn turned down the short hall, with slow steady steps toward the suite entrance on the private floor. "God, give me strength," she whispered and raised her arm up to knock then froze mid-air.

The door unlocked and opened. "Komm herein, bitte." Drexwyler stepped aside.

"How did you know I was here?" Madelyn scanned around the entry and spotted a surveillance camera in the upper-right doorframe. "Of course." She rolled her eyes.

Madelyn followed Drexwyler into the apartment. Merlot-colored drapes contrasted against the pale walls. Bright-yellow rays beamed through the large windows, revealing a mountain view. She sighed. The suite appeared bigger than her condo in California, complete with wet bar, furnishings and two master bedrooms.

"Have a seat." Drexwyler held out his arm, offering Madelyn a light-green chair in the sitting room. "Master Von Füssen will be with you in a moment."

Madelyn experienced a type of time travel whenever she encountered Leon and Drexwyler. She didn't know whether his mysterious way of living frightened or filled her with intrigue. Drexwyler closed the linen drapes, flipped on the lights and exited. Madelyn remained calm until he shut the curtains and now, she placed all her trust in God, considering it would test her renewed faith.

"You've finally kept your word." Leon entered the room, advancing with gliding movements. "Always a pleasure." He lifted her hand and pulled her toward him, placing his cool, taut lips against each cheek. Madelyn stiffened as his muted gray eyes stared at her face.

Her fingers slipped from his gentle clasp as she lowered herself into the chair.

"You're early." Leon slid onto the sofa across the coffee table.

"I hope you don't mind; I was passing the hotel on a walk around town."

He searched her expression after every word she spoke, examining the authenticity of everything she said. "On the contrary, I'll consider excusing your blatant disregard of our prior engagements."

Madelyn slid deeper into the chair, straightening her posture to maintain a look of composure. She made it this far and wouldn't change her mind now.

"Would you like a Kaffee?" Leon said.

"Yes, thank you."

"Mason, zwei Kaffee," Leon ordered across the room.

Drexwyler hustled behind the bar with the moves of a serious chemist concocting multiple ingredients.

"He seems less intimidating when he's making drinks as opposed to trying to run me down with a vehicle."

A low, deep laugh sneaked through Leon's closed lips. "He proves to be a useful servant, most of the time. I enjoy giving him menial tasks to aid in his self-esteem."

Leon laughing and joking? Madelyn didn't think it was possible for him to show different sides of his personality. Although, drawing out his sensitive emotions would take a fearless courage and she doubted her capabilities.

"I like you, Madelyn Brighton. You express your thoughts." He stared at her with an intensity to crack through concrete.

Madelyn pressed her lips, forcing a small smile. She needed to navigate the conversation carefully. *God, please give me the words to speak*. "I'm glad you appreciate my straightforward approach." She cleared her throat. "How are Gretchen and the boys?"

"They're quite safe. We positioned my men outside the family's house, ready to act at the first implication of danger."

"The whole situation sounds so dire."

"Meine Liebe, you are only figuring this out now?" Leon leaned forward; his eyes narrowed. "The situation is grave."

Madelyn's breath caught in her chest and she swallowed hard. "Shouldn't you involve the authorities?"

"For the best interest of everyone, we're communicating with consultants on a need-to-know basis. Frau Healy agrees with our proceedings and prefers to keep the integrity of her late husband's name confidential."

"I understand and respect your choice." The strength she possessed earlier slipped away by the second. The weight of his stare became unbearable, and the pressure forced her to glance in the opposite direction every minute or two.

Leon's lips slanted up at an angle. "The moment I met you I recognized your astute nature." The faint smile vanished. "I assume you've followed my instructions and brought my music."

Madelyn gulped the lump in her throat. "I-I did." She clutched the pocket of her cardigan, the shape of the aluminum tube visible. Leon shot an agile stare like darts nailing a bullseye. His eyes locked onto her hand and the opportunity to appeal to a responsive characteristic drifted further away.

"Although, I'd enjoy a conversation with you."

"You wish to converse with me?" he said in a tone laced with suspicion.

"Yes." Madelyn tilted her chin up and looked him straight in the face. "So, we can get to know each other better."

"I'm almost intrigued." Leon eased back and stretched his arms out, resting his elbows atop the sofa. He displayed a casual demeanor, even his attire of a lilac dress-shirt, unbuttoned at the collar and rolled cuffs, appeared informal for Leon's standards.

Drexwyler brought two cups of coffee in on a tray, setting it on the table between them. "Sweeteners?"

"Yes, thank you," Madelyn said.

Leon waved him aside. "The usual."

"As you prefer, cream, sugar and peppermint." He placed the cup in front of Leon.

Leon rubbed his clean-shaven chin as his eyes examined Madelyn's face. "Mason, that'll be all, you're dismissed for the rest of the evening."

"Sehr gut." He grabbed his coat and left the suite.

Her throat constricted as she sipped her coffee, alone with Leon. Although she didn't feel any safer with Drexwyler in the room. If she appealed to Leon's lighter temperament, she might sway him to consider her suggestion and yet the way he studied every movement concerned her.

"Please continue, I'm interested in developing our acquaintance through conversation, along with other possibilities for us to gain familiarity." Leon held his cup to his lips, his eyes peering above the rim.

Madelyn squirmed in her chair. On the couple occasions she encountered Leon, he always prided himself on showing formal manners. She prayed on the accuracy of her judgment. What was worse, Leon's displeasure or keen attentiveness?

"Your expectations of my knowledge in the language arts may be too high."

"Don't be modest. I'm sure whatever you lack in colloquy you make up for in nonverbal communications." He arched an eyebrow. "I know your profession requires impeccable listening skills."

Madelyn never told Leon about her job. Jake's assessments were correct, Leon gathered information on her in advance and she'd been fooling herself, meeting him alone to persuade his decision.

The caffeine from the coffee added to her anxiety, but if she kept calm, she'd get the desired answers. "What happened between you and Dr. Nolan?" Her voice faltered.

Leon set his cup on the table and rolled his eyes. "What an absolutely boring subject."

"I'm curious how you, being a reputable man of wealth and culture, partnered with Henry Nolan."

"Your words flatter me," he said in a stoic tone. "But come now, don't think you can use your psychoanalysis on me, you've yet to encounter a mind as brilliant as mine." His eyes flashed like lightning as he stood from the sofa.

"I wouldn't presume—"

Leon stepped in front of her chair and leaned closer. She sucked in a hard breath. "Don't fool yourself into believing your simple counseling techniques will work on me." His stern tone cooled into an icy warning. "Nevertheless, I'm impressed you attempted to perceive my mind."

A chill ran through her body as Leon scrutinized her every move. A massive knot twisted in her throat, and she did not speak.

"Let's start over again, shall we?" Leon lounged on the cushions. "Ask me what you truly want to know."

Madelyn managed a weak nod and rubbed her clammy palms together. "Why would Jake try and confiscate Mozart's music, when you were Henry's partner?"

"You're closer to the right question." He finished the rest of his coffee. "However, you really aspire to learn how your father became involved."

A flush of adrenaline coursed through her veins. Leon knew more about her than she accepted as public knowledge. What difference did it make? He made her a pawn in his plan, and she could end up facing the same fate as Sam. "If you're aware of my relation to Sam, why didn't you confront me at your hotel?"

"I needed additional facts about you to find out if you were blameless in the situation."

"Your philosophy is guilty until proven innocent?"

Leon shook his head. "You still don't comprehend because you wish to remain ignorant to the truth."

"Then enlighten me."

"You're correct, Dr. Nolan and I had a partnership. We agreed on our findings until Jake arrived. After Henry passed, the division became greater, and the team divided. For a hefty sum of currency, Clyde Zimmerman offered to sway the rest of the crew and support my decisions. However, Clyde had an ulterior motive. He stole my authenticated artifact and used the money to pay for an expert counterfeiter: Samuel Healy. I learned of his deceit after he boasted about his association with an art forgery racket." A vein protruded from his forehead. "The fool thought he was capable of deceiving me und now he's dead."

"Did you—"

"My hands are clean. Killing is an act of desperation and I'm not a desperate man." His eyebrows pinched together.

"Some of your actions appear desperate."

"That would be an interpretation of someone who doesn't value restitution." His expression lacked emotion, his eyes a fixed stare carved into ivory.

Madelyn refrained from deviating any further from the topic. "Do you know who murdered him?"

"The same person who used the opioid, Carfentanil, to kill Samuel Healy. A man that goes by the name of John R, the leader of an art forgers' group. He, along with his accomplices, have a precise three-stage method of enlisting a crew member from museums to alter an artist file, replicating the artistic piece or documentation, then proceed securing an art dealer for sales. They've proven successful for many years, having a person with access to tamper with evidence of findings, und they're able to offer potential buyers with proof of provenance."

Sickness swirled in her stomach. Despite the broken relationship with Dad, she grieved over the loss of his life. The confirmation he died by someone's hand distressed her, and she lost the nerve to finish the journey she started. "That's awful, thievery and murder all for a few sheets of old music?"

"Nein, for wealth."

"You're deplorable."

"Why spit your vulgarity at me? I already have plenty of financial stability, which I earned und worked hard to gain. The music belongs to me, because of my partnership and funding of the entire project."

"I believe you had help with your findings."

Leon leaped forward from the sofa, placing his hands on the arms of her chair and leaned in close. "Listen carefully, there will be no discussions. I've kept my word, now hand over the music."

Madelyn should have heeded Jake's warnings about Leon. She pushed her body hard against the back of her seat. With mere inches between them, she squeezed her arm from her side and dug into her pocket. Her fingers wrapped around the cool aluminum and her hand trembled as she revealed the canister.

Leon's eyes shined with an anxious fervor. A heaviness pressed on her chest. She didn't know if she chose the right thing. She didn't want to hurt and betray Jake but protecting Gretchen and the boys remained her top priority, even if it meant forsaking any relationship with Jake.

Madelyn grazed her upper teeth along her lower lip. "Can I please ask a personal favor?"

"You have such a pretty please, it's difficult to resist your request." He folded his arms across his chest. "Go on."

"My father wrote me a letter, expressing his deep regrets of the choices he made in the past and confessed the errors of his ways. Sam wanted to make amends and knew choosing to do the right thing would be his demise. He asked me to decide the fate of the music and clear his tarnished name."

"Are you able to supply the note?"

"No, I tore it up."

Leon scrutinized her face, studying her as if she were a new species. "I don't care about Samuel Healy's final request or last-minute pleas for a pardon. However, I care to hear your wishes." He slid his hands over her shoulders, bending close enough to feel his breath on her neck. "What do you want?"

Madelyn shut her eyes and coiled her fingers tighter around the tube. "Will you consider placing Mozart's music on display at Mozart's Museum?" Her words flew from her lips with a gusty sigh.

Leon stood and circled her chair, a lion ready to pounce. She sensed his towering stature and her smallness increased, powerless like trapped prey awaiting a predatory attack.

"There are very few people worthy of my attention." He paused in front of the armchair with a faint smirk. "I find your boldness an attractive trait." He asserted his dominance, cornering her and sat on the edge of the table. "You're a compassionate person. A reputable attribute that can easily be used against you."

Was this his admission of taking advantage of her or was Leon offering friendly advice?

"I'll contemplate your request." He rubbed his fingers together and slipped gloves on, preparing for transferring the artifact between hands.

Madelyn set the slender tube in his hands. With a gleam of triumph, his eager extremities twisted the tube open. Unrolling the delicate parchment, he licked his lips. His eyes scanned the paper, and he straightened the edges of the documents and held it up toward the lamp beside her chair. Leon glanced up, his thundering gray stare shuddered throughout her body, and he crumpled Mozart's sacred Agnus Dei.

"What are you doing?" Madelyn flung her arms forward, reaching for the music.

Leon balled the papers up in his fist. "This is a counterfeit." He stood with a heavy huff. "The same forgery Clyde passed off to me."

"No…" Madelyn shook her head in disbelief. "I don't understand. How?" Panic filled every cell in her body. "I thought—"

"Either your father betrayed you from the grave or the logical explanation, someone else deceived you."

A sharp pain plunged into her heart and her world pulled inside out. A cold sweat broke on her forehead. Madelyn didn't know what to think or whom to trust. She preferred an alternative explanation; Leon suffered from insanity and destroyed the original of Mozart's Great Mass. Her mind refused to accept any other truth.

"It's plain you believe Jake to be a trustworthy man." Leon settled back onto the sofa. "Interesting detail, John R. und Samuel Healy were close colleagues for many years, yet the bond of friendship didn't save Samuel in the end." He tossed his hair to one side. "The person you least expect will most likely stab you in the back."

Madelyn pressed a palm against her chest. The reality that Jake double-crossed her, struck with the force of a bullet. "Did you know before I came here?"

"Ja, I suspected."

Jake's true interest appeared clear—he only cared about the music. Out of goodwill or possibly guilt, he helped her out of physical danger and didn't abandon her in the countryside of Bavaria. The fault rested with her since she allowed herself to trust him. Madelyn hoped this time would be different, that Jake would be different. Leon toyed with her to an extreme, despite the fact she had a forgery. "Why go through all of this trouble and protect Sam's family?"

His expression softened with a cocked smile. "Naja, if I'd told you upfront, you would have lost the lesson."

Every time she asked Leon a question, the answers eluded her. "What is the lesson?"

With direct eye contact, he leaned forward, resting his arms against his knees. "Angriff ist die beste Verteidigung."

"What does that mean?"

"Attack is the best defense."

Madelyn gulped. "Whom do I need to attack?"

"Can you not guess?" Leon tilted his head downward, his eyes a stormy gray.

A prickly sensation covered her entire body. If possible, to choose any moment over the last few days to escape the whole fiasco, it would be now.

"You still have an obligation to your father to fulfill, the widow Healy to consider and those young, innocent boys."

"What do you have in mind?"

"You're the psychologist. I'm sure you can figure out how to sequester the music from Jake."

She couldn't fathom trying to trick Jake, even if he had lied. "I don't think I can do that—"

"You will." Leon hopped from the sofa. "I'm counting on you to make up for the distress your father caused me."

Leon's demands rang in her ears and she knew he meant business. The hope of reasoning with him was lost. An hour ago, she sat peacefully in the presence of God and now she was trapped in the devil's den.

Madelyn dropped her shoulders and exhaled aloud. "All right."

Leon leaned against her, brushing his face against her cheek. "Schatzi, I have not overlooked your predicament." The silky sound of his constricting words slithered through his teeth.

Hot blood flooded to the surface of her skin with his warm whisper, "I will be near, watching you." Smooth, soft lips glided along, planting a puckered peck on the corner of her mouth.

Madelyn hated herself for allowing Leon to take such liberties. She imagined he would enjoy it if she fought against him, adding fuel to the fire, and encouraging him to pursue further actions.

Leon stepped back and confronted her, his eyes lightened, revealing a silver lining of blue. He had the look of a different man. The man she prayed would overpower the haunting spirit that seemed to possess him.

Leon gazed with a firm, direct visual contact, almost mastering a technique that absorbed the essence of her being. Madelyn wriggled in her seat, evading the lingering look and in a matter of seconds, the burning passion that blazed in his eyes turned ashy gray.

Leon grabbed her hands, pulled her upward from the chair and held her against his body. "Unfortunately, you may need to use whatever strategies necessary." His facial expression contorted as if he were in pain. "To persuade Jake." He pursed his lips, as if wanting to spit the sour aftertaste of the phrase from his mouth.

Madelyn wouldn't dare believe Leon cared. She made many idiotic errors the past few days, but Leon's disturbance by his own suggestion must've been from the pure agitation of jealousy.

"I understand." If her words appeased him, perhaps he'd let her leave.

"I'm only asking you to sacrifice your virtue for the sake of integrity." Leon slipped his hand around her shoulder, escorting her toward the door. "Jake dishonored his father und yours." Locks of hair grazed across his shirt collar as he tilted his head. "I know you will not fail me again." Leon lifted her arm, pressing his lips against her wrist, with his piercing stare exerting elements of hypnotic powers. Leon desired to dominate her in every way possible.

"Servus." He directed her out.

Sinking in a pool of defeat, she glanced heavenward as he closed the door. Her mouth dried with the bitter truth; Leon succeeded and gained control of her, pulling strings that moved her like a marionette.

Shadows crept along the hall of the hotel as the sun set. Madelyn now had to confront Jake. Her heart throbbed with the agony that he never trusted her and withheld the truth. She foolishly believed they progressed beyond secrets. How long did he plan on leading her on? When did he switch the music? She shook her head and rode the elevator down to the lobby. Madelyn still refused to accept Jake being capable of such a deceitful scheme. She set him on a pedestal, as an admirable, dependable man. In her reconciliation with God, the truth revealed that she placed all her hope in the men in her life, rather than in God, and secured her downfall. Reality settled in, and she realized only God remained trustworthy.

CHAPTER TWENTY-ONE

"Where did she go?" Jake swiped a palm across his face.

"Well dear, she's an independent woman." Mom handed him an equine caddy as he stood at the entrance of the barn. "Come help me."

"Why did you tell Maddie about Leon and put ideas in her head?" He led his mare Brunhilda out of the stall.

"I did no such thing. Honestly, Jake, I only explained Leon's involvement with our family."

"He's not involved with us and Dad must've been out of his mind—"

"Jake Peter Nolan, bite your tongue. I understand you're concerned about Madelyn, but you can't control people or circumstances." She grabbed the flicker brush from his hands.

"I didn't mean—"

"I'm not finished." She brushed long, downward strokes along Brunhilda's left flank. "I love you and you have a wonderful heart for the Lord, but you sure can be thick in the head at times," she said, in a breathless tone.

Jake retrieved the grooming tool and lowered his voice. "I'm sorry."

Mom flipped her bangs from her lashes. "I know you're being protective, and you care for Madelyn, but you need to give everything over to God." She sighed and bent, picking up a bucket of feed.

"Did you say anything that would've encouraged her to go see Leon?" His mouth grew dry with the thought of her alone with him.

"What is the problem between you and Leon?" Mom placed a hand on her hip.

Jake hadn't seen that look since he was eighteen and told her he was moving to Boston. Mom had always been the empathetic parent and searched for the positive in any situation. Dad tended to remain busy with work and realism influenced his judgment.

"Please, tell me what you told Maddie." He dug the heel of his boot into the hay-covered ground.

"Leon isn't responsible for your father's death. Your dad was called home by our Lord and Savior."

"Yeah, I know..." Jake said under his breath. Although he needed to be angry with someone, he knew the Bible too well to blame God. Maddie's assessment of him was correct, that he felt liable for Mozart's Great Mass being stolen and leaving Dad in the first place.

He pulled his collar away from his neck. "But you don't know what Leon's capable of now."

"What do you mean?"

"The situation is serious. Leon is unstable and can't be trusted at all." If anything happened to Maddie, he'd never forgive himself. If only he told her about switching the music upon their arrival at the inn.

"Are you sure you're not too emotionally involved?"

"He threatened and forced us to his house against our will." Jake tossed the brush into a pail. "Still think I'm over-reacting?"

Mom flinched her head backward. "Were your lives in danger?"

"At times…" He shrugged his shoulders. "I told Maddie not to see Leon, but she left upset." Jake shook his head. "Did she give you any indication she'd go visit him?"

"It's possible." Her voice cracked, and she set the bucket down.

Jake gulped hard. "What did she say?"

"Let me see"—she drummed her fingers on her arm—"Madelyn asked if God extended forgiveness to everyone."

Jake swallowed the lump in his throat. "And?"

Her eyes widened, and she placed her fingertips to her lips. "She considered reasoning with Leon, but I didn't know I influenced her decision."

A sweat broke on his nape. Jake massaged his forehead as he processed the information and planned his next move.

"What did she plan on doing?" He turned, questioning himself.

"I'm sorry." Mom patted the back of his shoulder. "I'm sure Madelyn wants to help everyone, especially you."

A sharp sting pricked his heart. Everyone included Leon. The scriptures convicted Jake, like Jonah rebelling against sharing God's message of redemption with the people of Nineveh, Jake wrestled with God on whether Leon deserved grace. The truth of the gospels taught all fall short of the glory of God. Mom, Dad and Maddie all recognized extending mercy included Leon.

"I'm worried." He spun on his heels. "She left hours ago." Jake led Brunhilda by the reign and walked her into the stall. "Say a prayer. I'll go find Maddie."

A rush of blood surged to his heart and banged in his chest as he hurried from the barn.

"Be careful. I will be praying for all of you."

Riding up the elevator of Hotel Luxur, Jake clenched a fist. He inhaled a deep breath through his nose and exhaled through his mouth, relaxing his hands and shoulders. With a slight jerk, the doors separated at the top floor. Jake turned down the dimly lit hall and approached the entrance to the suite. His heart pounded with the same beat as his hand banging on the door. Jake rocked back and forth on his heels with quick short breaths.

Leon opened the door with a smirk on his face. "I can't say I'm pleased to see you," he said, in a deep tone, filled with sarcasm. "Go away, unless you've brought either my music or the lovely Madelyn Brighton back to see me." Leon didn't wait for a response and turned away.

Jake flared his nostrils and followed Leon inside the hotel suite, shutting the entrance behind him. "So, she came here?"

"Ja, she visited me earlier." He strolled across the room toward the bar. "Madelyn and I had personal matters to discuss."

Jake huffed and drooped his shoulders. "What personal matters do you have with her?"

"I'm a gentleman, I never kiss and tell." Leon poured himself a drink. "You seem tense. Can I get you a glass of wine?"

Jake sucked in a deep breath as his blood pressure surged. He slumped into the chair furthest from Leon to refrain from any vehement actions. "And as a gentleman, I can assume she is safe, and you didn't lay a hand on her?"

"I'm surprised by you, Jake." Leon shook his head. "You're in complete disarray over a woman you recently met. I haven't seen you this upset since Henry died."

"Don't speak about my father."

"By now, you must have read the medical examiner's report. I had nothing to do with his death. I think the credit goes to a higher power. I believe your Bible says, the Lord gave, and the Lord hath taken away." Leon glanced up with an arched brow. "I hope you don't lose faith in your God on account of me."

"No, faith allows me to remain patient, knowing God will deal with you accordingly," Jake said through gritted teeth.

"Always a model of the Christian principles." Leon laughed. "You should call upon your God for wisdom."

Jake chewed his inside lip and cracked his knuckles. "I don't need your advice on anything—"

"Yet, here you are asking me questions und searching for answers." With an iced drink in his hand, he sat down on the sofa. "I have no intentions of bringing any harm to Madelyn, I'm quite fond of her."

Leon placed his beverage on an end table and focused his attention on the chess board lying on the table between them. After a prolonged stare, he moved a black knight piece. "She willingly came to visit me." Leon hovered over the chessboard. "Und looks like I'm in a position to capture your queen."

"Please stop, we're not in a theatrical play," Jake said.

"Indeed," he said with a deliberate arch of his eyebrow. "Let us get to the crux of the situation."

"By all means." Jake crossed his arms.

"You're the one avoiding reality, attempting to live out the life of Dr. Henry Nolan all the while your individuality is slipping from existence."

"I'm not the one living in a fantasy. You live in a castle and have a manservant."

"Ja, that is my reality und as usual you attempt to deflect the facts." Leon advanced his pieces on the chessboard.

"What truths do you recognize?" Jake cleared his throat. A sinking weight pressed on his chest with the constant nearness of Leon in his life.

"I know more about you than you care to admit."

"You know nothing about me. You're blinded by greed and dissention. Your only strategies are intimidation by taking advantage of an ailing man and a sensitive woman."

Leon paused, placing his hand to his chin as he leaned backward against the sofa. "Let me get this straight, you came here to rescue her from me, a fate worse than death?" He shook his head. "Madelyn is far from vulnerable. You always aspire to play the hero and that is what I know of you, Jake Nolan."

What alternate universe did he enter, where Leon talked about truth, reality and called him out on his actions?

Jake relaxed his muscles and kept his expressions neutral. "I'm not playing the hero. I care about her wellbeing." Jake rapidly bounced his knee up and down after his last remark, he didn't want Leon to use his words as ammunition.

"Your feelings for Madelyn are beyond a concerned spectator." Leon's mouth cocked up at the corners into a sneer.

Jake waved a dismissive hand. "Whatever…"

"My friend, don't misunderstand, it's nice to see you finally have a greater love than work."

"I'm not your friend."

"We were friends at one time."

"No, you were just my father's conniving co-worker."

Leon stared at the game board. "I was like a son to Henry, we're practically family."

Jake shifted his lower teeth, relieving pain in his clenched jaw. "Seriously? It's bad enough, I had to come here and endure—"

"Hearing the truth?" Leon glanced up. "Face it, you're ashamed of your envy."

A forced laugh burst from Jake's lips. "Why would I envy you?"

"I provided the money und partnership Henry desired. You were a disappointment to him when you left to pursue your own ambitions. You let him down, same as you will fail Madelyn."

"Oh, shut up, Leon. I always supported my dad, long before you entered the picture. I'm still working to ensure the security of his legacy is not destroyed by you." He got up from the chair. "And I will not disappoint Maddie, I'm sending her on the first train out of here and getting her far away from you."

He needed to leave before Leon gathered any more leverage. Leon ignored him with his eyes fixed on the chessboard. Leon had him and Maddie strategically placed.

"Wise choice." Leon gave a crisp nod. "Send Madelyn on her way to avoid any competition. Like work, you were never quite up for the challenge."

Jake aimed for the exit. "I don't have a problem with a fair match, but you lie, cheat and steal." He stopped and pivoted toward Leon.

"I believe this is the time in our game when I say checkmate." Leon knocked the white king down. A thin smile spread across his face as he stood.

Jake opened the entry. "You better look again at the board, you're the only one playing the game." Leon's dark laugh ceased as the door slammed behind Jake.

The damp of the early evening wrapped around Jake like a heavy blanket although his thoughts weighed on him above anything else. He scratched his scalp, mumbling, as he reflected on what transpired between him and Leon. Provoking comments about truth, the difficult relationship with Dad and harboring deeper feelings than he cared to admit for Maddie. He shook his head, Leon, of all people, lecturing him on relationships. Leon didn't know about love or care for anyone other than himself.

A lightheadedness staggered his steps, and he quickened his pace. He still had trouble comprehending Maddie visiting Leon on her own. She ignored his warning and continued keeping secrets. Although he wasn't blameless, his mistakes glared him straight in the face. "This is all my fault," Jake muttered under his breath.

The moment he met Maddie at the church in Munich he knew he'd be in trouble. The minute he gazed into her big brown eyes. When she spoke in her defiant tone, holding her own while surrounded by men in a foreign country. He admired her strength and courage, asking probing questions about faith with a genuine curiosity. At times he caught himself staring at her with complete adoration. A lump swelled in the middle of his throat. He only cared about her safety and would talk her into leaving town the second he arrived home.

Jake envisioned her loose tresses framing her face and wanted to run his fingers through the silky strands. He gulped. So much about her intrigued him, even her shy smile whenever she noticed him gazing at her.

Taking a shortcut to the house, his thoughts gave him momentum, and he stomped through a wet grassy field. The trajectory of physical distance that separated them across countries added to his belief that she existed outside of his league and he didn't stand a chance.

At the front door of the inn, Maddie stepped into view. The porch light shined down and illuminated her figure as she basked in the moon's glow. The first sight of her weakened him in the knees. Her rose-tinted cheeks, the cool creamy luminance of her skin, and dark hair sweeping across her face with a rustle of the evening breeze. His eyes danced round her attributes, settling on her pale-pink lips. Jake longed to kiss and hold her in the moonlight.

"Kate said you were looking for me." Maddie maintained a low, stable tone.

"Yeah." Jake stood closer, enjoying the fine details of her facial features. "It was dangerous for you to visit Leon on your own."

"Leon proved I can trust him more than others I've met this week," she answered with a down-turned mouth.

Her austere glare smacked of regret for ever knowing him. Jake massaged his chest with a steady slowing of his heart. He couldn't endure the look of dissatisfaction on her face.

"I'm not exactly sure what you mean by that and I am concerned about you. What if you had been hurt? Leon might've…" Jake choked on the words and banged a fist against his thigh.

The possibility of Leon placing his hands or lips on her made his stomach nauseated. "I was worried about you."

"Or worried I'd find out you deceived me?" Maddie tightened her jaw and crinkled her eyebrows. "I know you gave me Sam's forgery of Mozart's Great Mass." She shifted her stance and folded her arms across her chest. "Did you switch it when you discovered it in my coat?"

A sudden coldness shot through his body, hitting his core. She had been hurt, but not by Leon. Jake dragged his fingers along her jawline. "I hoped—"

"I wouldn't find out?"

Taking a deep, pained breath, he lowered his gaze toward the ground. "I wanted to tell you the first night we arrived here. I tried many times, even this morning, but you walked away."

Maddie shuffled her feet back and he reached for her arm. "There will never be any trust between us," she said with a watery stare.

"Don't say that. You can count on me."

She sighed with exaggeration and gazed out the corner of her eye. Did his words hold validity for her acceptance and understanding? Jake developed a sincere care for her and didn't want anyone to hurt her, least of all him. "My priority remains to protect you."

Maddie flashed a wounded glare. "I think you've been protecting your interest in the music and knew all along Sam Healy was my dad," she said, with a flushed face. "And you were using me to get your hands on the music."

Jake shook his head. "You've got it all wrong." He maintained a calm tone to refrain from being combative. "I didn't learn about Sam being your father until you confided in me. Leon passed the forgery onto me when the men on the Vienna team duped him. After that Douglas and I tailed Leon and followed him to the church. I wasn't aware of you and your relation to Sam." He stroked her cheek with the back of his hand. "You see, we were destined to meet."

Maddie jerked away from his touch. "You're worse than Leon!" Her lips quivered as the words caught in her throat. "You made me feel…"

Jake grabbed her by the waist, pulled her close and gently tightened his grip as she tried pushing him aside. "What did I make you feel?"

Maddie tucked her chin downward, avoiding his gaze and her body trembled in his arms. He angled his head, desperate to see her face, stare into her eyes, and realize the depth of her feelings.

"Guilty"—she whispered—"after all our conversations about faith and forgiveness."

A sickness from his stomach swelled up into his throat. "You're right, I shouldn't talk about trust when I've been so untrustworthy." His limbs went slack, releasing her from his grip. "The longer I put off telling you, the more time we had together. I know it's selfish, but the look in your eyes is the reason I avoided this moment."

Maddie wrapped her arms around herself with a glazed stare. "I wish you said something. Anything."

"I thought I said enough." He peered into the darkness spilling out over the hills. "You'd already decided to see Leon, regardless of all the warnings to discourage you."

"That's not true. I told you, Leon gave me an offer I couldn't refuse."

A full minute passed for her words to settle into his mind. During the years he had known Leon, he witnessed plenty of women falling for his unique style, charm and wealth. He never believed Maddie the type to fall for his flashy pomp. How did Leon come out of this situation looking like the good guy?

Maddie trusted Leon would follow through on whatever he promised her. Jake wanted to tell her to forget any deal with Leon and give him a chance to prove his trustworthiness. If only she'd forgive his mistake and allow him to make it up to her.

To think, Leon's assessments of him were accurate. He did not protect Maddie—he let her down. She probably viewed him as a wolf in sheep's clothing. Jake shoved his hands in the front pockets of his jacket.

"I truly hope Leon gives you all he's promised."

She blinked long and hard. "I want nothing from Leon. I made my decisions for the sake of Sam's family. His wife and two boys were in danger from the guy who evidently was a friend of my father, prior to poisoning him. I had no other choice but accept Leon's aid in protecting them."

Jake shook his head. "How unfortunate I became distracted with believing I was the protective one." Perhaps if he hadn't allowed his feelings and bruised ego to hinder him from making the right choices, he would have spared them the tortuous visits to Leon. "I wanted to tell you the news this morning."

"What news?"

"Yesterday the authorities arrested the guy running the whole forgery scam. They charged him on multiple counts of fraud along with the murders of both Sam and Clyde."

Maddie stepped back until her body rested against the wood column on the porch. Her lips parted and she placed her fingers against her mouth. Why did she have to look so forlorn? Every time he thought he spoke words of encouragement; the desperation grew in her eyes and he achieved the exact opposite. Would sharing the details help build a case in his defense?

Divulging all his knowledge in the matter would show his willingness to be upfront and honest. Or maybe it was too late.

"Douglas told me the urgent update last night."

Her eyelashes lowered and her posture shrank. "Leon said the man still threatened Gretchen and the boys, posing a danger."

Jake reached his hand out, wanting to hold and comfort her. He froze and dropped his arm along his side. Why did he find it so hard to show his feelings? He wanted to ask her how she felt about him, but he feared the answer. No, she must hate and blame him for withholding so much information. Best to leave it all unspoken.

"Instead of helping you, it appears I added to your troubles."

Maddie shrugged. "It doesn't matter now. Sam's family is safe, and you have what matters most to you." She forced a grieved smile and turned, facing the front entry.

Jake extended an arm and blocked her grasp on the handle. "Maddie—"

"I need some time alone." She glanced over her shoulder. "And I'll leave in the morning."

Jake opened the entrance and stepped aside as she rushed inside, hurrying up the stairs. He kicked the mud off his boots on the edge of the porch and left them outside. As the door shut behind, Jake bumped the palm of his hand against his forehead. "I'm an idiot."

About an hour ago Jake had every intention of asking Maddie to stay and accompany him to the museum in Salzburg, but his actions pushed her further away. There was no way she'd forgive him and no chance of developing any sort of relationship. He'd been so focused on competing with Leon, he treated her like one of his artifacts that Leon would try to steal. Pride filled his ambitions and guilt of dishonoring his commitment to Dad drove him to the brink of obsessing over the music.

"Everything all right?" Douglas stepped out of the living room with his spectacles lowered.

"No, not really." Jake tossed his jacket onto the coat rack. "Maddie went to see Leon."

"Oh goodness, did he put half-crocked ideas into her head?"

"Actually, he told her the truth." Jake sighed and pressed his hair backward. "I should've informed her of everything when we arrived here." Jake walked and stood at the foot of the stairs.

Douglas closed the book in his hands. "Yes, well, honesty is always the wisest choice."

"The worst part is I kept encouraging her to have faith and trust, when ultimately I made it impossible for her to believe in me." He banged a fist on the banister.

"You considered Henry and the shock of a stranger—furthermore, a lovely young woman—ended up with the last of your father's work. I suppose that's enough to cause you to make a few rash decisions," Douglas said with a nod. "And although it doesn't excuse your actions, I'm sure given the time, she'll understand the choices you made."

Jake always considered Douglas a part of the family, but since Dad's passing, he'd taken on a parental position. He provided an older wisdom and Jake valued his input on both personal and business matters. Mom appreciated the active role Douglas instated for himself after Dad died. Jake figured Henry made Douglas promise to oversee the household if anything were to happen and Jake knew Dad would say something along the same lines as Douglas.

"I felt if I finished the project, in honor of my dad, he'd be proud of my accomplishment."

"You can rest assured that you completed that job years ago. Henry was always proud of you and said having you as a son remained his greatest honor."

Jake cleared the lump in his throat. "Thanks, Douglas." He turned and climbed the staircase.

"Jake, another thing."

He stopped and peered down at Douglas standing in the entry. "Yeah."

"I suggest taking time off, after your business at Mozart's Geburtshaus? Somewhere with plenty of sunshine. I hear sunny, Southern California is an ideal destination," Douglas said with a wink.

Jake forced a smile, turned and dragged his feet up the steps toward his room. The smell of roasted meat and potatoes failed to entice his lost appetite. His greatest concern now—making things right with Maddie—took precedence. He knew the level of betrayal cut her deep.

Douglas' suggestion sounded tempting, although unrealistic. Within twenty-four hours of meeting Maddie, he entertained the idea of getting away from it all—visiting California, after he completed his work in Salzburg. During their hike through the meadows he contemplated taking a longer route to Ruhpolding and extend their time alone together. There were moments he thought she wished for the same; responsive to his touch, prolonging a hug and a reciprocated kiss. Jake would be a fool to believe she didn't hate him after the deceit.

Entering the bedroom, he crashed into Dad's Barcalounger Mom moved from downstairs into the guestroom a year ago. He slumped into the soft leather and reclined, propping his feet up. He recognized Mom let no one occupy the room. Clothes he'd left last year still sat in the same drawers and two winter coats hung in the closet along with all his outdoor recreational gear. It was hard to grasp the circumstances at thirty-three while he felt eighteen again. Mom would say he currently acted that age too. He wouldn't argue that opinion especially the way he fouled things with Maddie.

The struggles launched when he attempted to take control from God over everything in his life—the manner he handled the breakup of his marital engagement, the divided work crew that sided with Leon and an outright hijack of Mozart's music from Maddie. His self-proclaimed entitlement to the Great Mass' Credo with Agnus Dei, blindsided his logic, reason and purpose. Scrambling to make sure everything worked out according to his plans, regardless of the outcome. Did he still trust God's providence?

In hindsight, he had no right to switch the original Mozart composition with the counterfeit when it fell out of her coat. Although he knew nothing about her at the time, it didn't justify his reaction, after all, Sam enlisted her into the situation without her knowledge.

Jake's chest tightened and he sat upright. Maddie struggled with the same burden, attempting to do the right thing for her family. He leaned forward, placing his elbows on his knees and bowing his head downward. Jake closed his eyes, massaging his forehead, focusing on his next steps going onward.

He prayed for forgiveness, asking God to take control over his life and guide his choices. Surrendering his pride, he sought deliverance from the bondage of iniquity. Meditating on verses of the Lord's faithfulness in the scriptures, he implored God to comfort Maddie and heal her heart. He gave thanks and praise, rejoicing in confidence that God always has a better plan.

CHAPTER TWENTY-TWO

The following morning, Jake gathered the nerve to approach and discuss his actions with Maddie. The floorboards creaked as he walked across the hall. He tapped his knuckles on the cracked door of the guestroom.

"Maddie?" He pushed it open, stepped inside and glanced around. She had cleared all her belongings from the room, leaving no trace of her ever staying at the inn. A pang thrusted into his heart. Her presence rolled into his world like an unexpected downpour after a year of drought and, similar to unpredictable weather patterns, she stormed out of his life forever.

The worst-case scenario he played out in his thoughts for most the night came true: she left as soon as possible, leaving with a deep regret of their lives intersecting. The heaviness of his heart weighed him down. Jake sat on the edge of the bed, resting his head into his palms and blew out a hard breath. Maddie didn't change her mind and still decided to leave, but he didn't give her any reasons to stay.

The way she left in haste made it clear she desired to flee from him and everyone involved. Jake racked his brain all night. What could he say for himself to clarify the position and choices he made? Every time he thought of an explanation for his actions, the awful truth refuted the excuse and revealed she deserved better—an honest, sacrificial man, rooted in his faith with an offer of security and a permanent residence. Jake only showed her deception and recklessness along with being a failure at relationships. The problem stemmed when work became a top priority and hurt those closest to him. The damage remained irreversible and all he could do is let Maddie go.

Jake pressed his palms into the mattress, pushing hard against the heaviness of disappointment added to his body. The back of his hand brushed against a pad of paper on the nightstand, knocking the handwritten sheets onto the floor. He crouched and picked up the embossed letterhead pages labeled, Hotel Füssen. Licking his lips, he examined the words jotted down. A number for a train reservation scrawled across the top accompanied with a confirmed 10:30 a.m. departure time. Their parting was imminent, she'd travel home, and nothing would stop her. Jake read the entire page:

The minute we crashed together,
Our universe expanded,
Stars infinitely brighter.
Any other street,
On a different day,
Missing the moment...

Maddie scratched out the following lines. Jake staggered back onto the bed and swallowed the lump in his throat. "Sweet Maddie."

Her words evoked raw emotion and tenderness, while the refusal to finish her thoughts and feelings exposed her frustration; with him or herself, he couldn't decipher. Should he rush downstairs, gather her into his arms, plead for forgiveness and invite her to stay? If only he could explain his sentiments and express himself with a hope that they would see each other again. Trying to sum up his emotions didn't seem possible.

Jake massaged his chest, putting her at a distance would help him with the clarity of his heart and allow for testing of his feelings. His thumb stroked the hard-pressed words on the page, and he flipped the paper top over.

Psalm 42:8: The Lord will send his faithful love by day; his song will be with me in the night.
I walked in loneliness,
No friend to be found.
I heard tales of true love,
Never to have known,
Deep in my soul,
A long-lost love.
Only to spurn,
Afraid of rejection and pain.
Better to guard my heart,
Walking my own path,
Refusing to look back.
Today I discovered the truth,
The Word pouring over me,
True love always pursuing.
A constant·burning for me,
Faithful as the rising sun.
Unfaltering, unwavering, unchanging love.
Now that I know true love,
I will never let go.

Jake tore the pages off, folded the paper and stuffed them into his back pocket. Whether she left the sheets unintentionally, he read them, and things appeared different. He felt different. If he approached her and handed over her personal writings, maybe she'd be angry with him for poking around the room and reading private stuff.

Jake blinked, and rubbed the corner of his watery eye. Maddie rediscovered her faith in God and softened her heart, revealing a genuine spiritual growth. Above anything, he prayed she would experience the truth of God's love and she'd know real peace. He had shown his own rugged faith, struggling to live out what he believed were Dad's high expectations, yet God lifted his burdens and emotions tugged at his heart. The crushing pain of dishonesty swelled in his chest cavity along with the realization that Maddie was leaving before he confessed that he cared about her.

Tormented with the agony, he longed to learn everything about her and the little time they shared made a deeper impression on him than he intended. His soul was heavier, the weight harder to carry than any affliction he wrestled with the past week. If he declared any feelings, she'd probably laugh in his face or slap him across the cheek, which at this point he deserved.

"Jake," Douglas called down the hall.

Jake left the guestroom. "Yeah, I'm coming."

"Good morning."

"Is it?"

Douglas tilted his head with a slight frown. "Sorry, but Madelyn is ready to depart for the station."

"I know."

* * *

Madelyn set her suitcase on the floor in the entry. "I've really enjoyed my time here." She hugged Kate.

"I've loved your company too. It's a shame to see you go so soon."

"It's for the best."

Kate patted her arm. "I know God will guide you. Have faith and it'll all work out."

"I think that requires a lot of faith."

"Matthew 17 in the Bible says, faith the size of a mustard seed can move mountains, and nothing would be impossible."

She smiled, then waved her hand to follow. "Come with me into the kitchen."

Madelyn trailed behind Kate through the dining area while she swiped crumbs off a table with a dishcloth that hung from the front pocket of her apron. Kate possessed a positive vitality, building more than a guest list for the inn, she constructed a welcoming environment, creating friendships and bonds with everyone that entered her home. Madelyn concluded the quietness in her condo would increase tenfold, upon arrival at her empty house. She surprised herself at how quick she acclimated to the company of others at the inn. Losing Jake wouldn't be the only thing causing her heart to break.

Kate pushed through the kitchen doors, grabbed a travel tumbler from the counter and handed it to her. "Fresh coffee to go."

Madelyn read the engraving on the outside of the mug: *Nolan Family Inn*. She sucked in a hard breath, glanced at Kate, and lowered her gaze, avoiding eye contact. "I will miss you."

"I'll miss you too and I hope you know you're always welcome here." Kate smiled.

A simple gesture turned into an unbearable, emotional moment and she still needed to face Jake. Didn't she hate him? No, after considering the circumstances and staying up most of the night thinking, Madelyn understood his choices, despite the outcome. The situation proved they were both guarded people, hurt and betrayed in the past.

At least Jake got what mattered most to him and he would finish Henry's work. After, he'd be free to pursue his next mission and adventure. A heavy sigh blew through her lips. She would have done the same thing. Her occupation carried significant importance and although it didn't involve physical danger, she endured emotional hazards on the job. If Jake confided in her earlier on their journey, then they'd be delivering Mozart's Great Mass to Salzburg together. Madelyn knew better than anyone that life isn't a fairytale and it's a struggle to survive.

"Kate, Madelyn?" Douglas cracked the door open.

"We're on our way." Kate angled her head.

Madelyn tucked the tumbler into her shoulder bag. "I guess this is goodbye." She shoved her trembling hands in the back pockets of her jeans. With a heavy-footed walk she followed Kate to the front entry of the inn.

"Where's Jake? He's driving Madelyn to the station." Kate glanced around the living area.

"I'm here." Jake marched downstairs.

Madelyn locked eyes with Jake and she felt the weight of her heart in her stomach. His stare pierced through her and it seemed like they were the only two in the room. She summoned all her strength to refrain from rushing toward him, confessing she forgave him and wanted to continue their journey. She found it unbearable to tear her gaze away. With each step her body surged with the awareness of how close he drew near and stood in front of her. The solidity of his stare crushed any barriers constructed to protect her vulnerability.

"You're ready to go?" His lips pressed together into a slight grimace.

The words heaped hot coals onto her head. Madelyn flinched at the dilemma of answering truthfully from her heart or saying what she must. She opened her mouth and Jake moved aside, grabbing his jacket.

His actions spoke loud and clear—he didn't even care to hear her response. Whatever she shared at this point wouldn't matter. Jake made up his mind and his heart; he never considered asking her to stay.

Kate stepped forward, pulling her into a side-hug. "Have a safe journey. I'll keep you in my prayers."

"Thanks, that means a lot to me," Madelyn said.

"Jake, can I get you a coffee or pastry to go?"

"No thanks, Mom, I'll eat later."

Douglas, Jake and Kate walked outside onto the porch. Madelyn paused inside, taking a visual snapshot of everything— every room, mentally absorbing all the images, etching each memory in her mind. The dark varnish hardwood floors, the front entrance filled with a warm welcoming, the guests gathered for meals in the dining area, the conversations in the kitchen, lingering scents of fresh-baked bread and cinnamon, the comfort of mix-matched furniture in the sitting room, where she and Jake shared a kiss. The thought set free a swarm of butterflies inside her belly, yet when she stepped outside the front door, the words from last night kicked her in the stomach.

"Sorry, Douglas and I can't come to the station. We have new arrivals later today," Kate said.

"I understand. Thanks again, for everything."

"Your suitcase is in the car." Douglas smiled and extended a handshake. "Cheers."

"Bye, Douglas." Madelyn placed her hand into his, tugging him forward into an embrace. His body stiffened before he relaxed and wrapped his arms around her. She stepped backward and turned away, keeping emotions under control.

Jake stood by the open passenger-side door of a pristine ivory-over-dark-gray, classic Mercedes Benz. No wonder the entire trip to Germany seemed like another time; lost sheet music from the 1700s, vehicles from other eras, castles, and living out a different version of herself.

Jake shifted his gaze, focusing on her eyes. "I would have driven you all the way to Munich," he said in a low tone.

"It's fine, and I'm sure you'll want to head out to Salzburg as soon as possible." She glanced toward the barn, turned, and climbed inside the vehicle.

Avoiding eye contact, she slipped across the smooth, light-tan, leather interior and glided a palm along the wood dashboard. Jake hopped into the driver's seat and slid the steel sunroof open.

"Did you restore this car, like your motorcycle?" She slinked down and bit her lower lip. It wasn't the best idea, bringing up the bike.

Jake sighed. "This is my dad's 1958 Mercedes Benz Ponton 220S Coupe." He started the car and drove down the gravel driveway. "He bought it when we lived in the States. I was ten at the time, so I helped a little, but mostly watched and learned. I remember flying out from Massachusetts to Indiana, picking up the vehicle from the original owner, and driving it back home in a car trailer." He shook his head and laughed. "The mishaps we had on that trip."

Madelyn grew fond of hearing stories from Jake and Kate about the Nolan history. Their reminiscing filled her with longings for a family that she buried deep inside. The feeling of an emotional bond cemented the harsh truth of the loneliness awaiting her at home. She choked down the sentiments and glanced at Jake.

"After a lot of thinking last night, I'm glad you have Mozart's Great Mass and can finish Henry's work." The wool-and-polyester blend of fabric grazed her knuckles as she curled the bottom hem of her sweater. "In my heart I wished for you to be the one."

Jake shot a quick glance, parted his lips, but said nothing as he refocused on driving.

Madelyn cleared her throat. "I mean, I always wanted you to have the music."

Jake pulled into a parking space at the Ruhpolding train station. He turned off the motor, twisting his torso, and revealing sullen eyes with lack of sleep.

"I'm really sorry." He inhaled and exhaled deep through his nose. "About everything. I didn't want you to get hurt and although I didn't want us to part on disagreeable terms, at least I know you'll be safe."

"I…" Madelyn winced, rubbing her cold fingers on her scalp as the sun beat down on her head through the open roof. She didn't expect a declaration of feelings and nothing changed, from the first day they met; he kept trying to send her away. "I better go, I don't want to miss my train."

"Right. I'll grab your bag." Jake stepped outside the driver side.

Closing her eyes, she pinched the bridge of her nose. What could she do to change things? This is how their story would end;

no happy ending, no epic romance, only the makings of real life, with struggles, heartache, deception and death.

Madelyn approached Jake at the rear of the car as he pulled out her suitcase and shut the trunk. She straightened her shoulders and grabbed the luggage handle. She prepared herself the past few days for departure and a final goodbye, but didn't picture it ending at a train station, under strained tensions. Now, her life had become an official cliché.

Jake hooked his thumbs on the front pockets of his jeans and rocked backward onto his heels. At a loss for words, he glanced around the parking lot. He wanted her gone and counted the minutes until her final departure.

"Well, it's been an experience, Jake Nolan." Her voice strained.

His lips pressed tight, and he looked over his shoulder. "You've got your ticket?"

"I printed it this morning."

He turned and reached for her suitcase. The warmth of his palm covered her hand as he gripped the handle. "There's about twenty minutes till the train arrives."

Madelyn tucked a corner of her lower lip under her front tooth and walked beside Jake. A couple days ago, she remained eager for him to drop her at a transportation location, so she could return home. Nausea swept over as they strolled toward the light-and-dark equant stone building. Sunlight gleamed off the second-floor window, reflecting into her eyes. She squinted, gazing upward at the brick-framed windows with pink geranium flowers blooming from boxes.

People rushed in and out of the glass doors of the station, the wheels of cases clanked on the cement. The chattering of the other passengers' greetings to their loved ones echoed throughout the room.

"Want to get a drink or snack before you go?" Jake gestured to a coffee cart.

"I'm all right for now, thanks." She ran her fingers along the engraving on the travel tumbler in her bag. An empty mug with his name etched on it was all she'd have left of Jake Nolan. Yet, she was leaving her heart behind in Ruhpolding.

He half smiled. "It's about a two-hour ride to Munich, with a stop in Traunstein."

Jake held the door, waiting for a couple to exit before leading the way out onto the concrete platform. Madelyn blinked several times while she stepped into a cloud of cigarette smoke outside. She glanced around, hoping Jake wouldn't notice her teary eyes.

Standing behind the yellow-painted line, a wind kicked up as a locomotive rumbled in on the opposite side of the tracks. In less than two minutes the train rolled out of the station. She flicked her gaze upward at the double-sided, numeric, hanging wall clock. Time was running out, and these were their last moments together. She didn't know what to say.

Madelyn looked at Jake, memorizing every fleck of light reflected and absorbed in the deep blue of his eyes. A few days ago, he was a stranger, and in a rapid procession of disasters, he had become a significant person in her life. He showed an honest faith through mistakes and flawed character—not that she didn't feel wounded by him switching the music—but the time they spent together, walking the alpine meadows and their meaningful conversations. What effect did she have on his life, if any at all? A red train barreled into the station, blowing strands of hair into her face and she shivered with a wave of cold.

"I guess it's a few minutes early," Jake said.

The prickle of tears stung, and she gulped the tight pinch in her throat. "Jake," she whispered under her breath. They spoke no words, yet they communicated much in one swift movement, as they embraced each other. She closed her eyes, hoping he wouldn't let her go. Her head pressed against his torso, she wanted to dive in and get lost within his soul, a sea to explore everything that comprised Jake Nolan, and know him inside and out.

Jake held one hand on her nape, while the other stroked her hair as he kissed the top of her scalp. She craned her neck upward from his chest, with their lips inches apart, Jake leaned forward, pressing his soft, warm mouth against hers. With a gentle kiss he enveloped her lips then sealed the gesture with a peck. Her face rested against his palm, with his breath on her cheek, she felt weightless and her knees buckled.

Madelyn lifted her eyelids and like the rising sun bringing new light, bursting onto the horizon, all her feelings for Jake emerged, yet she'd never see him again. He brushed a strand of hair away from her chin, allowing his hand to trail along her throat. He smiled with a gleam in his eyes. His gesture was as a goodbye kiss and nothing else.

The only promise between them was to deliver Mozart's Great Mass to Salzburg. Now that he had the sheet music, it broke the commitment. Any bravery or confidence she gained slipped away and the words piled on the tip of her tongue. The intensity of his stare revealed he perceived her feelings. Jake read her like the pages of a novel and with a mischievous grin, already knew the ending.

His glance shifted between her and the train. "Five minutes." He stepped backward.

"I…" Her heart hammered against her chest and words knotted in her mouth. "I wanted to finish my dad's request. I feel like I accomplished nothing by coming here."

"You accomplished more than you realize." His eyes shined with confidence. "And that's the first time I've heard you call Sam your dad. Isn't that what you set out to do? Put the past behind you and look forward to the future?" Jake spoke with the cool, courageous tone she wanted to convey.

"I guess I'm feeling the loss of my family. The bond you have with Kate and Douglas…" She lowered her gaze. "I miss having a family."

"You also found out you have two younger brothers." Jake slanted his head sideways with a thoughtful expression.

"Yeah, that's true. I don't know what I'm saying." She swayed on one foot. "Haven't felt myself for days."

"Hey, I'm sure you'll feel better once you're home. I've never met anyone as determined and focused as you."

Tears swelled from the ache of being let down gently. Why did she allow herself to get emotionally entangled? She failed to demonstrate her detachment from relationships. It seemed Jake wouldn't settle for anything less than exposing the truth—she needed people and relations in her life.

"All aboard," the train conductor called out.

Madelyn squared her shoulders, lifted her chin and held out a stiff handshake. "Bye."

No point in waiting for him to stop her from leaving, when he made it clear he conceded to send her home.

"Maddie." Jake inched closer, curled his fingers around her hand and pressed their palms together as he escorted her toward the carriage's sliding doors. Her tough exterior crumbled under his caress.

"Everything will work out." Jake gave a gentle squeeze and let go.

Madelyn nodded, picked up her suitcase, and boarded the train. She felt his stare but resisted turning and gazing into his eyes one last time.

CHAPTER TWENTY-THREE

Madelyn tugged her suitcase behind, searching for a seat in the carriage. She focused her attention on the opposite side to avoid catching a glimpse of Jake on the platform. Tossing her bag into an available spot by a window, she slinked into an empty four-person dinette and hung her head downward while sliding her hands over the smooth table.

The slow grind of steel on the tracks emulated the cry of her heart and the train whistle echoed the screaming ache inside. Tears pooled, and she dabbed the tips of her fingers in the corner of her eyes. She let herself get caught up in emotions, and on a daily basis she advised other women on refraining from getting carried away by feelings.

Jake was right; as soon as she arrived home and settled into her routine, she'd feel like herself again. Who was she kidding? She wasn't the same person from four days ago. So much changed—not just her perceptions about Sam and forgiveness, but the importance of relationships, her renewed faith in God, and opening her heart to love again. Although Jake didn't reciprocate the sentiment, for the first time in years, she awakened to the possibility of a romantic relationship.

A romance between her and Jake was laughable. They never exchanged phone numbers or contact information. Sure, finding the number for the inn seemed simple enough, but the fact Jake didn't ask to communicate in the future drove the painful truth into her heart: he had no intentions of ever talking to her again.

"Leaving so soon?"

Madelyn jerked her head upward. "What are you doing here?"

"You're surprised I'm here?" Leon unbuttoned his navy blue, hand-tailored suit jacket and sat in the available seat across the table. "Are your tears out of concern that you'd never see me again?"

She closed her eyes for a minute and prayed for strength. Did she feel equipped to handle another encounter with Leon now?

"I'm no longer of any use to you. Jake has what you want, so you're both free of any worry of me getting in the way of your plans." Madelyn turned and gazed out the window. "Too bad you wasted a train ticket."

"On the contrary, meine Schatzi, my treasure." Leon yanked off his leather gloves and covered her hand with his palm. "Collecting art and music are not my only passions."

Madelyn held her breath as his fingers curled, tightening his grip. A slow smile built, and he leaned forward with firm eye contact.

Heat crept up her nape. "Wha—what are you saying?"

"I'd like you to stay." His fair skin flushed with a shade of golden amber.

Her mouth went dry. "I don't know how to respond."

Madelyn slipped from his clasp and she pressed a hand against her abdomen. Leon said the phrase she longed for Jake to profess. Did she even take Leon at his word? She couldn't conceive Leon loving anyone besides himself.

"Please don't involve me in another one of your ploys to get Mozart's music from Jake. The flaw in that plan is believing Jake would care enough—"

"Now I see." His clammy palms dragged across the table as he reclined. "The feelings are mutual between the two of you."

Leon drew in a deep breath and exhaled out his mouth. "Jake is a fool for allowing the real treasure to slip through his fingers and wouldn't admit a greater love exists beyond sheets of music."

Madelyn's heart exploded with the possibility of meaning more to Jake than his work, but the fact Leon had been the person to taunt her emotions caused the excitement to burn into smoldering ash.

"Are you telling me you're foregoing your pursuit of Mozart's Great Mass to focus your attention on me?"

"There are many relics and artifacts to possess, but there is only one *you*." A translucent blue glimmered in his gray eyes, his lips relaxed and slightly parted.

Madelyn sucked in her lower lip. She wasn't sure if Leon was serious or trying to manipulate the situation again. Did he honestly have an interest or care for anything other than his possessions?

"I don't know if I can trust anyone after everything that's happened."

Leon narrowed his gaze. "Did I lie about any of the things that transpired up to this point?"

She shook her head with the accuracy of his statement. Leon had been the only straightforward person over the past few days. A hard breath escaped from her lips. "What is it that you hope to achieve with me?"

"Come away with me and you'll see."

Her muscles tensed with an increased pulse. "Where? I need to travel home. I have a life and a job in California."

"We'll go to Salzburg for an extended weekend. I have a property in the city, all expenses paid und naturally I'll provide you with your own private suite." Leon formed his hands into a steeple, resting his chin against his fingertips as he kept strong eye contact.

Keeping her cool, she swept her hair back from her brow. "Why would we go to Salzburg? The train goes to Munich."

"I thought you'd at least like to see your father's final request completed." He arched an eyebrow and curled his lips up to one side. "Aren't you on a personal mission to exonerate your father from his crime?"

A surprising calmness and peace filled her chest at the mention of Sam. She hadn't even dwelled on him since her conversation and prayer with Pastor Fredrick. God redirected her through the events in Germany and freed her from the chains of the past. "I didn't know you cared."

"I'm the one asking you to remain und I ensured the protection of your family. I'm a man of integrity. Regardless of what Jake may have told you, I pride myself on being an example of my people in Bavaria."

Right when she had hopes of Leon being a rational person, he made odd statements. Maybe she read too much into the comment and it was a commonality of rich individuals to make off-handed remarks. Leon must've had another scheme up his sleeve and planned to intercept the music from Jake in Salzburg; perhaps she'd stop him. Her head whirled with the speed of the train as she gazed out the window.

The landscape blurred with the blending effect of paintbrush strokes of mixed green and blue shades. If the opportunity to help Jake occurred by keeping Leon's desires and ambitions in check then she had to take that chance.

She wriggled her tingling toes and shifted in her seat. "All right, I'll go with you to Salzburg."

The train's automated recording announced the next station. Leon stood with a distant smile.

"This is our destination." He stared; his eyes smoky and fiery-in the gray of his irises. Towering above the table he reached and pulled the emergency cord. Screeching steel pounded on the tracks and the train slowed to a stop. Madelyn and the other passengers lunged forward then backward into their seats. Leon held the cable while maintaining a solid stance.

Madelyn glanced around in a panic. "What are you doing?" she said through gritted teeth. All eyes in the carriage glared at Leon.

"We're getting off here." Leon gripped her forearm and with a gentle pull, helped her out of the dinette.

"Why didn't you wait to get off at Traunstein?" She grabbed her suitcase.

"I like a certain aura of unpredictability to surround me." He waved his hand, instructing her to follow him through the connecting carriage and emergency exit.

Madelyn stared at her feet while passing by the passengers as their whispered complaints grew louder. Leon struck the door release lever and stepped down onto the gravel between the tracks.

"Halt! Komm zu mir bitte." The conductor rushed down the corridor.

Madelyn froze and whirled her head toward the man. She peered outside at the dense forest of spruce and fir trees, leading to the foot of the mountains. She didn't think Leon intended to harm her, but she worried about his lack of restraint.

"What are you waiting for?" Leon said.

Madelyn glanced over her shoulder as the conductor reached out. Her shoe inched forward and she lost balance. The weight of her suitcase thrust her outside, and she tripped on the foot plate, propelling her straight into Leon's arms. His slender body type deceived her, and he didn't budge with the force of the impact.

Madelyn opened and closed her eyes a few times as her brain swirled with the rapid movements. The man yelled out a few obscenities before closing the carriage doors. She tucked her limbs close to her sides and Leon rested his hands on her shoulders. With her neck angled downward, he slipped his finger under her chin, tilting her face upward. "How is meine Schatzi?"

Madelyn shook her head, regained her senses, and staggered backward. "I'm fine."

With a bitter smile he picked up her luggage from the ground. "Let's move away from the tracks." Leon traipsed the grassy slope.

The sound of the squealing train whistle made her body jolt, and she rushed down the verdant terrain to join Leon. Did she make the right choice going with him? Yes, even with the slightest prospect for helping Jake and Leon progress beyond their differences when rivalry blinded them. Leon stopped and set her baggage on the ground. His light-blond locks blew in the breeze and he stared out into the distance. He lifted his hand over his brow, shielding the sun from his vision.

"This way." He pointed toward the east.

Blowing out a heavy breath, her shoulders dropped. Madelyn had enough of the outdoor adventures the other day. "I don't understand why we didn't stay on the train."

"Since you left the comforts of my castle, I assumed you enjoyed wandering through the wilderness." He glanced back and walked ahead, leaving the suitcase at her feet. "Perhaps that is only with the preferred company of Jake?"

Madelyn almost regretted her decision going with Leon. He had a way of leading her to believe he was a deep, complex person whom others misunderstood. Although, he harbored a deeper wound beyond the loss of his parents at a young age and she wanted him to confide in her expertise. Pushing up her sleeves, she grabbed her stuff and hurried beside him.

If she connected with him and spoke in his terminologies, she had a chance at discovering his emotional ailments. "I'm accustomed to driving in the confines of freeway congestion. It's lovely out here, but I've done more hiking in nature this week than in my entire life."

"The Nolans have exposed you to those with primitive standards. I have unlimited resources." Leon offered a slight smile and straightened his maroon silk tie.

Madelyn grappled with figuring out when he was being humorous or serious. His demeanor sold a story of constant solemnity with a reputed arrogance. Frequently she caught him glancing out the corner of his eye. What response did he expect? A playful retort or defensive fighter? From what she experienced with Leon she'd guess all of the above.

Wading through knee-high reeds, they stopped at the edge of a thick area of trees. A less-than-visible dirt trail, with grass sprouting through the middle, hid any definite direction.

"Is this where we're supposed to be?"

"All in good time." Leon checked his watch. With an exaggerated sigh, he folded his arms across his chest and tapped his foot. The impeccable style of his clothes flaunted the money he had at his disposal. She couldn't picture him getting his hands dirty on any of his explorations. He demonstrated being in a position of directing and giving orders.

After a few minutes she sat on top of her suitcase. The rays of the sun poked like fire irons on the back of her neck. She tied her hair into a low bun and fanned herself with her hand. She surveyed Leon with the circling pace of a caged animal. Better to observe his mannerisms now and ask questions later.

As the bushes rustled, he snapped his attention toward the movement. A red squirrel scurried on the ground and hopped up a tree trunk. With a pinched expression, he massaged his temples and closed his eyes. He pulled out a pocket square, yellow-green with cream polka-dots, and blotted the sheen from his face. Rather than fuss with a proper fold, he shoved it inside beside a realistic, snow-white flower, worn through the buttonhole of his lapel.

"Are you wearing an edelweiss boutonnière?"

Leon glared at the dirt road and remained silent for over a minute before he answered. "Ja."

"Did someone give it to you or—"

"It was intended as a gift," he said with a slight frown.

"What happened?"

The color drained from his face. "She proved to be unworthy." The root of his pain flickered in his eyes and he turned away.

Leon of all people, a hopeless romantic? No wonder she felt drawn to him, she recognized the hurt and devastation of a broken heart. Madelyn hopped from her suitcase, knocking it to the ground and stepped beside him. She placed her hand on the hot, wool blend of his sleeve and brushed his forearm with a light stroke. He ignored her presence and stared off into the distance.

"Who was she?"

Leon flinched under her touch and his posture straightened. He moved his arm to his side and delivered a long, pained look. "A weakness und I assure you I'll never…" His eyes narrowed and peered at the dirt road. "Finally." He groaned under his breath.

A familiar black BMW rounded the bend of trees in a dust cloud. The tires crunched the gravel while maneuvering around potholes. The vehicle pulled up and stopped beside them. Leon picked up her suitcase and knocked on the trunk. The automatic doors unlocked, and Leon tossed in her bag then slammed it shut. He opened the back-passenger side for her and gestured with his arm to get inside.

"Hello, Drexwyler." Madelyn slid into the car.

"Hallo."

"Mason, the delivery of a casual greeting sounds rude." Leon closed the door and climbed into the front. "You're late."

"Entschuldigen Sie bitte, mein Fehler," Drexwyler said as he reversed and drove in the direction he came.

"Don't bother with an apology." Leon flipped on the air conditioning full blast. "Do you have a valid excuse for your tardiness? We waited several minutes in record-breaking heat."

"It wasn't a long wait and the fresh air was nice," Madelyn said.

Leon turned his head over his shoulder and gazed out the corner of his eye. "Your benevolence adds to your value, a true treasure."

Madelyn cringed whenever he spoke of her like a possession and if he implied it again, she'd kick his seat. She raised then dropped her shoulders and pressed her back into the leather interior.

Leon felt betrayed by a woman in the past. If a situation presented itself in Salzburg and Madelyn intervened, aiding Jake, she risked evoking Leon's feelings of resentment, which could turn volatile. She didn't want to destroy the little trust created between them. She grazed her teeth along her lower lip and prayed for direction.

Madelyn held onto the handgrip with the bumpy off-road ride for about ten kilometers until Drexwyler arrived at the A8 motorway. What kind of timeframe did she have to work with during the ride? The drive provided the opportunity to challenge Leon's linear thinking and help him accept responsibility for things in his control.

"You were telling me about the woman and the edelweiss—"

"Was I?"

Drexwyler hit the brakes. Madelyn lurched forward and the safety belt tightened across her chest, forcing her backward.

"I apologize, my foot slipped."

Her internal temperature and heart rate increased. She closed her eyes, took a deep breath and focused on the back of his head. *Treat Leon as a regular client.* "If we discuss the interconnectedness of everything from your past and surroundings in life, I can help you work toward personal growth."

"I advised you before to refrain from your psychobabble."

"I thought you enjoyed my company?" Madelyn said.

Silence lingered for over a minute until a heavy sigh escaped from his lips. "You're asking me to expose the secret annals of my soul und neglecting the professional etiquette of a practicing therapist." He rotated in his seat with a deliberate arched brow. "First, build a relationship."

"The last thing I'd want is to make you feel uncomfortable. We're getting to know each other, sharing personal details—"

"You prefer me to talk while you try useless scholarly techniques, taught by so-called professors holding a worthless PhD."

"Please don't mock the benefits of specialized therapy."

Leon turned and faced forward. "You misconstrue my remarks by assuming I'd choose to change."

Madelyn leaned closer as the belt stretched. "I think if we continue our conversation—"

Leon laughed. "Must I indulge your amateur methods of counseling for the next hour?"

"Not at all, if you find enjoyment in something other than degrading my profession."

The leather squeaked as she slouched into the back seat. Leon seemed amused when it was at the expense of humiliating someone else and communicating with him proved a greater challenge than she expected.

"Don't feel discouraged, you made real progress. You're the first therapist I've allowed to remain in my presence."

"I guess I'll consider myself lucky." She blew a stray hair away from her eye with the air filled in her cheeks.

Leon appeared to be an expert at evading any conversation about his personal life while managing at the same time to provoke a confrontation with mere words and took pleasure in the task. Madelyn rolled her neck, relaxing her muscles. She clung onto her newfound strength in her faith and prayed for a miracle. In the meantime, she would lead Leon to believe she was a pawn in his game.

"How about if I turn on music?" Leon pushed a button on the front console. "Die Entführung aus dem Serail by Wolfgang Amadeus."

The choice seemed fitting: *The Abduction from the Seraglio.* She wouldn't put it past Leon to have chosen that specific Mozart opera and feel inspired to live out the acts. Leon portraying the Pasha, Jake in the role of Belmonte and her as Konstanze? No, that's incorrect, Jake never professed his love, and she hoped, but doubted Leon would show mercy. An eerie sensation swept over Madelyn as if she were part of scenes in a performance orchestrated by Leon.

In the middle of the second act, during Ach Belmonte, Ach Mein Leben, Belmonte questions Konstanze's faithfulness, while she was alone with the Pasha. If Jake discovered she accepted an invitation from Leon to go away for the weekend, maybe he'd doubt her motives and intent. As much as she expressed a concern for Leon's wellbeing and connection to the Nolan family, she had to believe Jake would know her priority and heart remained true to him. Her eyes became heavy as she gazed out the window.

* * *

Leon twisted his torso toward the back seat. Madelyn had said nothing for over twenty minutes and Act II of Die Entführung aus dem Serail almost concluded. She kept her eyes shut as a few dark strands of hair swooped across her cheek. Even after he contributed toward her emotional turmoil, she trusted him, accepted the offer, and left herself susceptible to his proposals. His nerves responded with hypersensitivity whenever they touched, though he wouldn't dare open his heart. He hadn't risked getting close to someone since…

Leon shook his head with an uncertainty on whether he wished to arouse sentiments of love or fear. Madelyn would never see him for anything other than her captor and she already confessed having feelings for Jake. Better to remain alone and in control. The way emotions allowed him to taunt and manipulate served his purposes; most important, he still had a chance at retrieving his music. Jake and Madelyn were clay in his hands, ready to be molded however he pleased.

Once a collector, now a creator. Everything went according to plan. The calm of her breathing while she slept magnified her beauty—a demure physical attractiveness intertwined with a suppressed sensuality and an awareness of her seductive powers. He licked his lips, faced forward and closed his eyes, clearing his mind. A vision of Madelyn luring him down a long, dark corridor, her laughter echoing through the hall haunted his meditation. His eyelids flashed open as the opera hit a crescendo.

"O torment of the soul…" he whispered.

Mason focused on the road. "Welch ein geschick, O Qual der Seele."

"Ja, what dreadful fate conspires against us?" He swallowed hard.

Mason knew his place and wouldn't dare intrude on a moment of solitary thinking. The silent agreement was part of the original orders in his commission to serve the Von Füssen household.

Leon decreased the temperature then loosened his tie and wiped beads of perspiration with his pocket square. The main task remained for him to execute commands without delays or flaws.

"We're approaching A1. What are your plans?" Mason said.

"Take A10, south of Salzburg. It'll allow her a chance to dream."

"Are you going to contact Jake?"

"Shh, you'll wake her before it's time."

The comfort of music lulled him into a place of peace and spoke to his soul in a way no person reached the deepest part of his core. No matter her allures, he would never permit a woman to make a fool of him again. Leon would ensure she served his aim of ensnaring Jake into his trap and nothing else.

CHAPTER TWENTY-FOUR

Madelyn smacked her head against the window, awakening her as the car made a sharp left, then a right turn. The tires screeched as the vehicle swerved up the winding road of a mountain.

"Are you quite certain we're being followed?" Leon said.

"Positive. I noticed an automobile tailing behind us for the last thirty kilometers. I tried to lose the pursuer and turned at Tennengebirge pass," Drexwyler said.

"You Dummkopf, this is the only street access for the alp."

Why would someone follow Leon? He didn't have Mozart's music. Madelyn rubbed her head, thinking she'd been dreaming. Blinking her eyes several times, she gazed outside. Mountain peaks with evergreen trees and shrubbery stretched across a three-hundred-and-sixty-degree view as the car drove a steep incline. The sun reflected off the white-with-gray speckled limestone and shined a harsh glare into her vision.

"What's going on, where are we?" Madelyn said.

"Stille, I need to think," Leon said.

"Don't hush me, I—"

Drexwyler slammed on the brakes and Madelyn lunged forward.

"The sign states no vehicle entry past the gate."

Leon exhaled aloud. "I can read. You"—he pointed at Drexwyler—"stay here and try to detain whoever followed us. Madelyn, come with me." He exited the car, opened the back door, and grabbed her hand.

"What is the rush? Can't you wait and see if your assumptions are correct," she said.

"This is not the occasion for confrontations."

Madelyn glanced around and stared up at the peak. Nausea stirred in her stomach. "Are we climbing the mountain?"

"Your persistent chatter is clouding my judgment," he said, in a stilted tone.

"You invited me, so I must factor into your plans, and I'll keep talking until I get answers."

Leon didn't give a second glance. He continued to take long strides up the paved pathway and pulled her along. "As of today, you will not need to climb a mountain, there are aerial trams."

Her calf muscles tightened as she shadowed him up a steel staircase. "Ah, it doesn't look like the tram is operating. We should return to the car."

"I'll inquire with the man at the ticket booth."

"Wir haben geschlossen," the cable car attendant said.

Madelyn pushed past Leon and leaned forward, resting her elbows onto the counter. "Sprichst Du Englisch?" She refused to be unaware of what they discussed.

"Ja, I speak English."

"I'll translate, they're closed." Leon shot a hard stare and his nostrils flared as he tautened his lips.

Madelyn cleared her throat. "I guess we better leave."

The man pulled out a brochure. "Last cable car left five minutes ago. Regular operating hours are—"

"I don't care." Leon tossed the pamphlet back at him. "You'll send us up now." He stood tall above the attendant, staring down with a wild fury and entrancing eyes.

Had Leon mastered the technique of mind control?

The man scrunched his face. "What can I—"

Leon pulled out a hundred-euro banknote from his leather billfold and slammed it down on the counter. "Schnell, schnell." He snapped his fingers. "I'd hate for you to be responsible for any unfortunate consequences."

The attendant tripped over his own feet and stumbled out of the office. "I'll take you to the tram now." They followed the man for a brisk fifteen-minute walk. He slid open the door of a silver cable car, motioning for Madelyn and Leon to step inside.

"Danke," Madelyn said as he stood with wide eyes.

She walked into the suspended gondola and gripped onto the cool, chrome handrail. The doors shut and, with a sudden jerking motion, the haulage rope propelled the tram. She sucked in a quick breath, and her mouth watered with a queasiness rising in the back of her throat.

Leon peered below at the valley. "You can relax now."

Relax? She removed one hand from the handrail and rubbed her clammy palm against her thigh as the tram swung on the line. Her eyes fixed onto the floor. She wouldn't dare glance out the window.

"Now you oblige me with silence?"

"I…" She gasped and latched onto the rail tighter as the car bumped and joggled along the wheels pulling the system.

"Schatzi, you're afraid of heights," he said in a pacified voice and slipped his arm around her shoulder. "The ride is a few minutes."

Madelyn nodded and closed her eyes as she slowed her breathing. Leon clarified he possessed the capability of expressing compassion, for those he deemed worthy. The treatment of people he considered below his social standards, he demonstrated an act of superiority, which revealed an underlining struggle with insecurities. It made sense, with Leon experiencing the trauma of losing both his parents at a young age and his feelings about an embittered relationship with the mysterious woman that he labeled unworthy.

"We're here," Leon said as they slowed to a stop.

The doors automatically unlocked, and he guided her from the tram with his arm around her side. As she stepped outside onto the concrete, she opened her eyes. She swayed with a continuous sensation of the swinging cable car.

"I still don't understand what you hope to accomplish by coming up here."

"Enjoy the atmosphere. Smell that fresh air." He inhaled deeply through his nose. "Look around, you're at one of the top tourist attractions in the region." He spread his arms open wide.

Clean air filled her nostrils with the scent of minerals from wet rock. Madelyn expelled a hard breath and scanned the sights. The elevation must have been over five thousand feet. Mountain peaks, surrounded by swelling clouds ready to burst with moisture, and black birds circled overhead. She didn't feel confident that a small wooden railing, intended for security, would keep her from plummeting the staggering heights and thousands of feet to the ground below. She held onto Leon's hand rather than risk walking too close to the ledge. He forged forward, taking long strides and she hurried to keep up with the pace.

At the dizzying altitude the temperature dropped, and the wind chill blew right through to her bones. Madelyn longed for the sunshine and safety of the meadows they sat in an hour ago. Continuing a twenty-minute walk along the pathway, zigzagging up the curve of the mountain, they reached the last bend and stopped. Her legs tremored with the rigorous workout on her thighs and she bent forward, catching a breath.

Madelyn glanced out the corner of her eye and captured a glimpse of the river winding through the valley. She gasped and flicked her gaze upward at the arched rock formation creating a hole in the mountain's side. Oh good Lord, why did she depart from the train?

Leon turned in every direction as if he were searching for something or someone. He gave her hand a gentle tug. "Let's go."

Madelyn dug her heels into the ground. "What is this place?"

He halted with a slow, disbelieving head shake. "You still don't trust me?"

She crossed her arms. "I'm not moving until you tell me."

"Have a little faith, I wish you no harm." A sizzling glow lit his irises and one side of his mouth curled upward at the corner while he slinked closer with the moves of a snake spying its victim.

Madelyn quivered as he lifted her chin. Leon shook her nerves whenever he approached her with the ambitious look of a huntsman in his eyes.

"Inside is a world of ice giants." He stood close and leaned forward with his breath on her face. "At one time the Austrians believed it was the gateway to hell."

Madelyn stiffened and the hairs on her nape raised. A thick mass caught in her throat and she lost the chance to vocalize a response.

Leon stepped backward, his eyes two shimmering gray pools of melted metal. "Shall we proceed?"

"I, ah—"

"Gut."

Passing under the limestone archway they walked toward the double wooden doors. She looked over her shoulder, trying to decide which sight was worse—the perilous heights or the cave of the unknown.

Leon picked up two oil lanterns from a table outside the entry and lit the lamps. He yanked on the iron latch and a blast of cold air gushed into her face as she stepped inside the entrance. The force of the wind almost knocked her off her feet.

He wrapped his frigid fingers around her hand. "You're perfectly safe."

Madelyn shuddered and hugged herself with one arm in the subzero temperature. She held up the lantern and inched forward into the blackness. The door banged shut behind Leon and her body jolted with the thud. She felt him press against her back.

"Where do we go?" Madelyn stared onward, seeing nothing.

Leon raised a lamp above her head and illuminated narrow wood planks, leading to a set of stairs.

"Over there." He placed a palm on her shoulder and steered her steps.

She shuffled her feet on the wet floor and found it difficult to gain a steady foothold as he gripped her tight. Did he care about her safety or send her out in front, for testing the durability of the structure before subjecting himself to any potential dangers?

With the lantern outstretched at arm's length, Madelyn reached and grabbed the icy, metallic hand railing. In the darkness, her next footstep could be to her death. Each ascending step made the staircase appear never ending and the outside world farther away. She didn't see the ice giants Leon spoke about, but sensed they surrounded them. The echoing sounds of their footsteps, sporadic drips of water, and her pounding heartbeat in her ears filled the cave.

Physical fatigue wavered her balance and Leon supported her entire weight. In her weakness she leaned on the rail and scraped her knuckles against the craggy wall. Madelyn didn't feel anything. Either her fingers stopped trembling, or they were numb with frostbite.

Mountain and ice climbing existed for adventure seekers, and not the faint of heart. Yoga skills provided the flexibility, but she lacked muscular endurance to prepare for the current level of exercise. She couldn't imagine visiting this location as a vacation destination. They certainly didn't wear appropriate attire for the strenuous activity and for the first time during the visit to Bavaria she hadn't worn her coat.

Madelyn forced her eyes open and saw less now than when they entered the cave. No matter where she positioned the lantern, the tiny glow lit a minuscule few inches in front. Did he intend to bring them here all along and this was his idea of torture? If so, he succeeded.

She lost count, but they must have climbed around seven hundred steps when they reached the end of the staircase, and right before she collapsed with rapid, shallow breathing, as she clutched her chest. At the top, she gasped and hunched over, her lungs burned from the frosty atmosphere.

"We'll take a break," Leon said in a strained, unrecognizable voice.

He held his lantern at chin level, elucidating his high cheekbones, but darkening his eyes which gave him an unearthly appearance. A little light cast ghostly, blue shadows on the ice behind. She blinked several times to rid the image from her mind.

"Enjoying our adventure?" he asked.

"W-woo…would be better if it wasn't so cold." Her teeth chattered.

Madelyn still strained, adjusting her vision in the dark, and she flinched at the touch of his hand.

Leon drew her close. "You need to conserve your body heat."

If Leon didn't have access to thousands of bedrooms at his hotels, she would have thought he used this kind of tactic for carnal contact. She doubted it was part of an overarching plan since he wasn't dressed for the environment either. Madelyn shivered uncontrollably and understood the need to huddle together. She stepped and turned toward his open arm. He tightened his embrace, pressing her against his torso.

Leon raised the lamp, staring her in the face, his eyes bright and gleaming. She curved her chest inward and gulped hard. Didn't they agree their relationship would remain platonic during their trip to Salzburg? Her pulse quickened; hotness prickled across her collarbone and crept up her neck.

Taking a deep breath, he straightened his posture. "You're getting warm," he said, with a gratifying sigh.

As her body temperature increased, her face and ears burned. She licked her chilled, dry lips. "Why did we come here?"

Leon extended a limb and shined the lantern in front of them. "Look at these magnificent sculptures."

Madelyn shifted her shoulders and leaned toward the light. Massive stalagmites formed a circular display, something like an ice version of Stonehenge. Leon tucked his hand under her arm, guiding her along a level plank walkway, with no railing, and through a shimmering frozen tunnel.

A giant ice formation towered in the center of the largest area of the cavern. Strategically positioned lights, behind the water-stained limestone, irradiated an aquamarine icy structure. The climate created a rising sculpture and curled them into the shape of a crashing wave. Madelyn closed then widened her eyes as her eyesight improved with the additional light. Her nose twitched with her face pressed against Leon's wool suit.

Madelyn twisted in the opposite direction, tilting her head upward, and investigated the solid ice wall. She reached out and ran her fingertips against the frozen foundation. A tingle rippled across her skin. She tightened her hands into fists and shivered.

She swallowed the dryness in her throat. "Can we leave now?"

A thud echoed throughout the cave. Leon stood with a rigid stance; his eyes flickered. "We're not alone."

"Who—"

His hand pushed against the small of her back. "Keep moving."

A darkened archway led to an icy labyrinth. Leon halted, expelling his breath as he raised his lantern and searched in each direction. One tunnel emitted yellow-orange flickers of light. Leon's stiff finger poked her shoulder. She hobbled toward the glowing passageway. The exposure of her skin to the arctic temperature tightened the tendons in her feet and ankles.

"Maddie, where are you?" a distant voice amplified in the dome.

Her heart dropped into her belly and she froze while Leon clonked into her back, knocking his lantern onto the ground. The sound of stomping footsteps increased, advancing up the stairs and her pulse raced with the speed of his feet.

"J—"

Frantic, frozen fingers slipped across her chin, clasping over her mouth. Her lamp crashed and smashed on the wood planks. With a deep breath, cold air surged through her nostrils. She grunted and Leon pressed his palm harder against her lips while he fumbled with the other hand, folding her arms behind her back. Entangled within his grasp, she stumbled over his shoes, inching into a glacial burrow.

Her gaze wandered higher, settling on the crystal-clear stalactites dangling in the form of a chandelier then darted to a spotlight, flooding the cavern with a warm, amber glow. Worker lights encircled a repair zone. If they stayed in the well-lit area of the cave, Jake would find them.

Madelyn squirmed and wriggled under Leon's tight restraint. He leaned closer, pressing his body firmer against her backside and holding her tighter in his grip. She craned her neck, squeezing her shoulders free and pushing forward with all her strength. Leon staggered, loosening his clutch.

Madelyn broke away from him and tripped off the walkway. "Jake," she yelped in a shaky tone as she slid on the frozen ground. Fumbling, she regained her balance, but her shoes skated across the ice.

"I'm coming for you, hang on." Jake's voice grew closer.

"Stop," Leon growled under his breath while he glided along the icy surface. He latched onto her arm, slowing them to a halt, and almost pulled her down with his weight anchored to her side. Wrapping his arms around her waist he forced her to face him. Leon held her near enough to feel his breath on her forehead. She bent her arms against his chest, creating a wedge between them. Wasn't Jake coming for her or did she imagine his voice?

"Why have you betrayed me?" Leon's eyes widened and his eyebrows pulled tight together.

Madelyn lifted her chin, no longer caring about Leon's intimidation and bullying. He crossed the line, making it impossible to maintain a level of professionalism.

"I agreed to go with you to Salzburg. I didn't choose to freeze in an ice cave while being manhandled."

Leon cocked his head to the side. "I believed you trusted me."

"How can I when you act irrationally? If you compromised or considered anyone other than yourself then…"

His muscles relaxed, slackening his grasp around her waist. "What is it you want, Madelyn Brighton? Correct Samuel Healy's mistakes, go home to California, or experience life in a way you never knew existed?" He leaned closer, with a direct, probing stare.

A pinch in her elbow intensified, and she winced. What did she want? She wanted to forgive Sam while moving on from the past, personable relationships with no longer feeling abandoned and alone. How could she achieve her aspirations without exclusive reliance on people and circumstances? Leon spoke of a life she never knew existed; she experienced the truth of his statement earlier in the week. With faith and guidance, individuals were capable of change—Sam's transformation in character, fellowship in the community group at the inn, the revelation she was able to grow beyond her own self-imposed confines and discover that buried in the deepest alcoves of her soul, she retained her belief.

A sense of calm washed over her as if she emerged from water with easy breathing. "I want to strengthen my faith and dependence on God."

A dark laugh rumbled behind his closed lips. "We create our own destiny." The tension of his hold eased, his hands traveled the curve of her waist, and settled on her hips. "Stay with me, I'll show you."

"Step away from her." Jake's demand boomed throughout the grotto.

Leon spun her in his arms toward the voice and he appeared as a shadowy figure, standing on the pathway. Madelyn's chest expanded with a lifting feeling, ready to take flight. Jake's actions spoke louder than words—he did care and he followed through on his promises. He asked for trust but never earned it and with all her doubts she couldn't accept him at his word until this moment. As he stood, a few feet away, she trusted him now and forever. A surge of adrenaline streamed through her veins and she stepped a foot forward. With a forceful yank, she slammed back against Leon.

"How derivative, playing the hero again." He shook his head. "Typical of your behavior."

Jake shifted his stance and inched frontward. "You're the predictable one, I saw you board the train. Then all I had to do was find Drexwyler, since you go nowhere without your nanny."

Leon clenched his hands and tightened his squeeze. Madelyn's eyes shut as her shoulders slumped. Did Jake have a plan beyond verbal insults and one-upping Leon? There was no need for a rescue, and she trusted, by now, Jake knew Leon wasn't a true threat, unless provoked.

"I didn't have a chance to say goodbye to Madelyn. Being a real man, I confessed my desire for her to spend the weekend with me und of course, she accepted."

"It looks like you've had a bit of a scuffle. Are you sure you didn't persuade her by force?"

"All relationships have struggles." Leon turned with a pained stare and the skin bunched around his eyes. "Tell him how you willingly came with me."

Madelyn gulped down the knot in her throat. At least she wouldn't be able to see the look of disgust on Jake's face. "I agreed to go with Leon, but—"

"There you have it. You caused this whole fiasco, pursuing us out of jealousy." Leon threw a hand upward.

"I thought it was because you wanted this." Jake pulled a small titanium tube from his jacket pocket. "Mozart's music for Maddie?" He stepped onto the ice.

Madelyn felt Leon's body twitch as he crept backward. "I don't know, I've grown so fond of meine Schatzi." His hands crawled up from her waist and he crossed one arm over her chest while he caressed the backside of his other hand along her throat, trailing his fingers along her cheek. "The passion between us is hard to contain."

Jake scrunched his face like he swallowed vomit. "Okay, I'll make the choice simple." He shook the tube back and forth as if he were taunting a dog with a bone.

She prayed for a chance to see Jake again but not at the cost of his work. "Don't do it. The music has been an important mission for you and your father—"

"You're more important." His eyes locked onto hers, the corner of his mouth pulled up to one side.

The words set off an explosion of fireworks inside her heart. If he told her last night or at the train station, she would have shared her feelings.

"Don't be an idiot." Leon's heel scraped the ice, taking another step back with her secured against his hip.

Jake raised his arm with the music clutched in his hand.

"You wouldn't dare." Leon slackened his grip.

Madelyn glanced over her shoulder. A couple feet away, a short, red barricade and two narrow planks laid in position at the edge of a wide chasm in the ground, where constant water dripped from the stalactites.

Madelyn gasped, sucking the cold air into her lungs. "Wait—"

Jake threw the canister toward Leon. "Checkmate."

Leon reached out to catch it while his fingertips grazed the tip. In the silence the cylinder clanked like a pinball rolling along the ice. He lunged to his right, following the sound of the clanging titanium and with lightning-movement, knocked Madelyn off balance. She slipped with the lack of traction on her shoes, sliding until she slammed into a volcanic-shaped formation and smacked the top of her skull then bit down on her lip as she crashed into the icy structure. The bang vibrated throughout her body, and a buzzing sensation filled her brain that reverberated in her ears as she dropped to her knees. Throbbing pressure forced her eyes shut while she slumped onto the frozen floor.

"Maddie." Jake's boots squeaked as he rushed and kneeled close.

His nearness radiated heat and she trembled.

He slid his arm behind her neck. "Please open your eyes, if you can hear me."

Madelyn groaned while he elevated her head and rubbed his hand along her scalp.

"I'm getting you outta here." Jake removed his jacket. He laid her onto the cool leather of the folded material and the warmth of his lips pressed against her forehead.

With a crash of the barriers, Leon swore, and Jake jerked his body toward the noise. "I'll be right back," he said with a gusty sigh and caressed her hand.

Madelyn opened her mouth and tasted blood on her tongue. Her thought processing was delayed, and she lost the ability to speak. Her eyelids fluttered with the little physical energy and willpower she had left inside. A shooting ache bulleted through her brain as she turned toward Jake.

Jake grunted as he leaped and slid across the ice in time to grab Leon's arm before he went over into the abyss. "Don't move any farther or we'll fall." His voice strained while holding the weight of Leon.

Madelyn rolled onto her side and squeaked with her heart pounding in her throat. She outstretched her shaking limb, desperate to help. As she squinted, everything seemed hopeless and praying proved too difficult. She managed a whisper, "God."

The thin slats covering part of the ravine cracked, splitting the wood from the pressure of Leon leaning over the edge. "I've almost—"

The support gave way beneath Leon and the cavern consumed him. A ferocious bellow spouted from the cavity. Every cell inside her froze, and she blinked several times, ensuring she kept cognizance. Jake shot a quick glance at Madelyn then down at the icy ledge crumbling under his body.

"Oh sh—" Jake vanished in an avalanche of ice.

After the rumble of ice quaked underneath, her body shook with the aftershock of seeing Jake and Leon disappear. She whimpered and placed her palms on the frozen foundation, dragging herself along the slick surface.

A sharp breath expelled from her mouth and she choked on tears. Seconds turned into agonizing minutes of silence, yet the echoes of yelling rang in her ears. She pushed her body up onto her knees and crawled closer to the rift. There were no signs of them, and reality ravaged any hope with the repeated image of Jake falling flashing in her blurred vision.

She knew her trials would lead to the testing of her faith. Madelyn wrenched herself to the rim of the blackened fissure. Jake and Leon were gone.

What if ice trapped and injured them, or worse? Her quivering chin was a stone in the cold and her heartrate slowed. Dizziness coerced her eyes shut and she curled inward into a ball. The rawness in her throat burned as she regurgitated the sickness from her stomach. Ready to surrender consciousness, things became fuzzy and a panged howl reverberated as if others cried out from the depths of the icy crevices. The Austrian's original assumptions were accurate: the cave was the entrance to hell.

CHAPTER TWENTY-FIVE

Madelyn moaned as her head rang with a constant beeping beside the bed. She shifted in the stiff sheets and cringed while an intravenous needle in her arm delved deeper into her flesh. *For crying out loud, someone shut off the alarm.* The fluorescent light shined through her closed eyelids. It was better to appear unresponsive than face additional questions from the medical staff.

The hospital room door swooshed open and rubber soles squealed on the linoleum floor. Finally, a technician turned off the machine. Latex gloved fingers pressed her wrist, checking her pulse for about a minute. A blood pressure cuff inflated tight around her upper arm and the attendant lightly pushed a cold stethoscope bell below the cuff's edge. The hospital would have to admit her into the psychiatric ward if she didn't get discharged soon.

She kept her eyes shut as someone knocked and entered the room.

"Excuse me, Sprechen Sie Englisch?" The man closed the door.

"Ja." The nurse removed the blood pressure cuff and set Madelyn's arm back down on the bed.

The plastic ID band scratched her forearm along with a constant itch from the tape holding the IV in place. She twitched her nose and flared her nostrils as she inhaled the smell of sanitizer and the oils from her unwashed hair.

"I'm Mr. William Clark from the US Embassy. I received a call from the authorities and was given permission to ask a few questions about your patient."

Her throat tightened, and she swallowed, wetting the dryness in her mouth. Praying she'd hear any news about Jake and Leon, she raised her brow with her lids sealed.

"The doctor is coming in to speak with you."

The door creaked open. "I'm Doctor Hauzenberg." The doctor spoke fluent English.

"I need to gather a few facts." The man clicked the top of a pen. "Where and in what condition was the woman found?"

The events of what happened inside the cave remained fuzzy. Perhaps she had a few answers for the inquiries. She cracked her eyes to slits. The men stood facing each other. If she received information about Jake by eavesdropping, she'd avoid the details of the circumstances that led her into the ice caverns.

The nurse pulled her chart from a holder at the edge of the bed, flipped open the folder and handed it to the doctor before exiting.

Doctor Hauzenberg nodded. "The patient, Madelyn Brighton, was discovered alone, after business hours, and unconscious in the ice caves near Werfen."

Mr. Clark scribbled in his notepad and scratched his temple. "Do you know why she was in a restricted area?"

The doctor shook his head. "The paramedic reported a collapse in the structure of the cave."

"Are her injuries severe?"

Doctor Hauzenberg scanned the file. "We admitted the patient for a concussion, serious dehydration and mild hypothermia. The magnetic resonance image showed slight swelling between the cranium and cortex with no internal bleeding. We'll continue to monitor her vital signs and repeat an MRI scan. She's been in and out of sleep for the past seventy-two hours. We've continued an IV drip with 50mg of Demerol for pain and 20mg of Gravol for anxiety."

Mr. Clark's hand sped across the paper. "I gather she's responsive since you acquired her name. They told me over the phone she didn't have identification."

"She knows all pertinent information about herself." The physician tilted the patient chart toward Mr. Clark.

He jotted in his notebook and glanced at the doctor. "Who is Jake Nolan?"

Madelyn held her breath and her heartrate increased on the monitor. Good or bad, she needed to know what happened. Fatigue, drugs, or both, weighted her eyes, but she fought to keep her mind active.

The doctor said, "An attending nurse wrote it down in her records the other night. The patient woke in a panic, shouting the name and we decided to administer anxiety medication."

"Is Jake Nolan registered here?"

"Nein, we checked yesterday."

Mr. Clark clicked his pen and stuck it in his suit pocket. "I'll make an inquiry at the Embassy. In the meantime, keep me posted on her condition." Mr. Clark handed the doctor a business card from his notebook. "Please contact me when you sign her release. I need her to come into my office and answer a few extra questions."

Doctor Hauzenberg opened the door. "I'm her attending physician and will notify you as soon as we clear her for discharge."

"Thank you for your time." They shook hands, and both men left as the door hissed shut.

Madelyn strained, lifting her eyelids, and glanced around the room. Madelyn massaged her forehead, uncertain if the ache derived from the injury or the intensified feelings in her heart.

They hadn't even heard of Jake beyond her mentioning his name. What if they never discovered Jake and Leon? The blow to her cranium wasn't enough to forget the image of them falling into an ice crevasse. Everything seemed surreal and replayed in her mind like a scene from a movie, a tragic tale without a happy ending.

Part of her remained content lying in a hospital bed under sedation, yet her heart wanted to rip the IV needle from her arm and find Jake. Madelyn waned under the influence of medication and surrendered to the lull of the intravenous drip as her tears dropped with the same consistency. Did he survive or… She cried out, "Please God, let them be safe." She squeezed her eyes tight and curved her body onto her side.

*　*　*

Flames roared in the stone hearth, heating the living room. Jake shivered with an icy chill running through his veins as he paced the rug in front of the fire.

"It's a wonder you survived. What happened next?" Douglas' mouth slackened as he leaned back into the chair.

"The surface started to crumble, and I grabbed Leon's hand. The weight pulled us down at least a twenty-foot ice chute. The rest of the frozen structure toppled, and we crashed into an open cavern below." Jake glanced at Douglas and kneaded his forehead. "Everything happened so fast."

Douglas cocked his head. "Thank God you escaped barely scathed after being buried under ice."

Jake raised his right elbow in an arm sling. "Leon landed feet first and once he hit the ground, I wasn't sure if the cracking sound was the ice or the bones in his foot. Since he broke my fall, I smashed onto my side, resulting in the sprain along with a few bumps and bruises." He shook his head. "After the accident, I freed Leon, but we didn't make it far, I tried supporting him with one arm until all my energy drained and hypothermia kicked in. We waited for over an hour before the search and rescue team found us."

"Possibly they discovered Madelyn earlier and took her to a different hospital."

A tight breath bottled up in Jake's chest. He prayed they had saved her first. The last time he saw Maddie, she laid on the icy ground trembling and practically unconscious. With a gusty exhale he blinked long and hard. "I've been praying that is the case. She must be near Werfen and since Leon insisted that we have the best care, he ordered the paramedics to take us to his personal physicians in Munich."

"Leon must be grateful you risked your life to aid him."

"I was partly responsible for causing the accident." Jake pinched the bridge of his nose and closed his eyes. "The worst part is I put Maddie in jeopardy again."

Douglas blew an exaggerated breath from his lips. "In all the years I worked with your father, we stayed out of life-or-death situations." He threw his hands upward. "You've become a thrill seeker."

Jake scratched the stubble on his chin. Maddie said the same thing when she called him out on his behavior, after he promised to protect her and failed. He coughed as stomach bile sidled up the back of his throat. He turned and leaned on the mantel, gazing into the flickering fire. Finding Maddie and ensuring her safety were all that mattered.

"I'm simply thankful you're home." Mom entered the room and walked toward the chair beside the fireplace. "Douglas is right, you need to settle down. Now, sit and take it easy." She fluffed and patted the top cushion on the seat.

"How can I relax when it's been days and I don't even know where Maddie is?" Jake slammed his hand on the mantelshelf. "Calling the hospitals is pointless with patient confidentiality policies. I should be in Salzburg searching for her, instead of standing here."

"I understand, but you've done all you can for now and just arrived home this morning." She spoke in the same soothing tone from when he was a child.

Jake stared off toward the corner of the room. Mom and Douglas tried to comfort him, and he responded like a jerk. "I'm sorry I snapped at you. I feel useless and haven't done enough to find Maddie." He carved his fingers through his hair.

Mom stepped close and placed her hand on his arm. "I believe she is well, and you'll see her soon." She squinted and the fine lines around her eyes deepened. "I'm going to make tea."

Jake exhaled and forced a smile. "Thanks, Mom."

Douglas stood. "We all want to know Madelyn is safe. Katherine emailed a prayer request to our community group. I'll call Pastor Fredrick and ask him to reach out to the whole congregation."

Jake nodded. "I appreciate the prayers."

Douglas gave him a pat on the back and left the room.

Jake sat in the chair next to the fireplace and rubbed his palms over his face. "Please God, I pray we hear from Maddie soon."

Jake knew from the first moment he spoke to Maddie she would impact his life; the minute she contested his integrity, jumped from a castle window into a lake, compromised when it challenged her convictions and showed compassion for all people. Then, her reemerging faith in God and the prose she wrote solidified all the pivotal times they shared, creating a bonding relationship. His heart hammered and he couldn't deny their growing interest in each other.

Jake longed to regain the minutes she had been in his arms. Aware of stirring feelings in those moments, he wished she allowed him to hold her longer. What an idiot, acting so casually when he kissed her. Such a precious gift and with no guarantees he'd ever get that opportunity again. If given another chance, he'd make sure she knew how much he respected her and would do whatever needed to earn her trust.

"You have a telephone call on the mainline." Douglas stood in the doorway. "An American bloke, and the caller came up as a Salzburg number."

Jake hurled himself out of the chair and rushed from the living room into the kitchen. He flew by Mom in the dining area, almost knocking the tea tray out of her hands. "Sorry," he uttered under his breath.

His chest pounded while he jumbled picking up the receiver on the mounted wall phone. With heavy breathing he released the hold button. "Hello, this is Jake Nolan."

"Good afternoon, Mr. Nolan. My name is William Clark and I'm calling from the US Embassy. I'm contacting you regarding a personal request I received to update you about a woman named Madelyn Brighton."

A tight pinch swelled in his throat. "Yes."

"Ms. Brighton was admitted to Unfallkrankenhaus in Salzburg a few days ago and has been recovering from her injuries."

Jake placed his hand over his heart. "Thank God she's all right. Do you know how long she must stay?"

"They should discharge her today. When I visited the hospital, Doctor Hauzenberg assured me he would notify me when she's released."

Jake gulped. "You met her? What was her condition?" Jake inhaled and exhaled hard. "I apologize, last time I saw her she was mostly unresponsive."

"It's fine, I understand your concerns. She was sedated and looked as expected after an accident. The staff is keeping her strictly for monitoring," Mr. Clark said in a neutral tone.

He stepped backward and leaned against the wall. "If she didn't talk to you, then who told you to contact me?"

"The whole situation is rather peculiar." He cleared his throat. "They gave me your name at the hospital and wrote it in Ms. Brighton's chart when she inquired about you. Then, I returned to my office, and received a message from the Austrian Federal Government, instructing me to telephone you."

"I can't imagine how the Austrian Government got my name and information, but either way, I'm grateful for the update."

"A confidant advised the vice-chancellor to keep you well informed about Ms. Brighton's whereabouts and condition."

Jake stretched his neck to the side, trying to loosen the stiffness in his injured arm. Someone, a friend of the vice-chancellor. He drummed his fingers on the counter. The only person… His mouth fell open.

"Mr. Nolan, are you still there?"

The cord twisted, and he almost dropped the receiver as he twirled, entangling his arm. It was one thing for Mom to have a landline for the business, but she didn't make an investment in a cordless phone. "Yeah."

"I'll ring back once I have confirmation on Ms. Brighton's status," Mr. Clark continued in a flat voice.

"Thank you and I appreciate the update." Jake hung up. Gaping at nothing as he let out a huge sigh, he staggered into the dining area and flopped onto the wood bench. With a slight shake of the head, he blinked hard. He took a moment, allowing the information to settle and glimpsed at his watch. If he acted fast, he'd be in Salzburg by late afternoon.

"Any news about Madelyn?" Douglas strode into the room, wringing his hands.

"Maddie's recovering at Unfallkrankenhaus in Salzburg and I need to leave right away." Jake hopped to his feet and hurried into the entry.

Douglas spun on his heels. "Anything I can do for you?"

"Yeah." Jake scooped up the car keys sitting on the table by the front door and glanced at Douglas. "Can I borrow your mobile?"

He patted down his pockets. "One moment…"

Jake laughed under his breath. "Douglas, I got it." He picked up the flip phone lying beside the guest logbook.

Douglas held his open palms skyward. "I have little need for the confounded gadget."

"Please forward my calls to your number." Jake stared at the coat rack. His jacket…

"I will."

Jake shoved the device in his back pocket, opened the door and stepped onto the porch. His eyes flicked upward to a white letter envelope, with his name written across and taped on the post. He ripped it off and tore the top. A single key laid at the bottom. He examined it closer. With rapid blinking, he shifted his gaze toward the motorcycle parked in the driveway. His body tensed while he strode over and inspected the bike.

He ran his hand along the shiny new mirror, his fingers trailing the smooth, black leather seat, as he leaned closer, scoping out the straightened fender and restored taillight, all original parts.

"My R50," Jake gasped, shuffling backward a couple steps and clasped his hand to his forehead, pressing his hair down.

A tentative smile built in awe of God, the true hero, and the splendor performed in a person with an open heart. He removed the helmet hanging on the handlebars, set it behind and stuck the key into the ignition. As he started the bike and revved the engine, a flush of adrenaline surged through his body. The motor purred then roared with the influx of power.

Douglas walked outside onto the porch. "What's going on out here?" He squeezed his eyes shut then opened them wide. "Where did that come from? I thought you crashed your motorcycle?"

"I did. I'll explain later."

Douglas hustled toward the bike. "Don't be daft, attempting to ride with one arm in a sling."

Jake's senses heightened with the revelations of his motorcycle fully renovated, unexpected acts of kindness, and confirmation that Maddie was safe. After everything that happened—the injuries everyone sustained, losing the music and all his mistakes—nothing had gone the way he planned, yet everything worked out regardless of his failed, forced strategies. God always proved to be trustworthy. If he learned anything the past couple of weeks, it was to listen, be still and wait.

Jake bent his neck forward and slipped the sling off his shoulder. Extending his arm, he clenched his jaw and slowly inhaled and exhaled. He gripped the handles, the motor humming and ready for added mileage on the Autobahn. Jake throttled the engine, removed the key and tossed it to Douglas.

"Please tell my mother I'm taking the car to go see Maddie in Salzburg." He swung his leg off the seat and dug the keys out of his front pocket.

Douglas nodded. "Well done."

CHAPTER TWENTY-SIX

Madelyn reclined in a visitor chair beside the hospital window. The nurse removed the IV and freed her from the monitors. She refused to spend another minute in bed waiting for the doctor's sign-off for discharge. Showered and dressed, after she used the trial-size toiletries supplied, she combed through wet strands of hair with one hand while she tilted her head, pressing the phone receiver between her ear and shoulder.

Madelyn set the comb on the small table beside the bed and switched ears. Trying to call from the hospital room to a neighboring country provided an additional challenge. Her daily functionality became impaired without a cell phone, intensifying her disdain for technological dependency. The operator accommodated her long-distance calls and assisted her with getting in touch with Gretchen. Madelyn spent half an hour briefing her on the week's events and, most important, explaining the family was now out of danger.

Two minutes passed before the phone rang as she called Kate's inn. Her heart thumped with each unanswered ring. Voicemail picked up the call and a sudden onset of nausea rolled in her stomach. She took a deep breath. "Hi, it's Madelyn. I'm in Salzburg, waiting to leave the hospital, Un-fall-kran-ken haus. Sorry, I wanted to know if Jake made it home safely. I don't know where I'm staying tonight, but I'll try to call again later. And if Jake—" The rest of the message cut off with a hateful beep. She slumped into the chair, tormented by the image of Jake falling. If she talked to Jake, Kate, anyone… She smacked a palm against her thigh. Yes, Leon owned a hotel in Salzburg.

Madelyn glanced upward at the door and the nurse, Emilie, stepped into the room. "Doctor Hauzenberg cleared you for release. I have a few instructions to send with you. Do you have any questions?"

"Can I make another call before I leave?"

"Ja, I'll be back with a wheelchair and escort you out." Emilie set the papers on the table and left.

Madelyn requested contact for Hotel Füssen, and the connection to a local number took less than a minute.

A receptionist answered, "Hotel Füssen, wie kann ich Ihnen helfen?"

"Herrn Leon Von Füssen, bitte." She asked to speak with the owner of the hotel in a simplistic tone and bit the corner of her lip. Would the staff bother Leon with incoming calls from ordinary people?

"Einen Moment, bitte."

"Danke." It wasn't the best time to practice her basic language skills.

Madelyn rubbed the top of her head and scrunched her face, feeling the tender, swollen bump the size of a golf ball.

The employee came back on the phone line. "Herrn Von Füssen requested we forward his calls and messages to his Handy."

Madelyn's inadequate German must have prompted the woman to speak English.

"Thank you."

"I'll put you through."

A flutter bubbled inside her belly. If Leon survived, then Jake did too. The hold music silenced, and a dryness filled her mouth. "Hello? Anyone there?"

"Hallo," the reception answered again.

"I'm waiting to speak with Leon Von Füssen."

"I'll try again und if there's no answer, leave a message." Silence lingered for a few seconds before the sound of a click.

"Leon, this is Madelyn Brighton. I'm leaving the hospital in Salzburg, I—um, don't know where I'm going next, but I'll be at Gretchen Healy's for a few days. I want to make sure you and Jake are all right after the accident. Sorry, I'm still a little disoriented." Madelyn rushed her speech and gulped a mouthful of air. "I'll call or stop by the hotel later. Thanks." She held the receiver away from her ear and stared at the phone before she hung up. She blinked and shook her head. At one point she heard background noise, and possibly breathing on the line.

Emilie opened the door and rolled a wheelchair into the room. "All set to go?"

Madelyn nodded, picked up her release papers and sat in the wheelchair. Emilie wheeled her into the hall and stopped at the nurse's station. She remained so focused on finding out about Jake, she forgot about paying for her treatment. With a hard intake of air, she held her breath.

Emilie handed her a business card. "This man requested that you call him at the US Embassy."

A gusty sigh escaped Madelyn's lips. "What about payment for my care?"

Perhaps the US Embassy looked up her personal data or emergency contact information in her file. She never checked if her insurance policy covered out-of-country emergencies.

"All your medical expenses are paid."

Madelyn craned her neck over her shoulder. "How? Who—"

"I don't know." Emilie plopped a plastic bag onto her lap. "The paramedics brought this in with you on the day you arrived." She pushed her down the hall toward the elevator.

Madelyn opened the bag and pulled out Jake's brown leather jacket. She clutched it against her chest and ran her fingers along the distressed material, hugging the garment tight in her arms. His scent embalmed in the fabric, hints of citrus and musk. She closed her eyes. Jake had to be fine, she rejected any other possibilities or outcomes.

"Where will you go now?" Emilie backed the wheelchair into the elevator and pressed the first-floor button.

Although Gretchen offered to pick her up from the hospital, she refused leaving Salzburg without finding Jake. "I'll probably get lunch then take a short walk and stretch my legs. Any suggestions?"

"Walk Altstadt, the old town, tons of places to eat, museums and Mozart's birthplace—"

"Yes, Mozart's." Madelyn bobbed her head. How silly she didn't think of visiting earlier. The idea of touring Mozart's Museum comforted her and satiated a sense of closure.

As they exited, Emilie steered the wheelchair through the lobby and out the automated sliding glass doors. Madelyn squinted at the sunlight as Emilie rolled her down a ramp toward a row of flags at the pickup and drop-off zone. For the first time in days Madelyn inhaled the cool, fresh air, no longer trapped in a cave or hospital room.

Emilie stopped and moved from behind the wheelchair. She held out her hand and assisted Madelyn from the chair. "Here is a little money to help you get to your next destination." She handed Madelyn a small card with a fifty-euro bank note clipped on the back.

Every day for seven years she listened to the darker side of humanity and lost faith in the goodness of people. In the past week, she encountered warmth and generosity, even in the smallest of gestures. She finally opened herself up to relationships and experienced honest fellowship.

Madelyn glimpsed at the card with Emilie's email printed on the front. Her words piled on her tongue and she found it difficult to speak. "I don't know what to say." She moved closer and hugged Emilie. "Thank you, I'll keep in touch." Her voice wavered, enriched with emotion.

Emilie stepped backward and pulled out a folded piece of paper from a pocket of her playful kitten-printed scrubs. "Write your contact information. I'll let you know if I get any news." She unhooked the pen hanging from her lanyard.

Emilie waved at a taxi in the loading zone, opened the door and instructed the driver to drop Madelyn at Mozart's Geburtshaus. "Good luck, I hope you find Jake soon."

Madelyn jotted down her email and phone number. She handed it to Emilie before climbing into the passenger seat. "Thanks, bye."

Emilie waved as the taxi drove off.

The air vents blew a direct cold stream, aimed at her torso. Madelyn eased into the vinyl seats, tucked her legs close and wrapped her hands over her knees. She shivered and straightened Jake's jacket over her chest like a blanket. The inside lining turned out, revealing papers stuffed inside the pocket. She stared down then shifted a glance side to side. She chewed her inner, lower lip and yanked the pages out.

Madelyn unfolded the paper and discovered her handwritten poems. Heat swept up her neck and across her face. Jake read her simplistic outpouring of thoughts and feelings. An emptiness ensued—he knew of her affections and still sacrificed Mozart's music. Above anything she wanted to see him and share intimate details about each other. She believed their developing friendship showed potential for a deeper connection.

The vehicle stopped at Mozart's Geburtshaus location, the ultimate destination of her journey. Finally, she arrived, after failing her personal goal for delivering Mozart's music. She paid the fare and opened the back door of the taxi.

The driver handed her change and pointed down the street. "Mozart's birthplace is at Getreidegasse 9, straight ahead, on the left."

Madelyn counted the colorful paper Euros and slipped a few coins in her pocket. "Danke." She stepped out onto the pedestrian walkway and shut the door.

Ancient architecture of the city spoke through years of history crying out from the walls. The streets filled with stories of the past and present, all leading toward the future. She strolled the stone pathway, maneuvering through crowds of people. A man played the violin outside Mozart's Geburtshaus. Tourists circled for a photo with the role player dressed in Mozart fashion, wearing a satin suit, a crimson embroidered frock coat and an exaggerated white, powdered wig.

The yellow ochre exterior of Mozart's birthplace gleamed compared to the surrounding buildings. The structure shined, between the pale, beige stone edifice on each side—which she thought was appropriate and deserved. Rows of double-hung, trimmed windows lined the building at least five stories high. A long red-and-white Austrian flag adjourned below the roof, swaying with a soft, elegant flow of movement in the breeze.

Madelyn strolled under the arched doorway festooned with wrought iron and passed the open dark-wood door embellished with a brass lion head knocker. Climbing the steep, stone steps, she dragged her fingers along the steely railing. Her hands trembled, and she felt a special connection with Wolfgang Amadeus Mozart as if he sent a personal invitation for a visit.

At the entry booth, she purchased a ticket and continued without a guided tour. Navigating through the tight corridor she entered the Mozart family apartment on the third floor.

Madelyn glimpsed at the kitchen presentation: a stove, cooking utensils and shelves. Perusing each room, they presented historical gems around every corner. Portraits of Mozart, his father, mother and sister hung on the walls. She squinted, reading the posted descriptions and lost herself in a daydream as she imagined experiencing the museum with Jake. An intense pain bulleted through her chest and shot upward through her brain.

The wood floor creaked walking into the Geburtszimmer. The brochure noted Mozart was likely born in the bedroom. Pillars in the center exhibited mementos from the Mozart estate, with his enclosed child violin, attached to wiring, and created the illusion of mid-air suspension.

Wolfgang Amadeus Mozart's Piano Concerto K.488 played, her head twirling a dance while she ambled the perimeter into the next area, avoiding the large groups of people. Passing the piano in the middle of the room she proceeded toward the far wall. The articles showcased Mozart's time in Vienna. Madelyn scanned handwritten letters about Mozart's life and events in the city.

Her gaze gamboled over a page and settled on four sheets of written music. Her pulse increased, and she placed her palms on the fixture, pressing her forehead against the case. Medication lingered in her veins, thoughts still fuzzy and she blinked a few times. The dim light highlighted the title, Great Mass in Minor C, including the Credo with Agnus Dei and Mozart's signature dated 1783. Her eyes darted to the short description and credit line, 'Donated in Memory of Dr. Henry Nolan.'

A slight squeal caught in her throat. Madelyn straightened her posture, clasping her hands in front of her chest as she exhaled aloud. Thank God, Jake was safe and finished his mission. Guests peered over her shoulder, catching a glimpse at the new addition to the museum, but she stood grounded in the same spot. Although people gathered, she sensed a profound, private moment, involving everyone connected to the music. Whether positive or negative, it affected many lives.

Madelyn accepted she may never see Jake again, yet standing near his accomplished work made her feel close to him. She stared at the encased parchment, staff, clefs and ledger lines blurred together as tears brimmed in her eyes. A haunting sound of joy, relief and sadness escaped her lips.

A man stood beside her and spoke in a low tone. "Kann ich Ihnen helfen?"

Her muscles tensed and she swiped a finger under each eye. "I'm admiring the music on display."

"I'm Franz, the curator." He adjusted his round-rimmed glasses. "I don't mean to intrude, however, there are other articles to view in the museum."

"I understand."

"I'll leave you to enjoy the rest of your tour."

"No, wait." Madelyn grabbed his arm.

Franz stiffened and spun on his heels. His eyes widened and darted toward her hand, with the medical identification adorned around her wrist.

Madelyn released him and tucked her arm behind her back. "Excuse me." A nervous laugh crept up her throat.

"Yes." Franz smoothed the creases from the sleeve of his suit jacket.

She stepped away from the display case. "I was hoping you'd share how the museum acquired Mozart's Great Mass piece." Perhaps Franz met with Jake when the music was presented. She bounced on her toes.

"A patron from The Mozarteum Foundation Salzburg recently brought the artifact to us." He pushed his eyeglasses further up on the bridge of his nose. "The collection committee quickly accepted and agreed it belonged in our permanent collected works."

"Did you meet the donor?"

Franz flinched his head backward with a slight frown. "The person wishes to remain anonymous."

"Oh, right." She felt her heart shrink. If she heard about the encounter, Jake standing in the same room, speaking with Franz, she visualized the interaction in her mind and shared in the event. Madelyn should have been part of the experience, after everything that transpired.

"Now, if you excuse me."

She tilted her chin downward. "Please, if you could describe him, or something he said, anything at all that you can tell me…"

Her breath hitched in her chest and she clasped her hands together, holding back the urge to shake Franz by the arms. "We were in an accident and were separated. I intended to be here when he delivered the music."

"I'm sorry, the name is confidential. Although, I spoke with him briefly, a tall man, fair hair, and he walked with a cane."

A warmth spread throughout her body. Regardless of the hardships, Jake did it, his job completed, and she wished she could have seen his face when the music went on display, honoring Henry. It sounded like he sustained an injury, resulting in a need for a cane, but hearing of his accomplishment, he had recovered and now had peace. Gazing at the artistry wall, a smile built as she pictured Jake—his cobalt eyes shining with satisfaction, his dark… She rubbed the back of her neck. Light? Franz stated the donor had fair hair! Jake's jacket slid off her shoulder and onto the floor. Bending to pick it up, she flipped her head upward.

"Leon," she said in a muddled tone. Her legs wobbled as she erected her body and staggered backward, bumping into a pedestal, almost knocking over an artifact.

Franz extended an arm to block her fall. "Perhaps you should sit down."

Madelyn had a feeling Franz meant to protect the item rather than assist her. Catching her balance, she squared her shoulders and looked around the room, searching for answers. "Did the donor have someone with him?" Other than Leon's usual companion, Drexwyler. "Perhaps a co- donor?"

"He was alone. Are you positive you're acquainted with our contributor?"

"Um, yes." A queasiness rippled in her stomach and her mouth filled with saliva.

"Thanks, you've been very informative." Madelyn stared ahead and tottered in a daze into the next room. Where was Jake and did he make an agreement with Leon? She attempted tuning everything out, the crowds, the displays—she glimpsed out of the corner of her eye at a clavichord, shoes, and a wig. Picking up her pace, she followed the exit signs downstairs.

Madelyn wrestled with sorting out her feelings. Physical fatigue set in as she tried processing the information. She struggled with the fact Leon elected to be an anonymous donor of Mozart's music and honor Henry. Her steps slowed behind a group of people mingling in the mid-1700s re-created Bourgeois living room on the first level.

"Bitte warten Sie," a voice called out through the crowd.

The crowd parted, pressing against her arms. Madelyn peered over her shoulder as Franz rushed over with a heavy breath. "You are Madelyn Brighton?" Franz pinched his side and exhaled aloud.

"Yes—"

"The contributor instructed me to give this to you." He presented a small gift.

"Vielen Dank." Madelyn accepted the offer and smiled.

Franz gave a curt nod and scurried off. Madelyn stared at the antique hand-painted wooden box. As she examined the vintage case, she knew Leon expected her to arrive at Mozart's birthplace. A tightening in her chest constricted her breathing. Instead of gaining answers or securing a sense of closure, she left with additional questions and uncertainty.

Exiting the museum, she stood on the cobblestone street outside the market next door. An airstream jetted along the narrow passageway, whipping hair into her face. She slipped on Jake's oversized jacket as she paused in the shade of the buildings. Her head buzzed as the swarm of people bustling in and out of boutique shops and cafés on Getreidegasse. Her eyes skimmed the area for an available place to sit at the coffeehouse on the adjacent corner. Madelyn pulled out a chair and cringed as the iron scraped the concrete ground.

A tingle filled her limbs as she lifted the lid from the box and removed a linen note. She set the case on the table, her fingers fumbling as she cracked the wax seal. She unfolded the regency-style letter and read:

> *Dearest Madelyn,*
> *I'm relieved to find you are safe and are making a full recovery. Please accept my deepest apologies for any anguish and distress I caused you. I declare complete responsibility for the injuries you suffered, and I've financially covered your medical expenses. Don't hesitate to contact me if you require any additional treatment. Furthermore, I've sent your belongings to the Frau Healy estate. After the accident, I thought of you, and considered your request. My final deed was for you. I hope in time you will think of me kindly.*
> *Yours,*
> *Leon Von Füssen*

Madelyn gasped, clasping her hand over her mouth and held her breath for a moment. With a large exhale she laughed and cried at the same time, directing her eyes heavenward while folding her hands in prayer. Leon acted selflessly and demonstrated breaking free of the confines of the defining human condition. Beyond neurological wiring of the brain and conditioning, Leon proved redemption and a change of character were possible, like the transformation Gretchen witnessed in Sam and Svenja with her husband. She didn't know if Leon allowed God into his heart or was performing an act of contrition or revealing genuine compassion.

Madelyn refolded the letter and glanced inside the box. Leon's edelweiss boutonnière gleamed into her eyes. He moved beyond his past too. A bittersweet taste settled on her tongue. If Leon met her in person, she'd give him a wholehearted hug. Although an ache persisted in her heart with no mention of Jake, and yet she believed with every ounce of her being they would reunite.

Madelyn arose from the table and secured the gift box in the pocket of Jake's jacket she wore. She wandered the pedestrian walkway but didn't know where to go. Hang around the city for a couple hours, visit the local Hotel Füssen then take the train to Ruhpolding?

Strolling the street, her mind replayed recent events. So much of the last week played out like a dream sequence and impaired her rational thinking. One thing for sure, she gained a new perspective on people and renewed her hope for mankind. Regardless of the disenchanting testimonies she encountered daily at work, on her journey she observed the fruitions of God, and attested love, peace, kindness, and faithfulness prevailed.

Madelyn sauntered by the Old City Hall and passed several shopping options. Somehow, she had functioned without the consumption of coffee for several days. A five-minute walk led her to a charming square. With no purpose or intentions, she reached Mozartplatz.

Benches lined alongside the bronze-and-green tarnished Mozart statue. The sculpture a focal point in the center with yellow and purple flowers that flanked the pedestal. Madelyn loitered at a waist-high, black iron fence that bordered the monument honoring the composer. She stared at the figure. She'd leave Germany soon, bringing her journey to an end.

For the first time in years she risked her heart and dared to dream of something further than the life she had been living. Bitterness consumed over a decade of her life and now with a flicker of faith a real light filled her with encouragement. And against all odds, she ended up at her intended destination, with freedom from the past. Although her hands were empty, she gained a newfound purpose. She let go of Sam's previous deeds and connected with her unknown family, learning to cultivate relationships. Everything that occurred led her beyond a mission to escape her history, and experience eternal things—relations with God and people. A confidence surfaced, feeling she gained a deeper perspective for greater efficiency at work, with the guidance of her journey toward forgiveness and second chances.

Oblivious to the passage of time, she pondered her thoughts and only wavered her stance when she felt someone brush beside her hip.

"Nice jacket."

Madelyn's heart stopped for a moment and she sucked in a hard breath. The whole of her body a fluid movement as she turned toward his voice. "Jake." She thrust herself against his chest. Winding him, Jake burst out a gust of air.

"I missed you too." He embraced her, stroking the length of her hair.

Jake's heartbeat against her cheek reassured her it wasn't a daydream. She didn't want to move from the security of being wrapped in his arms, even though they stood in front of a focal point in the square. Earlier she thought she'd never look into his eyes again, yet God brought them together and Mozart played an instrumental role again. Jake loosened his grip and eased her head backward, revealing vibrant blue eyes, deep and inviting as a lake in July.

Sliding his hands up her nape, he cupped her face with his palms and leaned close. His kiss a single raindrop before the storm. Pressing his lips to hers, releasing heat, and fueling an electric thunderstorm the minute their mouths met. Two pools merging into a warm summer lagoon, drifting on ripples of gentle waves, a melodic rhythm almost dizzying, until emerging for breath seconds before drowning. She gasped for air yet felt filled with new life. Her heart a balloon, expanding and lifting.

Madelyn leaned into the cradle of his hands and found it impossible to tear her gaze away. "How did you find me?" she said in a raspy and unrecognizable voice.

"A certain person, with contacts in high places, told the US Embassy to call and give me an update on you. When I arrived at the hospital an overly excited nurse informed me you went to Mozart's Geburtshaus. I searched the museum, but was too late, until I spotted you walking Getreidegasse street." Jake winked and yanked on the shoulder of his jacket.

Meeting Emilie was a true blessing. A smile built, thinking of the friendships she made on her travels. She even valued her complex relationship with Leon. "Did you know about the music and dedication?"

Jake smiled and nodded. "Let's continue believing in miracles."

Standing with Jake in Mozartplatz was a miracle. It would be imperative to keep the faith, once she returned to California, and he traveled back to Boston, although at least they'd be in the same country. Madelyn didn't know what the future held, but discovered peace and contentment, no matter the circumstances.

"What's your next venture, now that the job's finished?"

"But I didn't finish. I promised to help you get back home safely." His eyes lit up, brighter than the sky on a cloudless day. His hands traced the outline of her arms and he laced his fingers between hers. "And I can't think of a better adventure than escorting you all the way."

Madelyn's pulse raced and her legs weakened at the knees. "I agree. Sounds adventurous, especially if it will be like your usual escapades."

Jake wiggled an eyebrow and grinned. "I'll do my best to keep the risky situations to a minimum."

"I'm willing to take my chances." Madelyn squeezed his hand and took a deep, savoring breath. A flood of warmth spread throughout her body. He included her in his plans—his words burst all doubt. And now that he found her, she trusted Jake wouldn't let her go.

The End

ABOUT THE AUTHOR

Victoria Marswell is a Romance and Suspense author. She started writing poetry and short stories in her early teens. Victoria majored in biblical studies at Hope International University and incorporates inspirational Christian themes into her writings. Victoria is a world traveler and sets her stories in the locations she has visited. At 17, she traveled to Germany and Austria where she was inspired to write, The Counterfeiter's Daughter. Victoria continues to travel the world; creating and writing romantic, thrilling adventures. She lived in Orange County, CA. for 38 years and currently resides in Portsmouth, NH.

Author Victoria Marswell's website: www.victoriamarswell.com
Follow the author on any of the social media platforms:
twitter.com/vicmarswell
www.facebook.com/vicmarswell
www.instagram.com/victoriamarswell

TO THE READERS

I hope you enjoyed The Counterfeiter's Daughter. If you did, please leave a review on Amazon, Barnes & Noble, iTunes, Kobo, Goodreads, BookBub, or wherever you enjoy leaving feedback. You can also like, follow and share my social media pages on Facebook, Twitter and Instagram. Reviews and sharing feedback are the greatest gift you can give to an indie author. I'm grateful for your support and thrilled to share my writing journey with you.

Would you like free and exclusive offers delivered directly to you?

Visit my website at www.victoriamarsell.com and subscribe to my newsletter, which will keep you updated on my current work, new releases, special promotions and free goodies. While visiting the website, please check out my additional pages; blogs, poetry and getting to know me. I enjoy connecting with my readers, so feel free to contact me on social media.